What reac
Spirit Bow: Th

MW00511365

"…excellently depicted the atmosphere of life in early 19th century America. The harshness of the wild and tense relationships between the generations of settlers and the Native Americans is felt especially when the protagonist lost his family. …**a gritty and unflinching novel that focuses on the human will to survive.** …will definitely evoke a myriad of emotions from readers. All in all, Spirit Bow is a moving and **substantial read from Lettis.**"

— *Five Star Review, Lit Amri, Readers' Favorite*

"…**a new voice for western fiction**… My book club will find **Spirit Bow** at the top of my recommendations."

—*5/5 Amazon, B. Williams*

"I was immediately drawn into the story. It was hard to put down. …many trials the characters had to go through to merely survive. I highly recommend this book."

—*5/5 Amazon, W. Gardner*

"A great book - a must read. I highly **recommend this book for Book Club members!** Congratulation's Mr. Lettis. I can't wait for the next installment."

—*5/5 Amazon, L. Hall*

"…an excellent historical novel. …**masterful** weaving of historical fact … and fiction."

—*5/5 Amazon, L. Sethmann*

"I very much enjoyed reading **Spirit Bow: The Saga of Sean O'Malley**. My sister bought this book for me and I am glad she did. **I look forward to more books by James Lettis.**"

—*5/5 Amazon, Jana*

"This book is a **wonderful** read, the first page sucked me in and I did not want to put it down. I would **highly recommend** reading this book."

—*5/5 Amazon, J. Conley*

"Wow!! Great book; well written. Begins as an easy read Western, but develops into more depth. **Marvelous!**"

—*5/5 Amazon, R.P.*

"**Great read**, get it now! …lots of attention to detail and historical events."

—*5/5 Amazon, C. Johnson*

"Just finished reading a 'great novel.'…**loved each and every chapter**. Please keep writing, you have a real talent."

—*P. Lindstrom*

"…liked it a lot. I like reading things that have some historical value. **It kept my attention even better than my Clive Cussler books do.**"

—*D. Bohrman*

"… hard time setting the book aside to do my housework. **Wow, what a story.**"

D. Magoon

"**Should be required reading for every high school student studying western expansion.**"

—*D.D.*

JAMES LETTIS

Spirit Bow

THE SAGA OF
SEAN O'MALLEY

ISBN: 978-1-54396-564-3 (print)
ISBN: 978-1-54396-565-0 (ebook)

*I would like to dedicate **Spirit Bow: The Saga of Sean O'Malley** to my parents, Lloyd and Myrtle Lettis. "Thank you for making education such an integral part of my life."*

Special thanks must go to my wife Celia, for her unwavering love, support, and encouragement through an author's ups and downs.

Thanks also to my editor and writing coach, William Greenleaf of Greenleaf Literary Services, for his suggestions and patiently teaching me a few of the finer points of writing.

My beautiful cover is a painting by Paul Sachtleben entitled, Silent Teepees. Paul has many beautiful and poignant paintings dealing with Native American Indians available on his website.

BOOK ONE

Nice Shot

CHAPTER ONE

Ohio, November 1819

The crust of the snow softly crunches under their moccasins as they kneel to examine the tracks. They have trailed their quarry now for most of the afternoon, and Sean knows they must be getting close. For much of the journey, icy sleet has been coming down hard from the darkened sky. Nearby flashes of lightning closely followed by rolling thunder warn of an intensifying storm.

Sean's grandfather, Tom O'Reilly, points out the sharpness of the print before gesturing up to the bare branches of the bush, where the big buck must have stopped to browse. It stands in contrast to the other bushes nearby, the ones still heavy with snow and ice. Sean nods in understanding. The two men have not uttered a word since they first set out after the buck. Grandpa uses a slight wave of his hand across the forest in front of them to indicate that the buck has to be close. Very close. The old man passes the Kentucky long rifle to Sean, whose eyes widen in surprise as he accepts the offering.

From the size of the prints, Sean knows this must be a big buck, and now he has become the one responsible for bringing it down. He can feel his heart beating harder in his chest as his grandfather steps aside and invites him to take the lead. As he moves past, the old man pats him on the shoulder. Sean is grateful for the show of confidence, but also nervous about how one bad shot could ruin everything. He feels confident that his aim will be true when the time comes, but for the moment, the anxiety and adrenaline are making his stomach churn.

Quietly through the snow and thick forest, Sean follows the buck's tracks. Soon, the wood begins to thin, and Sean spots faint movement in the brush ahead. He holds his hand up and takes a knee, preparing to fire just as Grandpa taught him. Through the falling snow and sleet, Sean can barely make out his target in the brush.

Grandpa moves up to kneel beside him. "Go on, boy," he whispers. "Take him."

Sean slowly unwinds the oiled rag that keeps the powder dry in the rifle's pan. He checks to make sure the flint is securely held between the pieces of leather. Then he cocks the hammer back and aims through the driving sleet. As he levels the sights on the center of the brown patch, he can see the rifle shaking. He takes a deep breath to calm his nerves. He holds the heavy rifle at the ready for a long time and hopes for a clearer shot, not wanting to miss. After a time, he realizes that he's holding his breath instead of breathing slowly, as his grandfather taught him. He exhales long and slow, lowers the barrel, and tells himself there has to be a better shot.

Sean senses his grandfather's frustration, but he tries to put it out of his mind. If he shoots now, there is no certainty. But if the buck steps out from the brush, Sean is certain he will not miss.

"Boy," Grandpa whispers in his ear, "if you ain't gonna shoot him, let me."

At the same time the old man starts to reach for the rifle, Sean sees the antlers rise. He quickly aims at the brown patch just below the antlers and fires. The powder in the pan flares and the rifle booms, spitting lead, flame, and smoke from the end of the long barrel. Through the acrid smoke, Sean sees the antlers drop.

Grandpa springs to his feet and draws his skinning knife as he jogs in the buck's direction. Sean stands and quickly begins to reload the old rifle. His excitement causes him to fumble the ramrod, so he pauses and takes a deep breath to calm himself. As he reloads, his grandfather's words replay in his mind. *An empty rifle won't do nothin' but make ya dead.*

A few minutes have passed before Sean finally catches up to Grandpa. The old man stands in front of a gravely wounded young

4

Indian, examining the warrior's bow and quiver of red-feathered arrows. As he looks closely at the markings on the bow, Grandpa mumbles something that sounds to Sean like "Spirit Bow."

A nice-sized buck lay in the snow just above the wounded Indian's head, a red-feathered arrow protruding from its side. It is obvious to Sean what happened. The young Indian had just lifted the buck to his shoulders when Sean saw the antlers and fired. He can see the lifeblood oozing out of the small bullet hole in the Indian's buckskin shirt. As Sean steps closer, the wounded boy's eyes suddenly open wide and he reaches a hand up to him.

"Grandpa!" Sean calls out. "Forget the bow and help me. He's still alive. We gotta do somethin'. For Gawd's sake, he's not much older than Jake!"

The old man casually kneels to examine the young Indian's wound. He runs a finger over the beadwork on the warrior's buckskin shirt. "Reckon the boy's most likely Illinois band. Might be Miami, but pretty far south for them. Ain't nothin' we can do for him now, Sean. Just gotta leave him be to meet his maker. Nice shot, though."

Grandpa looks up at the storm just as a stab of lightning cuts the darkening sky. All morning, they have watched the clouds piling up to the East, and now the sky is shrouded in black thunderheads. Sean sees his grandfather suddenly look down at the bow and quiver in his hands before thrusting them into his chest as if they are on fire. Sean barely has time to grasp them.

"You carry these," Grandpa says before pointing a gloved hand up at the dark clouds. "We can't stay here, weather's closin' in fast."

"We got what we came for." The old man steps over, lifts the dead deer to his shoulders, grabs the rifle from Sean's hands, and abruptly turns to leave. Sean is left holding the bow and quiver of arrows as he stares down at the Indian. The dying boy returns the gaze, all the while reaching up to him. After a short hesitation, Sean removes his leather cape from his shoulders and lays it over the boy's body. Then he turns and starts jogging to catch up with his grandfather, leaving the wounded boy to die alone in the snow and cold.

As they make their way home, the storm strikes with a fury that Sean has never experienced before. What started out as a soft snowfall that morning has now become a violent blizzard. The wind howls and shrieks like a tormented soul as it gusts through the trees and spits it's grating sleet. Branches sway whiplike, lashing out at them as they pass. It becomes harder and harder for Sean to see where he is going as he holds his arms up to shield his face. He stumbles along through the storm and icy forest as he tries to keep his fleeing grandfather in sight. Sean is confused because he is fairly certain they are heading in the wrong direction.

The storm intensifies by the minute. Flashes of lightning are so closely followed by the crackle and boom of thunder that they almost seem simultaneous. Sean pauses in awe as a slash of lightning splits the darkening sky into brilliant fingers of fire that momentarily illuminate the forest.

Crackle, crackle, kaboom!

These are the loudest sounds Sean has ever heard, and he has never been more terrified.

Crackle, crackle, kaboom!

Sean glances up just in time to see another bolt of lightning strike a tree near his fleeing grandfather. The tree explodes in a shower of sparks and splinters. Sean watches as Grandpa leaps away, drops the buck from his shoulders, and takes off at an even faster pace. Another close lightning strike forces the old man to veer in yet another direction. Sean can't beat back the strange feeling that the storm is following them home, attacking all the way.

In the dark and blinding weather, the young man falls farther and farther behind. Roots and vines claw at his feet and ankles, and he must struggle to keep his balance. He stumbles along until a brief lull of the wind allows him to stop again to look for the old man. Grandpa is nowhere to be seen.

Sean knows there is nothing he can do but push on in the direction he has been going, even if it may not be the right one. He tries to follow Grandpa's footprints but loses them in the failing light and blinding storm. His fear begins to get the better of him, merging with the cold to freeze his heart and seize his mind. In a storm like this, he knows he will freeze to death if he doesn't find shelter. Doubt creeps into his mind about his decision to leave the leather cape with the Indian boy. Idly, he wonders what Pa will think when Sean's frozen body is found without it. He tries to push the thought from his mind so he might study the sky and figure out the fastest way home. He knows he must keep moving, even though his body cries out to sit a moment and rest.

Finally, after what seems like hours, he sees through the trees and flashes of lightning what appears to be cleared fields. They might be his family's, but it doesn't really matter. Any cleared field means there is shelter close by. As he nears the edge of the field, the lightning strikes a large sycamore tree next to him.

Crackle, crackle, kaboom!

The tree explodes in a blinding flash of sparks, sound, and scattering splinters.

Instinctively Sean leaps away from the explosion, but his foot catches on a vine and he falls backward, striking the back of his head hard on an exposed root. In the same instant, a huge limb splits from the sycamore and comes crashing down on the path in front of him. The branches scratch the side of his face and tear a hole in his woolen shirt, gouging his side.

He lies still in the snow and slush, stunned and bleeding. When he tries to push himself up, he discovers that the limbs of the heavy branch have him pinned down tightly. He shouts feebly for his grandfather to help him, but the howl of the wind swallows his words. The back of his head begins to throb, and cold and alone, he slowly loses consciousness.

CHAPTER TWO

Ohio, July 1821

"*Nice shot!*"

Sean gasps as he snaps awake from his nightmare. His nightshirt is damp from sweat, partly from his dream and partly from the summer night's warmth. He wonders if anyone in the cabin has heard him cry out. He peers across the darkness of the loft to where his older brother, Jake, softly snores. He wishes that he, too, could sleep so soundly.

Sean's cornhusk mattress rustles as he sits up. He knows it is useless to try to go back to sleep, for his nightmare is still too vivid in his mind. This is a recurring ghost, this vision of the dying Indian boy's wide eyes and outstretched hand, and it is always followed by Grandpa's words. "Nice shot."

Sean sits and listens as the rain lightly hits the roof's shingles a few feet above his head and the thunder echoes across the valley. Of course, the summer storms are a blessing to the scorched Ohio Valley, but Sean also knows that the thunder triggers his ghostly nightmares. It has been that way now for almost two years, ever since he accidentally shot the Indian boy.

He counts himself lucky that his father and brother were able to locate him before he froze to death that night. Grandpa adamantly refused to go back out in the storm, but he was able to tell Pa and Jake where to start looking. Somehow in the dark Pa found Sean pinned under the old sycamore. The way Pa tells the story, Sean still held the bow tightly in his hands even as his father carried him home. Pa asked him once about the lost cape, but Sean just shrugged and Pa never asked again. For two years, Sean has tried to push away the memories of that hunt, to hide them somewhere in a dark corner of his mind, but by now, he knows he will never succeed.

Sean rubs the scar on his side as he listens to his brother's soft, rhythmic snoring. As he listens closer, he hears a few snorts coming from his grandparents' side of the cabin. Recently it occurred to Sean that somehow the stormy night two years ago was even more terrifying for Grandpa. He wishes things could be the way they were before that terrible night. If only they had turned back when it started to snow.

The rain finally ceases its patter on the shingles as the storm moves past. Sean hears the old red rooster greeting the faint morning light. He tugs his damp nightshirt over his head, pulls on his wool trousers, and slips into his linen shirt. With his shoes clutched in his hand, he quietly climbs down the loft's ladder and heads for the cabin door. He stops to lift the bow and quiver of arrows off the row of pegs near the door before he turns the wood block latch and steps out into the predawn light.

The air feels fresh and clean as he begins his long jog. Always hopeful, Sean carries the bow in one hand as he jogs up to the wagon road that will eventually wind its way into town. He promised Ma that he would go to the mercantile to get a loaf of sugar before Jake's birthday. He isn't sure of the date, but he knows the birthday has to be getting close.

As he jogs, he passes many dark and quiet farmsteads along the road, with only an occasional warning bark breaking the predawn stillness. After a while, a few cabins display the flicker of candlelight, the folks inside beginning their preparations to face the day.

Sean thinks about his grandfather's caution about not letting anyone see the bow. He tells himself that if he doesn't see anything to shoot through the next stretch of forest, he will have to hide the bow and quiver of arrows before entering the outskirts of town. Fortunately, he has done this many times before, and has located the perfect hiding place.

Around the bend, he finds the hiding spot in a hollow log just off the road. Carefully he hides the bow and quiver before resuming his jog toward town. As he reaches the outskirts of the tiny community, he ducks off the road and into the shadows of a small cherry orchard. The nearby house is still dark, so he quickly picks as many of the ripe cherries as he can hold in the front of his upturned shirt. He would like to pick some apples, too, but that will have to wait, as they are not yet ripe.

When he reaches the town's first building, Sean is pleasantly surprised to hear the blacksmith's heavy hammer rhythmically pounding. Sean has always thought of himself as an early riser, but nothing like the blacksmith, for it must take at least an hour to get the coals hot enough to do any kind of work in the smithy.

Sean pokes his head through the open doors and nods to his friend Newt, who is working the giant bellows. Like most of the other boys his age, Newt stands taller than Sean. The two have known each other for three years, ever since Newt's family arrived in town and bought the old rundown barn. Newt is the very first African Sean ever saw, and next to his brother, he considers Newt his best friend.

Their first meeting was by the river when Sean spotted Newt fishing for catfish. Sean still remembers being astonished by Newt's black skin. Taking it for a disease of some sort, Sean kept his distance at first. But then, after they sat and fished for a spell, it seemed clear that Newt wasn't sick at all. Later, Newt would admit to Sean that he had thought the same thing about him—that with all his freckles, Sean was the sick one.

On the day of their first meeting, Sean wet his fingers and tried to rub the black off Newt's arm. His new friend did the likewise, trying to scrape Sean's freckles away with a chip of wood. They closely examined each other's hair as well—Sean's curly and bright red, Newt's black and kinky. Afterward, they sat there making up stories about why they looked the way they did, and they laughed and laughed. They have been best friends ever since. Sometimes they get to fish together, but most of the time, Newt has to work at the smithy, so they just talk as he works. Sean does most of the talking, while Newt mostly just listens.

Sean has tried to teach Newt to read a little, but Newt hasn't taken to letters much. Of course, scratching out words in the dust of the smithy isn't really an ideal teaching method. Sean has always been sorry that Africans and Indians aren't allowed to go to the white school. He has never understood what the teacher thinks may happen if Newt and the Indian girl in town attend school, but Pa once told him to forget it because it just wasn't gonna happen.

Sean recalls the first time he saw the sign that Newt's pa put up: Blacksmith. Back then, Sean thought the word referred to a black man named Smith.

There was a time when Sean was sure that the heat of the fire must have had something to do with the blackness of Newt's and his father's skin. It was just like when Ma left a roast by the coals too long. But then, for the life of him, he couldn't figure out why Newt's ma's skin was dark, too, since she was never near the fire.

"*Africans come from a land on the other side of the earth,*" Ma had tried to explain. "*They're from a country called Africa, a place that has thick jungles, lions, zebras, and elephants, and is hot all year long. All the people are black-skinned there.*"

But how did their skin get black in the first place? Sean wondered for a long time after that. Only after he thought on it a spell did he finally arrive at the answer on his own. He didn't know what to think of Ma's descriptions of lions, zebras, and elephants, but when Ma said Africa was always hot, it became obvious. Africa must be closer to the sun. The people there are black because they're slowly getting burned up.

On this day, Sean greets his friend before taking a seat on a log stool near the fire. He dries the sweat from his shirt, eats a few of the cherries, and watches Newt work the big bellows. Newt's father, Big John, is absolutely the biggest man Sean has ever seen. Big John's muscles ripple and shine with sweat as he works the heavy sledgehammer with ease. Sean's own father is tall and lanky. Big John must be twice Pa's weight, Sean thinks. He wonders if Big John has been working the bellows since he was a kid. That at least might explain his muscles.

"You think I could work 'em bellows for a spell?" Sean casually asks his friend.

Newt hesitates a moment in his rhythm and looks over in his father's direction before shaking his head.

"How 'bout if I let you eat the rest of 'em cherries?" Sean asks. When he catches Newt's hesitation, he adds, "They're really good."

Newt looks again at his father, who is busy pounding on a piece of red-hot iron. Then the young man gazes back at the ripe cherries Sean has piled up on the table. Newt finally nods, and they change places. Newt eats cherries while Sean pushes and pulls the great bellows up and down. After a spell, what at first looked like fun turns out to be really difficult. Sean grits his teeth as he struggles to move the big bellows and gain a rhythm.

"Newt!" Big John hollers after a few minutes. "Git back to work. Fire's goin' cold!"

The dutiful son jumps to retake his place. Sean is left winded as he watches his friend work. Newt gives him a smile that seems to suggest that a few minutes at the bellows just isn't enough to master the technique necessary to keep the fire going.

Sean decides that it is time to head out. He leaves the last few cherries for Newt, then gives his friend a nod and waves to Big John before stepping through the open door and into the sunlight. The skies have brightened and the sun is breaking clear above the horizon. Sean passes a heavy wagon standing just a few paces from the door. Somehow, he failed to notice it when he first entered. One axle is missing a wheel and is propped up by a stump of wood. Maybe this is what Big John is working on, Sean thinks. He wonders if the big blacksmith lifted the heavy wagon up by himself to set the stump.

Sean hasn't seen a traveling wagon in these parts of Ohio in quite a spell. Most folks moving on around here simply float down the nearby Ohio River. It has been ten years since Pa helped the militia defeat the Shawnee Indians at Tippecanoe in 1811, and Pa has told him that all the usable land around Pleasant Valley is taken.

He looks the big wagon over, figuring that this must be one of those Conestoga wagons he heard about in school. Boy, it sure is big, he thinks. Sean tries to peek inside, but he isn't tall enough. He is about to climb up on a wheel and take a look inside the wagon when he glances over at the open door to the shed and sees Big John glaring out at him. From the look the big blacksmith gives him, Sean decides that maybe this isn't such a good idea after all.

He nods to Big John and turns to make his way up the street to the mercantile store. He passes the half-finished brick church the town has been working on for the past two years. It doesn't look like anything has been done since he last saw it three weeks ago. People are just too busy on their farms to be making bricks to build a church, he thinks. He supposes that the church will have to wait until after the spring planting.

The moment Sean pushes in the front door at Johnson's Mercantile, the tiny bell rings above his head. He looks up to locate the ring's source. He is certain that the bell wasn't there last year, but the store has changed hands since then. What a good idea, he thinks as he opens and closes the door a few times to test the bell. Finally satisfied with its workings, he turns his attention to the dimly lit interior.

The floor is stacked high with heavy bags of supplies, and the shelves are full of all manner of newfangled gadgets. Most of the items crowding the shelves or hanging from the ceiling and walls he recognizes, but some are goods he has never seen before. Sean studies a couple of gadgets, trying to determine their purpose. He glances nervously around for Will Johnson, a local kid he has never much gotten along with, but he only sees a short man that he assumes must be Will's father. Mr. Johnson is busy restocking shelves along the far wall. The shape of the man's body reminds Sean of a pear.

Sean turns to walk over to the counter, where he is truly amazed at what he sees. Sitting on a stool behind the counter has to be the fattest person Sean has ever encountered. Her beady little eyes watch him as he cautiously approaches. She picks up another cookie from the well-stocked plate sitting on the counter in front of her, then stuffs the whole thing in her mouth.

"Somethin' I can help you with, boy?" asks the huge, sour-faced woman as she chews.

"Ma sent me to fetch a loaf of sugar," Sean replies. He isn't sure why, but he suddenly feels pity for Mr. Johnson. He notices a number of crumbs resting on the plateau of the woman's enormous bosom, probably waiting to be devoured at a later time.

"Aren't you the O'Malley boy that's been causing so much trouble 'bout?" Mrs. Johnson asks.

"I don't know nothin' 'bout no trouble," Sean answers softly. "But yes, I'm Sean O'Malley. Ma told me to put the loaf on her credit."

The woman pulls out a worn brown notebook hidden somewhere between the ample folds of her dress and slowly pages through it. Sean's eyes are drawn to the huge folds of fat hanging from her upper arms and down over her elbows. He watches the folds jiggle as she turns the pages of the notebook. Finally, after finding what she has been looking for, she looks back at him and shakes her head. "I'm sorry, boy, but you O'Malleys done reached your limit."

"But it's my brother's birthday in two days," Sean pleads, "an' Ma needs that sugar for his sweet-potato pie."

The woman hesitates before she rises, slowly manages to turn her massive body around, and reaches a ham-hock arm up to the shelf behind her. She brings down a loaf of brown sugar and stuffs it in a small cloth bag. As she turns away, Sean takes his opportunity to deftly grab a handful of cookies off the plate and drop them down his shirt front.

The woman hands the cone-shaped bag over the counter to Sean. "You tell your ma that this be the last credit I can give her. Tell her she owes almost sixteen dollars."

"Thank you," Sean says as he accepts the bag. "And I'll, sure enough, tell Ma what you done said."

As he leaves the store, he catches a glance of Will sticking his head out from the back storeroom. Sean feels a bit sorry for him, having met his parents for the first time, and that feeling makes him think maybe he should stay a spell and chat. But in the next heartbeat, he decides that it might be best to head back over to the blacksmith and lay low a few hours before heading home. Besides, he wants to see for himself if Big John can really lift that wagon.

CHAPTER  THREE

Dusk has fallen by the time Sean nears his family's farm. The quiver of arrows retrieved from the hollow log are slung over his shoulder, and he carries the bow in one hand while the bag of sugar dangles from the other hand. He can only hope that the sugar is still good after sitting in the sun for a spell. After he left the blacksmith, Sean spent some of the day hunting along the river, but mostly he just sat. He might have come home directly to get the sugar to his mother, but he needed to clear his head and tend to his battered face after his unexpected fight with Will.

He was glad Big John had come along to put an end to the fight, but he still can't quite figure out why it started in the first place. He has replayed the moment in his head a hundred times by now, but he is no closer to the answer. One moment, he was calling out his hello to Will, and in the next moment, he was in the middle of a violent tussle.

When the cabin comes into sight, he tosses away the wet moss he has been holding against his cheek and split lip. Dang, but it sure does hurt like the dickens.

He sees his older brother getting in a few last swings with the ax against the roots of a huge stump still stubbornly holding out in the middle of the freshly plowed field. Two mules stand idle in their harness, their chains wrapped around the stump. Sean shakes his head as he realizes that Jake has been working on and off on that stump now for the past two weeks.

He is just about to call out to Jake when a pang of pain in his lip reminds him that he is trying to hide his bruised face. Besides, someone else catches his eye before he can holler out. A man and a woman stand in the door of the cabin, and only one of them Sean recognizes. The one he knows is his mother, and Sean's heart skips when it comes clear that the other is an elderly Indian. It isn't unusual for one of the friendly locals to come by begging for a little coffee or sugar, but Sean has never met this particular Indian. So, curious, he starts jogging toward the cabin, completely forgetting about his face, or about the bow he holds in his hand.

Ma, being a Christian woman, has just given the old Indian a cup of coffee. As Sean arrives, she is trying to explain to the Indian that she doesn't have any sugar. A moment of hesitation enters Sean's mind as he frets on whether he should reveal the contents of the bag in his hand.

He is so caught up in this thought that he doesn't realize the mistake he has made until it is too late. The moment the old Indian turns to face him, it occurs to him what he has done. A seizing sort of dread creeps up his spine. Suddenly, his battered face feels like the least of his worries. He tries to move the bow behind his back, hoping it won't be noticed, but it is no use.

The old Indian smiles and slowly nods as his gaze catches the bow. Then, wordlessly, he reaches out his hand as if asking permission to examine it. With his eyes downcast, Sean is just about to hand the bow to the old Indian when he hears a hollering from inside the cabin.

Grandpa, thoroughly drunk again, rushes through the door, yelling and carrying on so brashly that Sean jumps back in fright. The old man waves his arms crazily as he barks something at the old Indian in a language Sean doesn't recognize. Sean suspects that the language is Shawnee, but he knows he will never get a chance to ask without provoking Grandpa's ire.

The Indian shrinks away when Grandpa raises the clay whiskey jug he's holding and threatens to hit the old warrior with it. The old warrior drops the cup of unfinished coffee and backs away, that silly grin still pressed on his face. When Grandpa starts at him again, the old Indian hightails it across the field before vanishing into the forest.

Not wanting to face his grandfather's wrath, Sean stares at the spot in the trees where the Indian disappeared. But he can feel the old man's gaze hot upon his cheek, and his mother's as well, and he knows he can't shy away any longer.

He can feel his heart pounding in his chest. The pain in his face redoubles as he turns teary-eyed to accept the blame for what he has done.

It is the angriest that Sean has ever seen his grandfather. The old man looks down at his precious corn-whiskey as if offended that Sean's actions would force him to risk injury to its container.

Grandpa doesn't say anything in front of Ma, but his glare says enough, and when he shakes his head in disgust, it is about enough to break Sean. He knows that in forgetting to hide the bow from the Indian, he has really messed up.

Ma just stands there, clearly dumbfounded about why Grandpa would react this way. But then, whatever confusion she holds about the incident fades when her gaze finds Sean's face.

Before she can say anything, Sean slips past the adults and goes to the woodpile. His instinct tells him that if maybe he goes about his business as if nothing has happened, they will forget the incident and return to their routines. He gathers up a load of firewood and clutches it high on his chest to help shield his face as he steps back past his mother and into the cabin. He hears his grandfather take a long pull from the jug as Sean bends to drop the load of wood in the bin next to the fireplace.

Patches, the old family dog, ambles over to greet him with a sniff and a whimper before reclaiming his spot under the rough-cut kitchen table. Deaf and nearly blind, the dog circles a moment in search of the perfect spot before whimpering again in the effort to lie back down. Patches used to be a good hunting dog, but now seldom has the energy to get much farther than a few feet outside the cabin.

Sean is surprised when he turns back to find that his ruse has worked. Grandpa, drunk as he seems, has ambled back to his bed, and Ma is busy preparing supper. Sean smells something delicious emanating from the kettle on the iron spider beside the coals. As Ma kneads biscuit dough, Sean's mouth starts to water at the thought of sourdough biscuits, honey, and a bowl of venison stew. He hasn't eaten but a handful of cherries, a few stolen cookies, some wild strawberries, and a few dandelions he found along the river, so he's famished. He watches her a moment as she kneads the dough.

In the corner of the room sits Sean's grandma, her mind ever wandering among tangled and confused memories. She hasn't uttered a clear word since the night Sean was found nearly frozen in the forest.

A few days after they found him, Jake told Sean that Grandma jumped up and yelled, "Praise the Lord," before crumpling to the floor. The doctor told Pa that she most likely had a stroke, but Sean doesn't know exactly what that means. He only knows he doesn't want to catch it, so he has kept his distance ever since.

Grandma sits and sings quietly as she rocks in the old rocking chair, both the words and the tune of her own making. Ma has to walk her out to the outhouse four times a day or she'll pee or mess herself. Grandpa doesn't even want her in bed with him at night, but Ma insists.

The rocker Grandma uses is the O'Malley family's only store-bought piece of furniture. It was a wedding gift to a grandma Mary over eighty years ago, and it has been passed down ever since. Sean reckons that his sister, Becky, will probably get it next.

Grandpa, old and tired, as well as drunk, now lies nearby in one of the two visible beds. His disheveled, iron-gray hair hangs down to his broad, thick shoulders. Life has been hard on him, causing him to become increasingly bitter in his old age. As far as Sean can see, Grandpa has no visible ailments. He just suffers from old age, superstitious fear, and a growing dependence on the jug at his bedside.

Ever since that terrible night two years ago, Sean has done his best to stay clear of Grandpa when he's been drinking. But as the old man leans over to grab his jug for another swig, he catches Sean's gaze and glares at him. Sean can see that, even though he may have avoided the immediate confrontation, it will be a long time before Grandpa stops being mad about the bow and the old Indian. An old flintlock pistol rests by Grandpa's side. That is something Sean has never seen before and wonders where Grandpa had it hidden. He watches out of the corner of his eye as Grandpa tilts the jug up for another sip before returning it to rest under a protective arm. Sean can feel the old man continuing to glare at him.

"If ya insist on goin' 'round with that bow, boy," Grandpa bellows from across the room, "then why ain't ya shot nothin' today? Ya done lost your touch?"

Sean ignores the old man's harsh questions. He doesn't want to let on that he sat by the river all day tending to his bruised cheek and split lip.

Becky sits near the fire, playing with the wooden doll Pa carved for her some weeks back. Like Sean, Becky has freckles, curly red hair, and green eyes. Sean watches in amusement as she talks to the doll and straightens the little homespun indigo dress Ma made for it from scraps of cloth left over from the dress Becky wears. Becky's matching indigo bonnet hangs on one of the pegs by the door. Pa carved the doll out of some driftwood he found on the river bank, so it is exceptionally smooth. This isn't the first doll he has carved for his daughter, but it is certainly his best work. Pa has always been an excellent carver, but the detail of this doll's face is so lifelike that even Sean has to admire it. Becky, meanwhile, is so absorbed in her imagination that she isn't even aware that her brother has entered the cabin, or that her grandfather is hollering at him.

"Sean O'Malley," Ma says, beckoning for him, "come over here this instant!"

Now you're in for it, he thinks as he reluctantly shuffles over. He knows Ma won't be steamed about the bow, but she has spied his face again for sure.

With her flour-covered hand, his mother turns his face from side to side, examining his bruised cheek and cut lip. "What you gone and done to your face this time? Was it that Sawyer boy again?"

"Ah, Ma, it ain't nothin'," Sean shrugs, struggling to turn his face away from her hurting grip. "Will Johnson an' me just had us a little tussle, that's all. Really ain't nothin' to fret on Ma."

"Don't you go telling me it isn't anything," Ma corrects, before giving a sigh. "You have a split lip! That's the second fight this week. First, you're off fighting with Sawyer, and now this Will fella. It's a good thing you're hardheaded. Folks will soon start asking what kind of offspring I be raising." She frowns and folds her arms across her chest.

"Besides, ain't Will Johnson that big fella? Father owns the mercantile store? What was this ruckus about, anyway?"

Sean grits his teeth, uncomfortable about the subject. "I had to fight 'em, Ma. He didn't leave me no choice. He called us no good Irish trash. Called Grandpa a liquored up ole drunk. Said Ohio be better off without no drunken Mick trash!" He throws a nervous glance over at Grandpa, who has raised himself up on his elbows, the better to hear. "He also called me a spotted runt! I ain't no spotted runt! I hate these damn freckles! How come none of 'em other fellas ain't got no freckles?"

Ma brushes his red hair back with her hand. "I don't like bein' made fun of no more than the next, but that ain't no reason to fight—especially not anyone as big as Will Johnson. 'Sides, freckles are a gift from the Lord above. Because Ireland is mostly covered in mist, God sprinkled a little magic dust down on us, giving us freckles. That's just his way of reminding the Irish of the beautiful stars in the heavens above." Ma teasingly fluffs Sean's hair with her fingers. "And this beautiful, flaming red hair is for us to see the beauty of the sun at sunset."

"Yeah, yeah," Sean tries to imagine telling that to Will Johnson. His jaw aches just at the thought of it. "I done heard it all before, Ma. I just wish ya done shut me up indoors when God did all the sprinklin'. And it don't make no never-mind how big Will is, anyway. Ain't no one gonna call me no spotted runt. I ain't no runt!"

"Jenny," Grandpa says, pushing up to a seated position, "y'all leave the boy be now. He's gotta learn to take his lumps and bruises if'n he's gonna grow up to be a man. Shawnee bastards sure whooped me a few, an' I was a might younger than Sean. Didn't do me no harm. Anyway, sounds to me like that there Will fella deserved the lickin' the boy gave 'em."

Sean puffs out his chest, half proud and half glad that the subject of the fight seems to have made Grandpa forget about the mistake with the bow.

Ma sends a stern warning glare at her father-in-law before turning back to Sean. "I still want you to stay away from that Johnson boy." As if trying to change the defiant mood hanging over the cabin, she offers him a sympathetic smile. "Maybe the day after tomorrow you can take

Grandpa's rifle and go see if you can shoot us a turkey for supper—a nice big fat one. I'm pretty sure Jake would rather eat turkey for his birthday than one of 'em old scrawny chickens. Tomorrow, though, I'd like you to help Jake on that stump."

Sean, relieved that the subject has been changed, smiles at his mother. "Know just the spot. Saw some fresh sign the other day when I was fishin' catfish up river a bit. I think I'll take the bow too. No point in wasting good powder on a turkey."

Apparently satisfied, Ma returns to her cooking.

"Ma, I almost forgot." Sean grabs the cloth bag he set down beside the woodpile and carefully hands it to his mother. "I got ya the sugar loaf ya wanted. Sorry, but it got a little busted up in the scuffle."

She takes the sack and sets it on the table. "I'm sure it will do just fine, thank you." She turns back to the biscuit dough, and Sean snatches a wooden spoonful of stew from the kettle. Ma shakes her head and frowns, but does nothing to stop the raid.

"Mrs. Johnson said ya owe sixteen dollars," Sean says. "Says she ain't gonna give ya no more credit. An' she says she wants the bag back, too."

"I know, I know. Thank you for remembering."

"I think that woman may be bigger than our sow."

"Sean O'Malley, that sure ain't a nice thing to say." She gives him a stern look. "Mrs. Johnson's just got an eating problem, that's all."

After a moment's pause to lick the wooden spoon clean, Sean replies, "I'm not so sure, Ma. Looks to me like she done eats just fine." Setting the spoon aside, Sean asks, "Ya think Pa will be home from the Harris place soon?"

Sean's ma tries to hide a smile as she answers, "You know good and well the Harris place is eight miles up the road. I 'spect he'll be along soon enough, for sure by Jake's birthday dinner. Other than that, he'll be here when he gets here." She pauses at the sounds of someone at the wash bucket outside. "Sounds to me like Jake's here now."

A moment later, Sean's older brother pushes the door inward with an elbow and steps through, bare-chested and drying his hands on the dusty shirt he is carrying. His hands end up just a shade cleaner than when he started. His leather suspenders hang at the sides of his knees. Sean watches Jake, who is tall for his age, move about the cabin. The slight shadow of a mustache adorns Jake's upper lip, and his tanned, well-muscled chest and arms make Sean dream of the day that he, too, will boast the features of a man—a day when Will Johnson will think twice about tauntin' him.

Jake pulls a homemade three-legged stool over to the open door to catch the breeze before sitting down. There, he pulls his damp linen shirt back over his head. He takes a good look at his brother before turning back to complain to his mother. "I've been thinkin' hard an' long on it, Ma, an' it ain't right that Pa be up at the Harris place." He brushes his brown, curly, shoulder-length hair away from his face with his hand. "After all old man Harris' says about us bein' Irish an' all, Pa goes off an' I get stuck with all the plowin' an' other work 'round here! Damn heat's enough to shrivel parts of a man all up."

"That what ya are now, boy, a man?" Grandpa's voice booms out from the corner. "Quit your snivelin'! Startin' to sound like that good for nothin' son of mine, your lazy uncle Jack.

Jake shoots a hateful gaze in his grandpa's direction but doesn't bother to reply. Like Sean, he has learned that it isn't worth the energy to fight a battle of words with the old man.

"That no good lazy bastard son of mine hightailed it just when we had us a trifle bit of work to be done." His grandpa pulls the stopper on the corn whiskey and tilts the jug back again.

Ma moves over next to Jake and whispers loudly enough for Sean to hear, "Don't you pay no never-mind to Grandpa's carrying on. He doesn't know anything. Just a mean, hateful old man, letting the corn liquor do all his talking. I do know for a fact that Pa's mighty proud of you and thankful for your help, and so am I. You be doing a man's share right now, and we're both grateful." Ma continues on a little louder. "Us being Irish and all is probably the reason Pa's there. Pa and I done hashed it over. We decided if you kids had to grow up hereabouts, it was best to beat down this Irish nonsense. Best way to stop people being mean and all is with a little kindness. That's what the Good Book says."

By the end of her point, her preaching has taken on a tone musical enough to snap Becky out of her game with the doll. The little girl looks back at her mother and nods as if confirming a point she isn't nearly old enough to fully understand.

"The Good Book must have been written by men sittin' in the shade," Jake replies softly, "with a sea breeze a blowin' an' a cool mug a lemonade in their hands."

"That'll be quite enough of that, Jake O'Conner!" Ma says in a raised voice. "Don't you be mocking the Good Book." After taking a deep breath as if to calm herself, she continues. "Besides, y'all be fifteen come tomorrow, and that's practically a grown man in my mind. I'm sure a little ax work and plowing can't get you down none. Your pa's probably just one or two more days, I think y'all can survive."

"The boy's spot-on for once, Jenny," Grandpa says. "Pat's wasting his time helping out over there when there's work aplenty 'round here."

"I don't see ya doin' nothin'," Jake mutters back in the old man's direction, "just laying around all day, bitchin' an' complainin'." Then, to no one in particular, he adds, "Might help if them damn mules did a little more pullin' instead of me doin' all the pushin'. All that diggin' an' choppin' an' that old stump ain't moved a plum inch."

Sean's heart skips when his brother turns to look at him.

"Did ya whoop him?" Jake asks.

Puffing out his chest, Sean tries to act as tough as possible. "Will Johnson called me a spotted runt, an' we had us a little scuffle. Guess I showed him, though. I was givin' him a pretty good lickin' when Big John stepped in an' saved him." After waiting for his brother's reaction, he adds, "Will called ya a Mick bastard too!"

"Sean O'Malley!" Ma hollers. "I'll have no such words in this house. You're starting to sound like Grandpa."

"Yessum, Ma," Sean responds while keeping his eyes locked on his brother.

Jake appears lost in his own thoughts as he mutters to Sean, "We'll see who the bastard is 'round here! Next time I see him, I'll—"

"Jake O'Conner!" Ma cuts in. "I said that'll be enough. Y'all know I don't hanker to that kinda talk. Especially not in front of Grandma and all. Besides, y'all got enough work to do 'round these parts without goin' about wasting your energy on that there Johnson fella!"

Jake gets up from his stool and faces his mother. "It may not be tomorrow, but Johnson's gonna get his. Sorry for cursin', Ma, but ya know good an' well that Grandma don't know half of what's goin' on in front of her face."

"Boy's spot-on again, Jenny. Woman here don't hear nothin'. Just keeps on singin' whatever it is she's singin'. 'Bout enough to send a man to an early grave." Grandpa takes another quick sip, then pats his jug and continues. "If 'n it wasn't for missin' me corn-sippin's here, I'd probably been under already."

"Don't y'all go talking 'bout 'Lizbeth like she ain't here, Tom O'Reilly. I won't hear of it." Ma throws her towel down as she directs her anger at the old man. "She's been a fine lady. Just had her a long and hard life. She deserves a little peace in her last years. She's certainly earned it, living with the likes of you—your just plain ornery! She shoulda left you when you ran off your own flesh and blood. If I had my say, Patrick woulda threw your sorry ass out long ago."

With a look to Jake, Ma takes a deep breath to calm herself. "Go on out and fetch me some water. And look in on that chicken coop too. Sounded to me like something was trying to get at 'em last night."

Jake grabs the bucket and walks out the door, mumbling just loud enough to be heard. "Why do I always gotta do all the work 'round here? What's wrong with Sean? Always, Jake, do this, an' Jake, do that."

"Your brother will be helping you tomorrow."

Sean watches his brother walk out the open door before turning to his mother. "Ma, why do 'em fellas call me 'Mick,' that ain't my name?" As he waits for her reply, he takes Jake's place on the vacated stool by the open door.

"That's just a way for being mean and all. 'Mick,' refers to somebody that comes from Ireland."

"But I didn't come from Ireland. I was born right here in this cabin. I thought ya said Great-Grandpa fought against the Redcoats in the War for Independence. We've been here a long time."

"When times get hard, some people look for someone else to blame their short-comings on," Ma explains. "Anyone that's a little bit different is an easy target for hate and blame. Now folks blame their troubles on the Irish. A few years back, it was the French, and before that, the Germans."

Sean is a bit confused by her answer. After a short pause, he abruptly changes the subject. "Ma, ya think I'm ever gonna grow? It's hard bein' the smallest fella 'round. Even that new kid Tom is taller than me, an' he's only ten."

Ma wipes her hands on a rag and takes his hands in hers. "Sean, its like I told you before. Boys all grow at different speeds. Some fast, and some, like you, a might slower. It's all the Good Lord's will. You just have to be a little more patient."

"Yessir," Becky says without breaking concentration on her doll. "Have to be more patient."

Sean might have chuckled at his precocious sister, but he is too busy being sullen about his size. "I've done been patient," he says in frustration. "What if I don't ever grow none?"

"You will. Besides, there are certainly worse things than being short." Ma pats him on the shoulder. "There are plenty of things you do right now that Will Johnson don't hold a candle to. Like the way you can shoot the eye out of a squirrel with the rifle and your skill with the bow." She ruffles his red hair. "Just look at the way you can run like the wind. Ain't no boy 'round can come close. Just you wait. I feel it in my bones. You'll shoot up past Will and be a head again taller. Both my brothers are near six foot, and just look how tall your pa is. It'll happen, son. Now go on and wash up, supper's 'bout ready, and see what's keeping your brother with the water."

As he ponders his mother's words, Sean slowly does as he is told and wanders out the cabin door.

CHAPTER FOUR

Two days later, by the predawn light of the full moon, Sean easily jogs the familiar wagon path toward the Scioto River. He carries the heavy Kentucky long rifle in one hand while the bow and quiver of arrows are securely slung over his back. The forest on either side of the wagon road is dense with pine, cedar, spruce, and hickory, with the occasional sycamore. Periodically, Sean jogs past cleared fields planted in barley, corn, or wheat.

Closer to the river, the road becomes darker as the river's mist begins to block what little light the moon offers. At the river's western bank, the wagon road turns south and winds down to the nearby ferry crossing. At this turn, Sean leaves the road and heads north, plunging deeper into the wilderness. He quickly locates the faint game trail that follows along the river's bank. Trees and brush appear as dim silver shadows in the whitish mist. The full moon still hangs high in the sky, but it sheds little light on the trail. The overhanging vegetation and thick mist hugging the ground along the water's edge hinder visibility in the predawn light. Sean stumbles along upriver for a mile or so.

He can't recall ever noticing how many roots and tangles of vines there are along this trail. Seemingly with every other step, they reach out to catch his moccasins or tug at his woolen pant legs. Then again, the last time he came this way, it wasn't in the faint light before dawn. He tells himself that maybe he should have stayed in bed a little longer.

After following the game trail along the water's edge for another twenty paces or so, Sean suddenly stops. He has been lost in his thoughts, but he is sure he heard something—something out of the ordinary that has alerted his senses and broken the early morning stillness. Could it possibly have been voices? As a precaution, he moves a couple of steps away from the river's edge and quietly settles back into the thick brush to listen. Who else would be out here at this time of day? There it is again, he thinks. It is voices, and they are coming from upriver. But are they coming from the path or the water?

He can't tell, so he pushes himself farther back into the brush as he stares upriver for the source. Sean wishes he had time to check the powder in the rifle's pan, but he can't take a chance now. He didn't think to wrap the oilcloth around the firing pan when he left the cabin this morning because it wasn't raining. But he's fairly certain that the powder will be damp from the river's heavy mist, rendering the rifle worthless.

Suddenly, a canoe appears out of the mist, glides silently by just a few feet from the bank, and disappears back into the mist downriver. The faint sound of paddles dipping in and out of the water is lost within seconds of the canoe's passing. A few heartbeats later, a second canoe slips by like a ghost in the gloom. Like the first, it silently appears out of the mist, only to vanish moments later.

Indians! Sean realizes.

He stays hidden and motionless for a few more minutes before stepping cautiously forward to the river's edge. He looks and listens for a short time but hears nothing further. Quietly he takes the powder horn, wipes away the damp powder in the rifle's pan with his thumb, and then freshens the pan with dry powder. He waits a few more minutes, then turns to continue on the trail upriver. As he continues on his way, he wonders where those Indians could be headed.

Another half mile upriver, a fallen old hickory tree looms up out of the mist, blocking any further progress along the river's bank. Sean turns away from the river and begins to work his way through the tangle of underbrush. Just as his grandfather taught him, he is careful to avoid stepping on dead leaves that might rustle or small twigs that could snap underfoot and give away his location to any game nearby.

With the old hickory tree having assured him of the correct location, he now confidently finds a spot to sit, concealed in the brush overlooking a small clearing. Sean had success here just last month when he killed a doe, so he knows there is a game trail that follows a gentle slope down through the clearing to the river's edge. Turkey sign is everywhere—feathers, prints, and droppings.

As he sits, he cups his hands and blows his breath quietly on his fingers to ward off the chill. He didn't really notice the cold until he settled in to wait. He shivers as the dampness of the river's mist and his own sweat from his three-mile jog begin to chill him to the bone. Thinking back, he wishes that he had listened to Ma's advice and brought the small blanket she suggested—or at the very least, his new leather cape. He often has to learn the hard way not to scoff at her suggestions. About all he can do now is clamp his fingers under his armpits and pull his knees up tight to his chest.

Sean thinks back to the two canoes of warriors that passed by earlier. There was very little light, and they were obviously hugging the river bank for navigation. Where could they be heading this early in the morning? He thinks there were three warriors in each canoe, but he can't be certain. And was that really war paint on their faces? He thinks so, but again, he isn't sure. It was pretty dark when they came through, and he only caught a fleeting glance as he hid in the shore's underbrush while they glided past. He shudders at the thought of what might have happened if they had spotted him.

There really hasn't been any local Indian trouble in the past few years. Leastwise, none that Sean has heard of. Everything has been quiet around the settlements. The only real Indian troubles people talk about have been happening farther to the Northwest. Sean wonders again where those Indians were headed so early in the morning. If not for one of the warriors breaking the stillness with chatter just moments before they glided by, who knows what his fate might have been?

Sean glances across the small clearing toward the eastern mountains in the distance. Although not quite dawn yet, the horizon slowly brightens. The storm clouds hanging over the mountains begin to glow a dark pink around the edges to highlight their angry gray interiors. A second summer rain would be very unusual. Sean chuckles to himself. Generally, this time of year he would have given anything to find a cool spot to take shelter from the heat. But today, he is cold and can't wait for the sunrise.

Grandpa often told him about blocking discomfort from his mind. *"Discomfort is just a state of mind, boy,"* he often said. *"Concentrate on something else, something special."*

Sean looks down at the bow lying across his knees. He holds two arrows loosely in his left hand. About half of the arrows in the quiver were original and had bright red feathers. He studied the red feathers on one of the arrows he holds and wondered where the Indian boy had found the red birds. Out of habit, he already checked the straightness of the arrow shafts when he withdrew them from the quiver, even though he didn't need to because he knew they would be straight and true as ever. Months ago, Grandpa showed him how to straighten shafts with heat and steam and how to make arrows during the winter. The new ones Sean made recently were tipped with iron. There are only a handful of the red-feathered arrows left.

As he looks down at the bow, Sean feels proud that Grandpa so readily entrusted him with it. Even counting the old Kentucky long rifle, that bow is the only thing Grandpa truly values—well, that and the jug of corn whiskey.

Grandpa's words bounce around in Sean's head: *"Your rifle's only as good as your powder, but a bow now, it'll see you through hard times. Learn to use the bow an' arrow, an' ya won't ever run out of food."* Sean thinks about how if the rain actually does come today, Grandpa's words will certainly ring true.

The back of the bow is covered in soft doeskin and painted in intricate designs. Grandpa pointed out that under the glued-on leather, there would be glued-on elk or bison sinew to give the bow added strength. Sean knows how powerful it is because he still can't pull the sinew bowstring all the way back. Still, he can admire how the whole bow is covered in beeswax that the maker had polished to a fine shine, and how the boy who had been carrying it had thought to keep a second bowstring in the bottom of the quiver. Grandpa referred to the weapon a number of times as a Spirit Bow, but he had never explained just what that meant.

Sean glances over at the old Kentucky long rifle leaning against the tree next to him. Pa said they were made in Pennsylvania, which struck Sean as strange at the time, because why would they call them Kentucky long rifles if they are made in Pennsylvania?

Grandpa has never said where this rifle came from, only that he acquired it when he was living with the Indians. Sean turns the rifle to look again at the silver nameplate on the stock. The nameplate is well worn, but he can still clearly make out the name, E. Jackson. He has always wondered just who E. Jackson was.

Though he knows he can't use the rifle now with the Indian canoes so close by, Sean checks the prime of the pan again, just in case. The powder is still dry.

The rifle and the well-waxed bow across his knees bring back fond memories of the long hours in the woods with Grandpa. They are all fond memories, that is, except for the last time he hunted with the old man. Grandpa always seemed to cherish their time together, as well, teaching his grandson the ways of the wilderness. It is almost as if Grandpa and the forest have an understanding between them—his knowledge of the wilderness is that thorough.

Of course, Sean would have liked his father to teach him, as well, but Pa really doesn't know much about the ways of the wilderness. *"Didn't have the knack,"* as Grandpa often puts it. Anyway, Pa always seems too busy. Sean has never held it against his father any, not with how hard Pa works and all. His father is just a farmer, simple as that.

Pa always agreed that he had farmer smarts. Ask about when to plant a crop or when to harvest—anything about farming—and Pa will have all the answers. He occasionally shoots a deer or a bear, but they pretty much have to come to him, begging to be shot. For all Grandpa's encouragement, Pa and Jake just never did take much to the woods. That fact always seemed to gnaw at the old man, the idea that his stepson and eldest grandson don't enjoy that special freedom one feels when alone in the woods. *"Your wits against Mother Nature,"* Grandpa liked to say.

The way Pa tells it, Uncle Jack has always been at home in the woods, but Sean has never met his uncle Jack. Jack actually isn't even a blood uncle, but everyone says it is complicated, so Sean just refers to him as his uncle and leaves it at that. Uncle Jack left home before Sean was born, back when Grandpa and Pa were still living down in Kentucky. Uncle Jack is half Shawnee, born during Grandpa's stay with the Indians.

Where Pa and Jake never showed much interest in the woods, Sean couldn't get enough. Grandpa once told him he had a special instinct for the woods that few white boys shared. The old man called it *"a callin'."*

Grandpa learned most of his wilderness skills when he lived among the Shawnee. They had saved his life and adopted him into the tribe. Grandpa has told Sean many fascinating tales about growing up with the Indians. At least they were good up until the time Grandpa had his falling out with the Shawnee chief, Tecumseh.

Sean has often wondered why Grandpa refuses to talk about that incident, other than to say that it had something to do with the Kentucky long rifle. It sure is obvious by now, though, that his grandpa has *"no use for the red heathens,"* as he often says. He has never had a good word to say about them.

Grandpa's time with the Shawnee made the wilderness his second home. He is as comfortable in the wilderness as any Indian and quick to share his knowledge with his grandson. Grandpa can tell the sex and age of a deer just by seeing its tracks. Or how many men have passed by on the trail in the past few hours. Or how to set a trap to get only the best pelts. As for his marksmanship, there isn't a man around that can match him with that Kentucky long rifle.

Sean's thoughts flash back to the last time he and Grandpa hunted together—back to the day that triggered his nightmares.

It has now been almost two years, but the image is still as fresh in his mind as if it happened yesterday. It seems that the more Sean tries to forget it, the more vivid the memory becomes.

"Nice shot!"

He can't seem to forget Grandpa's words. The old man spoke them as if Sean had shot a squirrel or something instead of an Indian boy. *"Nice shot!"*

To Sean, that was the worst shot of his life.

His eyes begin to tear up. He wipes the dampness on his sleeve. He recalls how the snow started early that day, and how, just after he shot the Indian boy, the storm struck with a fury he had never experienced before. The snow, sleet, and wind intensified to a whole different level as he and his grandfather made their way home. The flashes of nearby lightning followed by the crackle and boom of the thunder and the fury of the wind made it the scariest day he had ever experienced. Now more than ever, Sean is convinced that the storm followed them home, trying to kill them on the way. It was pure luck that it didn't, pure luck that Sean survived despite being left behind by his grandfather and despite freezing under that fallen branch for hours before Pa and Jake found him. In his mind he still can feel the bitter cold.

Sean still isn't sure whether Grandpa's desire to leave the wounded Indian boy had more to do with escaping the furious storm or an unspoken fear of being found by other Indians. More than likely it was a little bit of both. The old man has never mentioned that day since—not the dying Indian boy, not the terrible storm, and especially not the Spirit Bow. He wishes he knew what Grandpa meant by *"Spirit Bow."*

In any case, Sean is certain that the incident was the reason for Grandpa's drastic change in behavior. The old man no longer has anything good to say to anyone, and he takes to the whiskey jug with a vengeance. Sean sure does miss his old grandpa, partly because he is scared of the new one.

That terrible day has had a huge effect on Grandma too. Ever since, she has spent her days just humming and rocking. Sean wonders if Grandpa told her about the Indian boy. Is that what triggered her change, not some old stroke? Sean can't be sure, but he thinks so. One thing he does know: Grandpa didn't tell Ma and Pa about it. When Pa asked about the bow and quiver of arrows, Grandpa lied and told him he had traded his knife for them. But Sean saw the old man throw the knife into the woods as they made their way back to the cabin. And why did they take such a long, roundabout way of getting home? Even through the furious storm, it looked like Grandpa was trying to hide their tracks.

Sean can't even get Grandpa to go fishing with him now, much less hunting or out to check a trapline. Grandpa refuses to get out of bed most days except to visit the privy, and even that isn't very often. It is almost as if Grandpa is afraid to be outside. Lately, it is always, *"Get away with you, boy! Don't you see I'm busy?"* Sean never sees anything that could be occupying the old man but that clay jug. When his Grandpa raises his voice, Grandma doesn't even miss a beat in that nonsense song of hers. She just sings a little louder.

After that day, Sean became the main supplier of meat for the family. He is very proud of that, but he still wishes that Grandpa would go hunting with him again. Maybe if Grandma were to die, then his real grandpa would come back to him and rejoin him again in the woods. Thoughts like those make Sean feel strange inside. He knows he shouldn't want Grandma dead, but he sure does miss the time spent in the woods with Grandpa.

Sean's thoughts are suddenly interrupted by the sight of a large turkey standing a few feet into the meadow. It must have emerged from the thicket on the far side. The gobbler struts boldly for a few paces, puffing itself up in search of a hen. As the big bird blows low-pitched purrs from deep in its chest, Sean wonders how long it has been standing there while he was lost in his thoughts.

The turkey suddenly stops its display as it senses danger. It just stands there, staring in Sean's direction, straining to pinpoint the source of its fears. Slowly, Sean nocks an arrow and raises his bow. His actions are slow, very deliberate, as he knows the turkey's eyesight is keen. As he slowly draws back, the turkey ducks back into the brush, lost from view. Sean's shoulders sag at his failure to get a shot off. He continues to remain perfectly still, easing off on the bowstring's tension. He begins to wonder how he will explain to Ma about how he missed Jake's turkey because he was daydreaming and forgot to nock an arrow.

The sun breaks through the clouds building up on the horizon, and the mist finally begins to lift. Sean rests his head on his knees, vainly trying not to get lost in his thoughts again. He wonders whether the bully, Will Johnson, has ever even shot a turkey with a bow and arrow. Perhaps Ma was right. Maybe he can do some things better than the other boys.

His arms and body ache with stiffness from sitting still. He wonders how long he has been waiting. He tries to judge the time from the angle of the sun across the river.

As he studies the distant riverbank, he thinks, one of these days, I'm gonna build me a raft an' look 'round that far side of the river.

He decides to only wait a few more minutes. Maybe he can try somewhere else. Not wanting to return empty-handed, he considers his options. He could try to shoot a deer on the way home. If he takes the long way back, cutting north through the woods, he might get lucky.

Just as he starts to rise, he catches sight of the big gobbler once again in the clearing.

This is crazy, Sean thinks. How long has it been there?

He slowly brings his bow up and draws back the sinew string. He aims and fires quickly, confident that the big bird will not get away this time. The bird jumps once and then flops around a moment before lying still. The arrow has pierced the bird in its breast and passed clean through.

Sean looks around at the surrounding woods. All remains quiet and still as he listens for any danger signals from other birds, signals that might indicate another presence nearby. Hearing nothing out of the ordinary, and satisfied that he is alone, Sean steps into the clearing. He picks up the turkey by its feet and looks it over appraisingly. It is a large bird, maybe ten pounds. Sean breaks out in a big grin at the thought of how proud Ma will be of him.

After searching the leaves and brush until he finds his arrow, Sean gently wipes the blood off on the wet grass. He carefully smooths the arrow's feathers and then replaces it and the other arrow in the quiver. The bow secured over his back, he picks up his rifle in one hand and the turkey in the other and begins his long jog back home. As he runs, a light rain begins to fall.

Sean covers the distance at an easy pace. He thinks back to what Ma told him yesterday about his ability to run great distances effortlessly. Even Jake can't stay with him for very long once he settles into his pace. He wonders how he might be able to get the boys in town to chase him. Then he would show them who is the runt.

CHAPTER  FIVE

By the time Sean approaches the cleared fields of his family's farm, his flannel shirt is soaked through with sweat and rain. He is careful to avoid the lightning-split sycamore tree at the edge of the field. Excitedly, he breaks from the woods into the field where his brother has been working on the old stump.

He notices that the mules are standing in their harness next to the stump, so he calls out, "Jake! Jake! Where ya at? Look what I gotcha for your birthday!"

When there is no response or sight of his brother, Sean turns to look in the direction of the cabin.

Maybe Jake went back to the cabin when it started to rain, he thinks. But why are the mules still in harness? Ma must have called him to help with some other chore. He'll be back.

Sean sets the turkey down, cups his hand to his mouth, and hollers again, "Jake! Where ya at?"

A roll of thunder drowns out his last words as it echoes across the valley. The sudden thunder makes him jump, and he nervously looks up to scan the darkening sky. The rain begins to fall harder.

It is not like Jake to leave the mules tied in harness, especially out in the rain. Sean is beginning to get a little concerned. He picks up the rifle and turkey and jogs over the muddy field toward the family's cabin. As he approaches the cabin, he feels more and more apprehensive that something is amiss. Everything appears still and quiet. Not a soul is moving about outside—not entirely unusual, given the afternoon thunderstorm, but still eerie. Sean feels some relief when he faintly hears Grandma's singing.

"Ma!" Sean hollers. "I got one, Ma. I got a really big one."

No one replies, and no one comes to the cabin door. All is quiet in the yard as the rain begins to drum louder on the cabin's shingles. Even Grandma's singing momentarily stops.

Sean rounds the trunk of the old hickory and stumbles over the sprawled body of his brother, Jake. He drops the turkey and kneels by his brother's side. The back of Jake's shirt runs red with blood and rainwater.

"Quick, Ma, Jake's been hurt!" Sean yells as he slowly turns his brother's body over. His eyes grow wide, and he lets out a gasp as he sees the broken stub of an arrow protruding from Jake's chest. He grabs his brother's body by the shoulders and gently shakes them. "Jake! Jake! Wake up. Ya can't die. Wake up, Jake!"

When no response comes, Sean shakes more violently before collapsing back on the seat of his britches. He sits there in the mud and rain, his brother's dead eyes staring blankly back at him. A rush of tears overcomes Sean.

He draws his knees up to his chest and rocks back and forth in shock, mumbling, "No, no, no."

Lightning flashes and thunder explodes in loud, rumbling booms. Crackle, crackle, kaboom!

Sean glances up again at the storm gathering in its intensity just overhead. For a split second, he wonders if this could be another nightmare—wonders if he will soon wake.

Only a few moments pass before Sean suddenly grabs the rifle and struggles to his feet. He darts behind the trunk of the old hickory tree. The rifle is useless in the rain, so he leans it against the trunk of the hickory and pulls the bow from his shoulder. He nocks an arrow from the quiver and quietly peers around the tree trunk at the door of the cabin. For the first time, he notices the splintered door standing partway open. It hangs inward at an odd angle from one leather hinge. On the outside of the door are six bloody handprints.

His mind jumps back to the canoes he saw passing on the river. Could this be an attack by the same warriors that passed him in the mist?

Grandma's singing resumes as Sean slowly approaches the cabin's open door. At the door, he leans against the cabin wall and listens intently. He hears the sounds of the rocker and Grandma's soft singing, but nothing else.

Sean cautiously peeks around the doorframe into the dim light of the cabin's interior. Listening to Grandma's serenade, he steps through the shattered door and slips quietly inside. He slides along the wall just inside the door as he allows his eyes a short time to adjust to the interior's dimness.

He looks toward the sound of Grandma's voice in the far corner of the cabin. The rocker is quietly squeaking as the crazy song continues. Oddly, the old woman can't seem to remember the tune. He quietly steps over to her side. The front of her dressing gown is soaked in blood that weeps down from her head. Sean is shocked to find the top of her scalp torn and bloody, with a flap of skin hanging down on her forehead.

She's been scalped! He realizes in terror.

As if sensing that she is no longer alone, Grandma stops singing and continues in a soft hum. She turns her head and smiles at Sean as she rocks gently, back and forth, back and forth, lost in the far reaches of her mind.

Sean turns toward the nearby bed and sees the bloody figure of his grandfather. Multiple arrows pierce his body. They look familiar somehow. Sean glances down at the arrow strung across his own bow and recognizes that the red feathers are identical to the ones protruding from his grandfather's chest. There is no question that these are the markings of the Indian boy's tribe.

A small, circular puddle of blood has formed on the floor by the side of Grandpa's bed. It catches Sean's eye as another drop hits the center of the pool. He stares a moment at the puddle's perfect roundness. When another drop gently lands, Sean's eyes are drawn upward in search of the source. Grandpa's hand hangs over the edge of the bed, and it is missing several fingers. Sean stares in shock as another drop of blood forms at the end of one of the bloody stubs. He watches as the blood swells at the stub's end before dripping to the puddle below. Sean turns and scans the room. "Ma! Where ya at, Ma?" Under his breath, he utters, "Please, Gawd . . ."

But in the back of his consciousness, he already knows what he is going to find. On the far side of the room, partially hidden by the over-turned plank table, Sean sees his mother's bare legs. Her body lies on the floor beside the bed that she and Pa shared. Sean rushes across the room to kneel by her side.

The sight of her torn clothing and bloody body causes Sean to gasp and stagger back. He realizes instantly that she is dead. In his haste to back out of the cabin, his foot catches on a crumpled piece of leather. He recognizes his old cape as he loses his balance and stumbles back-ward through the broken door. He sprawls awkwardly in the mud just beyond the step, then he scrambles on his hands and knees back around the trunk of the hickory.

There, he draws his knees up to his chest, holding them tightly with both arms. He notices the blood on his hands for the first time and wipes them furiously on his wet pants. Only then does he think of little Becky. He wants to go back into the cabin and look for her, but he can't. He's too afraid of what he might find.

A sudden, violent rush of bile comes up from his belly. He leans over to his side and vomits. For what seems like forever, Sean contin-ues with dry heaves, as if his small body is working hard to turn itself inside out. When the retching finally ceases, he leans back against the tree trunk. He stares off across the field, through the heavy downpour, and to the woods beyond. His eyes are wide open, but his mind regis-ters nothing at all.

"I killed 'em. I killed 'em," he begins to mutter over and over in his grief and guilt.

The sudden afternoon thunderstorm gives one last flash and chuckle of a rumble as it moves off to the West. The rain begins to lessen as Sean remains in the mud, mumbling softly to himself, numb to emotion.

Sometime later, Sean's mind vaguely registers the screams coming from the cabin. At first, he fears that the Indians have returned. But then he hears the muffled sounds of sobs drifting out from the cabin's broken door.

From out of his dreamlike trance, Sean finds his shoulders being shaken. "I killed 'em. I killed 'em," he mumbles to the shadowy form holding his shoulders. He hears the shadow say something, but the words make no sense to his mind. He whispers to the shadow again, "I killed 'em," in hopes that the shadow will go away.

Sean feels his shoulders being shaken again, and the shadow slowly starts to come into dim focus. He thinks he sees his father. But how can this be? Has he really just been dreaming all along?

He hears the shadow say, "Where's Becky? Have you seen Becky? Sean! Have you seen Becky?"

It sounds like it might be his father, but Sean's mind fails to process just what he is asking. Something about Becky?

"I killed 'em," Sean mumbles again.

Pa jerks his head back, looking surprised at Sean's words. Then he drops back down and waves a hand in front of Sean's face. Before Sean can react, his father pulls him into his arms and holds him tight. Tears roll down Pa's cheeks as he sobs.

Somewhere locked away in Sean's mind is the vivid ghost of an Indian boy reaching up for help, the memory always followed by the words, "Nice shot."

CHAPTER SIX

Ohio, March 1822

Sean O'Malley clenches his fists at his sides as his father, Patrick, leather hat tucked under his arm, swings open the cabin door, stoops his tall frame, and steps outside.

"It's okay, Sean," the young woman standing next to him says. "I already done checked, an' there ain't no Indians 'round."

Sean has been dreading this moment, but now, ever so cautiously, he takes a deep breath and follows his father out the door and into the bright light. He squints against the glare of the morning sun. When his eyes adjust, he scans the edge of the forest butting up to the family's cleared fields. Satisfied that there is no immediate danger, Sean looks around the cabin's yard. He has refused to step out of the cabin for months. He notices a few determined wildflowers have forced their way through patches of lingering snow, and where the snow has already melted, new grass and flowers blanket the damp earth.

Sean draws in a deep breath of the cold, fresh air. His anxiety about being out in the open gradually begins to fade, and he finds that he is glad to be outside again. He knows that if Pa had not threatened to leave without him, he would not have had the courage to leave the cabin at all.

A big bay stallion catches and holds Sean's eye as it stands quietly a few feet from the cabin's door. Sean thinks it must be the biggest saddle horse he has ever seen. His family has never had a riding horse. The horse swings its head over and looks long and hard in Sean's direction before turning back. The stallion is accompanied by their two mules, one packed and the other standing easy, fitted only with a saddle and appearing to enjoy its momentary good fortune. Pa moves over to the pair of mules and holds the saddled one steady as he indicates for Sean to step forward. As Sean starts forward to do so, he suddenly turns and runs back into the cabin, scattering a few roaming chickens that managed to survive the winter's cook pot. Moments later he reappears holding Becky's indigo bonnet, which he stuffs down the front of his shirt. With Pa still holding the reins, Sean swings up onto the mule's saddle.

Sean gazes for a moment over at the spot where he last saw Jake's body. In the old hickory tree above the spot, some jays are scolding a squirrel. The squirrel in return maintains its innocence with a steady chatter of its own. Sean notices the pen adjacent to the cabin, where the sow relaxes as her piglets fight for prime suckling positions.

Scores of bright yellow chicks follow the mother hens being kept in the nearby coop, scurrying to jump in any time one of them scratches up something of interest. Sean remembers how his sister, Becky, used to chase last year's chicks around, and this makes him wonder if Indians keep chickens.

When the young couple emerges from the cabin, Sean's daydream breaks and he stiffens in the saddle. They are not much older than Jake was, and Sean has enjoyed their presence for the short time they have been in the cabin. They seem like good people, but he still hasn't accepted the idea of another family living in their home and taking over their farm—the place where his mother, grandparents, and brother have been laid to rest. The thought that this young couple will be staying while he and Pa are leaving causes Sean to choke up. He looks on and swallows his emotions as Pa shakes the hand of the young man and tips his hat to the young woman.

It proves difficult to hold back the tears when Sean thinks about what will happen if Becky somehow manages to escape her captors and find her way back to the only home she has ever known. How will his sister react when she encounters a new family living in her mother and father's cabin? What will she do when she learns that everyone she has ever loved, is either dead or gone?

But Pa has been clear about these kinds of thoughts. *"Becky won't be coming back,"* he has told Sean more times than the boy cares to recount. *"The Indians have either killed her or taken her to their village, where they will likely adopt her into their tribe and eventually marry her to one of their own."* Pa had told him it was not that unusual. *"As much as we wish it will be different for Becky, it is pointless to hold out hope."*

Sean has often thought about the possibility of Becky escaping, but his father has always had an answer for that too.

"The moment anyone hears of a young, red-haired girl lookin' for her parents, someone will send for us," Pa had said. *"But, she ain't been seen in any villages nearby, Sean, so I think it's time you accept the fact your sister ain't never coming back."*

Sean thinks back to that terrible night when they lost everything and everyone they love. He can still see the big thunderheads, can still see his grandfather lying there with his fingers dripping into the pool of blood. Still see the red feathers on the arrows.

Pa had taken him back to the cabin after finding him in the yard. There, Sean had watched as his father unsuccessfully searched for the pistol by Grandpa's bed. He remembered the smell and scorch of the gunpowder on the bedcover that suggested his Grandpa had gotten a shot off before he died. That suspicion was confirmed when Sean followed his father back into the yard, and they found the start of a blood trail.

Pa had tracked the blood trail to the bank of the Scioto River, a half mile downriver from where he had shot Jake's turkey. Sean remembered his heart sinking when he saw Becky's doll. The one her father had whittled for her so carefully and so lifelike that it sometimes enticed him to join in his sister's games.

Sean recalled Pa crouching down beside the doll and passing his fingers over the mud. There, Sean had seen the pair of drag marks indicating that two canoes had launched from this spot. He could hardly breathe as he then realized these were probably the same two canoes he had encountered during his hunt. He might have fallen back into a stupefying panic if his father hadn't paused to examine the doll.

"No blood," Pa had said, and he had sounded somehow relieved despite the tears in his eyes. *"Doll's dress is clean, but the head is missing."* For the moment at least, he had shared his father's sense of relief. No blood anywhere on the doll meant that Becky was probably still alive. But, where was the head? Why the Indians would have spared her, he couldn't say, but as long as she was alive, there was a chance they might someday find her. He had watched as Pa removed the doll's indigo dress and stuffed it inside his shirt.

"The river drains into the Ohio just a few miles down," Pa had noted. *"From here, they coulda gone off in any one of three directions."*

Pa had said it as a means of tempering their hope that they would ever find Becky again, but Sean knew even then that he himself would never lose hope. That remained true even after the search parties spent a better part of the next two weeks on a search that turned up nothing, and it is still true now as he sits on his mule and waits for his father to say his goodbyes. Sean reaches up with the back of his hand and wipes away a tear from his eye.

He watches now as the woman steps forward and hands Pa a small cloth sack. "Thought ya might fancy some biscuits an' blackberry jam," she says.

"Thank'e kindly," Pa says as he turns and ties the sack securely behind his saddle. "They sure won't go to waste. Like I said, as soon as we find my brother, we're heading to Oregon Country." Patrick swings his leg up over the saddle of the big bay. "We'd best get on the road an' start lookin'. Mighty big country out yonder."

"Good luck to y'all on gettin' to Oregon," the young man says. "Heard tell it's a right pretty spot. Me an' the missus sure can't thank ya enough for what ya done for us. We know the place is worth more than what we paid, so as soon as y'all get settled, send word so's we can send ya some more for the farm."

Pa nods again as the young man hands up the Kentucky long rifle. Pa rests it across the crook of his arm.

The young woman throws a glance back at Sean and steps up closer to Patrick. "Hope to heaven he gets better. Was a heap terrible thing he done saw, we'll pray for him."

At the words, Sean turns away and gazes across the fields.

"Mr. O'Malley," the young woman adds, "don't ya fret none 'bout your missus an' all. I'll tend to your family's graves like they were me own."

"Ya take good care of that horse now," the young man says. "He's young an' still a might frisky, but I think he's gonna be pretty special. God be with ya."

"Thank'e kindly," Pa says again, "your words mean a lot. Reckon it's gonna take some time with Sean, though. Doc says there ain't nothin' wrong with him that a change of scenery might not cure, just too many bad memories for him here. Sure do hope he's right. Y'all take care now. It's a good farm. It'll do right by you if you work it hard."

Pa turns his new horse and slowly leads the way up the path. Sean stares blankly ahead as his mule lunges forward. He holds the reins, but it doesn't matter much, since his mule's lead rope is tied to Pa's saddle. As he leaves behind the only home he has known, Sean slowly turns to look back at the cabin. The young couple raise their hands in a final wave. Sean shows no acknowledgement as he turns his head away to gaze out over the partially cleared field where the old stump still stands, then out at the dark forest beyond.

As they climb halfway up the rise to meet the main road to Pleasant Valley, four fresh graves lie just off the beaten trail. It is a pretty spot under a large oak tree overlooking the small valley that once made up the O'Malley homestead.

Pa turns his horse toward the graves, dismounts, and walks over to his family's final resting place. His hat in his hand, Pa kneels beside his wife's marker. After pulling a few new weeds and tossing a small, broken branch off the grave, he bows his head. "Well, Jenny dear, its time to say goodbye. I don't reckon we'll be passin' back through these here parts again. Gotta take our boy away and get a fresh start. Doc says otherwise he ain't never gonna talk no more. You know I love you. That I'll always love you."

Sean watches his father scoop up a handful of loose dirt and pause a moment before tossing it back onto the grave.

"See you in heaven, Jenny, me bonnie lass." After standing to look briefly at the other three graves, Pa turns and remounts his horse.

"Sean," he says, imploring him once more, "wouldn't you like to say goodbye to your ma, at least?"

Sean stares at his father a moment before dropping his gaze a little to stare back across the field to the forest beyond. Ever so slightly, his guilt overwhelming, he shakes his head.

With a grunt and a nudge of his heel, Pa starts his horse up the path toward town. The mules follow as Sean turns to stare at the family graves as he passes. His thoughts are buried deep in the shadows of his mind as a tear runs down one cheek. He wipes it away with the back of his linen sleeve. The words come to mind, but he is unable to say them out loud: Sorry, Ma. I'm so sorry. It should be me laying there. Them Indians came for me, not ya an' Jake. An' Becky, I promise that if you're still alive, I'll find ya.

CHAPTER SEVEN

Swollen by the heavy spring runoff, the Ohio River runs high, fast, and muddy. Sean watches a pair of tree limbs get caught in the swirling eddies, gaining momentary respite before continuing their journey downriver from an unknown source to an unknown destination.

"I think it best that we follow the wagon road west to Cincinnati," Pa tells his son. "When I went to buy supplies an' settle up with the Johnsons, folks there reckoned it to be just a little over a hundred miles or so. Maybe five or six days' easy travel." As if an afterthought, he adds, "I saw Newt, Sean. He asked me to say goodbye, an' he wished you well."

Sean's eyes tear up at the thought of his friend. He dabs at his eyes with his fists before staring out over the muddy river. Newt was the only one to stop by after the massacre, and he misses his friend.

With all the swollen streams, it takes seven days before the two travelers reach the outskirts of Cincinnati. The young city is by far the biggest concentration of humanity Sean has ever seen.

As he leads the way into the bustling city, Pa turns back to look at Sean. "Some folks claim that ten thousand people live here," he marvels. "Really hard to imagine that many folks wanting to live so close together. I wonder what your grandpa would say. He left Ken-tuck because people were crowding him, gettin' within a mile."

They try to ride as close to the riverbank as they can, but this proves difficult. The farther into the city they go, the harder it is to even see the river. Warehouses line both sides of the streets, some extending right down to the river's edge with a dock of their own.

"I'm going to try to get me a job on a riverboat heading downriver," Pa says.

They find a side street running between the warehouses back toward the river, and they turn down it. Sighting the river's bank again, they ride past one busy dock after another.

"Son, will you look at that?" Pa says as he points out over the Ohio River. "It's one of 'em newfangled paddlewheel steamboats! Never thought I'd ever see one of them."

Sean's eyes are already wide open as he stares at the hustle and bustle of the men working the docks. He turns to briefly look in the direction his father indicates before gazing back at the men again. Many of them are black-skinned African slaves. Sean has heard of such a thing, but until now, he has never actually seen a slave. He notices that some of the slaves even have their ankles manacled and chained to one another in pairs.

Pa spots a flatboat tied up to a nearby dock and nudges his horse over. Men are busy unloading the boat's cargo onto waiting wagons. Other wagons stand nearby, ready to be unloaded. Pa dismounts and hands the reins up to his son. "Wish me luck."

Sean nods his head and sees his father take a deep breath before approaching a short, round man who appears to be in charge.

"Excuse me, mister," Pa says. "Got a second? Me and my boy was hopin' for a ride downriver. We need to reach St. Louie, an' I'm willing to work. You don't happen to know where I might find a boat needin' a hand, do you?"

The short man removes a fat cigar from the corner of his mouth and looks the big farmer over. He apparently likes what he sees. "I'm heading down that-a-way myself as soon as I get loaded back up. Who be asking?"

"Name's O'Malley, Patrick O'Malley, an' my boy there's Sean."

The potbellied captain looks over at Sean and then eyes Patrick up and down again. "Sorry, but I ain't lookin' for no Irish, too much trouble."

"Mister, I'm a hard worker, an' I don't drink none. It looks to me like y'all could use another strong hand." Unwilling to give up so easy, Pa adds, "We maybe could even pay a little bit too."

"Well, I am on a tight schedule, though I ain't never met no Irish that don't take to the bottle. Tell ya what. I'll take ya down to the Mis-sip. Ya can help with the unloading an' loading up again, an' I'll take ya for ten dollars. Up front. Y'all have to sleep on the deck, though. Ain't got no room left below deck."

"Ten dollars?" Pa turns his back on the man and reaches into his pocket to pull out the necessary coins. "If y'all can make room for the animals, you got a deal. I'll buy the feed. You won't regret it none. I'm a hard worker."

To Sean, it seems that the man realizes he has some leverage as he places the cigar in the corner of his mouth.

"Them animals take up space," the man says. "With the animals, that'll be another ten dollars, an' the first sign of liquor, off ya be."

Pa reaches back into his pocket for another ten dollars and hands the coins to the small man before shaking his hand to seal the deal.

"Looks like we'll be goin' to St. Louie." Pa smiles up at his son and slaps Sean's leg. "An', I ain't gonna have to build no raft." He chuckles. "Hell, I don't even know how to build a raft. Plus, we don't have to sell the horse and mules. We need to celebrate."

Sean stands by the railing of the big flatboat as it floats down the Ohio River. He carefully counts the sixteen pieces of hard candy still in the bag. Pa said the store clerk in the drugstore back in Cincinnati called them Salem Gibralters. They have a sweet and sour, lemony taste and look like little, hard lemons. Sean is certain he has never tasted anything so delicious in all his life. He has been determined to make them last by allowing himself to eat only one a day.

As he watches the banks of the river glide by, Sean reckons that they have been on the journey now a little more than three weeks. He glances over at his father, only to see Pa smile back in his direction. He knows Pa has been watching him, but nothing has changed. The world crashed down on him on the day he found most of his family dead, and he knows it was all his fault.

These lemon drops are about the best thing to happen since they left home—well, that and the time Pa got knocked off his horse by the low branch and rolled down the riverbank into the muddy Ohio. Sean can't help but give a little smile at the memory. He probably smiled back when it happened, too, because Pa came up sputtering and cussing until he looked up at him and caught the grin. With that, Pa pointed at him, slapped his hat on his pant leg, and started laughing.

It took Pa and the six slaves another two days to finish unloading and then reloading the big flatboat in Cincinnati. Sean had studied the slaves as they worked. One of them didn't seem to know any English and was always being whipped. Each time the lash landed, the slave would stop working, stand up tall, and stare at the man with the whip, a look of pure hate and defiance on his face. That usually brought on another lash, but the big man didn't seem to mind. Swollen welts crisscrossed the man's back. But his chest was even more puzzling to Sean. The big slave appeared to have healed scars and raised dots in an intricate pattern all over his chest and shoulders.

When Sean's father comes over to stand next to him, it breaks Sean from his memory. "Never thought it would take this long to get down to the Mis-sip," Pa says. "Wasn't countin' on so many stops along the way."

Sean looks down at the three slaves working the oars on this side of the boat. They are pulling hard on the long oars to keep the unwieldy flatboat in the middle of the current. He points hard at the slave with the raised scars, then looks up at his father questioningly as he motions with his hands to his own chest.

"Captain told me he just bought him," Pa says. "Some kind of big chief back in Africa. Captain says now, that if he had it to do over, he never woulda bought him. Been nothin' but trouble."

Sean moves his hand back up to his chest.

"To show his bravery an' position in the tribe," Pa explains, "he was cut an' then had ash rubbed in the wounds to make the scars bigger." He looks down at his son before adding, "He's a far braver man than I am."

Pa nods over to two trappers who boarded at the last stop. "Let's go over an' talk to 'em fellas an' see if they know anything 'bout your uncle Jack."

One of the two men glances up suspiciously as Patrick and Sean approach. The other is busy cleaning his pistol and doesn't bother to glance up.

"Howdy," Pa says to the trapper, who nods in response. "We're looking for my brother. Headed out to trap goin' on fourteen years back—fella by the name of Jack O'Reilly. Thought maybe one of you might have crossed paths with him."

The trapper cleaning his pistol simply shakes his head, and continues working.

The other answers. "Plum never came 'cross no Jack O'Reilly. It's a big country, though. Might lucky if he ain't gone under in that length of time." He pauses to scratch his beard. "Fourteen years is quite a spell. If y'all scurry up to St. Louie, I hear tell there's an outfit might be gettin' ready to push out west." He nudges his partner's shoulder with his knee. "Quince, what's the name of that fella that's wanting a hundred men to head out to 'em Rockies?" Not waiting for an answer, he says, "I remember now. Ask for a fella named Ashley. William Ashley, he might know something 'bout your kin."

"You two plannin' on joinin' up?" Patrick asks.

"Nah, we done seen enough of 'em mountains," answers the man cleaning his pistol. "Pretty sight to behold, but too damn cold. Cold enough to freeze your ears clean off. Other parts, too, if ya catch my drift. Nah, we seen the elephant, so we're done. Planning on settling down a little ways downriver. Hoping to do a little trading."

When it occurs to Sean that his father is getting ready to leave these men, he tugs on his sleeve and gives him a look that implores him to ask just one more question—the one that has been heavy on both of their minds for months now.

Pa sighs and nods his understanding. "Y'all ain't by chance seen a young girl with red hair an' green eyes during your travels, have you? My daughter, was kidnapped by savages, and we think she may still be livin' with 'em."

The trapper with the gun looks up and shakes his head mournfully.

"Nah, I'm afraid not, mister," the other says. "Lotta tribes out there too. Too many to know for sure."

The crack of a whip brings an end to the conversation as the four snap their attention over to its source. Sean follows Pa over to look at the three slaves starting to maneuver the flatboat with the long sweep of their oars. The sweat running down their bare backs is occasionally diverted from course by a raised welt or an old scar.

Sean sees the fat overseer standing beside the slaves, a cold pipe clamped tight between yellow-stained teeth. The man pats the side of his leg with a short, curled rawhide whip. As the man uncurls and raises the whip to deliver more encouragement, Pa catches the man's wrist from behind.

"We ain't in that much of a rush," Pa says as he releases the man's wrist. He turns his back to the man and looks to the far bank.

The overseer glares at Pa's back with anger in his eyes. He glances around as if checking to see if the captain is watching. Then, after curling the whip up, he pulls out a plug of tobacco from inside the front of his shirt and bites off a chaw. He drops the remaining plug back into his shirt, then yells back down at the three slaves. "Pull, ya black bastards!" Under his breath, he mutters to Sean, "Ain't worth the food we feed 'em."

Having overheard, Pa frowns in disgust at the overseer, who smiles and slowly turns to spit a long stream of tobacco juice into the muddy water. Some of the spit hits the shoulder of one of the slaves manning the oars. Sean watches as the black spittle slides down the man's arm, hangs there a moment, then drops away into the dirty water. He sees the slave's fist tighten on the oars in reaction, muscles bunching in his forearms.

The overseer wipes his mouth with a well-stained sleeve, then turns his attention back to Pa. "I've seen ya been a good worker an' all, but 'round 'bout this here neck of the woods, fella don't go pokin' his nose in other folk's concerns." After spitting again for emphasis, he continues. "Kinda rude to be offerin' up advice to one that don't need it an' sure as hell don't want it. Might end up stiff an' floatin', if ya catch me drift."

"Just didn't 'spect to see no slavin' out here," Pa says, "least not this far north." He shakes his head. "Can't get it right in my mind to be ownin' another human being."

"Then best get a grip on it. 'Em folks up in Washington just done settled it." He pauses and looks questioningly at Patrick. "Ya have heard of the Compromise, ain't ya?"

Sean glances away and spots the small, fat captain approaching.

The overseer turns his attention back to his job and slaps the coiled whip against the boat's railing. "I said, pull, ya no good for nothin' black bastards!"

"That lad of yours sure is quiet," the captain says as he takes a spot near Pa on the railing. "He ain't sick or nothin', is he? Been a heap of sick 'round 'bout—yellow fever and such."

Having overheard the captain's comments, Sean glances at his father. Then he returns his gaze to the slaves.

"No, he ain't sick none," Pa says, "just quiet." Then, as if an afterthought, he adds, "Lad's seen a heap too much misery for a young-un. Just ain't yet found the right words. Anyway, nothin' wrong with quiet." Pa nods in the direction of the man with the whip. "Be good if more folk took up the habit."

The captain removes his cigar from his front pocket and chomps down on it. Then he pulls out a rag from where it was tucked behind his leather suspenders and loudly blows his nose into it. All the while, he stares hard at Sean. Seemingly satisfied that the boy is indeed not a threat to his health, the captain stuffs the rag back in place and looks toward the far shore. The stub of his unlit cigar bobs in the corner of his mouth. "Saw ya havin' some words with Culpepper," the captain says, slowly shaking his head. "Not a good idea, he's kind of set in his ways, if ya know what I mean. He gets the job done, though."

"I wouldn't be surprised if you woke up one morning an' found Culpepper missin'," Pa replies. "Men can only take so much abuse, slave or free." Glancing at the slaves straining hard on the oars, he adds, "They may be just slaves, but I've seen their pride too."

"Ya may be right, but that's why I hired Culpepper; to whip that pride out of 'em. Time will tell which comes first."

Pa slowly shakes his head at the captain's remarks. "Been lookin' for me brother," he says, changing the subject. "Haven't seen him since he run off the farm back in Ken-tuck nigh on fourteen years back. Said at the time he was headed to the Shine'n Mountains to be a trapper, fella by the name of Jack O'Reilly."

The captain shakes his head and removes the cigar from his mouth. "Gawd, man, fourteen years is a long time to hold on to your hair in these parts. I reckon he's donated it to decorate some heathen's lodge-pole by now."

"Figure it'd take a mighty hard Indian to get at Jack's hair. I remember he had a certain orneriness about him, as well as bein' a half-breed himself."

"Maybe so, but there's plenty more savages than Christian folk, and quite a few of 'em are a might feisty in their own right." The captain, seeing no reaction from Pa, adds, "Big country to get lost in."

Two days later, they finally reach the mighty Mississippi River. After the two rivers join, it takes another hour to steer the boat to the Mississippi's western bank. When the flatboat finally bumps the bank, the slave that Patrick momentarily prevented from getting whipped jumps to shore to secure a heavy line to a nearby tree trunk. Three large planks of wood are laid from the boat to the shore to act as a gangway for the animals.

Sean leads the big stallion off the same way he led him on. He rubs the agitated horse's nose and massive head in reassurance before blindfolding him. When the horse calms down, he turns his back to the stallion and places its nose over his right shoulder before slowly walking forward. The big stallion follows as long as Sean continues rubbing its nose and head with his hands. In this way, the horse follows him off the boat.

"Looks to me like you've made a real connection with the bay, son," Pa says afterward. "Looks to me like it's somethin' right special."

After the animals and their meager gear are unloaded, the captain walks over to Patrick. "Y'all sure as hell seem damned determined to get yourselves scalped. Well, suit yourself. St. Louie lies north, maybe five, six days' hard ride. Just follow the river an' y'all can't miss it." The captain looks over at Sean. "These here parts ain't no place for no tenderfoot."

"Reckon he's gotta learn sometime," Pa says. "Besides, we've come a fair piece already, an' been through some mighty rough country." He nods to Sean. "Boy's a might tougher than he looks. Obliged for the concern, though."

"For his sake, I hope your right." After the captain shakes Pa's hand and re-boards the boat, he adds, "Y'all try to hang on to your hair now. Remember, as the sayin' goes, it's the ones ya don't see that ya have to worry 'bout. Good luck to ya, Pat. I have to say, for a gawd damned Irish Mick, ya did have a bit of work in ya after all."

As the slave begins to untie the mooring rope, Sean hurries over to him and hands him his last two pieces of hard lemon candy. He looks up at the big slave and points to him and then up at the chest of the scarred slave on the boat. The slave nods his head in understanding. Sean turns and walks back over to the mules.

As they repack the mule and saddle their mounts, Sean can't help but turn and look downriver at the flatboat disappearing around a bend. He feels his father's hand on his shoulder.

"It's gonna be okay, Sean," Pa says. "We're gonna be fine."

Sean hopes his father is right, but a cold shiver shoots down his back. He can't help but think about Becky again, about how every mile they travel away from the farm is just one more mile standing between them reuniting with her. It seems clear now that, even if she ever does come back, she will never be able to find them. He wants to say all this to Pa—and has wanted to say it for some time—but every time he tries, his heart fills with hurt.

Sean and his father ride north, following a faint path along the West bank of the Mississippi. The first day out, they skirt around a small Indian village of two tepees and a few blanket-covered willow enclosures. The few inhabitants they see at a distance don't appear to be in very good shape. Still, Pa tells his son that it would be better just to steer clear of any encounters at this time.

A few days later, they ride up to what could barely pass as a homestead—just a small scratch in the ground up by Cape Girardeau. They find a young widow struggling to survive in a harsh land. It is obvious to Sean that she is having a tough time of it. As Pa talks with the woman, Sean watches her three kids step out from behind the outbuildings to stare at the two strangers. He is amazed at the loose rags hanging from their thin bodies, and about how filthy they appear. He thinks that they are almost as dirty as the hogs being raised behind the privy.

The woman seems excited for the company. She kills a chicken and fixes her guests the best meal they have eaten since they left their farm. Pa tells Sean that the lady's name is Mary, and at the table after supper, she describes her plight.

"My Bob kilt himself last winter workin' with the ax. He was cuttin' wood for one of 'em newfangled steamboats when he cut his leg. Cut it bad, down to the bone, he did. Didn't last through the winter once the gangrene set in. Ain't no doctors here 'bout, so we all just watched him slowly die.

"He goes an' brings us all the way out here from our nice home in Virginny to this godforsaken piece of dirt, an' then he goes an' does that!" Mary starts to cry as she continues. "Now what am I to do? Five dollars! Five dollars is what the damn steamboats leave ya for a pile of wood. Five dollars is the price of my Bob's life? Three small kids, an' the oldest not yet seven. Just what am I gonna do now, Bob? What ya want me to do now?"

Sean looks over at his father.

Pa finally says, "Mary, maybe it be best to flag down a passin' flatboat. Them hogs will more than cover your passage."

"Yeah, then what? Got no place to go. I ain't got me no people here 'bout." After a short quiet spell, she turns to her three kids. "Y'all head on out an' use the privy an' then get on up the loft." She turns back and looks at Sean. "Do ya think I could talk with your pa here for a moment alone?"

Sean doesn't move. He doesn't want to leave his father with this woman, and he certainly doesn't want to go outside alone, where who knows what might be lurking.

Pa turns to him and says, "Son, I'll be along in a bit. Maybe you can go an' get us a fire goin' at the campsite."

Sean's eyes open a little wider as he looks from his father's face to the widow Mary. He doesn't move.

Seeing his son's hesitation, Patrick nods toward the door. "It's all right, son. Just wait outside. I'll be along shortly."

Finally, Sean reluctantly rises from the split-log bench and walks to the door. He glances back at Pa with a scared expression and slowly closes the door partway. While kneeling down beside the partially open door, he listens to their conversation.

"Pat, is there somethin' wrong with that boy?"

"Nothin' that the Good Lord an' a bit of time can't get right. He come upon his ma, brother, an' grandparents butchered by Indians."

"Oh my! I'm sorry to hear that."

Sean watches through the crack in the open door as Mary gets up and starts gathering the wooden bowls together.

She abruptly sets them down and moves over to stand behind Patrick. She places her hands on his shoulders and rubs them up and down his muscular arms. "I was just thinkin'," she says haltingly. "Y'all ain't got no woman, an' I be needin' a man an' all. Maybe ya might consider stayin' 'round a bit longer. I'm a pretty good cook, an' I know I can please a man between the blankets. Make ya feel real good an' all."

Dreading his father's answer, Sean puts his hand over his mouth and shakes his head. Thinking, no, Pa, no.

Patrick gently removes the young woman's hands from his shoulders as he stands. Turning to face her, she barely comes up to his shoulders. "I'm sorry, ma'am. It's not that I don't appreciate the offer none, an' you sure can cook an' all, that's a fact, but it's just not a good time for me—not just yet, anyway."

Mary steps up closer, putting her hands on Pa's chest. "Y'all might not got no feelings for me now, but I reckon that could grow with a bit of time."

She starts to move her hands downward when Pa takes her hands again in his and softly says, "Just not the right time." He abruptly turns and walks out the door.

Sean stands and hugs his father tightly around the waist as he steps out onto the porch.

Patrick and Sean stay on and work the next day. They help the widow Mary by splitting a pile of firewood and repairing the leaky roof.

That evening, over chicken soup, Pa once again suggests that Mary flag down a passing flatboat. "You bein' still young an' all, an' there ain't bein' many women 'bout in these parts, if y'all get to a town, you can have your pick of the fellas."

The next morning, the O'Malleys saddle up early, and Mary hands up a small cloth sack to Pa. "Just a small thanks for y'all helping me out," she says. "Little slab of bacon an' some hard-boiled eggs. Now that ya had a chance to sleep on it, ya sure y'all won't reconsider me offer? Got two hundred acres bottomland here. Bob thought good things would come of it. Ya really don't have to go lookin' no further."

"Thank'e kindly, Mary, but I 'spect me an' Sean got us a hankerin' to see Oregon Country. We'll be movin' on. Best you take your boys downriver to a town. You won't make it out here alone. You can always come back when you find the right fella. You got the deed, so the land ain't goin' nowhere."

She reluctantly nods as they turn to ride off.

CHAPTER EIGHT

Over the past two days, they have passed many wagons, pack-horses, buggies, and riders, both coming and going, as they approach the bustling city. Three days after leaving the widow Mary, the narrow path they've been following became a wider wagon road that now veered inland, away from the river. They passed fertile farms, one after another, as they drew closer to St. Louis. All told, it took them five long days before reaching the outskirts of the city.

As they ride into the city itself, St. Louis appears only half as big as Cincinnati, but it is still a grand sight to behold. Sean points to the banners and flags hanging from the buildings and shrugs his shoulders up at his father.

"Maybe they're gonna have a parade," Pa says, looking up at a red, white, and blue bunting on a nearby balcony. "Almost looks like a Fourth of July celebration, only it can't be July yet."

Patrick and Sean continue to ride slowly down the main street, totally in awe at the size and number of beautiful buildings. Some buildings that Sean points out are a full three stories tall. He cranes his neck to stare up in wonder as they ride past. And all the glass! Everywhere he looks, there are glass windows. Back in Pleasant Valley, a person had to be pretty well off to have a glass window. Pa often promised Ma they were gonna get one, but it never did happen. Their old cabin had an oilskin window that let in some light, but Sean remembers how you couldn't really see anything out of it—just shadows and such.

Sean turns his mule as Pa veers over to speak with an older man cinching up a packhorse in front of a mercantile store.

"Me an' my boy be wonderin' what all the flags an' such are for?" Pa asks. "Is there gonna be a parade or somethin'?"

"Son, y'all must have been out in the woods a spell. 'Em flags have been up now for almost a year." The man continues to cinch down the packhorse's leather straps. "Missouri done become a state of the Union back in August of '21." The man hawks up some phlegm, leans over, and spits into the dust. "Been a long time coming, too, so we had us one hell of a shindig. The so-called Missouri Compromise finally let Missouri in as a slave state, though most folks 'round these parts don't take to slavin' much. Still, statehood was quite a celebration."

"Much obliged to you." Patrick nods in thanks and turns his horse to continue deeper into the busy city. They pass men and women of all types—black, white, and even a few Indians. The order of dress runs the gamut, from men decked out in suits with string ties and fancy boots, all the way to those dressed head to foot in buckskins. Nobody seems to take notice of Sean's and Pa's gawking as they watch the city folk going about their business.

"Let's head on down to the docks an' see if we can get a job," Pa says. "Might as well try to save what little money we have for gettin' on to Oregon."

They make their way down to the docks along the Mississippi and pull up in front of a tall, thin, bald man overseeing the unloading of one of the numerous flatboats tied up.

Sean stares at the man in astonishment. His mind flashes back to Ma's old pole scarecrow in the vegetable garden. Sean doesn't think he has ever seen anyone so thin. He feels sorry for the poor man, and if he had been carrying anything at all to eat, he would have offered it to him.

The thin man glances up at Pa a moment before returning his gaze to the roll of papers he holds in his hand.

Pa dismounts, holds his hat in his hand, and addresses the man. "Mister, we just rode into town, an' I'm lookin' to find me some work. Me boy here, too, if'n you might know of anythin'."

"If you're willing to help unload the flatboats, I can use another strong arm. Don't know about the boy, though. Seems a bit on the scrawny side." The bald man doesn't seem to want to lose out on hiring

59

a man of Patrick's stature, because he quickly adds, "Tell ya what I'll do. I'll give ya four dollars a day an' take the boy, on a trial basis only, mind ya, at two dollars a day. And I'll even let you sleep in my warehouse for the time being. Corner of Gravois and Chouteau, half a block up. My man Cotton's there. He'll show ya where to sleep an' all. Start work promptly at sunup tomorrow. How's that sound to ya?"

Pa nods.

The man extends his hand in Pa's direction. "Name's Dawson, but most folks 'round 'bout call me Skinny, for some reason. I'll answer to both."

Sean gives his father a slight smile as Pa steps forward to shake Skinny's hand. "My name's Patrick, an' my son's name is Sean. Don't you worry none 'bout Sean, Mr. Dawson. We'll both give you a solid day's labor. What did you say those streets were called again?"

Sean can hardly believe it, but he has his first paying job. He watches his father get better directions as Skinny uses a stick to draw a small map of the streets in the dust. Five minutes later, they are standing in front of a rough-cut plank warehouse. Sean can barely make out the words Gravois Street Timber Co. crudely painted across the front of the building in faded, whitewashed letters.

After dismounting, Pa hands his reins back to Sean. The boy follows his father up to the big double doors of the warehouse, where Pa leads him inside.

"Hello?" Pa hollers. "Anybody here?"

Sean watches his father stand there a minute, letting his eyes adjust to the dim light.

"Mista, can I help ya?" a voice asks from somewhere within the shadows.

Pa turns in the direction of the voice. An elderly black man steps over and into the light of the open doorway. He holds a large twig broom.

"I'm lookin' for the Dawson warehouse," Patrick says.

"Well, then, Mista, I reckon ya found it. But Mista Dawson ain't here now. He be down at the North Docks. Tall, skinny fella, ya can't miss him, 'less he turns sideways."

Pa shares the old man's chuckle. "You have a good point there. We just met him, an' you're right, Mr. Dawson don't cast much of a shadow. You must be Cotton. Mr. Dawson told us we could sleep here for a spell. Me an' my boy Sean here start work tomorrow."

Cotton nods.

"Maybe you could tell me where I could find a fella named William Ashley," Pa says. "And perhaps you could also help me find a place to stable the animals."

"The animals are easy," Cotton replies. "Two blocks up an' two blocks over is a stable. The fella's name is Dan somethin'. Don't let him charge no more than forty cents for the lot or your gettin' cheated." The old man rubs his beard and thinks for a moment before adding, "Don't recollect I heard tell of no Ashley. What's he do?"

"I'm told he's outfittin' a group of trappers. Heading out west to 'em Shine'n Mountains."

"Come to think of it," Cotton says as he rubs his white beard in thought, "I did hear tell 'bout some fella buyin' a heap of supplies—mules too. Best bet is to ask up on Carondelet Street. Just look for the street name with the most letters. Longest name in town. That's how I find it." He pointed to the far corner of the warehouse. "Y'all can bed down over in the corner there. Hang any food y'all have up by a rope so the rats don't get at it. I got a couple of cats somewhere hereabouts, but 'em rats can be mighty tricky. Privy's out back. Mista Dawson don't allow no fires in here, so I cook out back, an' y'all welcome to join me. Folks 'round about call me Cotton, but you already know that. I'm a free man. Mista Dawson done free me. He now pays me five dollars a month an' all the rice and beans I can eat to look after this here warehouse." Cotton gives Patrick and Sean a big smile. "Been savin' to buy me boy free. He be slavin' on one of 'em flatboats workin' the rivers. I see him time to time—give him a holler now an' again, I do."

Sean jolts up straight as Pa nods to the old man and steps in the door's direction.

"We'll just get our gear," Pa says, "and then we'll see to 'em animals."

Patrick and Sean step over to unload and stow their meager belongings in the corner Cotton pointed out. They don't have any food to hang up, and Sean is getting really hungry.

When they are all settled in, Pa turns to ask Sean, "How 'bout we eat in one of 'em restaurants we passed when we rode in? Ain't never ate in no restaurant an' might not get another chance. What do you say, son? You wanna give it a try? We can drop the mules off at the livery on the way."

Sean's eyes open wide in anticipation and excitement. He nods as his father smiles back at him.

Patrick leads his son down to the river's edge to wash some of the trail dust and grime off. "Can't have people thinkin' we no-account bums, now, can we?" Patrick says as he splashes some water in his son's direction. "Your ma would turn over in her grave."

After combing their hair back with their wet fingers, they head back up to find what Sean recalls as Car-something Street.

They drop the mules off at the livery before riding double down Carondelet Street, which also happens to be the very street they first rode in on. They tie the horse up to a hitching post in front of a watering trough, then start down the street's brick sidewalk in search of a suitable place to eat. They pass a number of upscale establishments with posted menus that Pa seems to have difficulty deciphering. He says he isn't sure what the fancy-named dishes are, but he sure can't believe the prices.

He puts his face to a few of the windows to look in. His gaze is met by fancy-dressed folks staring back from their window tables. "Not even our Sunday best would be good enough in there," Patrick says as they walk past yet another restaurant.

Frustration is beginning to mount on his father's face just as Sean tugs on his sleeve and points at a small wooden sign nailed on the corner of the building. The name Ma Tucker's Home Cooking is burned into the wood with an arrow pointing down a narrow alley. They stand and watch the restaurant's door for a few minutes until a man dressed in a flannel shirt and leather britches steps out.

Pa nods down to Sean and smiles. "Looks like Ma Tucker's might be just the spot."

Through the door, they step into a large, noisy room. Six oil-burning lanterns hang from the rafters. A young man carrying food out to the tables points over at two open spots at the end of a bench. "Have a seat," he tells them. "Gramps will be with you in a minute."

They sit where directed, facing one of four long plank tables. All four tables are full of working men busy with talk and eating. Sean makes a quick survey of the room with his eyes. He catches his father's attention and lifts his chin in the direction of one of the customers. At first, Sean assumed that this customer eating with a big knife and a wooden spoon was a man, but he realizes now that she is actually a woman. Everyone seated is generally dressed the same—either buckskins, homespun, or some combination of the two. The person in question wears buckskins. The only thing that gives her away as a woman, is that she's the only one without a beard.

Eventually, an elderly man with a stained apron steps over and sets two clay cups and a jug of slightly discolored water in front of Sean and his father. Next, the man digs a couple of forks out of the pocket in his apron. After wiping them off on his dirty apron, he sets them beside each of their cups. "Welcome to Ma's," the old man says. "Y'all can call me most anything, but I generally only answer to Walt. Can't say as I've seen you two gents here before. We ain't got no menu, supper's whatever Ma's cooking. Beer's a nickel, and supper will run you two bits, and twenty cents for the lad. Today we got buffalo steak with taters and carrots, smothered in Ma's gravy. Sorry though, but we plumb run outta biscuits. Gotta get here a might earlier for the biscuits. They tend to go fast.

"I can hold on to your rifle back in the kitchen," he adds, pointing up to a sign on the wall. "Ain't no firearms allowed in the dinin' room. One gunfight was enough. The knife you can keep." He holds out his hands, waiting for Patrick to pass him the rifle.

Patrick hands over the Kentucky long rifle to the old gent. "Buffalo steaks sound good to me. Patrick's my name, and my boy here is Sean. Hold off on the beer. This here water will do right fine with us."

"Apple pie and coffee will run y'all another nickel, but Ma does make the best apple pie this side of the Miss-sip. You can let me know later if'n you got any room." After looking down at the old flintlock Patrick has handed him, Walt adds, "Haven't seen the likes of one of these in a spell." He turns to look at the nameplate, and his eyes widen. "Where you boys say you're from?"

"Come down from Ohio. Hopin' to make our way out to Oregon Country."

"Nameplate here says E. Jackson," the old man says. "Funny, I knew a fella in Kentucky a ways back by the name of Elijah Jackson. He went and got himself kilt by the Shawnee."

Before responding, Patrick glances over at Sean, furrows his brow and gives a subtle shake of his head. "Well, we're from Ohio. Must be more than one E. Jackson around. This here rifle belonged to my step-pa. He had it when he married my ma. Don't rightly know where he might have come upon it."

Walt shrugs, still examining the rifle, gives a little grunt and heads out the back door to the kitchen, carrying the rifle.

Patrick pours two cups of water from the clay pitcher before he turns to the man across from him. The man is obviously hungry, given how he leans over his plate of food protectively. He doesn't hardly have a chance to finish chewing one bite before shoveling in the next. Everyone at the table has their hunting knives in one hand and a fork or spoon in the other.

Patrick waits until the man pauses to take a breath before saying, "Looks like the food must be pretty good, eh?"

The man glances over and takes a long drink of beer before wiping his beard and mouth on his stained sleeve. "Yeah, ya might say it's tolerable, but everything's good when your hungry. Bit pricey, though, for buffalo. That's the first beer I've drunk in a long spell. Been off trappin'."

"Trapper, you say?" Pa says quickly. "I'm lookin' for a trapper—me brother. You don't happen to know a fella named Jack O'Reilly, do you? Passed this way ten or twelve years back?"

"Trapper? O'Reilly? Nah, ain't never heard of no O'Reilly, an' I know most of 'em. Might he go by another name?"

When Pa shrugs, the trapper turns to the others seated at the tables and loudly asks, "Any of y'all heard tell of a trapper goes by the handle of Jack O'Reilly, this 'ere fella's lookin' for his kin?"

The room drops silent for a moment before a grizzled, windburned old mountain man sitting at the next table over finally chimes in. "Y'all might look in on a trader down on . . ." He pauses to rub his beard, thinking deeply. "Maybe down on Lafayette Street. Yeah, Lafayette I think. Trader's name of, let me see now . . . German fella . . . maybe Schmidt. Yeah, pretty sure it's Schmidt. He could've heard something." The trapper raises a finger. "And I did hear tell of a group of a hundred trappers fixin' to join up with William Ashley. Yeah, so ya might check with Ashley too. Be goin' me-self if me knees would behave. They don't much fancy the cold no more."

"Thanks for your help." Pa touches his hat in the old trapper's direction. Then he turns and pats his son's arm. "See? I told you, Sean. Everything's gonna work out. We'll head on over to the trader's after supper and check it out." He gave Sean a big smile. "What do you say we splurge a bit and split a piece of Ma's apple pie?"

Patrick secures his rifle in its holster and then reaches down to pull Sean up behind him on the big stallion. After turning the horse, they slowly make their way down to Lafayette Street under the directions Walt gave them just before they left Ma's. Sean pokes his father in the back and points out one marvel after another as they pass.

It soon becomes obvious that Lafayette Street marks the far edge of St. Louis. The closer they ride to the trader's, the louder the noise grows. Sean becomes a little anxious when his father pulls out the rifle and rests it across the crook of his arm. A large number of trappers have gathered in the street in front of the trading post, where a small rendezvous carries on in a raucous fashion. Sounds of fiddles, juice harps, singing, and laughter permeate the air. Occasional gunfire disrupts an otherwise joyous atmosphere. As they ride closer, they see piles of equipment between wagons, and tents set up right in the street.

Sean's heart leaps when through the crowd he catches a flash of red hair. He cranes his neck to look through a gap in the gathering as Pa keeps the horse moving. Finally, the men blocking his line of sight part, and Sean sees the red hair once more. To his excitement, the hair belongs to a little girl with her back turned to him.

He pats Pa on the back frantically, wanting to show him the girl who might be Becky. But the moment Pa turns, so does the girl, and she's not a girl at all. She is small, to be certain, but she is much older than Becky.

"Something wrong, son?" Pa asks.

Sean just hangs his head. He is sorry that the woman is not who he thought she was, but the most disheartening part of it is the realization that he is always watching for Becky, even when he isn't fully thinking about her. Idly, he wonders whether she will always remain just on the edge of his thoughts.

They work their way through the maze of equipment and humanity, and Sean marvels at the fascinating sights all around him. As he turns, he is first to see the two drunken riders coming right at them. He hits his father hard on the side and then holds on tight as one of the racing horses gallops by, just missing them. Their startled stallion moves sideways and rears, causing the second rider's horse to suddenly veer off to avoid a collision with the bigger stallion. The drunken rider is thrown from his saddle and lands awkwardly in a pile of equipment and furs.

Sean is somewhat surprised that he and his father were not also thrown when the stallion reared. He continues to hold on tight to his father's waist as their big horse prances around nervously.

The fallen rider struggles to his feet in a drunken stupor and pulls a huge knife from his belt. Sean is terrified. His eyes open wide as the drunken man starts to stagger in their direction, only to stop a few paces away.

"Why didn't ya get outta me way, ya stupid plow-boy?" the man barks. He stands there tossing the huge knife back and forth from hand to hand. "That race just cost me a ten-dollar gold piece. Now this here Tennessee Toothpick is gonna have-ta collect it outta your hide!" With the knife held high, the man staggers another step forward.

To Sean's surprise, his father turns the stallion and levels the old flintlock at the man, cocking the hammer back in the process. "Mister, we ain't lookin' to cause no ruckus, an' this ain't nothin' but a squirrel gun. But unless your lookin' to add another hole to your face, you might want to consider puttin' the knife away and backin' off a bit."

The trapper hesitates. Even when drunk, staring at the wrong end of a rifle tends to sober a man up. This particular man stoops to pick up his fur hat, bangs the dust off against his pant leg, and angrily points the blade up at Patrick. "Don't be thinkin' this be the end, cause it ain't. There'll be another time. Prairie's big—mighty big—an' I got me a long memory. There'll come a day y'all gonna be sorry ya done met up with Jean Larrieu." He turns to reach for his lathered horse's reins, mumbling to himself as he fumbles to replace his knife in its sheath.

Sean looks up proudly and holds on tighter as his father nudges the stallion forward. After winding their way farther through the makeshift encampment, they draw near a small group of men gambling on a buffalo robe in the dim light of a nearby gaslight. As they approach, a heated argument suddenly erupts. Two men jump to their feet as the other gamblers dive for safety.

The smaller of the two combatants holds a whiskey bottle in one hand while fumbling awkwardly for his knife with the other. He curses in a mixture of French and English. "Vice estes menteur et tricheur! You'll no cheat . . ."

The taller man doesn't give the little trapper the chance to complete the threat. As the Frenchman fumbles to draw the knife from his belt, the working end of a hatchet is buried deep into his chest. The hatchet appeared in such a blur that the Frenchman momentarily stands and looks down in disbelief at his misfortune before slowly sinking to his knees. As Sean watches, the whiskey bottle slips from the trapper's hand and onto the buffalo robe as he topples to his side. One of the nearby gamblers reaches over to rescue the whiskey before much of the precious liquid has had a chance to spill.

Pa nudges the flanks of the stallion with his heels, and they slowly move through the gathering crowd. Sean continues to watch over his shoulder as the taller man steps forward, uses his foot to hold the dying man down, and yanks his hatchet free. The dying man's mouth flows with blood. Sean faintly hears a gurgling sound as he struggles for air. When the killer twists the knife from his victim's hand, Sean can plainly see that the dying man is missing two fingers.

Sean's mind flashes back to his grandpa's mutilated hand. Had Indians done the same thing to this man too? Before he even has time to process what he is seeing, the tall trapper slices off the left ear of the dying man and then cuts his throat.

"I'm sorry you had to see that, son," Patrick says as they finally ride up to the trading post. "That ain't right, someone should do somethin' 'bout that."

The trading post is a simple structure with rough-cut plank walls and a canvas roof. On one side, the canvas is rolled up a few feet in an attempt to capture the slight breeze coming up from the river. Sean slides down off the horse before his father swings his leg over and dismounts.

When his father tries to hand him the reins, Sean shakes his head vigorously. The killing has scared him, and he searches the darkness around him. He isn't about to stay here alone and hold the reins.

Patrick ties the reins to a post, puts his hand around his son's shoulder, and they duck through the canvas door. As his eyes adjust to the dim light, Sean studies his dark surroundings. The air is thick with tobacco smoke. A couple of men are leaning on a makeshift bar off to one side of the room. They stare over at him and his father. Finally, one hits the other on the arm, and they turn back to their drinks. Sean hears them laugh as one glances back in Sean's direction before laughing again.

He watches his father step over to the other end of the makeshift bar. A small man with spectacles perched on his nose is busy behind the bar, engaged in a heated argument with another trapper. Sean marvels at how the spectacles can stay there, pinched on his nose. He notices that both men are similarly dressed—buckskin britches and woolen shirt. The only difference he can see is that the trader's clothes are cleaner.

The trapper's voice becomes louder and louder in their dispute over money. Pa waits patiently until the argument finally tapers off. After much gesturing and angry words, they seem to have finally settled on a price for the pelts resting on the counter. The trader reaches into his pocket and slowly counts out a stack of coins and sets them on the plank bar beside the furs.

After a moment's indecision, the trapper grudgingly picks up the coins, bites into one, and drops them into the small leather pouch tied around his neck. The trader reaches down behind a bale of furs and pulls out a bottle of watered-down rum, which he offers to the trapper. Pushing the offered bottle aside, the trapper grabs a bottle of good whiskey from the shelf behind the trader's head. Two burly men standing quietly behind the trader immediately take a step forward. The trader raises his hand and shakes his head, stopping their advance.

Sean notices the trapper's hand drop to the hilt of the skinning knife at his belt, a sight that makes him wonder if everything in St. Louis is settled with a knife or a hatchet.

The trapper seems to have a slow turn of mind and backs up a couple of paces as he warily watches the three men behind the counter. He mumbles something about the true birthplace of the trader's mother, then abruptly turns and bumps hard into Patrick.

"Get outta me way!" The big trapper pushes Patrick aside with the hand holding the bottle as he makes his way out of the tent.

The trader's men step up to hoist the new furs onto a rather large pile already behind the plank bar.

Sean watches as his pa steps forward, "Evenin."

The trader glances up at Patrick above the spectacles for a moment before looking back down at the few furs still on the bar.

After wiping his hand on his pant leg, Patrick extends it in an offer to shake, "Name's Patrick, Patrick O'Malley."

The trader ignores the outstretched hand, and Patrick withdraws it.

"Me an' my boy here be lookin' for a fella named Schmidt."

"Ya a friend of his, are ya?" The little trader looks Patrick over above the spectacles.

"No, but I was told he might be able to help me."

"Well, ya found him. Don't look like your fixin' to sell nothin', though, so it ain't likely I can help y'all that much."

"I'm tryin' to find me brother. Fella up at Ma's place said you might know him. Brother's name is Jack O'Reilly."

The trader looks back down at his work. Without glancing up again, he finally replies, "Nope, can't say as I know no O'Reilly. Course, that sounds like a Christian name, and not many here 'bouts keep to their Christian names. Most folks in these parts ain't exactly lookin' to be found, for one reason or another."

The trader turns to get himself a drink. With a nod, he pours Patrick one too. Sean watches with curiosity as his pa picks up the offered drink and salutes the trader before bringing it up to his mouth.

"That'll be a nickel," the trader says.

Caught by surprise, Patrick sets the glass down and fumbles through his pocket to fish out a nickel.

"I do know a couple of fellas that go by Jack," the trader says. "Did, anyhow. Hung one here last spring for killing a fella and stealin' his Hawken. Guess ya might say he don't count no more." As if talking to himself, the trader adds, "Just don't take kindly to stealin', horse nor rifle. Whipped him good, then stretched him out hard." The trader pours himself another shot of whiskey, not bothering to offer any to the tall farmer in front of him.

"I'm new 'bout these here parts, an'—"

The men at the other end of the counter cut Patrick off by breaking out in laughter. Sean frowns at the men, and they stare back.

"Don't pay them any notice."

Patrick ignores the men's laughter and continues. "Like I was sayin', I just rode in, an' I ain't lookin' to get hung. What exactly is a Hawken?"

The trader turns back, chuckling. "It's a rifle, man, a rifle. The best ya can buy around these parts. Made right here in town, too."

"Just where might one get his hands on one of these Hawken rifles?"

"Brothers by the name of Jacob an' Samuel Hawken make 'em. Opened a shop up on Soulard Street back in '15. Make 'em all by hand. Good Hawken will bring down most anything movin' on the plains, man or buffalo. Hear tell they have a new fifty-caliber in the plannin' stages. William Ashley himself told me he already put in his order."

Patrick sets his empty glass down on the counter and turns to leave. Sean can see that his father is dejected, so he nudges him and holds up two fingers.

Sean notices his pa's brow furrow a moment before he turns back to the trader. "You said you knew a couple of Jacks. Is there one you ain't strung up yet?"

The trader busies himself wiping out the two glasses with a dirty rag. "Might be Hatchet Jack, but ya wouldn't want to claim no kin to him. A half-breed with a real mean streak."

An expression of hope crosses Pa's face. "Where might this Hatchet fella be? You seen him in town recently?"

"He's here 'bout somewhere," the trader replies. "He traded some bales in here just yesterday. Top-notch pelts, too, but Jack ain't none too friendly. Runs with a little French Canadian that don't talk much. Short fella missing a couple fingers. Trappers call him Frenchie. They both like the dice, so most likely if they ain't lit out yet, they'll be where the dice are rollin'. 'Spect ya might have ridden right by 'em."

Patrick turns to his son, and they nod at each other.

As they turn to leave, the trader cautions, "But I really wouldn't wanna disturb him none. Hatchet don't take kindly to bein' disturbed during his gaming. Hell of a quick temper, right crazy fella, and boar-grizzly mean. Seems to have a natural gift for killin'. Seen him get drunk an' kill two men at once with that hatchet. I mean, they didn't even have a chance."

After thanking the trader, father and son duck out the canvas opening and walk over to the horse.

Patrick levels a serious look on Sean. "I need you to stay back away from the circle of men, hold the horse, an' stay still. I'm gonna try to talk to him."

CHAPTER NINE

With his father walking in front of the horse while Sean rides, they wind their way back to the men and their noisy game of dice. Patrick turns and tells Sean to stay where he is before he makes his way closer to the gamblers.

Sean nervously glances at the trappers crowded in around him. With the old flintlock at his side, Pa looks totally inadequate compared to the heavily armed men gathering near him. Most of these trappers have one or two pistols tucked in their belts and carry heavy-caliber rifles, and as far as Sean can see, all have some sort of large knife. But, the most frightening thing he notices is that they all appear to be drunk.

The crowd of men quiets down as a detachment of blue-coated soldiers stationed in town from Fort Belle Fontaine push their way through to the gamblers. Sean leans forward to better hear over the bustle. The soldiers move the crowd back a bit before forming a semi-circle in front of the gamblers. All their rifles are now pointed in the direction of the seated gamblers.

A short lieutenant steps a little closer to the gamblers. He appears to be quite young and noticeably nervous. "Wha-wha-what happened here?" he asks, pointing to the body lying a few feet to the side in a pool of blood. The lieutenant's eye twitches, and his face screws up as he fights to get his words out.

After a moment of silence, one of the gamblers looks up. "Frenchie here tried to withdraw his b-b-bet and went f-f-for his knife." With each stutter, the trapper's mouth twists up. "Jack here just showed him the er-er-error of his wa-wa-ways." The trapper winks his eye a few times during the last stutter.

The gathered crowd of drunken mountain men roars with laughter at the lieutenant's expense. The soldiers present start to laugh a little, too, until a quick glance from the lieutenant reminds them of their rank and place.

"You sayin' this is self-defense?" the lieutenant says. "For God's sake, man, the fella's had his throat cut! And what happened to his ear?"

One of the other gamblers glares at the lieutenant. "Hell, General, the Frog asked for that. Frenchie was moanin' an' groanin' an' such. Jack here thought he said, 'Finish me.' Y'all know how hard it is to understand them frog-eaters' gibberish." He quickly adds, "Fair fight, though. Frenchie was just a might slower, that's all. Probably on account of him givin' 'em Dakota bucks a couple of his digits back on the trail. Never should have gone an' done that, no, no. Don't know why Jack here wanted his ear, though. Y'all have to ask him."

Sean sees Jack turn to glare up at the lieutenant. The crowd grows even quieter now as they catch Jack's look. The lieutenant meets the stare just as Jack winks. The men that see him roar with laughter. Sean sees that even his father can't hold back his smile.

The lieutenant's eyes widen in surprise before he regains his composure. "Mister, I think ya need to come with me."

The soldiers raise their rifles, with the business ends pointed in Jack's direction.

Jack holds up his left hand and slowly reaches into the front of his buckskin shirt with his right. He pulls out a dirty piece of tightly rolled leather tied with a thin piece of rawhide and hands it up to the young officer.

"What's this?"

"Read it," Jack answers.

The lieutenant loosens the rawhide and unrolls the brown paper inside. "I can't read this. It's in French."

With a disgusted look on his face, Jack slowly shakes his head. "Turn it over."

The crowd roars with laughter.

The lieutenant flips the paper over and reads to himself. When he is finished, he turns back to Jack. "Show me the ear."

Jack pulls out the leather pouch hanging around his neck and passes it to the lieutenant, who peers inside. Apparently satisfied, the lieutenant hands the paper and the pouch back to Jack.

"Seems to be in order. Come up to Belle Fontaine to settle this. I'll let the captain know." With that, the lieutenant turns to his men and nods that it is time to go. He pauses and turns to Jack. "Ain't ya at least gonna bury him?"

Without looking up from the dice, Jack answers. "We'll be long gone 'fore we notice the stink. Ya want him dug, dig him yourself." He shrugs. "Save a lot of time, though, if ya just toss him in the river an' let the fish finish him. Might be the bones make it downriver to them other Frogs in Orleans."

The lieutenant hesitates before turning to his men. "Smiley, you and Reynolds take the body to the cemetery and bury him." As he turns to walk off, he adds, "And I best not hear no splash."

Sean watches two soldiers step over to drag the body off.

The lieutenant turns and yells, "Pick him up!"

One of the soldiers silently mimics the lieutenant's last words before following the order. The other muffles a snicker.

Some of the gathered trappers slowly break up, laughing among themselves as they return to their camps. The dice game regains its serious nature. Sean nudges his horse in closer to better hear the conversation.

"What's all the interest with the Frog's ear?" one of the gamblers asks.

Jack shoots the man a dirty look before returning his attention to the game. "Little Frenchie 'ere got himself all liquored up an' kilt a couple men trapping up in Canada. One bein' his Hudson Bay brigade captain. Company posted paper on him—dead or alive. I figured I'd work him till we cashed in." Jack let out a big chuckle before adding, "I reckon we done cashed in."

"That's mighty cold, Hatchet, even for you," one of the gamblers says. "I mean, him bein' your partner an' all."

When the gambler stands, Sean notices how Jack's hand reflexively drops to the hatchet on his belt. The boy tenses in fear that he might bear witness to another murder.

"I've had 'bout enough fun for one night," the other gambler says. "I ain't pitchin' no dice with scum that would kill his own partner."

The man takes a few backward steps before turning away into the night. Only once he is gone does Jack drop his hand from the hatchet. The other gamblers keep quiet, and the dice game resumes.

Sean hopes that his father will walk away from this evil man, as well, so he is a little surprised when he hears Pa say, "Jack? Jack O'Reilly? That be you, Jack?"

Jack stirs ever so slightly at the sound of the Christian name. He slowly raises his hand up to the hatchet once more as he turns to stare up at the tall man standing behind him. "Been called a lot of names, but ain't heard that one in a spell. Who the hell are ya?"

"Can't say as I recognized you at first," Pa says, "what with all that hair an' such. Fella still oughta recognize his own step-brother, though, even after fourteen years. It's me, Jack. Patrick O'Malley."

Sean closely watches Jack's face and is relieved to see a slight smile.

"Well, I'll be damned," Jack says. "Might far from Ken-tuck for a social call. Ain't the old man got nothin' for ya to do?"

"Ain't called Ken-tuck home since you up an' skedaddled," Pa says. "Moved on up to Ohio, where your pa was kilt by Indians, year ago April. Lizbeth died in May." Pa pauses as if to wait for Jack's response. When none comes, he points to Sean, "That's my boy, Sean, over on the horse. Is there anywhere we can sit an' talk a spell?"

"I'll be back shortly, boys," Jack says. "Y'all keep the dice hot."

Sean watches as Jack and his father move off toward the river. He can't hear them, but he watches as they talk awhile. Before long, some of the gamblers yell over at Jack, and he returns to the game. Pa walks over, and Sean slides off the horse to allow his father to remount before pulling Sean up behind him.

"Jack agreed to talk with us after supper tomorrow," Pa says. "I know you must think he's crazy, an' probably a little scary, but I still think he's our best hope of gettin' to Oregon. Now let's get this horse to the livery an' hit the sack. We got us a long day tomorrow."

The morning breaks clear and bright. After eating a little piece of buffalo they managed to save from last night's meal, Pa and Sean find Skinny standing near a large flatboat. Skinny directs a couple of slaves unloading some rough-cut timber into two wagons nearby, one of them empty and the other partially full.

"Mornin', Mr. Dawson," Patrick says as they walk up.

"Next time y'all show up after sunup, it won't be such a good mornin'," the skinny man says as he looks toward the sun above the horizon. "Because y'all won't have a job—at least not with me. Now help these lazy bastards unload the boat. And call me Skinny."

"Yes, sir, Mr. Daw . . . I mean Skinny. And you'll see that me and Sean will give you a good bit of our sweat."

Sean follows his father down to the boat, where they immediately help unload.

All day long, the men carry rough-cut planks and logs from the boats to stack into the waiting wagons. Within a few hours, everyone but Sean has stripped to the waist. The hot sun beats down and the air grows more humid as the day wears on. Their only respite is a short break at midday to eat a quick meal. Pa and Sean only have a small piece of leftover meat from last night's dinner between them. They cut it in portions, and Pa gives Sean the bigger piece.

As he chews the last bite of meat, Sean looks over at Skinny, who sits in front of a big basket of apples. Skinny catches him looking and holds up two handfuls of apples with a questioning look. Sean's eyes widen as he nods. Skinny brings over the apples and passes them a handful.

Skinny wipes his glasses as clean as he can on his sweaty sleeve, then gestures at the apples. "Y'all have to eat around the worms some, but they're tasty. The apples anyway—don't know so much about the worms. Got a tree out back of me place. No idea how it got there, but it sure do make for some good apple pie and sauce."

They finish unloading the last wagonload of timber just before sundown. When the work is done, Sean doesn't think he can lift another board. Skinny hands Pa five dollars and starts to walk off.

"Wait a minute, Skinny," Pa says. "I thought you said four dollars for me and two dollars for Sean."

"I did, but y'all started late." Skinny shrugs. "So I knocked off a dollar. We'll see y'all tomorrow, prompt at sunrise like we agreed on."

Sean can see that his father is upset, so he takes his arm and pulls him away before he says something he might regret.

"That's a cheatin' son of a bitch," Pa says softly to his son. "That's what he is. Hell, we worked twice as hard as those other two." He pauses his stride, takes Sean by the shoulders, and looks him in the eyes. "Son, don't you ever cheat a man like that. Always be true to your word."

Sean nods in understanding.

They make their way over to Ma's again for dinner. There, they find that the menu is the same as the night before: whatever Ma has been cooking. But once again, it is good, as well as filling. Sean is famished, as he has never worked so hard in his life, so he wipes his plate clean with a last piece of biscuit. He isn't sure he will be able to work like that every day, but he sure will try. He doesn't want to let his father down.

Sean watches Pa wipe his plate clean as well. Then Sean catches his eye and glances at a man wolfing down a piece of pie at another table.

Pa smiles and gestures for Walt to come over. "We're gonna need two pieces of apple pie an' coffee for the both of us. And do you think you could make up a couple of biscuits with some buffalo slices for another two bits?"

"I think that can be arranged," Walt answers before heading back outside to the kitchen.

After they finish their pie and coffee, Walt brings them a cloth bag with their sandwiches. "Ma said she wants the bag back."

Pa nods in thanks.

Together, father and son head over to the Hawken brothers' shop on Soulard Street. Just like Walt's directions said, the shop isn't far. The eldest Hawken brother greets them at the counter and asks what he can do for them.

"We come for one of 'em grand fifty-three-calibers we heard so much 'bout in town," Pa says with the narrowed gaze Sean has only ever seen him use during negotiations.

"Well, ain't this your lucky day," Hawken says. "Orders usually weeks out, but we happen to have one right here meant for a fella who turned up dead yesterday."

Pa gives Sean a knowing glance before shrugging and asking for the price. To Sean's pride, when the elder Hawken makes his offer, Pa rebuffs it expertly.

"I heard you were honest men," Pa says, "but you seem to be takin' me for a rube."

After some hemming and hawing, Pa counters with a much lower offer. "Now you an' I both know the fella who ordered that gun already put in a down payment. Only fair for that total to get shaved off the price."

They trade good-natured barbs before arriving somewhere in the middle of their two positions.

Finally, the elder Hawken turns to holler back over his shoulder at someone working in the shadows at the back of the store. "What you think, little brother?" he calls out. "We square?"

There is a long, uncomfortable pause before the younger Hawken finally speaks. "Square," he says simply.

"Now hold on," Pa says with a sour expression, "your forget'n the cartridges."

The elder Hawken shrugs. "Fine. How 'bout I throw in fifty paper cartridges to sweeten the deal?"

Pa turns slowly and winks at Sean before accepting the offer.

As he watches his father pass the money over, Sean swells with pride at how his father bargained so well. When it is over, Sean and his father step out of the shop with a brand new .53-caliber Hawken rifle, some lead bars, a bullet mold, a bag of powder, and the fifty paper cartridges.

Outside, Pa smiles. "Didn't rightly have us much choice, did we, us both needing a rifle an' all."

Sean gives his father a big smile and hug as he thinks about the Kentucky long rifle actually being his now.

Once free of his son's embrace, Pa counts out what little money they have left. "Gonna have to make that the last big purchase for a while."

Moments after they return to the warehouse, Sean heads over to the corner to lie down. He is so tired that he has already forgotten about his uncle's visit. When Jack enters the warehouse a few minutes later, he arrives with company. Jack has a cord tied around his wrist and connected to an Indian woman's wrist on the other end. In this way, the woman walks a few paces behind. Pa takes them out back to sit next to the dying coals of Cotton's dinner fire.

Sean crawls quietly over to sit along the wall near the open door to listen. He watches through the rough-cut plank wall's cracks as his father adds wood to the fire and sets a coffeepot on an iron spider to heat. Sean tries to see the Indian woman sitting behind Jack, but he can't make out much. She looks to be Sean's mother's age. She has long black hair, and she wears furs from neck to ankle, but there isn't much else to see. Sean thinks about how hot she must be in those furs.

When she looks at the wall in his direction, Sean startles at the thought that she must have heard him, despite how quietly he moved over to eavesdrop. It doesn't seem possible that she could have sensed his presence, and yet she continues to stare at his hiding place. Through the dim firelight, Sean notices the bruises on her face.

"Jack, I'm hopin' we can sit and talk a spell," Pa says. "Kinda catch up, so to speak."

"Right sorry to hear 'bout 'Lizbeth," Jack replies. "She was a good woman. Tried to do right by me. Tried to stop the bastard." He moves a few coals around with a stick as he stares into the fire. "Thought many a night on different ways to kill him. Somehow it just don't seem right I wasn't there to see Pa's end. Kinda feel cheated."

"I remember how Pa beat you, Jack. Know how it must have pained, an' I'm sorry, but, that's done an' past now."

"You don't remember nothin'!," Jack snaps as he glares over at Pa. "It ain't your back all scarred up from his whip. Old man never laid a hand on ya, an' ya weren't even his own flesh-n-blood!"

Sean's forehead leans against the rough-cut wall as he listens and watches. He is wide awake now, to be sure.

"Beat me so hard," Jack says, his anger clearly building. "So hard I couldn't even lay down. His own flesh-n-blood. Damn him to hell. How I wish I'd had the courage back then to kill him." Now Jack slumps and his tone softens. "I just had to run off. Couldn't stand it no more. How could he do it? His own son?" He hesitates before adding, "I shoulda run off sooner."

After a long period of silence, Pa quietly says, "Its over, Jack, done and past. Now we need to talk about here and now." Pa laces a rag around his hand and picks up the coffeepot. He pours two cups, one for Jack and the other presumably for the Indian woman.

Jack takes one of the tin cups but ignores the other. "Don't make no sense wasting good coffee on a squaw. Coffee be scarce 'round here. Most of these bastards are so liquored up on whiskey or rum, they wouldn't know what to do with good coffee." He sniffs the drink deeply before taking his first swallow. "Y'all said ya needed to talk some, so get on with it."

Sean watches his father blow on the coffee before taking a sip. "Once you run off, Ma an' Pa packed up an' moved to Ohio. That was back in '06. Don't exactly know why, but Pa was really eager to get outta Ken-tuck. Whatever the reason, that was my lucky day, because when we moved to Ohio, I met Jenny O'Conner. She was so pretty. Just like an angel an' not quite seventeen. Her city-boy husband had died the year before an' left her with a two-year-old son named Jake. Kinda hard to imagine, but this city boy fell a tree right on himself. Snapped his neck like a twig. Never did meet him, but obviously not one for the frontier.

"I married Jenny that very summer. My own fair bonnie lass! We moved in with Ma an' Pa, an' was real happy too. Had us another beautiful boy an' the sweetest little girl the Good Lord could ever dream up.

Sean came along a year after we wed. Then we were blessed with little Becky, who we waited eight years for. You done seen Sean, an' your gonna like him. He's a hunter just like you. Both of 'em were born with my family's beautiful red hair an' green eyes."

Sean watches as his pa reaches into his shirt and pull out the doll's indigo dress. He wipes his eyes with the cuff of his shirt. He has never heard Pa talk this way about him and his sister. He feels ashamed now that he ever hated his red hair. He stands, wipes his eyes again, and steps through the open door.

"Here's my boy now," Pa says with a smile, as he pushes the doll's dress back into his shirt. "Sean, this is my long-lost step-brother, your uncle Jack."

Sean turns to the man and nods once in acknowledgment.

Pa holds up the coffeepot. "How 'bout a little coffee?"

With another nod, Sean picks up an empty cup.

After Pa pours the coffee, Sean walks over to the Indian woman and offers it to her.

Jack leaps to his feet and angrily knocks the cup aside, splashing the hot coffee over Sean's woolen pants and the squaw's furs. "What the hell ya think your doin', boy?" He raises a hand as if to strike Sean, but then hesitates.

"Stop it, Jack!" Pa hollers.

The grizzled trapper straightens up and returns to his seat.

Sean retreats back to his hiding spot just inside the warehouse.

"Don't you ever let me catch you striking my son," he hears Pa say. "What the hell's wrong with you? He didn't do nothin' wrong."

"Best tell him to keep clear of Jack's affairs," Jack calmly replies. Moments later, he continues as if nothing happened. "Ya said something 'bout Ma an' Pa bein' kilt by Injuns?"

Sean listens and watches from his hiding place as his father stares at his step-brother for a few moments. He hopes that his father won't say anything else, and will instead make Jack go away, but after a time, Pa answers.

"Yeah, they were. Sean was the first to find 'em—his ma, brother Jake, your pa, an' my ma. Ma was still alive but scalped. She had lost her memory some time before that, an' she died of infection a month later. We never did find little Becky. We think she must have been taken."

"Almost sounds like an 'eye for an eye' kinda thing. Y'all didn't have no Injun trouble before the attack?" Jack asks. "Maybe kill one? Wouldn't put it past the old man."

"No, no problems at all," Pa answers. "Your pa hadn't even been out of the cabin much for two years."

"Where the hell were ya when all this was happening?" Jack asks. "What y'all doin' out here if ya can't fend for ya own any better than that?"

With a glare at his step-brother, Pa's face reddens. "Jenny sent me down the road to help out on the Harris farm. Tom Harris was laid up with a broke leg an' needed some plantin' done." Pa takes a deep breath. "You don't think that frets me every night? Why wasn't I there?"

The two step-brothers hold a long gaze between them.

"We weren't 'spectin' no trouble," Pa says. "My boy Sean hasn't mumbled a word since—nary a word. Somehow he blames himself for our troubles, an' he wasn't even there. The doctor told me to take him somewhere else. Anywhere else, just so it's far from Ohio. So I got to thinkin', what about Oregon Country? They said it was real pretty, an' enough land for the takin'. Rumor has it that Astor's men found a pass over the Rockies. Thought maybe you could help—that maybe you done been there?"

"Can't say that I have, an' I sure ain't thinkin' on goin' neither. Might say it's a bit of a ways, with a big ole desert plum stuck in the way." After a sigh, Jack changes the subject. "Sorry to hear 'bout your wife an' family, though—that's tough. I reckon Lizbeth weren't kilt on account 'em Injuns thought she was spirit touched. If y'all kill someone spirit touched, ya release their evil spirits an' they can move into your own body. Good riddance to the old man, though. Hope 'em Injuns cut him up but good!" He takes a long, slow sip of his coffee before adding, "Ya try to find your little girl?"

"Course I did!" Pa says, his voice raising momentarily. "After Sean an' I did some trackin' an' the trail ran cold, folks an' militia searched for weeks. Didn't find a trace—not so much as a whisper on the wind. Checked villages fifty miles in all directions, but nothin' was found."

"Well, I reckon she'll survive," Jack says. "Her red hair probably saved her."

Upon hearing the words, Sean's heart starts to pound in his chest. Becky might still be alive after all! With that thought, his determination to find her redoubles.

"The Injuns would hold that hair in mighty high esteem," Jack continues. "Be big medicine. Tribe most likely just took her in, with her bein' so young an' all. Probably gave her to a family that had just lost a daughter. 'Member, I'm half Injun myself. Plenty worse things than growin' up Injun. Many a day, I wish I still lived with 'em. Tried to go back once, but they wouldn't have me."

"If it was so good, why'd Pa up an' leave?" Pa asks. "He used to tell lots of good stories about the Shawnee, but neither of you ever said why you left 'em." He reaches over and refills Jack's coffee cup.

"If ya 'member when I was livin' with y'all back in Ken-tuck, I didn't exactly know much English. Can't say as I really want to talk about livin' with the Injuns now, either." Jack sips the hot coffee and stirs the fire with a twig before tossing it in. "Let's just say the tribe blamed the old man for somethin', an' he in turn blamed me."

Sean strains to listen as Pa sets his empty coffee cup aside and pulls out his clay pipe from his shirt front. He begins to stuff the bowl with tobacco from a small pouch as Jack eyes the tobacco bag.

"Is that the real stuff?" Jack asks. "Not none of that Injun mix?"

Pa tosses Jack the small bag. "Right outta Ken-tuck," he answers.

Sean sees Jack's eyes close in clear appreciation as he opens and sniffs the contents of the bag.

"You can keep the bag if you tell me 'bout living with 'em Indians," Pa says. "I'd sure like to know what its like, considerin' my Becky an' all. Might ease my mind some to know how they might treat her."

Sean's ears perk up as he leans closer to the wall. He can sense that the Indian woman with Jack still knows he is eavesdropping.

Jack stuffs the sack in his shirt. "It was good—for a boy, anyway. Girls had to do lots of chores, but I never saw one mistreated. Boys spent their time preparin' for battle, huntin', an' standin' sentry. What more could a boy want? I had me a brother too. He was two summers older. The Shawnee called him Squirrel, on account that he was always laughin' an' chatterin' like a squirrel. He hadn't earned his warrior name yet. I was called Hatchet, not 'cause I was a warrior, but 'cause I cut me leg playin' with a hatchet when I was around five summers. Funny how that name came back 'round."

"Where's your brother now? Have you ever seen him again?"

"He's dead!" Jack answers loudly. "But, yeah, I do see him from time to time—in me dreams. He mostly forgives me, but other times, he tries to kill me. Kinda wavers 'tween the two, ya might say."

"Forgives you? Forgives you for what? Did you kill him?"

Sean holds his breath to better hear his uncle's reply.

Jack takes a last sip of coffee before turning the cup over and setting it by the fire. "The white militia attacked our village. We didn't know the reason at first. We thought maybe another tribe did something to set 'em off. White men can't tell the difference, ya know, or they just plumb don't care. To most whites, an Injun is an Injun. Anyway, I must have been 'round eight summers when they attacked. I remember the yellin' an' shootin' an' all—Ma grabbin' me an' me brother by the arms an' us running for the canoes. Of course, Squirrel wanted to stay an' fight the whites, but Ma wouldn't allow him. We made it to the canoes all right. I was tossed into a canoe with Ma, Squirrel, an' another warrior. As we started downriver, the warrior was shot an' the canoe flipped over. I couldn't swim none, so I held on to the canoe the best I could. The river was cold an' fast, swollen from snowmelt. I was really scared, an' yelled out for Ma or Squirrel to save me." Jack took a deep breath before continuing. "Squirrel had already made it to the bank, but he tried to swim back out to me. He didn't make it. I watched him get pulled under by the current. He looked right at me. Eyes got real big an' all, like he knew what was coming. Then, just like that, he was gone. I never did see Ma. We never found either of their bodies neither. I somehow managed to hang on until the canoe got caught up on some overhangin' branches downriver.

"When Pa came home, he blamed me for killing Ma an' Squirrel. Said I acted like a coward. Said he was ashamed to call me his son. That's when the beatings started." Jack chuckled. "Chief Tecumseh learned later that the white militia hadn't made a mistake at all. It turned out that Pa and a handful of others had ambushed some white wagons. Tortured an' massacred ten white settlers just passin' through on their way west. Pa an' Tecumseh had 'em some words, an' we were banished from the tribe. Turned out that Pa was the one responsible for my ma an' Squirrel bein' dead—not me."

Pa looks stunned as he stares back at his brother. "I knew Pa had a fallin' out with Tecumseh, but I never knew what it was 'bout. That explains why he wanted to leave Ken-tuck so bad, an' where the long rifle came from." He pauses before saying, "I'm sorry you had to go through all that."

As Sean turns and leans back against the wall, he can't get the nameplate on his rifle out of his mind, E. Jackson. His own grandpa massacred white settlers to come by it. He takes a deep breath and softly starts to cry.

"Pa was right in one respect, though," Jack says. "If I hadn't been a coward an' called out, Squirrel would still be alive. I know that now. One thing though: no one has ever called Jack a coward since." He looks over at his step-brother and adds, "Once he learnt me the lesson, Pa shoulda stopped. He really shoulda stopped beat'n me." He throws another stick on the fire. "Anyway, how do ya think your gonna make it to Oregon?"

"Hadn't really thought too much past just findin' you. Since it seems you can't help none, maybe I could latch on with that Ashley fella—maybe as a mule skinner or something. Here tell he's lookin' for men."

"Yeah, he's lookin' for men, all right—trappers, mountain men. Hard men with experience. Men he don't have to babysit. Not a dirt farmer, an' pretty damn sure not your boy there. Ya saw the boy cringe when I lost my temper. What do ya think he'll do when real Injuns come at us?"

"I'll just have to show Ashley I can handle myself," Pa replies. "I know your wrong about Sean. You just surprised him, that's all. He's a might tougher than he looks. He knows the woods, an' he's a good hunter. He did most of the hunting back in Ohio. With bow or rifle, your pa taught him well."

"That was the woods back in Ohio, not out on the plains or in the Rockies." Jack sarcastically adds, "Maybe I can ask the Injuns to announce when they're coming, so he's not too surprised an' all."

Sean catches the scowl on his father's face.

"How much did ya get for the farm?" Jack asks, changing the subject.

Pa hesitates before replying, "Five hundred dollars. Sold it to a young Christian couple. They promised to send me two thousand dollars more in a couple of years, once we get settled in Oregon."

Sean thinks Jack must have noticed his father's hesitation, because he certainly had. He wishes that Pa had not said anything, or at least had said that the money was gone.

Jack gazes over at his brother with a look of total disbelief. "How big a place was it, anyway? I thought ya said it was a farm or something."

"We had a hundred sixty acres, twenty miles west of Portsmouth, one section up from the Ohio River. I know it was probably worth more—two or three times more, maybe. But I got what I needed to get here." Pa shrugs. "They're good Christian folk, an' I believe 'em when they say they'll send some more money when they get a crop in."

"The hell ya say?" Jack asks incredulously. "Y'all seen the last of 'em, an' they know it. Be fools to send anything more. Never get to ya even if they did try to send it." As he stares at the dying fire, Jack stirs a few embers around with a stick. "Tell ya what I think. Ain't no good hookin' up with Ashley, even if he was dumb enough to take ya on, which he ain't. He's headed to Green River country. That's south, an' y'all need to go north to take Astor's pass. I'll take y'all as far as the western slope of the pass. From there, your on your own, bein' that its desert an' all, an' Jack here don't do no desert. Cost ya five hundred dollars up front."

"I ain't got no five hundred dollars," Pa says. "Even if I did, I'd still need to buy supplies an' all. I can send you double what your asking once I get the money from Ohio."

"Cold day in hell when that happens. Ya just said ya got five hundred for the farm. How much ya got left?"

Pa turns away from his step-brother and pulls out a leather pouch tied to his belt. He carefully counts out the contents, then tucks the bag back in. "Three hundred eleven dollars," he says after some hesitation.

Jack sits and thinks for a minute before replying. "We're startin' out a might late for Oregon. I'm heading up north to trap the Powder River country. Maybe sell the squaw back to her Crow people. Y'all can winter over with me on the Powder an' help with the trapping. Then we'll head out to Oregon Country with the spring melt. I'll keep the winter pelts for payment. We'll split the cost of supplies."

"Looks like that Schmidt fella has some trade goods," Pa says. "I can probably trade the mules to him for some of the supplies. Might be—"

"The hell ya say?" Jack interrupts angrily. "Ya never said nothin' 'bout no mules. Don't ya get nowhere near that conniving Schmidt bastard. Be better to sell 'em mules to Ashley. I hear tell he needs some. Better yet, let me sell 'em, since you're likely to go soft in the head again. And, yeah, we need supplies. Trade goods, like knives, steel arrowheads, needles, mirrors, beads, bells, and colored ribbons. Besides that, we need powder, lead, nails, canvas, wire, coats, blankets, flour, beans, bacon, salt, sugar, coffee, an' whiskey. But I'll do the buyin'." Jack chuckles. "Actually, it's your lucky day, since me partner just donated his outfit and horses. He had a couple pistols an' a nice rifle ya can use. Good Hudson Bay camp knife too. We'll need to get another rifle for the boy. That squirrel gun ain't much use out here. Ya got one good horse, but we need to get at least four more."

"I done already bought myself a rifle today," Pa cuts in. "Got it from the Hawken brothers over on Soulard Street—fifty-three-caliber."

"Maybe your brain ain't totally full of mush after all. Frenchie put in an order for that same gun last year." Jack holds up a finger. "But just don't go buyin' nothin' else. Give me the three hundred now an' we can meet up again in two days. Where are 'em mules, anyway?"

Sean watches as his father hands over most of his money.

Jack slowly counts it before stuffing it into a leather sack. "I have a camp up the river a ways," he says when he's finished. "Y'all need to come up an' watch the supplies. I don't trust 'em other bastards 'round here none. Tell that dock fella that tomorrow's your last day, that y'all quit. I'll meet up with y'all here tomorrow evenin'. I need to stop in at the fort in the morning an' settle up on Frenchie. Then I can start picking up the supplies we need an' take leave of this overcrowded rat hole. Hopefully set out in two, maybe three days tops."

Sean watches his father extend his hand to shake on the deal, but Jack just sidesteps his brother on the way out. Sean scurries over to the corner so it won't appear like he has been listening. His father comes in a few minutes later.

"I really didn't want to give him that money," Pa says, "but I reckon we don't have much choice in the matter." He sighs. "I gotta head over to the livery an' let Dan know Jack will be by for 'em mules in the morning."

CHAPTER TEN

The next day, Patrick and Sean arrive a good bit before dawn to work the docks. They unload and load the seemingly endless number of flatboats. All Sean keeps thinking as the day wears on and the sun scorches the land in blistering heat is that this will be their last day on these docks. It is the only thing that carries him. Before they started, his father told him that they would wait until the end of the day to tell Skinny about quitting.

When the end of the day finally comes, Sean watches as Skinny counts out four silver dollars and sets them in Pa's hand.

Pa calls Sean over before telling Skinny, "Sean earned 'em. I think it only fitting that he get 'em. Stick out your hand, son."

Sean breaks out in a big smile as Skinny counts and then drops the two silver dollars into his open palm. This is the first time he has actually been paid for a job.

Skinny turns to walk away, but stops and takes a step back when Pa calls over to him.

"I wanted to let you know that we won't be comin' back in the mornin'," Pa says. "We're headin' on out."

With that, they leave Skinny standing and seething. They make their way over to Ma's for supper.

When they return to the warehouse after their meal, Cotton is standing patiently outside, watching over the pile of their meager belongings. "Mista Patrick, I'm sorry, but Mista Dawson says y'all can't sleep 'ere no more. He seemed plenty mad too."

"That's all right, Cotton," Pa says. "We'll be leavin' St. Louie shortly, anyway." He turns to Sean and says, "I guess I'll go an' get the horse while you pack up our stuff. I'll be right back."

By the time Sean has bundled their belongings together, Pa has returned with the horse. They finish tying their belongings behind the saddle just as Jack rides up a few minutes later. The Indian squaw follows behind on another horse. Sean and his father are both surprised to see the mules still tied to her saddle.

"What happened?" Patrick asks. "Didn't Ashley want 'em mules?"

"We have to get back to me camp," Jack replies. "I bought the supplies, but I wasn't able to trade 'em mules. Ashley said he wouldn't trade for no stolen mules. We had us some heated words. But that's okay, I just saw another fella ride into camp with a string of ponies. I think I can barter some with him. But I gotta do it now before he trades 'em ponies."

"I'll go with you," Pa replies as he mounts the stallion. "Sean can ride back to camp with the woman and watch the supplies." Without waiting for Jack to respond, Pa turns to his son. "Sean, swing on up behind the squaw there and go with her to keep an eye on the supplies."

Sean slowly shakes his head as he turns to look over at Jack. He doesn't want to get that close to Jack's squaw. He's afraid of what might happen.

"Go on, boy, an' do as your pa says," Jack yells over. "She ain't gonna do nothin'. Keep her tied up if ya want. We won't be long."

Jack unties the lead ropes and rides off with the mules. Pa hesitates a moment before turning his horse and riding to catch up with his step-brother.

Sean turns and looks nervously up at the woman, her hands tied as she sits stoically on the horse. He is left alone with an Indian for the first time, and he doesn't like it. He picks up his long rifle, takes a tentative step closer, and notices that her lip is cut and swollen and her eye is bruised and puffy. She looks down from the saddle and reaches her tied hands down to him.

Does she really think I'm going to untie her hands, or give her the rifle, Sean wonders?

She gestures with her hands again and nods her head up and to the back of the horse. Sean finally understands that she is offering to assist him up behind her on the saddle. He accepts her helping hands, then struggles up one-handed while holding the rifle securely in the other.

When they arrive at Jack's camp, Sean slides down from the horse and reaches up to offer her a hand down. She shakes her head and swings easily down from the saddle. He hesitantly starts to reach toward her face in concern, but she jerks her head away. But when she turns back, she must see the tenderness and genuine concern in his eyes, because she smiles faintly.

Sean points for her to sit before he walks down to the river's edge. He knows from experience how much she must be hurting. After setting the rifle down on the bank, he wades into the cool water and reaches along the river's bottom. Soon he pulls up a goodly amount of the soft moss growing on the submerged rocks. He returns to camp with a big handful of moss, which he gestures for her to hold against her cheek and eye. She takes the wet moss from his hands, smiles faintly, and does as he indicates. She nods and says something unintelligible back to him. He assumes that she is probably thanking him.

An hour later, Patrick and Jack ride back into camp, leading four good-looking horses. Sean walks over and tentatively rubs the neck and head of a beautiful pinto.

"Some nice horses," Pa says. "A half-breed called Two Knives stole 'em from some Cheyenne. I think Jack here just kinda stole 'em from Two Knives. Made one hell of a barter. Even got Two Knives to throw in ten dollars' silver, to boot." He gives a little chuckle before adding, "Two Knives took a likin' to my red hair. Joked that he'd like to add a little color to his lodgepole. Sounded to me like Jack and Two Knives have some nasty history goin' back between 'em."

Sean listens to his father as he moves from one horse to another, studying each in turn.

"You look like you're pickin' out a horse, son," Pa says. "But you don't need a horse, 'cause you already got one. The stallion already done chose you a long time back."

Sean's eyes grow wide as a big smile breaks out across his face. He rushes to hug his father.

They leave St. Louis early the next morning, generally following the left bank of the Missouri River. They travel with nine horses between them. Jack takes the lead with Patrick close behind. Sean rides the stallion side by side with the Indian woman. Behind them trails a string of packhorses, Sean leading two and the woman leading the other three.

"Movin' out cross-country cuts the distance between the big bends in the river," Jack explains as he leads them onto the plains. "Follow 'em gullies an' draws whenever ya can, if they lead in your general direction. An' be sure to move off the ridge lines as quickly as possible too. No point in makin' yourself a target. Might take a little longer gettin' there, but it's a might better than bein' dead."

Jack slows his horse to ride alongside Patrick. While turning in the saddle so Sean can hear, he says, "The Injuns in these parts are on friendly terms with the whites. Call themselves Osage. Not near as warlike as some of the bands we'll be crossing paths with farther on. Most Injuns farther out would rather skewer ya than talk to ya— Comanche, Cheyenne, Lakota Sioux, an' Blackfeet ain't too friendly toward white folk.

"Damn Hudson Bay Company makes matters worse by trading guns only with the Blackfeet, just to keep 'em from tradin' their furs with good folk like us. 'Em Blackfeet havin' guns while the other tribes don't has caused a big problem. Makes 'em tribes that don't have guns that much more unpredictable, 'cause now they need to get 'em to survive."

Jack points a thumb in the direction of his squaw. "Everyone else calls her people Crow, but they call 'emselves Apsáalooke. Seen some Crow warriors reach down and pick up a lance stuck in the ground at a full gallop. All 'em tribes do that with their wounded. Two warriors ride up an' pluck a wounded man right off the ground at a gallop. Ya can't help but admire that. But they still ain't gonna last long without guns."

Sean doesn't understand what Jack said about the Crow and Apsáalooke. Why would the white man name her tribe after a bird?

"I think you just said osage," Pa says. "Sean's bow was osage. You think it came from all the way out here?"

Sean nudges his horse to move up closer. The thought makes him think of Becky again, causing his heart to skip with the hope.

"Did Pa tell ya that?" Jack asks.

Sean's father nods.

"Hell, Pa was just talkin' 'bout the osage tree the bow was made from, not the Injuns that made it. I was just lookin' at that bow last night while Sean was waxin' it. How'd Pa come by it, anyhow?"

Sean holds his breath, anxious about how his father will reply.

"Said he traded some Indian for it," Pa says dismissively. "Traded a skinnin' knife, I think he said."

"That's a load of horse dung," Jack replies. "Ain't no Injun gonna trade that bow for no skinnin' knife, that's a Spirit Bow—strong medicine. From what I could make of the beadwork on its back, I reckon it was made for somebody important, maybe a chief's son, an' that boy sure as hell ain't gonna go trading it, leastwise not for no skinin' knife. Especially not to some white man! No, I 'spect Pa more'n likely kilt the boy for it. Fits his nature too. Maybe that's why you were attacked."

Sean's heart beats faster with his uncle's reply.

"That's not the story I heard," Pa says. "'Sides, it ain't likely he kilt no Indian around Portsmouth while he was out hunting with his grandson here."

"That right, boy? The old man trade a knife for the bow?" Jack looks back at Sean as if to judge his reaction.

After a short hesitation, Sean nods once.

"Anyway, what do you mean by Spirit Bow?" Pa asks.

Jack is still looking at Sean questioningly. Finally, he turns back to answer his step-brother's question. "When a high-rankin' boy, like a chief's son, is determined by the tribal elders to be ready for the tests of manhood, his father makes him a bow. Not just any old bow, mind ya, but a special bow—a Spirit Bow. I've heard tell that some of these bows are many moons in the makin'. The best ones are always made from the wood of the Osage orange tree, like Sean's bow. That tree ain't easy to find, an' it sure as hell ain't easy to cut. Damn hard wood! The chief then takes the finished bow to be blessed by the tribe's head medicine man in a special ceremony. The medicine man conjures up all the chief's ancestral spirits into the bow to help the boy in his quest for manhood. With the help of this Spirit Bow, the boy is then sent out into the wilderness to live by himself an' seek a vision. Hopefully, the bow's spirits will guide him in this quest. Only then can the boy return to his people as a junior warrior."

Sean's father turns and glances back at him. When their eyes meet, his father's brow wrinkles up questioningly. Sean pulls his horse up and stops, wanting to put a little more distance between them. He's sure now that his father is suspicious, and he doesn't want him to see his shame.

It took a while, but Sean finally figured out what the Indian woman was trying to tell him: her name. Her name is Chimalis. When he finally pieced it together, a smile lit up her face.

They have been riding side by side ever since they left St. Louis, and she has been pointing to things and teaching Sean the Apsáalooke word for whatever she indicates. At first, the words sounded like gibberish to him, but as the days have passed, he has begun to comprehend more and more. Recently Chimalis made it into a game. She says a word, then waits until Sean points to the word's meaning. She sometimes shakes her head and softly laughs at his answer. But when he gets it right, she breaks into a smile. He is slowly beginning to learn Apsáalooke.

Finally they draw near to the small trading post known as Lohman's Landing, a place located along the South bank of the Missouri at the point the muddy river makes a big, lazy turn. Sean stares at the raised tepees scattered along the riverbank. As they get closer, he starts to pull out the Kentucky long rifle from its scabbard.

Jack seems to notice, because he turns to him and says, "'Em Injuns be the Osage I told ya 'bout. Lazy buggers. No need to concern yourself 'bout 'em."

They ride past a few scattered structures made of adobe or logs and mostly topped with sod roofs. They finally pull up to the hitching post in front of a bigger log structure. The two men dismount and tie off their horses.

"Best ya stay put out here," Jack says to Sean and Chimalis as he points to the corner of the log structure. "There's a waterin' trough 'round the side there. Look after the gear an' water 'em animals."

Sean and Chimalis ride around to the watering trough, dismount, and pull the packhorses up for a drink. A few Indian kids run over to stare. Sean figures that they must be curious about his red hair, so he takes off his hat and shakes his head. The kids jump back, their eyes and mouths wide open. Chimalis says something to them in sign language, and they turn and flee in panic. Sean wonders what she could have signed to frighten them so.

Jack and Patrick come out of the trading post and walk their horses over to drink.

"I known it weren't true," Jack says, "an' to think they almost had me!"

"Weren't true 'bout what?" Pa asks.

"Just some fellas back in St. Louie sayin' this place was gonna be the new state capital of Missouri. Said it was gonna be called Jefferson City, in honor of Thomas Jefferson, and the son of Daniel Boone himself was gonna design it."

Sean's eyebrows raise as Jack chuckles loudly.

"I just asked the fella inside, an' he laughed an' said he heard that story too. Said it had to be a joke. I knew 'em fellas was pulling me leg. What a bunch of hogwash," Jack says, "an' I almost fell for it."

Sean looks around at the few run-down log buildings and adobe cabins scattered about, then thinks back to the beautiful brick buildings in St. Louis. In his view, there is no comparison between the two. He can only see one glass window in this whole place, and half of the inhabitants around here are Indians.

That night, Sean joins his father in the trading post, where he searches for more of that lemon candy. He has been thinking about that candy for the past few days, and plans on using one of his silver dollars to buy every piece of it they might have. He is depressed when he doesn't find any. The place only carries a few basic essentials.

They ride out at first light the next morning, and for a number of days, the little party continues to encounter other travelers. As the days pass, however, the number of encounters dwindles. The wagon ruts they have been following over the prairie are becoming fainter with each passing day, until one day the ruts vanish altogether. Some of the eastbound travelers they meet have loaded packhorses, but there are no more wagons.

Eventually they run into a party of Osage Indians heading east to trade hides and dried meat at Lohman's. Jack seems pleased to restock their own supply of dried meat and acquire a little pemmican by trading two steel needles and a couple of mirrors. The Indians sign that they plan to continue on to St. Louis, to see for themselves the white man's stone town.

"They'll probably joke about the square brick buildings," Jack says as the Osage ride off. "How only the stupid white men would want to live in one place, in tiny stone rooms, while the Osage are free to move from one beautiful spot to another as they wish."

Sean thinks that the Indians have a pretty good point.

They continue to follow the Missouri River in a northwesterly direction, and there continues to be plenty of game. Each evening, as the men set up camp, Sean takes his bow out to hunt and is proud of the fact that he almost always comes back a short time later with the evening meal. Since leaving St. Louis, he has brought back to camp some Canada geese, a couple of deer, and many plump rabbits. To Jack's clear surprise, Sean even snagged a beaver with a wire snare. Chimalis excitedly prepared the tail, rubbing her stomach as she smiled at him. Sean was a little skeptical at first, but after finally trying a piece of the roasted, fatty meat, he thought it tasted great.

As the days stretch on, so does the landscape. Prairie grasslands spread away in every direction. Mostly flat or slightly rolling, the prairie is featureless except for a few cottonwoods bordering the occasional meandering streams. Other than these few twisted ribbons of trees, the prairie offers little variety to greet the riders each morning. Sean hasn't seen a soul since they left the Osage party nine days ago, and Jack says that is just the way he likes it.

Midmorning the next day, Sean looks up from listening to Chimalis to see Jack galloping back down from a rise in their direction. He is still some distance away, so Sean and Chimalis trot their horses over to stand next to Pa. As they wait for Jack to ride up, Sean sees his father cast a look around, probably searching for someplace to take shelter if the need arises. Sean follows his gaze but doesn't see anything but open, rolling grassland. Sean reckons that the nearest trees are a hard ride north to the Missouri River. They have been cutting across overland to avoid a big bend in the river.

"Ain't sure, but could be trouble ahead," Jack calls out as he abruptly pulls his horse up next to them. "Damnedest thing, don't rightly know what to make of it. Couple of ridges over are some fellas lazing 'round a buffalo chip fire. Looks to be two trappers an' three Injuns. Couple packhorses with 'em."

"What's so strange about that?" Pa asks.

"Don't rightly know," Jack says as he scratches his side. "Just got an itch tellin' me somethin' ain't right. Why would trappers be sittin' 'round in the middle of the prairie at this time of day? Almost looks like they're waitin' on somebody."

"What you want to do?" Pa asks.

"First off, check your powder an' flint," Jack replies, nodding to Sean as well. "It would take most of the afternoon to head up to the river an' go 'round 'em. 'Sides, if they are waitin' on someone, there might be others watchin' down by the river. No, I think we'll just mosey on over real casual-like an' see what they're up to. Sean, hop on down an' fetch Frenchie's rifle an' pistols out of the packs. Give your pa an' me a pistol each an' make sure the rifle's ready along with yours. I want you an' the squaw to stay back about fifty paces with the packhorses. When I tell ya, dismount an' stand behind your horse. Be ready to use 'em rifles at the first sign of trouble. If it comes to a fight an' ya don't have a shot at a man, shoot his horse. Reload behind your horse an' just keep shootin.'"

Sean nods his head in a desperate attempt not to let his uncle see how terrified these instructions have made him feel. His knees shaking, he walks back to one of the packhorses to pull out Frenchie's rifle and pistols. He hands one pistol up to his pa and the other up to Jack. His hands are unsteady as he loads the rifle, checks the flint, and primes the firing pan with fresh powder. He then pulls the old Kentucky long rifle from the stallion's saddle scabbard and checks its prime before replacing it. Sean sees that his father and Jack are re-priming all of their pistols and rifles as well. When he's finished with his own task, he remounts and nods over to Jack. He can only hope that Jack doesn't notice how much he feels like losing his breakfast.

"Boy," Jack says to him, "if there's too many of 'em an' ya gotta run for it, head back to that little dry wash we passed earlier. There were some fallen trees. Make your stand there." He raises his chin in the direction of the wash. "We'll join ya if we can."

"I thought you said there were only five," Pa says tersely.

"That's all I seen," Jack says. "Doesn't mean that's all there are. It's the ones ya don't see . . ."

". . . that'll kill you." Patrick finishes for his step-brother.

"Pat, if it comes to shootin', shoot the trappers first. They're better shots an' have better guns." Jack turns to the others. "Have your rifles in your hands. Y'all ready to ride?"

They all nod, and the little party sets off again. Sean's stomach feels like it's being tied in a knot. He remembers what he overheard his uncle say back at the warehouse—about what Sean would be able to do if they ran into a threat from real Indians. Well, these are real, and he's scared to death. He tries to reassure himself with the thought that maybe Jack's itch is simply his fleas acting up. Sean sure hopes the Indians are friendly. He's not sure he can really kill a man, even an Indian. He sees in his mind the image of the dying Indian boy reaching a hand up and hears his grandpa's words. *"Nice shot."*

Jack points above the second rise, where Sean can barely make out a faint curl of white smoke rising in the distance. Jack lifts his head up to sniff in a long breath of air. Then he holds a hand up below his nose and makes a couple of waves with it toward his nose. "Smell that smoke?" he asks Sean.

Sean sniffs the air again, but really can't smell anything. He shrugs and shakes his head. He would never even have seen the smoke if Jack hadn't pointed it out.

Jack laughs at his nephew. "Just funnin' with ya, neither can I. But ya can see it, though, can't ya?"

Sean nods once as they nudge the flanks of their horses to walk on. When they gain the top of the rise, Sean finally sees the men gathered around the open fire. Their horses are hobbled and grazing nearby.

"Cock your rifles now and ride in as if you're unconcerned," Jack says. "And stay calm. If they mean to do us harm, we don't want to alert them that we're ready. 'Sides, we may not be the ones they're waitin' for. But Pat, if it looks like trouble, shootin' first is always the best option. Be ready to follow me lead."

About fifty paces away, Jack nods for Sean and the squaw to stop. As Jack and his father ride on, Sean and Chimalis dismount and casually move between their horses to watch. Sean sees the men at the campfire stand as the two approach.

Sean watches Jack hold up his hand in greeting as he and Pa stop their horses a little ways out from the campsite. Jack casually dismounts, and as soon as his foot hits the ground, his rifle booms over the back of his horse. Sean gasps as one of the two trappers is slammed backward by the lead ball's impact and falls to the ground. The group's horses all try to bolt and one of Jack's pistols booms a second time.

Pa looks alarmed on his startled horse, but he doesn't hesitate to lift his rifle and fire. Once the shot is away, Pa jumps from the back of his horse. The second trapper reaches for a pistol and takes a wild shot, knocking Jack's hat from his head. Jack drops his rifle and empty pistol and pulls two pistols from his belt. He fires them, one after the other, at the second trapper and one of the three Indians. He wounds the trapper but misses the Indian. Two of the Indians bolt for their horses, but the one Jack missed charges Pa with a drawn knife. Sean has no chance for a clean shot as he watches the Indian charge.

Sean sees his father's horse rear back as Pa throws his heavy rifle into the face of the charging Indian and yanks a pistol from his belt. Pa barely has time to cock the pistol as he raises it and fires from his hip. The lucky shot hits the warrior in the neck, and he crumples at Pa's feet.

Sean fires a quick shot with Frenchie's rifle at one of the Indian's horses as the warrior cuts the hobbles, preparing to mount. Just as the warrior swings up onto its back, the horse collapses under him. The second warrior, having cut his horse's hobbles, gallops over and gives his companion a hand to swing up behind him. The two vanish over the rise as they make good their escape.

Sean and Chimalis quickly mount up and ride over to Pa and Jack. Just as they arrive, Jack slams his hatchet into the back of the wounded trapper's head.

"Load 'em guns, an' make it quick," Jack tells them as they dismount. He works fast to reload his rifle and pistols. When he is finished, he starts looking through the trapper's pockets.

"Why'd you fire like that so soon, Jack?" Patrick asks. "They seemed friendly 'nough an' all."

"Ya tellin' me ya didn't recognize Two Knives?" Jack replies. "He just as much promised ya he was plannin' on killin' ya. Turns out, we were the ones they were waitin' on. We just kinda surprised 'em a little."

Sean excitedly points to the first trapper Jack shot. Pa steps closer to see what Sean is pointing at. The dead man is sprawled out on his back with a big hole in his chest.

When Pa bends a little closer over the dead man, a look of recognition blooms across his expression. "Is that the fella that pulled the knife on us back in St. Louis?"

Sean nods.

"Amazing, him coming all the way out here just to get himself kilt over a ten-dollar horserace."

"French trapper called Larrieu." Jack says and then speculates, "Larrieu probably heard back in St. Louis that Two Knives carried a grudge, as well, and figured why not team up and settle two grudges at once. We must have said something about where we were headed when we traded 'em mules." Jack shakes his head, "Pretty stupid of him trustin' Two Knives. If we didn't kill Larrieu, Two Knives certainly would have." Jack picks up his hat and pokes a finger through the hole in the top. He scans the horizon and scowls. Then, without another moment's hesitation, he pulls out his knife, grabs the nearest man by the hair, and starts gliding the blade across his scalp.

Sean flinches when he hears the sucking pop as the scalp comes free and he sees the gummy, bright red blood clinging to the man's skull glisten in the sunlight. He tries not to think about how his own grandmother had to endure this same brutal act while she was still alive. He turns away as he finds that he can't keep watching. Still, he hears the grisly sounds as Jack finishes with the first man and casually scalps the other two.

When Jack finally finishes, he turns to Pa and sarcastically asks, "How the hell did ya manage to fire your rifle point blank an' miss everything? Now Two Knives is still out there somewhere, an' he's really pissed off."

"I wasn't 'spectin' you to just start in shootin'," Patrick replies. "Anyway, you missed one too."

"I told ya to be ready!" Jack turns to survey the camp. "Let's go round 'em packhorses up an' see what we got."

CHAPTER  ELEVEN

Sean and Chimalis continue to ride side by side and lead the pack-horses. Pa now leads the little party. Jack seldom remains with them for long, as he has taken to riding out to scout the country for hours on end. Sean watches as Jack rides up to Pa after his latest foray, talks quietly with him for a few minutes, points out a few distant land-marks, and then turns to ride off again.

This arrangement is fine with Sean, as there seems to be less tension when his uncle isn't around. Chimalis seems to have taken a liking to Sean, who has tried his best to treat her with respect and compassion. Sean knows that Jack is still abusing her because he sometimes sees fresh bruises on her face. He wonders how a man could treat a woman like that. What makes him so mean?

While they travel, Chimalis continues to point out various objects and speak their names in the Apsáalooke language. Although Sean still hasn't uttered a sound in reply, he now quickly points to things when he hears a word he knows. He now understands that her name means "bluebird," and that her tribe has some sort of connection with birds, but he still can't seem to figure out what that connection is.

"Platte River's a half day ahead," Jack says the next time he rides up. "Knew we had to be gettin' close. We'll follow the Platte for a week or so, then cross over an' swing north. No more fires for a while. We're headin' into Lakota Sioux territory."

They reach the little river late that afternoon.

"Looks like the Platte ain't much of a river," Pa says as they pull up to the bank, "leastwise, not after the Missouri."

The little river's flow is no more than a trickle in late summer. The cottonwoods and aspens lining its bank are just beginning to change color. Although the days are still warm, there's a hint of autumn in the air, and the nights are getting cooler.

They travel a few days along the Platte under an unyielding and oppressive heat. Finally, on the fourth day, Sean sees lightning flash in the distance. He listens to the soft rumble of the thunder as it rolls across the prairie. The horizon begins to darken.

Jack rides up a few minutes later. "Looks like we're in for a wet night. There's a spot up a ways that might be a decent place for a campsite."

After a short ride, Jack turns his horse to trot over to a large, fallen tree. Sean and the others trail after him, and at the site, they unload their gear while Jack directs Chimalis to lead the horses into the shelter of the nearby trees.

"This will do," Jack says as he surveys the grounds, "no fires again tonight, an' not for at least a couple more days. In a few more days, we should be free of Lakota country, an' then we can shoot us an elk or buffalo an' have us a feast.

"Pat, help me drag that big limb over here by this fallen tree. Don't pay to get careless. Not likely we've been seen, but Lakota don't much fancy attacking a good defensive position. Much rather fight out in the tall grass, where their horses give 'em an advantage."

Sean steps over to help drag the heavy branch alongside Jack and his father.

"Might call 'em Lakota a lot of things," Jack adds, "but ain't likely to call 'em stupid."

"We ain't seen nary an Indian since 'em Ponca we came across nine, ten days back," Pa says. "I thought you said the Lakota mostly kept farther north."

Jack scratches his beard before kneeling behind the fallen tree to test his line of fire with an imaginary rifle. As he stands, he turns to Patrick and answers. "I did, but if ya ain't seen 'em, ya don't rightly know where they be, now, do ya? It's the ones ya don't see that will most likely kill ya. 'Sides, could be raidin' parties out lookin' for horses most anywhere. Because of what Frenchie did to Little Hawk, any one of 'em Lakota would love to get their hands on us. It'd be big medicine."

"Don't rightly see what a dead Frenchman's got to do with us," Pa says. "He's dead an' buried, or more than likely, he's fish food in the river. This here dried jerky's gettin' downright tiring."

"Injuns don't see things that clear," Jack answers. "They don't exactly love me, neither, since I kilt a few myself, an' I still have the Crow squaw."

They remove their bedrolls from the packs before stacking the packs in a semicircle around the back of the fallen tree, as added protection. Chimalis has tethered the horses to a long rope strung between the nearby cottonwoods. She has left each enough lead rope to eat a sufficient quantity of the high grass and the new cottonwood growth.

As they settle down to another cold meal of pemmican and dried meat, Pa asks the question that Sean has been waiting to hear. "Just what did Frenchie do that raised the ire of the Lakota? I thought the Lakota were supposed to be friendly."

Jack continues to chew as if giving some thought to Pa's question. "Well, first off, ya gotta know that the Lakota don't take much of a spark to set off. They don't take too favorably to the white man to begin with. Kinda like the Blackfeet in that respect. Anyway, the idiot Frog went an' kilt the wrong Injun, that's what. Up an' kilt the big chief's grandson."

Sean joins his father in biting off a big chunk of the meat.

"While back," Jack continues, "Frenchie an' me was makin' our way down from a pretty little valley up Canada way. Headin' out, plannin' to trap the Yellowstone when six young Dakota bucks came upon our camp. They'd been raidin' on the Crow, out lookin' to count coup an' steal horses. I was off tryin' to rustle up some meat at the time, but from what Frenchie told me later, they wanted to trade the squaw here for some whiskey."

Sean notices Chimalis glance over at Jack before quickly looking away. He wonders just how much English she understands.

Jack takes out a small jug and tilts back a long swallow. After knocking the cork back in, he replaces the clay jug next to his buffalo robe. He wipes his mouth and beard on his buckskin sleeve. "Frenchie tried to tell 'em we were dry, but they didn't believe him. Hell, the damn Frog was liquored up most of the time, always singin' an' drinkin.'" Jack laughs heartily. "Hell, I almost shot him myself a couple of times, just to get a little peace an' quiet. Anyway, 'em bucks knew he'd been hittin' the juice, and they got in a bit of a scuffle. Frog shot one an' put his Hudson Bay blade in the back of Little Hawk," Jack nods at the knife at Patrick's side, "the very same blade you're wearin' now. Anyway, I heard the shot an' headed back. Smelt 'em Injuns before I heard 'em." He nods before continuing. "They found the jug, all right, an' was havin' a party at Frenchie's expense. Had him all hogtied to a log an' was cuttin' him up, knuckle by knuckle. Gotta hand it to the man, though. He was cursin' an' laughin' almost as much as they were.

"Me? I just walked right in an' shot the three of 'em." With a nod to Pa, Jack pats the two pistols tucked in his belt. "That's why a couple pistols come in handy. Gave 'em a little taste of me hatchet too. Reckon they were a might surprised. But one of 'em got off in the night, and it's mighty tough tryin' to locate a gut-shot Injun in the dark. We figured he must've hightailed it back to his people." Jack took another long pull on the keg before biting off a big piece of buffalo jerky. "I saw it right off," he continues, with his mouth full, "when I was helpin' myself to their hair. Frenchie had gone an' kilt Little Hawk, big chief Wa-na-ta's grandson. We was in big trouble." Jack takes a quick glance at Sean, "Little Hawk weren't much more than a couple years older than Sean here, so we lit out at first light. Gathered up what ponies we could find an' rode out hard. See, Injuns read sign real good. Even if that buck didn't make it back to camp, they'd figure out what happened, especially with Little Hawk bein' stuck in the back an' all.

"After Frenchie's little shindig, we thought it prudent to change course an' head to St. Louie." Jack gave a little grin at Patrick and Sean. "Worked out kinda lucky for y'all too. Now we're in Lakota territory, or close to it. Close cousins of the Dakota. The Lakota are also known as the Teton Sioux. Sure as hell, they know all 'bout Little Hawk. Word travels fast out here on the plains."

Pa looks over at the squaw. "Seems to me you done saved Chimalis, not Frenchie. How'd he end up with her?"

"Frenchie claimed he traded for her! Bragged he traded two an' a half digits for her. I told him he made a lousy trade, but right then, I thought it best to ride an' not argue. Long as he had his trigger finger, he was more useful to me alive than dead. 'Sides, I still had the paper on him. There'd be time enough to settle up later. We've done settled."

Sean shivers, not wanting to look at his uncle.

"Best turn in," Jack says. "Gotta get an early start. Pat, ya got first watch. Wake me in a bit."

After taking another drink from the jug, Jack gathers his rifle and robe and moves a few yards off. He returns to drag Chimalis and her blanket over with him. Sean hears a few slaps and low grunting sounds from Jack's direction before all is silent except the sounds of the frogs and nearby cicada. Off in the distance, a night owl hoots, closely followed by the rumble of distant thunder. A strange tingle shoots up and down Sean's back as he closes his eyes and involuntarily shudders at the sound of the thunder.

A stab of lightning lights up the sky as the thunder crackles and booms overhead. Sean feels the rain on his face and hands. He stares down at the ghost of the Indian boy, who stares back at him with dead eyes. A dead hand slowly reaches up to him.

"Nice shot. We gotta go. We gotta go now!"

Sean feels his grandpa tugging at the back of his shoulder.

"But we can't just leave him," Sean says over his shoulder, back at his grandpa. *"We can't go yet. We gotta help him."*

A sharp slap across his face jolts Sean out of his nightmare. He reaches for the rifle lying beside him under the leather cape. It must be Jack, he thinks. Must be time for my watch. He sits up, rubbing the sting out of his cheek. Why would Jack hit him?

"Boy, we gotta go," Jack says as he shakes Sean's shoulder again. "Somethin' bad happened to your pa."

It's still dark as Sean opens his eyes. His mind slowly focuses on the shadow of his uncle kneeling in front of him.

"Sean, your pa's been kilt," the shadow says. "Ya fell asleep on watch again, an' Pat got himself kilt by Two Knives. Pat must've heard something out by the horses, an' went to have a look."

What is his uncle talking about? No one woke him for watch, so he couldn't have fallen asleep. His father can't be dead. Sean sits there in the dark and rain, trying to clear his mind. Could he still be dreaming?

"I heard your pa yell, an' I went out an' kilt Two Knives myself. There must've been three of 'em, 'cause one got away with your pa's scalp. I think the stallion kilt the other when they tried to lead him off. Ya know how finicky that horse is 'bout bein' led. Found the buck's body a little ways out, face nearly stomped right off, but no sign of the stallion."

This can't be happening, Sean thinks. I must still be dreaming.

"If you hadn't missed shootin' Two Knives out on the prairie when you had the chance, your pa would still be alive," the shadow of his uncle says. "Now we gotta get outta here. If ya want to say goodbye to your pa, he's over there."

Sean rises and follows the shadow over to what had been a dry creek bed next to their camp. A trickle of water is now beginning to make its way down the center. Pushed up under an overhanging bank, the shadow shows him what appears to be the body of his father. Sean crawls under the overhang to look in the dim light. It looks like his pa, but how can it be? He sees the stone knife protruding from the body's chest. Sean moves away, sitting down in the wet gravel and trying to make sense of it all.

Jack starts to stomp on top of the overhang, caving in rock and dirt over the body beneath. As he continues to stomp the overhang down, he explains to the distraught boy, "This here is the best grave we can give him. Now we gotta ride, an' fast. There are probably other Injuns lurkin' 'bout. They came for our horses, but now they'll be after our scalps." In a few minutes, Jack is finished with the makeshift grave. "That's gonna have to do. At least I made it a little harder for the wolves to get at him." Jack turns to Sean and pulls him to his feet, roughly pushing him in the direction of camp. "Now let's get the hell outta here. Pack it up."

Sean staggers ahead, his mind unable to absorb it all. Is he now responsible for killing his father too? Did he really fall asleep on watch? His mind is in a swirling, confusing fog.

When Sean stumbles into camp, he doesn't even notice the stallion quietly standing next to his sleeping robe. Sean staggers over and collapses on his robe. He stares at his father's empty buffalo robe a few feet away.

"Pack it up, boy, we gotta go," his uncle repeats before turning to gather his own gear.

When Jack walks away, Chimalis rushes over to Sean's side. She kneels beside him, takes him by his shoulders, and holds him tight to her breast. Sean begins to sob uncontrollably as he hugs her tightly in return. She breaks the embrace and looks into his eyes, shaking her head side to side. Sean has the feeling that she wants to tell him something, but he isn't sure just what it is.

Jack walks over and grabs Chimalis by her hair and jerks her backward. She falls hard to her back, but quickly stands up and backs away. She looks at Sean again and shakes her head before turning to the horses.

Jack kicks out at Sean, catching him in the ribs. "I told ya to pack up!"

The stallion whinnies hard and begins to rear up, flailing out with his front hooves. Jack moves away from the boy, reaching down for one of his pistols. Chimalis jumps between the agitated horse and Jack.

"Hell, we don't have time for this," Jack says as he retreats another step back from the stallion. "Quit your snivelin', boy, an' pack it up. Now!" He pushes his nephew again, hard, driving him to his knees.

Dazed and shocked, Sean staggers back up and begins to gather his gear. The stallion rears again, but Chimalis quickly calms it back down.

"Woman, you finish with 'em packhorses."

The rain now falls heavy on the camp. After starting for the horses, Jack abruptly turns and comes back. He avoids the stallion and walks up to Sean, who is staring at the creek's bank a little way off. He can't take his eyes off the pile of earth and rock under which his father now lies.

"Reckon these belong to ya now," Jack says as he hands Sean his father's Hudson Bay knife and pistol. "Your pa sure as hell don't need 'em no more. Best learn to use 'em a might better than your old man did. I'm keepin' the Hawken. Call it a guide fee. I'll keep Pat's silver, too—leastwise, till ya light out on your own. Ya got eleven dollars coming to ya."

Sean crumbles into shock.

"Boy, life's short an' hard," Jack says. "Ya gotta be harder to survive it, 'specially out here. Flowers don't last long on the prairie. They get trampled by the buffalo. Best get your head 'round it, 'cause this ain't no country for the fainthearted. Now, like I said, get your gear together. We gotta ride." He starts to walk off, but then turns back a second time. "An' keep that loco horse away from me or I'll shoot it."

The rain comes to an abrupt stop as the three ride off at sunrise. In the distance, the thunder gives one final, rolling rumble like a deep-throated chuckle as the storm moves on.

CHAPTER TWELVE

It has taken some weeks for the crippling grief that Sean felt over the death of his father to finally harden into a heavy knot in his belly. The fear, though, has yet to leave him. The attack that took his father's life had come so suddenly, that ever since, he has pondered how, just like his father, Sean's own life might end at any moment.

His only reprieve from the pain and fear throughout their long overland journey has been Chimalis's frequent lessons in her native tongue. Her words are always soft and soothing to his mind. Even though Jack no longer rides off to leave them alone, her constant contact has kept him from falling even deeper into depression. Sean has the strong feeling that she wants to tell him something, but he doesn't know what it could be.

Even so, he has proven himself an apt student of the Apsáalooke language. He is beginning to grasp a good deal of what Chimalis is saying. The challenge compels him, and he is pleased by her agreeable nods whenever he correctly connects an object to her words.

Over the past few weeks, from a distance, they have seen a few small bands of Indians along their journey. Fortunately, these Indians have not been war parties, but are simply travelers that seem reluctant to get too close. Jack explains that they probably know that trappers have long guns and are well armed, and most Indians prefer to avoid such things. One small band, however, makes an exception.

"We're gettin' close now," Jack says in reference to his long search for a tributary of the Powder River, "real close."

SPIRIT BOW: THE SAGA OF SEAN O'MALLEY

The travelers are just beginning their descent from a high ridge when Sean catches Jack's smile as he points out the small stream in the valley below.

"Bet y'all thought Jack was lost," Jack says to no one in particular. "Bet y'all thought Jack couldn't find it, didn't ya?"

They start the animals down the gentle slope toward the stream below.

As they begin to move through the last stand of trees, Jack suddenly raises his hand to stop. He beckons for Sean to ride up to him. "Buffalo," he whispers, pointing through the pine, cottonwoods, and aspens below. "Take the bow boy an' see if ya can get us some supper."

Sean swings a leg over the stallion to dismount. He pulls out the bow and quiver of arrows from one of the packhorses and silently moves off into the stand of trees. His movements are slow and precise as he closes in on the grazing animals. Fortunately, he is upwind from the shaggy beasts, and they continue their grazing unconcerned, totally unaware of their danger.

Sean nocks an arrow as he silently makes his way closer to his chosen target. A year-old calf concentrates its attention on the sweet grass of the meadow. Sean's arrow penetrates deep into the calf's side, just behind the front shoulder. The calf immediately lets out a cry of pain and attempts to run, but its front legs buckle and it crashes to its side. The animal's legs twitch in death spasms, dead from the arrow through its heart.

As Sean moves up to the calf's side, he spots Jack and Chimalis riding clear of the last trees and arriving in the small meadow running along the stream. Sean checks his quarry, killed with one arrow penetrating to the feathers. The moment his company arrives, Chimalis smiles at him, dismounts, and walks over to stand by the buffalo's head. She kneels, places a hand on the animal's head, and chants a few words that Sean recognizes as intended for prayerful thanks.

Jack tethers the packhorses nearby and hands Chimalis a knife so that she can begin butchering the calf. "Nice shot," he says to Sean as he admires the calf lying beside him. He moves off to start gathering firewood for the coming feast.

The words are the last thing Sean wants to hear, as they cause the memories to flood back into his mind. He remains seated, staring at the calf as it stares back at him through dead, glazed eyes.

The afternoon sun is dipping low on the horizon, and buffalo steaks are sizzling by the fire when an old Indian man steps forward to stand in front of the nearby trees. Sean is the first to see him, and he moves quickly grab his rifle leaning against a nearby log. He is just starting to lift the rifle when Jack pushes the barrel back down. The Indian doesn't flinch.

The Indian has a bloody rag tied around his head. After watching their camp for a few more minutes, the man starts walking slowly toward them. As he does so, a small group of followers quietly materialize from the trees to slowly walk behind him. Jack grabs his rifle, and Sean again raises his.

The old man hesitates, then stops for a moment upon seeing the raised rifles. He holds up a shiny bronze medallion hanging from a rawhide strip around his neck. He raises his other hand open in front of his chest in a clear gesture that he is unarmed. He starts loudly talking while pointing to the medallion, and then begins to slowly walk forward again.

An old squaw follows close behind him with three, small, dirty children hanging on to the back of her stained leather dress. Next comes a boy—Sean thinks he must be ten or eleven—who leads the band's lone horse. The horse pulls a travois upon which lies a wounded man. They all stop at a polite distance of about ten paces away.

"Shoshone!" Chimalis yells as she rushes forward to crouch beside the wounded man. "Shoshone, no shoot!" She calls out, "Sean, water. Hot water." She doesn't wait to start tending to the wounded warrior.

Jack and Sean look at each other, Jack's expression matching the total surprise Sean feels at having heard his friend speak English. Jack nods toward the fire, and Sean steps over to bring Chimalis the pot of hot water. Sean carries the rifle with him as he approaches.

She pushes the rifle barrel down as he hands her the water. "Shoshone, friend," Chimalis says, holding the index fingers of each hand entwined.

Sean nods in understanding.

The old man who led them continues to babble, all the while pointing at the medallion and then at the butchered carcass of the buffalo lying on the grass by the fire. He gestures insistently, bringing his hand up to his mouth and then pointing to the hungry children behind him.

"Looks like he wants to trade," Jack says, lowering his gun, "The medallion for the rest of the buffalo. Ya the one done kilt the critter, so I reckon ya can do what ya want with him. We've got all the meat we can use for now."

Sean looks over at the hungry children cowering behind the Indian woman and nods his head in the old man's direction. The old man smiles and removes the rawhide cord from around his neck. He walks up to Sean and hands him the medallion while placing his other hand on Sean's shoulder. The Indian solemnly says something that Sean doesn't understand, then finishes with a pat on his back.

The old Indian motions for the others to come and carry the remains of the buffalo calf away. When they try to take the hide, as well, Jack waves the rifle.

"No," he says, "not the hide, just the meat." The rifle pointing the chief's way makes the message loud and clear.

The old Indian says something to his small group in Shoshone, and they leave the hide.

Chimalis is still tending to the wounded warrior, so Jack motions for the old man to sit down on the log near the fire to talk sign.

Sean watches as Jack asks the old man what happened to his band. "Are Lakota war parties in the area?" Jack says aloud as he signs.

Over the next few minutes, Jack translates to Sean what the old man signs in reply. "He says his name is Cameahwait, a big chief of the Shoshone an' friend to the white man. He was leading his band southeast to hunt buffalo when they were attacked by Blackfeet ten nights ago. The Blackfeet warriors were many, with many rifles, while the Shoshone only had bows and lances. The Shoshone fought valiantly, but were no match. He saw at least two of the Blackfeet fall dead from their mounts before he fell himself."

At this point, the old chief pauses to lift the bloody rag around his head and show a crusted furrow of a bullet wound. He nods, and Sean has the feeling that the old man is proud of his wound.

Jack picks up the sign talk again as the chief replaces the rag and continues his story. "The Great Spirit determined that it wasn't his time to die. His grandson dragged him off in the dark an' hid him. The Blackfeet burned their camp an' rode north in the morning. They found the other Shoshone in the mornin' an' gathered whatever they could find from the burned camp. The chief here says he's pretty sure the rest of his band were kilt or taken captive. They lost all they had when they ran. Now they're tryin' to locate other Shoshone to the South, but they must travel slowly an' the children are hungry. They've only eaten a few roots and nuts, an' one wolf kill with a few scraps of meat."

Cameahwait points to the boy standing by the horse.

Jack tells Sean, "That is his grandson. The old man claims he will be a great warrior someday."

The old Indian rises and holds his hands up in Sean's direction.

"He thanks you for the meat," Jack says. The old woman has started to gather wood for a fire, but Jack shakes his head and tells them they can't stay. "Take the buffalo an' go," he says before signing something to the old man and waving with his rifle that they should leave.

The Shoshone load the meat onto the travois, setting it next to the wounded warrior, and begin to walk off through the trees. They are chattering and moving at a quicker pace than when they first approached, the anticipation of a real meal seeming to give them renewed energy.

Before he passes into the trees, Cameahwait turns to Jack and asks in a combination of words and sign, "Do you know a trapper named Toussaint Charbonneau or a Shoshone woman named Sacagawea? Sacagawea is my sister, and I have not heard from her in many seasons. I think they live in St. Louis."

Jack shakes his head in reply.

The old chief nods in thanks, then turns to catch up with his party.

Sean watches the small band vanish from view into the trees as quietly as they appeared. Only then does he relax, lean his rifle against a log, and rejoin Jack and Chimalis as they tend the roasting meat.

After the three have eaten their fill, Jack gets up and says, "Pack it up. We ain't gonna sleep where we ate—leastways not with thievin' Injuns nearby."

They stuff the remaining roasted buffalo meat in leather pouches and mount up. They ride down the middle of the stream until it starts to cascade down a steep descent. At this point, the light has faded, and they make a cold, fireless camp.

"Not likely the Blackfeet would linger in Shoshone lands," Jack says to Sean. "But no reason to take a chance. Did ya notice how the old chief kept glancin' over at the horses during our talk?"

In the morning, they each cut off a chunk of buffalo roast for breakfast. As he eats, Sean pulls out the medallion and studies it.

"I was surprised the old chief gave up that medallion so easy," Jack says. "I've seen one before. Tried to melt it down to make shot for me rifle, but it wouldn't melt. Couldn't get the fire hot enough."

Sean can see that the heavy medallion is old. The images on both sides are considerably worn. As he studies one side, Sean can barely make out the words Peace and Friendship inscribed over a hatchet, with a peace pipe crossed over it. On the other side, he sees a bust of Thomas Jefferson, but the words around the edges are too worn to read.

"That medallion you're holdin' is called a Peace Medallion," Jack says. "They were given out by Louis an' Clark back in '05. The expedition handed 'em out to all the chiefs they met along the way. Gave 'em all a medal an' a flag, most likely in exchange for keepin' their hair."

Sean takes one last look at the medallion before looping the leather cord over his head and tucking it inside his shirt, next to Becky's bonnet.

CHAPTER THIRTEEN

Three days after their run in with the Shoshone, they finally reach the western bank of the Powder River. Sean watches closely as Jack searches each small tributary along the river's edge.

"Jack found it," Jack says as he rides up. "Take the horses into the river now, an' follow when I turn. Stay in the middle of the stream when we make the turn."

Jack leads them up a small tributary, all being careful to keep the horses in the middle of the small mountain stream. They continue to follow the stream bed up through a narrow, steep-sided valley. A short time later, the valley widens out to reveal a pretty little meadow.

"There it is," Jack says as he points across to the far side of the meadow.

Sean and Chimalis strain to see just what it is that Jack is pointing at. Then Sean sees it. Nestled between two large pines and behind some willow bushes are the ruins of a long-neglected log cabin. As they make their way through the lush grass of the meadow, they pass remnants of a broken down, rotting corral. Sean can see that the cabin's roof has fallen in, with most of its support logs broken or rotted away.

He is somewhat surprised when Jack doesn't stop, but rather, rides right past the cabin and over to the nearby cliff face behind. They halt their horses near the cliff, where Sean spots a small stream of crystal clear water bubbling up from the rocks at its base. The water cascades down into a still functioning, man-made rock basin. The runoff from the basin flows down a narrowly cut channel through the old corral and meadow to the stream.

"I trapped here five or six winters back," Jack says. "Me an' me partner built this here cabin by the spring. Looks like the spring's still runnin' pretty good, so I reckon this is as good a place as any to hunker down for the winter." After looking around at the ground around the spring, he adds, "Don't appear to me that anyone's been up here. Don't see no tracks."

They ride down to the ruins of the cabin and dismount.

Jack walks over to push on the log walls. "Seems solid enough," he says. "Needs a good bit of work, but a sure might easier than startin' from scratch. Boy, take 'em animals over to that stand of trees near the creek. We'll make camp there till the cabin's ready. Woman, help with the unpackin'. I'm gonna scout 'round for any sign of trouble."

Over the next ten days, they set about making the small, one-room cabin livable. They focus their attention first on the collapsed roof, with Jack cutting new poles while Sean and Chimalis clear away the fallen debris from the previous roof's cave-in. They are careful to save any scraps of hide still remaining so that they might reuse them on the new roof. They all help drag the cut poles from where they lay in the nearby forest, bringing them over to the cabin.

"Boy, climb on up an' sit on the high wall," Jack directs Sean. "Me an' the squaw will hand 'em poles up to ya. Use that log ladder I cut to get up there."

Sean moves the ladder over to lean against the inside corner of the log wall. The ladder is simply a length of pine with the branches cut off a foot away from the trunk on opposite sides and cut flush with the trunk on the other two. Not a perfect ladder, but certainly adequate for the job at hand. They maneuver the long cross-poles in place, the ends extending past each wall four or five feet. Then they set the cut branches from the evergreens crosswise over the poles. Finally, they cover the whole roof with canvas, the leftover hides from the previous roof, and six inches of cut sod from the meadow. The roof takes them two days to finish.

"Did your pa teach ya how to chink the walls of your cabin back in Ohio?" Jack asks.

Sean nods.

"Best get at it, then," Jack says. "Use the place where we cut the sod. Looked to be plenty of clay there. Look 'round an' see if ya can find any moss. Otherwise, you'll just have to use grass. Chimalis can help me with the door." He turns to the woman. "Where'd ya stick that buffalo hide?"

She looks back at him with a blank stare.

He slaps her hard across the face. "Hell, woman, Jack knows ya understand what he's sayin'. Why ya gotta go an' provoke me that way?"

Sean wants to stop Jack's abuse, but doesn't have the courage to stand up to the big, savage trapper.

"What ya lookin' at, boy?" Jack yells over at him as he holds up his clenched fist. "Ya be wantin' some of this too? Go get that mud like Jack told ya, an' get back to work."

They finish the cabin a couple of days later, and Jack and Sean start working on the corral. They attach one side of the corral to the back wall of the cabin, where they also attach a lean-to against the cabin's wall. This will allow the horses a chance to get at least partially out of the winter weather.

During his breaks from working on the corral, Sean has taken to watching Chimalis's efforts with the fire pit. He gets the sense that she is following the lessons she learned from building fires inside a tepee. On the first day, she digs out a hearth in the middle of the cabin's floor and lines it with stones she carries up from the nearby stream over the course of the next two days. Sean has marveled at how she is always careful in selecting only certain kinds of stones. Through their broken communication, he gathers that she knows of certain kinds of stones that might explode in a hot fire. Sean thinks she also explains that certain stones will help keep the cabin warm even after the fire has been banked down for the night.

When her stone-gathering task is finally finished, Chimalis spends the next day on the roof, where Sean watches her cut a good-sized hole through the sod and canvas directly above the fire pit. Afterward, when she lights up the fire, she looks pleased to see the smoke rise and pass through the opening above.

Sean and Chimalis spend the next few days cutting dead, standing trees and hauling the dry wood back to stack in one corner of the cabin and under the cabin's two overhanging roof lines. While they work, she chatters away in her native language, and he is beginning to understand more of what she says.

By the end of one of these days, Jack has gotten roaring drunk and doesn't seem to take kindly to how close Sean and Chimalis have become. "You think I don't see what your doin', boy?" he barks.

With wide eyes, Sean raises both hands to indicate that there is no offense meant by anything he does—at least when it comes to Chimalis.

"This here is Jack's woman," Jack says, swaying drunkenly.

Sean watches in fear as Jack staggers toward him and raises his hand as if to strike. But then, at the last moment, the big trapper stumbles past, and his blow meets Chimalis's cheek. Stunned, Sean stands back for a moment while Jack strikes her again. He wants to help his friend, but his feet feel as if they are rooted to the floor. Only when the third blow lands and she cries out does Sean leap into action. Jack reaches back once more, and Sean grabs him by the elbow, holding him back from striking the whimpering Chimalis. Jack turns with fury burning in his eyes and lashes out.

When the punch lands, Sean stumbles backward. Even as he catches his balance against the wall of the cabin, he thinks about how strange it is that it didn't even hurt. But in the next heartbeat, the pain comes. It is a throbbing, searing sensation surrounding his eye. Sean picked up more than his share of bumps and bruises back on the farm, and he had endured a black eye or two in his fights with the boys in town, but this is the first time in his life that an adult has ever hit him. He can't help but marvel at how much more it hurts than young Will's feeble punches.

Just as he collects himself, he braces for another blow from Jack, but when he looks up, the trapper is dragging Chimalis off into the trees. The last thing Sean sees before they disappear is his friend's pleading gaze. Not since he saw his father lying lifeless in the grass has he wanted to help someone more than he wants to help Chimalis, and like that day, he feels overwhelmed by his own helplessness.

A week later, Sean loads the cut wood on the travois behind one of the two horses. He is still hurting from yet another bruise on the side of his face where Jack struck him the night before. The big trapper seems to be getting more and more unpredictable in his behavior. Thinking back to last night, Sean can't even recall what he said or did to trigger Jack's wrath.

Sean has grown concerned about all the crazy conversations Jack has been having with himself, as if someone else is standing there talking to him. He can sense that Jack is getting more than a little stir-crazy, and he knows that he must find a way to get Chimalis away from him as soon as possible. Either that or Sean will have to kill him—one or the other. The only trouble is, he isn't sure whether he is capable of escaping his uncle, much less killing him. He does know one thing: whichever strategy he tries, he will only get one chance.

Sean has seen Chimalis's fresh bruises over the past few weeks as well, and he knows that if he is going to pull off one of his plans, he will need her help. But can he really trust an Indian? What if she gets scared and says something to Jack?

Before he can ever answer that question, he always reminds himself that he has no idea where they would go, even if they did manage to get away.

Sean wakes early to go fishing down at the Powder River. After a few hours, when he returns to the cabin and hands Chimalis two large trout. She smiles and tells him something in Apsáalooke. He understands the word for "thank you," but is not entirely certain of the rest. Something about fire. He smiles back at her and pats his stomach.

Besides fish, Sean has been able to bring down three deer with his bow since arriving at the cabin five weeks ago. He is afraid of shooting the rifle—afraid of the attention the sound might attract.

Along with eating some delicious roasts, Sean watches and learns as Chimalis smokes and dries most of the venison in small strips for the winter. She talks to him about pemmican, but he doesn't completely understand what she means. He remembers eating pemmican on the journey out from St. Louis, but really doesn't know how it is made.

Sean avoids getting too close to Jack, and he tries not to do anything that might ignite his uncle's temper. Jack still lashes out at him from time to time, but most of the abuse is now verbal.

One evening, shortly after Sean killed his fourth buck, Jack walks over to him and tosses him a small box of steel arrowheads. Sean is busy with Chimalis at the time, scraping and fleshing out the deer's hide they have stretched out on an upright frame.

"Good shootin', boy," Jack says as Sean catches the box against his chest. "Now get us some more." He then turns and walks back to the other side of the cabin.

Sean opens the box and smiles at the razor-sharp steel arrowheads inside. He looks over at his uncle, who is watching him, and nods in thanks. Sean can't remember Jack ever doing anything nice before.

Chimalis says something and nods in the direction of his quiver. Sean puts down his bone scraper and takes the box of arrowheads over to sit by his quiver, carefully pulling the arrows out.

Of the twenty arrows left in his quiver, all but two bear the iron tips that Sean or his grandpa fashioned onto them long ago. Sean picks up and studies the two original arrows he still has left. He looks at the colored markings on each and the bright red feathers as his mind flashes back to the arrows protruding from his grandpa's body. He looks closely at the black obsidian arrowheads, seeing how their maker carefully chipped and then secured them to the arrow's shaft. Sean often has been tempted to break the two arrows and throw the pieces into the fire, but for reasons unknown, he has never been able to bring himself to do it. He carefully drops the two arrows back into the quiver and turns his attention to the others.

For the next fortnight, after completing his work fashioning split-wood beaver hoops or fleshing out and stretching hides, Sean works on his arrows. He switches out the old iron arrowheads with the new steel ones. He works late into the night, sitting by the fire for what little light it offers. Changing the tips on the other eighteen arrows turns out to be a painstakingly slow process. More than once, Sean's fingers wind up bleeding from small cuts he gets from the steel arrowheads. Finally, he looks up from the last arrow, beams over at a smiling Chimalis, and drops the arrow into the quiver.

His task is done. He has finally finished. Or so he thinks.

Chimalis smiles and holds up one finger. Sean watches, puzzled, as she carefully removes one of the arrows from his quiver. She has been boiling some chokeberries in an iron kettle and has allowed the liquid to cool. She now carefully dips the arrow's feathers in the dark liquid. After a short time, she withdraws the arrow, and the feathers are as bright red as the original two still in the quiver. Sean's face breaks out in a wide smile and he gives Chimalis a quick hug. She beams back at him, and leans the dyed arrow against the wall to dry as Sean hands her another.

A short time ago, through sign language, Sean had tried to convey to Chimalis his desire to honor the young warrior he had accidentally killed, but he did not think she understood. He just wanted one small gesture that might appease the boy's spirits. Now, she has shown him a perfect way, by keeping his arrow's feathers dyed a bright red. He hope's the boy's spirits will approve.

When all the arrows have been dyed, Sean smiles over to Chimalis. He nods his head. Now he is done.

CHAPTER FOURTEEN

The fall trapping season has begun in earnest. Jack has already scouted all the nearby tributaries for the best locations. The beaver and other fur animals have all grown their thick winter coats.

"Let's go, boy," Jack yells over at Sean. "Time to pay for your keep."

Sean mounts his horse and leads the trap-heavy packhorse after Jack, who guides them out of the corral.

When they reach the first site Jack has chosen, they dismount and Jack begins to show Sean how to trap beaver. Sean turns out to be a fast learner.

"Looks to me like ya been trappin' before," Jack says. "Looks like me ole man taught ya well."

Sean doesn't acknowledge his uncle, and instead finishes setting another trap by baiting it with the foul-smelling castoreum oil that attracts the beaver. Then, as evening approaches, he sets yet another wire snare along a faint animal run.

"Pa teach ya how to do that too?" Jack asks.

Sean shakes his head as he arranges some cut branches on the ground to serve as barriers that will help funnel the animal into the waiting snare. He has grown weary of Jack's constant surveillance.

"Well, I'll be damned, boy," Jack says. "I didn't think ya were that smart."

Yes, you will be damned, Sean thinks.

First thing each morning, the two set off to check the trapline for any catches during the night. More times than not, they find a drowned beaver or a wire-snared animal or two. They spend the remainder of the day skinning, soaking, scraping, and stretching hides. Sean works alongside Chimalis, stretching the hides onto the wooden willow hoops they have been making each night for the past month. Trapping and preparing the hides is a cold, hard, repetitive job. Wading the icy streams chills Sean to the bone.

After a month, a break in the daily routine finally comes.

"Day after tomorrow," Jack announces one night after supper, "I'm gonna take the horses an' see if I can bring down an elk or two before the first snowfall. So, boy, we're gonna pull the traps tomorrow. Still plenty for ya to do. Just keep workin' on 'em pelts."

When Sean glances over at Chimalis, he can sense his uncle's bubbling anger.

"Don't y'all be gettin' no crazy notions, now," Jack warns. "There ain't nowhere to run." He chuckles. "'Specially if ya ain't got no horses."

Jack leaves a little after sunup two days later.

"Y'all best have 'em skins strung up when I get back," he warns before riding off.

Sean and Chimalis stand by the cabin, watching as Jack rides off. Once he has disappeared down the stream, Chimalis takes Sean's arm and motions that he should follow her. She leads him in the direction of the spring. After moving along the cliffside away from the spring, she pauses in front of a small slide of rocks. She looks a moment at Sean, then steps over and removes a leather bag of venison jerky from behind a rock. She holds it out to him, speaking in Apsáalooke while signing with her fingers that they should run.

The first feeling to leap into Sean's mind is fear. Of course he has been pondering for weeks now how they might escape. He has daydreamed about it often, in fact. But now that he sees for certain that Chimalis shares his desire, he isn't sure whether he is ready. He wants to get away from Jack, but he isn't sure whether he and Chimalis can survive in this dangerous wilderness, especially with winter so near. Even if they manage to evade Jack's tracking, how will they weather the snows and fend off the wildlife and Indians?

But then, something in her smile calms him. She has surprised him many times on this journey, and he can sense that she has more than a few more surprises to share with him. She is more capable than she looks—and far more resilient than Jack would ever be willing to believe.

So Sean returns the smile and slowly nods. Chimalis carefully replaces the leather bag behind the rocks. She is still talking in Apsáalooke and gesturing with her hands. Sean understands when she says the Apsáalooke word for "horse," and also understands that her gestures mean that they must be patient. Suddenly, more than anything, he is just happy that she wants to leave. He nods, smiling as he steps forward and gives her a hug.

The next morning, the bay stallion comes trotting back into the corral. Sean walks over to the big horse and rubs its nose and neck in greeting. The horse whinnies in response to his touch. Sean looks over at Chimalis, and he is sure that they are both hoping for the worst. Maybe Jack has run into trouble, Sean thinks hopefully. Maybe Indians got him!

Jack dashes his hopes as he rides in late the next day, all smiles. He is leading five horses, all loaded down heavy with meat. His smile changes when he sees the big stallion. He pulls out his rifle from its scabbard as he dismounts and strides toward the bay horse. "You big son of a bitch," Jack says as he starts to raise the Hawken. "Ya done seen your last days."

The big horse takes a step in the hated man's direction, beginning to bounce a little up and down on its front legs, ready to rear up.

Sean runs in front of his horse, waving his arms, shaking his head, and hoping that the terror displayed on his face will plead loudly enough for Jack not to shoot.

"Ya best get outta Jack's way, boy" Jack hisses. "Or your gonna die right here with that damned horse."

Sean shakes his head and stands his ground, his hands held in front of him as if they might somehow stop a bullet.

After a moment's standoff, Jack slowly lowers his rifle. He walks over to Sean and backhands him across the cheek, knocking him to the ground. "Boy," he says as he glares down at Sean's prone form, "keep that horse away from me. He ain't welcome here no more."

The horse takes a step back and rears up, flailing at the air with its front hooves.

Jack takes a step back as Sean gets up and grabs the horse's lead rope with his hands.

"Woman," Jack hollers to Chimalis, "tie 'em other horses in the shade of 'em trees over there, an' fix Jack up some vittles. I'm hungry 'nough to eat the stripes off a skunk." He starts to walk toward the cabin, then abruptly turns back to Sean. "Boy, after ya get that horse outta Jack's sight, start gatherin' some wood down by the stream. We got us a heap of meat to smoke."

They intend to burn the fire nonstop for three days and nights, with Sean or Chimalis tending it every moment. Over a bed of hot coals, they place wet, green boughs of spruce to make a dense, hot, aromatic smoke. The racks of thinly sliced meat are covered with hides and wet blankets placed over the smoky racks. Chimalis has hauled their sleeping robes down from the cabin so they can sleep nearby as they tend the smoky fire. They can't allow the fires to go out or allow the drying meat to be stolen by night scavengers.

As they sit around the first night's fire, eating thick and juicy elk steaks, Jack tells Sean about the hunt.

"Gawd damn stallion was trouble from the start. Broke free an' run off just a couple hours out. Took the two mares that were tied to him. He don't seem to take to Jack none." Jack tilts back a long swallow from his jug. "Don't 'spect we'll be seeing 'em two mares again.

"Shot 'em buffalo 'bout a day's ride south. Saw a smear of dust in the sky over the rise before Jack saw 'em." The big trapper pauses to take another drink of whiskey. "Knew the dust was either buffalo or Injuns, an' Jack didn't smell no Injuns. Just crawled on up the rise an' there they were. Closer than here to the cabin they were, just standin' 'round snortin'. One hell of a dumb animal, they be." Jack brings the steak up to his mouth with his hands and bites down, slicing the piece off with his knife. The meat's juices run down and through his beard as he chews. After a few more chews, he continues with the story. "Yeah, real dumb brute. Kilt the first one an' 'em others didn't even move. So Jack powdered up an' kilt him another. Hell, I could've kilt the whole lot if Jack had him a notion to. Thought about killin' a couple more just for the tongue, but then thought, why waste good powder? Took me the rest of the day an' part of the next, skinnin' an' cuttin' 'em up."

Sean adds more logs to the fire before laying a wet spruce bough over the top. When he takes his seat again by their small campfire, Jack resumes the story.

"Jack come up on the elk real sudden like on the pass headin' home. All the searchin' for elk he done, an' that damn elk just walks up. Lucky Jack was downwind, 'cause that big bastard just stepped out in front. Didn't even have to get down from me horse. Hawken dropped him right where he stood. Mighty fine gun."

Jack stands up from the fire a few minutes later, grabs Chimalis by the arm, and pushes her in the direction of the cabin.

"Boy, I best not find that fire cold in the mornin'," he says as he stumbles toward the cabin, whiskey jug in one hand while he pushes his squaw in front of him with the other.

Sean is even more certain that his uncle is going crazy.

Two days later, the meat is dried and stuffed into buckskin bags that Chimalis sewed together for the purpose. As they carry the bags up to the cabin, Sean sees her toss one of them behind the woodpile. They tie the rest of the bags up near the smoke hole in the roof, both to keep the mice out and to continue to dry the meat. Sean later notices Chimalis duck out the cabin door with the empty leather water bucket. He knows that the freshly dried meat she dropped behind the woodpile will soon join their hidden cache in the rocks by the spring.

Over the past few days, Sean has watched while Chimalis works on a pair of buckskin britches for him. His own wool ones are in poor shape, as well as being three or four inches too short. She has been using two of the deer skins from Sean's kills for the task.

Sean watches as she carefully pushes the needle holding the deer sinew through the soft hides. Her stitching is neat and tight. Every so often, she holds them up to measure the correct length next to Jack. This way, the trapper will think she is making them for him. Because of this, he has allowed her to use the steel needles from his trade goods. When Sean spots her hiding some of the needles, she tells him softly something that he understands to mean "mother and sister."

He smiles at her in understanding—she plans to give the stolen needles to her mother and sister. Are they nearby? He asks himself. Is Chimalis planning to escape to her people? What about me?

CHAPTER FIFTEEN

Chimalis has been harvesting a variety of berries since late summer. Sean has not recognized any of them, but he certainly has enjoyed eating them. Today, as she hands him two large leather baskets, she talks excitedly. Sean listens carefully as she speaks, and is pretty sure she is telling him where to find the berries they are going to pick. He also thinks she says something about pemmican.

Sean carries his bow and quiver of arrows slung over his shoulder as they walk down the valley toward the Powder River. He thought she had said the berries were up the hill on the left bank, but they had just walked past the fallen log bridge that would easily take them across the stream. He steps up and taps her on the shoulder, looking at her questioningly and pointing back at the fallen log.

She breaks out in a big smile, and he then realizes that she had been testing him in his understanding of her language. They turn back to cross the log bridge and begin to climb the shale rock slope on the other side. He has seen bushes growing up near the top of the rocky slope, but until now, he had no idea they were berry bushes.

After they climb partway up the treacherous slope, they spend the better part of the morning picking and eating delicious small red berries. The whole sunny slope is full of ripe berry bushes. They brought some smoked meat for their midday meal, but neither Sean nor Chimalis could possibly eat anything else, having gorged themselves on berries.

With their baskets brimming, Chimalis leads the way carefully down the loose shale slope. As usual, she is chattering away, and Sean recognizes the word 'pemmican' a few more times. They are both concentrating on the loose rock as they cautiously place their feet, trying not to slip and spill their baskets. Sean glances ahead and is the first to see the approaching bear slowly making its way up the slope. He and the bear both stop at the same time, staring at each other.

Sean has seen bears before, but never this close. Even though Sean holds the high ground, the bear looks incredibly large. The broad muscles in its shoulders tense at the sight of him. At first, there is something like a flicker of fear in the bear's black eyes, but then they narrow with murderous intent.

A surge of electricity running through him, Sean quickly sets his berry baskets down and reaches for the bow slung over his shoulder. Chimalis, unaware of the danger, continues to talk and pick her way down the slope. Sean utters the first sound he has made in nearly two years, a loud grunt from deep in his throat.

Chimalis stops and looks back at him, her eyes widening in surprise. He now has the bow in his hand and is reaching back for an arrow. When she spots the frightened look on Sean's face, she turns to see what has alarmed him. The giant bear has resumed its struggle up the slope and is now less than twenty paces away. There, it pauses again to stare up at the two obstacles blocking its way. It grunts a warning and sways its head from side to side.

From the sheer size of the bear, it is clear that it has spent the past days and weeks following its instincts to eat as much as possible in the shortening days before winter. It rises up on its hind legs to survey the slope above, perhaps looking for another way around or just checking to see what else might challenge its path to the berries.

Slowly, Chimalis lowers her baskets to the ground and steps backward up the slope. As she moves, she talks softly to the bear as if offering the berries she and Sean just finished picking. Sean wonders if this will make the bear content, but he suspects that he will need to fire. He nocks an arrow and begins to draw back on the bowstring, pulling it back to its maximum for the very first time. Fear seems to seize Chimalis in the next moment, for she stumbles and falls backward, only to start sliding down the loose shale toward the bear.

The bear, still standing, meets her advancing challenge with a mighty roar. Sean releases the arrow and instantly reaches back to pull a second from the quiver. The first arrow penetrates the large bear's chest, leaving only a few inches of feathers protruding. Roaring with pain and anger, the big bear's paw swipes at the object of its pain, breaking off the small, protruding piece of arrow. It turns its attention back to Chimalis, who is quickly approaching just as another arrow buries deep into the bear's side.

The big brute jerks violently at the source of the new pain, causing another rockslide that carries it down the slope. Sean allows himself a moment of hope that they have won the battle, but then the bear regains its footing and starts to lumber sideways out of the slide. The brute takes one last glance up at its adversaries before it stumbles and begins to roll, head over tail, down the slope.

Chimalis is finally able to stop her slide a few feet beyond the point where the bear had been standing. Sean watches as the bear tumbles downward, finally coming to rest hard against a big boulder at the bottom of the slope. Chimalis rises and carefully makes her way back up to stand in front of Sean, her face wet from the terror. She reaches up to put both hands on Sean's shoulders and bows her head to touch her forehead to his chest. She says something softly that Sean does not fully comprehend—something about Akbaatatdía. He's heard her use the word before, many times, and is pretty sure it refers to her god. She looks into his eyes for a moment before they both pick up their baskets of berries and resume picking their way carefully down the slope.

Upon reaching the dead bear, Chimalis takes Sean's baskets and sets them aside. "Go back to the cabin," she tells him slowly. "Bring horses."

He pauses for a moment to marvel about how he completely understands her instructions. Then he jogs up the valley to the cabin.

When Jack and Sean return with the horses a short time later, Chimalis is already well along in the process of skinning the big bear.

Jack dismounts and steps up to view the bear. He turns back to Sean and gives him a congratulatory slap on the shoulder. "Well, I'll be damned, boy," he says, slapping Sean's shoulder again.

Chimalis stands and reaches out her bloody hand to give Sean something hidden within her closed fist. Sean puts out his hand and she drops a bloody object into it.

"Akbaatatdía," Chimalis says again.

Sean holds the piece of arrow closer to his face and is surprised to see the obsidian arrowhead tightly attached. The arrow that killed the bear was one of the last two originals—one of the two that Sean had wanted so badly to break and burn.

Did the bow's spirits play a part in saving our lives he wonders?

CHAPTER   SIXTEEN

For two days and nights, Sean has sat restlessly in the small cabin as the snowstorm raged. It has been difficult enough to find ways to pass the time without worrying about the stallion. Sean has told himself that the small corral in the forest should hold up against the elements, but that is not his only concern. Soon, the stallion will run out of food. Sean hopes that the storm will abate some tomorrow so he will be able to carry more of the cut grass over to his horse.

Jack snores heavily as he leans against his buffalo robe on the cabin's wall. The fire in the pit Chimalis created flickers softly, the single cook pot hanging over it empty and awaiting preparation of the evening meal. Sean sits in one of the cabin's three chairs while Chimalis crouches beside the pot as if thinking about what to cook for supper. The two of them have been cautiously watching Jack drink from the whiskey jug throughout the day. They have tried their best to avoid him in the cramped cabin, but that has proven difficult, given that it is only a one-room structure. Ever since Sean killed the bear last month, his uncle has been treating him a little differently, and Sean is growing apprehensive. Jack has been more vocal in his abuse toward him and more physical in his abuse of Chimalis.

Suddenly, Jack wakes from his stupor and waves the arm he is not using to hold the jug. "Jack don't know why he keeps either of ya 'round," he mumbles drunkenly. "All ya do is eat his food an' steal his trade goods. Y'all don't think Jack knows 'bout 'em arrowheads an' needles ya done stole?" He smiles, pauses to take another drink, and then continues his ranting. "Damn right Jack knows. Jack keeps count. Jack knows y'all ain't no better than 'em damn thievin' red heathens."

As Sean watches tensely, Jack seems to drift off again before letting out a loud snort that wakes him up once more.

"Damn brother of Jack's never did stand up to the old man," he hollers. "Hell, that farm money shoulda been mine to start with. Jack knew damn well his cheatin' brother had more money. Had another five hundred dollars, Pat did—me own brother!" Jack sets the jug down and rubs his hands together. "Damn near freezing in here an' Jack gets stuck with a no-'count squaw an' a shut-mouth kid. Jack ain't heard a lick of white man talk goin' on four months!" He picks up and throws a small log across the room at Chimalis. "Fix Jack somethin' to eat! An' not none of that crap ya made yesterday neither. Possum tastes better than that stuff."

Sean's heart is still pounding in his chest when Jack turns his attention to him.

"Just what the hell did old Pat wanna go to Oregon for anyway?" Jack grumbles. "I hear tell its gettin' right thick with folk. Ruskies, Brits, an' Yankees all livin' together like fleas on a coon. All the while stealin' the land from the red heathens that already live there! That ain't natural, livin' so close together an' all. Can't go a day without runnin' into ya neighbor." Jack pauses to take another pull from the jug. "That ain't no way for a fella to live—'specially if he has a chance to live in this here paradise. Gawd's country, that's what she is—the Shine'n Mountains. By Gawd, the Rockies be the jewels of the earth!"

The look on Chimalis's face as she glances back at Sean matches the fear in Sean's heart. The tension in the room rises palpably.

"It's that damn Astor fella's fault!" Jack rants on. "He an' his American Fur Company just couldn't leave well enough alone. Had to go an' blab about that South Pass an' all." Jack points over at Sean. "Tell ya the Gawd honest truth, boy. 'Fore ya hit Oregon Country, ain't nothin' but desert, hardship, an' pain. Once ya get there, if ya ever do, not only do ya gotta watch out for 'em red heathens, ya gotta watch out all 'em other bastards as well. Gawd damn that Astor fella to hell, gettin' folk all lathered up and all. That land ain't worth crap. Can't grow nothin' but trees." Jack emits a scornful bark of laughter. "Hell, boy, we got plenty of trees right here!"

Sean feels a lump form at the back of his throat. What was Jack talking about Pa's money for? The implication that Jack thinks Pa was a liar makes Sean want to stand up, stride over to his drunken uncle, and slug him in the mouth. Instead, Sean shrinks into his chair, knowing that trying something like that would only get him beaten again, if not killed.

A mocking sort of laughter pours from Jack's mouth. "Well, boy, ya done plum outta luck, 'cause ya ain't gonna make it—not with this here trapper. Soon as the snow clears, I've a mind to take ya sorry ass down the hill ta Santa Fe an' sell ya to the one-eyed Mex trader there. Might be able to get me a couple-three jugs."

It takes all of Sean's strength to keep the tears that form in his eyes from spilling over his lids.

Jack's laughter redoubles at the sight of it. He laughs so loud and so long that he tumbles into a coughing fit that he chases away with a long, awkward swig from the jug. "Damn it, woman!" he drunkenly hollers. "Where's 'em vittles?"

Later that night, Sean wakes to a loud scream. In the dim light of the banked fire, he sees Chimalis trying to defend herself from Jack's violent, drunken rage. Jack picks up a small log from the woodpile and begins to beat her around the head and shoulders.

Her struggles cease as she loses consciousness from his blows.

As he mumbles inaudibly, Jack pulls out his knife. "Jack'll teach this no-'count squaw to talk back! I'm gonna skin her!"

Sean jumps from his fur pallet and rushes up from behind to grab Jack's knife arm. Jack is momentarily knocked off-balance, but quickly regains control. He strikes Sean a blow with his free hand, knocking him across the room. As Sean crashes into the far wall, he overturns the unlit lantern on the table. The lantern's oil spills on the floor near the fire pit.

"Jack'll take care of you next, boy," Jack yells. "Just as soon as he's finished skinnin' this here squaw!" He turns his attention back to Chimalis.

Sean recovers his senses as Jack kneels over Chimalis with the knife and starts to cut her buckskin dress. Sean leaps up, grabs a log from the pile by the door, and charges across the room. As he brings the log down across the head of his unsuspecting uncle, he cries out for the second time in nearly two years. "No! No more! Leave her be!"

The blow stuns Jack, who falls across Chimalis's unconscious form. After a moment, he starts to rise up. "Your in a heap of trouble now, boy," he mumbles. "Jack here is—"

He can't finish, because just as Jack turns his head, Sean delivers another heavy blow to the side of his face. The broken stub of a tree branch gouges deep into his drunken uncle's eye socket.

This time, Jack collapses unconscious on top of Chimalis.

Sean scrambles to pull the unconscious trapper off of his friend. "No! No! No more!" he cries out hysterically. "Ma! Ma! You're gonna be all right, Ma! I'm here now, Ma."

Sean sees Chimalis start to regain consciousness while he is yelling and tugging on Jack. As she struggles to free herself, he gives one hard, desperate heave against Jack's body and finally manages to push him off. Jack's body rolls against a pile of heavy traps, knocking them into the fire's bed of coals. A shower of sparks erupts from the fire pit, causing the lamp oil to leap into flame.

Sean is so concerned with saving Chimalis that the flames don't immediately register in his consciousness. The flames quickly spread over the floor to the corner wood supply. In a matter of moments, the corner of the cabin is engulfed in flames.

Chimalis is the first to react as Sean helps her to her feet. She yells something, and together they attempt to smother the fire with blankets. When it is clear that the task is hopeless, she turns and drags Sean's heavy bearskin sleeping robe over to the door. Once there she begins to pile loose furs, the two high-caliber rifles, the powder horns, the possibles bags, and the shot bags onto the bearskin robe.

But when she tries to open the door, it doesn't budge. Jack made the door to open to the outside, leaving it blocked by two days of heavy, windblown snow. She calls out for Sean's help as the cabin is filling with smoke. Together, they throw all their weight against the door. Sean feels the two middle planks bend but not break. The door won't open. They are trapped inside.

"Knife, knife!" Sean yells out to her in Apsáalooke.

Chimalis scrambles on all fours over to Sean's gear, where she retrieves the heavy Hudson Bay knife and returns to hand it to him. Sean uses the knife to cut through the heavy buffalo hide Jack used as a hinge. When it is free, he pulls hard on the edge of the door, and it begins to move slowly inward. Chimalis scrambles to help him, scraping the top of the door against the log above. The door finally gives, opening inward. When the opening is wide enough, Sean motions for Chimalis to go through. He then pushes the big bearskin bundle through the opening as she pulls from the outside to help. He gives one last shove and the bearskin is through. He watches as she drags the heavy bearskin away from the cabin.

Then, just as Sean begins to squeeze through the opening, she runs back, screaming at him, "Boots! Throw out the boots and coats near the door."

Sean understands her meaning and tosses the boots and fur coats out onto the snow. Suddenly, he realizes that there are two more items he has forgotten, so he steps back into the burning cabin. The smoke is thick, and the flames have increased with the opening of the door. He drops down to crawl back on hands and knees to his pallet of furs. Leaning against the wall beside his sleeping furs is the Spirit Bow and quiver of arrows. By his pine needle bed lies Becky's indigo bonnet. Sean grabs them both and makes his escape.

Sean and Chimalis sit in the snow, coughing as they pull on their heavy winter moccasins and coats. They regain their breath as they sit in the freezing snow and watch the log cabin become totally engulfed in flames. The heat from the fire stands in stark contrast to the incredible cold. It serves as a harrowing reminder of how very vulnerable they are out here in the elements—about the severe conditions they now face without shelter, without a safe place to sleep, and without a means to prepare their food.

Chimalis presses a handful of snow against her head above her eye, right where Jack struck her with the log. Sean notices how her arms and hands are cut and bleeding from fending off Jack's attack. He has given little thought to rescuing Jack, and he doubts that Chimalis has, either. As far as Sean is concerned, his uncle is well on his way to burning in hell.

As this thought plays out in Sean's mind, Jack comes crashing and coughing from the flaming cabin, barreling through the open doorway. He carries his hatchet in one hand and the old Kentucky long rifle in the other. His buckskins and hair are both aflame as he collapses in the snow in front of them, rolling and flailing about in the snow as he smothers the flames in a mist of white steam. He continues to lie in the snow, holding his bloody eye socket and head. Dazed and drunk, he lies there as the flames devour the remainder of his worldly possessions. He is not even aware that Sean and Chimalis lie only a few paces behind him, sheltered by the dark.

Sean stands, picks up the Hudson Bay knife and starts to move toward Jack. Chimalis grabs his arm and points to the horses, which have bolted free of the lean-to in their terror. They are now breaking down the corral and running off into the darkness. Sean pushes through the deep snow and makes several unsuccessful attempts to grab the lead rope from any of the horses as they bolt past. He turns and trudges dejectedly back to Chimalis.

Out of the darkness, the bay stallion silently walks over and nudges him in the back with his big nose. Startled, Sean turns to rub the loyal animal's nose and neck, and the horse returns the greeting with a series of soft whinnies.

Behind them, the roof of the cabin collapses with a crash and a shower of sparks and flame. Jack attempts to stagger up to his feet again but collapses back down to his hands and knees.

Chimalis says, "We have to go—now."

Sean picks up the heavy Hawken rifle and raises it to take aim at Jack's back. Chimalis stops him, pushing the barrel slowly down and shaking her head from side to side. Jack slumps over as he passes out, facedown in the snow.

After opening the bearskin, Chimalis picks up the other rifle, powder horn, and shot bag. She hands Sean the Hudson Bay knife he dropped when he dashed after the horses.

They are preparing to leave, when suddenly Chimalis pulls on Sean's sleeve and whispers, "Meat."

Sean watches as she pushes her way through the knee-high snow toward the hidden cache by the spring. She returns with three leather bags, two full of dried meat and one full of the pemmican she made last week. She smiles at Sean, and he nods. At least they won't starve.

The stallion is skittish. It shies nervously away whenever the bearskin is brought too near. It quickly becomes clear to Sean that one of them will have to walk and carry the bearskin while the other rides.

They make their way over to the stallion's corral and pick up the saddle, which they find protected from the weather by an elk hide cape. The three bags of food and the second rifle are secured to the horse's saddle. Chimalis mounts the horse, wraps the elk hide around her shoulders, and heads off into the dark as Sean follows with the heavy bearskin, the Hawken rifle, and his bow and quiver. He follows the stallion's broken path through the snow for a few paces before taking one last long look back.

Jack remains facedown in the snow. From this distance, Sean can't tell whether he is breathing, and the thought makes him question once more whether he should turn back and finish the deed. But then he remembers the look in Chimalis's eyes, and he understands. She does not want Sean to become a killer. Even if a part of Sean disagrees about sparing such a lousy life, there is another part of him that is grateful for Chimalis's mercy. Besides, Jack is unconscious, without provision, and half-buried in the snow. The moment Sean turns to depart, he will have consigned him to his fate. The boy can't imagine a more fitting end for his uncle.

And so he returns to the stallion's path in the snow, leaving the fire to swallow what is left of the cabin. They are free.

BOOK TWO

Man of Peace

CHAPTER SEVENTEEN

As Sean approaches their shelter, he marvels at how well Chimalis has hidden them. While she is huddled under the heavy bearskin, he can only faintly see her through the trees. Their shelter looks like a big, snow-covered boulder in the early morning light. The stallion stands motionless nearby, tethered under a pine tree, as the snow continues to fall.

They ended their push through the dark and snowy night only a short distance from where they began. They pushed for six hours through heavy snow in an unintentionally circular route. Their exhaustion and cold forced them to make a quick winter shelter, and Sean is just now returning from a fruitless effort to find dry firewood.

When he returns to her, he ducks under the bearskin and resumes his spot, sitting together on the elk hide over a pile of cut pine boughs. They sit face-to-face with their heads resting on the other's shoulder. Their rifles act as tent poles to support the heavy bearskin dome they sit under, fur side in for added warmth. Sean's body aches, his joints stiff and sore, but he is grateful they are still alive.

The next day's dawn breaks clear and sunny, the storm finally ended, after four long days and nights. After an hour or two of waiting and gathering warmth, Sean finally stirs. He stiffly stands and watches the fresh snow slide from the mound as he jostles the bearskin. They have survived their ordeal through two bitterly cold nights. The snow has acted as insulation, and their body heat in the small, enclosed area has kept them from freezing to death.

Sean stiffly stretches his cramped limbs and takes a good look around. He still has no idea where they might be. He picks up the heavy Hawken rifle and examines it closely. It doesn't appear that the cold has had any effect on the firing mechanism.

Sean steps over to check on the stallion. The horse is standing easy in the snow-well created by the big pine's overhanging branches, and seems to be suffering no ill effects from the storm. The big bay's thick winter coat has served him well.

When Chimalis drags the bearskin over near the stallion, the big bay becomes agitated, and its nostrils flare at the scent of the bear.

"You hold horse," Chimalis says to Sean in Apsáalooke. "Talk to him. Rub his nose and soothe his head. He knows you, trusts you."

Though he doesn't comprehend all of her words, Sean does understand what she wants him to do. He steps closer to the horse and begins to stroke the stallion's head and nose. He softly reassures the horse that it has nothing to fear. Chimalis slowly brings the bearskin over and rubs the fur side on the horse while she, too, speaks soothingly. Slowly she pushes the bearskin up and over the horse's back, all the while rubbing its shoulder and talking softly. The horse begins to prance nervously around, but they continue to reassure its safety. After a few nervous moments, the stallion begins to relax.

A little while later, Chimalis announces, "We need to go. Jack will look for horses, maybe find our tracks. We will go north. I think Jack will go south. We need to find shelter and food for horse." Sean doesn't entirely understand and she motions for him to ride the stallion. "We take turns, but you ride first with bearskin. Horse belong to you."

Now that they can actually see the sun and the distant, high mountains to the West, they continue to travel in a northwesterly direction. They alternate riding and following the horse through the snow. They eat a little as they travel, consuming the high-energy pemmican and pieces of dried elk or buffalo.

By late afternoon, Chimalis has ridden the horse in among a stand of cottonwood trees. She dismounts and turns to Sean as he walks up. "We will stop here," Chimalis says. "We eat. Horse eat."

After looking around for grass and seeing nothing but snow, Sean asks in broken Apsáalooke, "What horse eat?"

With a smile, Chimalis pulls the bearskin from the horse's back as the bay gives a little nicker. She carefully spreads the bearskin under the cottonwood trees. He draws closer to her just as she steps up to the nearest cottonwood tree and shows him how to use the knife to strip its bark. Sean watches intently as she separates the inner bark from the outer bark, then tosses the inner bark on the bearskin. Next, she cuts new-growth twigs at the end of the branches within her reach and throws them onto the bearskin as well.

She turns and hands Sean the knife. "Horse eat the new tree and inner skin," she says. "Don't take all the skin off the tree. Only skin one side. Understand?"

Sean nods, then begins to strip the bark from the cottonwood trees. He separates the bark, placing the inner bark on the bearskin and discarding the outer. He also cuts the new growth twigs to add to the pile.

While he works and the horse begins to eat, Chimalis sets about doing another task. She has borrowed the knife from Sean to cut a number of thicker green branches from the trees.

Sean watches her as he takes the time to eat. "What are you doing?" he asks in English.

"Make big moccasin for snow," she answers.

Sean recognizes some of the words but still doesn't understand their meaning. He continues to watch as she works. Within a short time, he understands completely, as she has fashioned two sets of crude snowshoes. She has bent and tied the green cottonwood branches together with pieces of fringe leather cut from her buckskin shirt, dress, and leggings. She then weaves green branches in a crisscross fashion and attaches them to the green hoops. When at last she seems satisfied with her work, she helps Sean tie them on. She uses strips cut from one of the furs she has carried under her coat. The two wanderers are now able to walk on the surface of the deep snow.

Chimalis points up to the sky, where Sean sees gathering storm clouds. He slumps at the thought that this will be a short break in the weather.

After picking up and reattaching the meat pouch to the horse's saddle, Chimalis points to the bearskin full of cottonwood bark. Sean picks up the four corners of the skin and drapes it over his free shoulder like a big leather sack.

"We go now," Chimalis says. "Look for a hole to sleep in. Good more snow come now. Jack no find tracks."

"Cave," Sean answers in English. Then, switching to Apsáalooke, he rubs his hands together and adds, "Fire, cold."

"Cave, yes," Chimalis says in English as she mimes digging. She switches to Apsáalooke to say, "Maybe we no find. Then we make cave."

They search for someplace to take shelter before the threatening skies open up again. Chimalis stops and gestures a little ways up the mountainside, where Sean spots a snowdrift that has piled high from the blowing wind. There is also an old gray snag of a tree a short way up the mountain.

"Dead tree," Chimalis tells him. "Good wood for fire. I dig a hole in the snow. We no get cold."

Within minutes, they reach their destination by the old snag, and Chimalis starts to dig into the snow bank. She uses a branch to loosen the snow and then scoops it out with a piece of bark from the dead tree. Before long, she has a good start on a small snow cave. As she continues to dig, Sean moves over to the dead tree and begins breaking off dead wood around its base.

Suddenly the snow gives way under his weight, and he tumbles through its crust. Startled and stunned, he shakes his head to clear his vision. It returns slowly, and he finds that he has fallen into a small cave under the roots of the old snag. It is dark and dank down here, but he can see clearly that there is room enough for both of them, and there is even space to make a fire. He scrambles to his feet and claws his way out, hand over hand up the slope of frozen earth created by his fall.

"Come here," he yells to Chimalis. "No dig cave. I found cave."

She grabs the two rifles and hurries over. Sean is about to go back down into the cave when Chimalis reaches out to grab his arm. "No, you no go," she says. "We must wait. Maybe animal living in cave. First, fix gun, start fire, then look in cave."

Sean checks the loads on the two rifles, then shows her how to cock and aim the one he hands her. They both start to gather wood, breaking branches from the old snag. Chimalis takes the flint and steel from Sean's possibles bag and pours a little gunpowder from her powder horn onto some dry shavings. With a spark from the flint and steel, the gunpowder flares and a small wisp of smoke dances away from the faint flame. She carefully nurses the flame along by adding more shavings and lightly blowing on it.

Once the fire is burning strong, she tosses down a few burning brands into the dark opening at their feet. They wait, rifles at the ready. When nothing happens, Sean tosses down a few larger pieces of burning wood. Still, nothing happens.

Sean finally says in broken Apsáalooke, "Sean has been in cave, animal no there. I go in."

He shrugs off her restraining hand on his arm and slides down into the cave, rifle cocked and ready. He gathers the burning brands of wood together into a small fire and looks around. The cave appears empty but damp, and he finds nothing of note to indicate that it is inhabited. He crawls back out and begins to throw more dry wood down into the mouth of the cave.

Soon they are settled in for the night beside a nice fire. They have moved the fire farther back into the cave, away from the opening to avoid any drafts of wind. Sean has just finished piling a large stack of wood near the fire before he takes a seat beside Chimalis on the elk hide cape. They eat from the bags of dried meat and pemmican. Sean listens for any sign that the stallion might sense trouble. They have left the horse tethered out of the wind, and last Sean saw it, it was chewing contentedly on the last of the cottonwood bark and twigs.

"Tomorrow, you look for meat," Chimalis says as she chews. "No shoot gun. Lakota hear. Jack hear. Better to use bow. No hear bow. If we go to my village, we need more meat."

"Crow?" Sean says in English, surprised at her suggestion. "Crow Indians? Jack say they kill me. He no like Crow—says Crow no like white man."

"Jack hate Indian," Chimalis answers in English before switching to Apsáalooke. "Sean no need worry. The Apsáalooke no hate white man." She slowly rises to her feet, picks up her rifle, and cocks it as she gazes into the darkness of the cave.

Sean, alarmed by her movements, gets to his feet and picks up the Hawken. "What is it?" he asks, staring into the darkness. "What do you hear?"

Not understanding him, she motions for silence. "We not alone," she whispers in Apsáalooke.

Sean, sensing the tension in her voice, cocks his rifle as Chimalis bends to pick up a burning brand from the fire. She tosses the burning stick back into the darkness. The sparks and sound of the wood hitting are answered with a few low woofing sounds. The faint glow of the fire brand dimly lights up a dark form in the cave. Two eyes swaying side to side reflect back at them. They both take a step back as the eyes raise up and a monstrous roar shatters the stillness of the cave.

Before Sean can call out to her, Chimalis jerks up her rifle and fires into the darkness at the beast. The boom of the rifle in such an enclosed area is deafening.

The huge beast lets out another roar as it drops to all fours. It hesitates in its charge toward the fire as Sean aims for its eyes with the Hawken. Just as the bear begins to charge, Sean's rifle fires with another loud boom, sending sparks, flame, and lead back into the darkness.

Chimalis screams as the huge beast engulfs her in its massive bulk and slams her to the ground, silencing her. Sean draws his knife and jumps to her aid, plunging the knife into the bear's shoulder. He stabs a second and third time before realizing that the bear is not moving.

Cautiously, he jabs at the animal's head with his knife, not quite ready to accept that the mighty beast is truly dead. Finally satisfied, he attempts to push the bear off her. It takes all of his strength to even budge the heavy head, but he is finally able to roll the bear to the side just enough to pull her motionless body free. He kneels beside her, not knowing if she is dead or alive. But when he listens with his ear close to her mouth, he is relieved to hear the faint sounds of her breathing.

She is covered in blood, but he quickly determines that it has come from the bear. Her arm is pinned beneath her, and from its unnatural angle, Sean can see that it is broken. He moves quickly to find two pieces of wood from the pile that might be suitable as splints. Next, following the lessons his grandfather taught him when he was a boy still learning the ways of the woods, he cuts long strips of elk hide to use as binding.

He returns to Chimalis and wastes no time setting the break. He places one foot against her armpit, then grabs her wrist and pulls hard to try and straighten the broken bones before splinting and binding the arm with the elk hide strips. He is pleased that she remains unconscious during the process.

When it is finished, not knowing what else to do for her, Sean gently lifts her and lays her down on the bearskin near the fire. Chimalis remains unconscious through the night, softly moaning and tossing as she struggles with the terror of her dreams. Sean sits by her side and keeps the fire going between his occasional periods of fitful sleep.

He keeps the cave warm throughout the stormy night, and finally Chimalis awakens midmorning with a soft moan. Sean watches as her good hand immediately moves to the splint on her broken arm, then up to feel the lump at the back of her head.

Sean has kept busy since early morning by skinning the huge bear. A large chunk of bear meat is roasting on a green stick leaning over the fire. The dripping fat sizzles as the drops hit the hot coals. He stops his work and hurries to her side.

"Sean, maybe I call you, 'Man Who Kills Bears,'" she says as she stares up at him.

He reaches for her hand. "You scare me. Thought bear kill you." He points to the big bear's carcass and smiles. "You wanted meat," he says in English. "We got us a passel of meat now."

Outside, the howl of wolves close by makes Sean pause.

"I go see horse," Sean motions and says. He picks up his bow and quiver and climbs out of the cave. In the dim morning light he is surprised to see the big stallion gone. "Horse gone," he calls back to Chimalis. "I look."

Even up close, the stallion's hoof tracks in the fresh snow are hard to see through all the wolf tracks around them. Sean is frightened at the thought that the wolves he has been hearing in the predawn darkness may have found their meal in the big stallion. Instead of trying to track the horse, he turns and heads in the direction of the howling wolves.

In a matter of minutes, he has spotted the wolves through the trees. As he cautiously approaches, he sees that the big stallion is indeed the pack's intended victim. They have the horse cornered between a cliff on one side and tightly bunched trees on the other. The horse's legs are bloody where it has been bitten, but it appears to have given back much in return. One wolf's body lies bloody on the snow in front of the horse.

Sean nocks an arrow, draws back, and takes aim at a large black wolf limping back and forth in front of the horse. The other wolves are cautiously moving in from the sides. Sean lets loose the arrow, and the moment the black wolf yelps, the others are startled. The black alpha wolf dies instantly as Sean's arrow strikes home. This seems to confuse the other wolves, for they hesitate in their attack. A big gray wolf pads over to her dead mate and gives him a nudge with her muzzle. It sniffs at the arrow protruding from the dead wolf's side.

The gray wolf follows its mate into wolf hell as Sean's second arrow strikes its mark. The rest of the pack instantly scatters when the gray wolf drops dead on the snow. Sean strides toward the horse and retrieves his arrows from the bodies of the two dead wolves.

"It's okay, big boy," Sean says. "I'm here now, and they ain't gonna hurt you no more." He tries to speak soothingly as he approaches the terrified horse. "You're gonna be just fine."

The stallion is agitated and in pain from bites on its legs, but upon seeing and hearing Sean's voice, it begins to take a tentative step forward. The horse noticeably limps, but does not object as Sean walks him back to the cave.

"Chimalis," Sean yells as he approaches the cave. "Wolves hurt horse."

She emerges from the cave and walks over to inspect the stallion's wounds. She runs her good hand up and down each leg. "Leg be good. Horse need rest." She picks up a handful of snow and shows Sean how to rub it gently up and down each of the wounded legs. "Snow good. Stop hurt. Help clean wounds."

As Sean follows her instructions, he talks softly to the big stallion. Chimalis turns and disappears back into the cave.

Sometime later, the horse seems to have calmed enough that Sean feels comfortable returning to the cave to see if he can lend Chimalis a hand. He finds that she has dug a small hole in the ground next to the fire. She has filled the hole with a piece of hide from the fresh bearskin, flesh side up. In so doing, she has formed a makeshift bowl. Just as Sean arrives, she is returning from the bear's carcass, where she has collected several large pieces of fat that she drops into the makeshift skin bowl.

"What Chimalis doing?" Sean asks in broken Apsáalooke.

She ignores him, busy as she is with her task. She gathers a few reddened stones from the coals and uses them to render down the fat until it is a smooth, cream-colored liquid. Carefully she removes the hot rocks and allows the fat to cool. When the solution is cooled to the point where it has just started to congeal, Chimalis gathers up the makeshift leather bowl, and Sean follows her out to the horse.

As she gently rubs the warm fat on the horse's wounds, she says in Apsáalooke, "White man gun call wolves last night. Wolves know gun's thunder mean meat. White man always takes little and leaves much. Wolves no stupid, they learn that they eat much when gun's roar. Not like Indian, who leaves no food for wolves." She looks over at Sean before adding, "Now you must watch horse. Wolves come back."

"Give wolves bear meat," Sean replies. "They no eat horse. We no carry all."

Chimalis gives this some thought before shaking her head. "Sean watch horse. Horse need rest. We feed wolves when we leave. Wolves stay, we go."

For the next four nights, the two travelers alternate keeping watch while the stallion regains its strength. The pack grows cautious after Sean kills another wolf during the first night. They continue to howl each night but maintain their distance, staying just out of clear sight—only shadows moving to and fro among the trees.

Chimalis continues the bear fat treatment, and the horse's legs rapidly heal. On the second night, she calls Sean over and starts to apply bear fat to his shoulder-length red hair. Initially he tries to stop her, but then she tells him, "Sean will be a Apsáalooke warrior. A warrior's hair is very big medicine. You no can cut. Men of the Apsáalooke all use bear fat to make hair shine. Long and shiny."

Each morning, Sean goes out with the knife and bearskin in search of cottonwoods. He patiently peels the bark and collects new-growth twigs to feed the big horse, and the horse continues to get stronger. He always carries his bow and quiver, for he senses the wolves' presence nearby. He knows that they are still in the vicinity by the nightly howling, but he never actually sees another.

Each evening, Chimalis applies bear fat to his hair, brushing it with her fingers. She adds another coat of bear fat to their moccasins and heavy coats each morning and night. Sean marvels at how, by thoroughly rubbing the fat in each time, Chimalis eventually makes the moccasins and coats completely waterproof.

CHAPTER EIGHTEEN

On the fourth morning, Sean is out searching for more cotton-wood trees when he starts to cross the small stream in the valley below. It has been covered with a thin layer of ice since they arrived, but today it flows free.

When he finds an overhanging stream bank, he unlaces his snow-shoes and lays the bearskin robe on the snow near the overhang. He lies down with his stomach on the robe, pushes his sleeve up, and slowly reaches into the icy water. He tries to remember what his grandpa taught him as he carefully moves his hand into the current under the overhanging bank. Finally, he feels what he has been searching for, the faint movement of a trout's tail. His fingers delicately move up the trout's belly until they feel the soft flutter of the front fins. Suddenly, he clamps his fingers down hard just behind the fish's head. With his catch secure, Sean pulls his hand out of the icy water and tosses the large trout onto the snow. He rubs his cold hand back and forth against the fur of the bearskin to warm it.

Within a short time, he has tickled two other large skinny trout, which now lie on the snow beside him. Sean thinks how happy Chimalis will be with the change in diet as he cuts a green branch from the nearby bush and pushes it through each trout's gills, to make for easy carrying.

As Sean kneels back down by the water's edge to wash the slime from his hands and quench his thirst, he glances up to see an Indian sitting silently on a horse, less than thirty paces away. The Indian is dressed for winter, his black shiny hair chopped short and uneven. Two feathers hang from the left side of his head. Across his back is a quiver of arrows, but Sean is more concerned by the one nocked in the bow the Indian holds in his hands.

Sean's heart thumps wildly in his chest as he glances down to his own bow and quiver lying just a few feet away. He knows that he will not be able to reach them in time.

When the warrior's gaze follows Sean's to the bow, he begins to raise the one in his hands. But then the warrior hesitates as if he feels something is amiss. He eases up on his bowstring and lowers the weapon. Finally, he raises his hand in the sign of greeting—an open palm facing forward.

His heart racing, Sean replies in kind.

The Indian nudges his horse forward, his eyes darting from side to side as if searching for any other danger.

Sean slowly stands, careful not to appear threatening.

The warrior stops about ten paces away and eyes Sean from top to bottom. He finally reaches behind, pulls out a fur, and tosses it onto the snow at Sean's feet. "Cold, wrap fur around shoulders," he says in a strange mixture of Apsáalooke and broken English.

Sean does his best to reply in Apsáalooke. "Thank you. No need." Sean points down at his bearskin.

The warrior's brow wrinkles in surprise. He grunts in understanding. He studies Sean for a moment, seemingly confused by his red, shoulder-length hair. His eyes search up and beyond the boy in front of him to study the surrounding country. Then he raises his chin in question.

Sean's gaze follows the Indian's to the faint wisp of smoke on the hillside above. His heart is beginning to slow a little as he makes the sign of eating. "Eat?" he asks the Indian.

The warrior stares at him for a time before reaching behind his back again. He brings out some dried jerky and holds it out in offering to Sean.

Sean smiles, shakes his head, and raises his hand in refusal. He holds up the three fish and points up to the smoke on the hillside. "You eat?" Sean asks in Apsáalooke.

The Indian nods and grunts in understanding.

Sean secures his quiver and bow over his back, then picks up the bearskin in one arm and the fish in the other before starting up the slope. Purposely, he turns his back to indicate his trust. He listens as the warrior dismounts and follows, leading his horse up the slope.

After passing the remains of two wolves, the warrior secures his horse next to the stallion and takes a moment to admire the big bay.

"Good horse," he states in English.

As they near the mouth of the cave, Sean calls out in Apsáalooke, "Chimalis, three to eat."

She steps from behind the dead tree, her rifle level at her side. Despite the splints, she points the rifle at the warrior's chest. The warrior abruptly stops. She motions with her head for Sean to move to her side.

Sean looks on as she studies the warrior's face.

Her eyes narrow and then grow wider. She slowly lowers the rifle. "Red Knife?" she asks.

The warrior nods, then tentatively asks, "Chimalis?"

"We have not seen each other in many seasons," she replies warmly. "It is good to gaze upon your face again. I hope Little Snake and your mother are well. But tell me, why are you here—is this not Lakota land? Our enemy would not take your trespass lightly." Her attention shifts to the fish in Sean's hand. "Come in out of the cold, and we will eat and talk. We have meat, and now fish too." She disappears down into the cave.

Sean starts down behind her before stopping and turning back to Red Knife. The warrior takes one last look around before grunting and following them inside.

The flames warm Sean's chilly hands as he sits on the bearskin at the edge of the fire pit. It looks as if Red Knife has finally eaten his fill of the roasted bear meat. Sean's hunger remains as he waits for the fish to broil on the green sticks tilted over the coals. Chimalis offers Red Knife some hot water from the skin basin, and he readily accepts.

"How you know Red Knife?" Sean asks Chimalis in Apsáalooke. "Why does he ride alone in Lakota land?"

Red Knife stares at Sean with a look of puzzlement on his face. "I, too, have many questions," he says as he wipes his hands on his buckskin pants. "I ask you, and you ask me."

Sean nods in agreement.

"My heart is still heavy with my loss," Red Knife says. "Lakota kill my woman, Summer Breeze, and take my son, Black Bear, many seasons ago. Love and joy are now missing from my heart, and my spirit is lost and wanders. I still cut my hair in mourning." He adds as if an afterthought, "Now I only live to hunt and kill Lakota." He turns to look over at Chimalis. "You are not safe here. Lakota look for me."

Chimalis passes each of them a stick of broiled fish.

As they eat, Sean asks Red Knife in English, "How did you learn to speak English?"

"My father white trapper. Good man. He live with Apsáalooke up on Big Horn River. He killed by Blackfeet when I small boy. My uncle, Little Snake, tell me white man talk is good to remember. I talk trade with white man for Apsáalooke." He nods to Sean. "Why you talk Apsáalooke?"

"Chimalis taught me Apsáalooke when white words left me," Sean answers in broken Apsáalooke. He then asks, "if you are both Apsáalooke, why do whites call you Crow?

"Apsáalooke is how we call ourselves. We also call ourselves, the Children of the Large-Beaked Bird or Bird People. The early fur trappers thought we were talking about the crow bird. Crow became our name to the whites and our Lakota enemies. Apsáalooke is too hard to say."

Sean points to the warrior's necklace, not knowing the Apsáalooke word for necklace. "Animal bones?" he asks.

Red Knife holds up his necklace to admire before answering in English. "Animal bones, yes. Blackfeet and Lakota animal bones. Cut off fingers of my enemies. Put much fear in enemy, and they no hunt so good in next life. Do you like it?"

Sean stares a moment before shaking his head and looking away.

"Now you tell me," Red Knife says to Chimalis. "Why are you here? What happened to your face and arm, and why am I eating bear?"

"Dakota caught me during a raid on our hunting camp," Chimalis explains. "The warriors were out hunting buffalo. Young Dakota bucks killed three old women and boy." She takes a deep breath. "I was not so lucky. They took me with the horses. Trappers then take me from Dakota, trappers named Frenchie and Hatchet Jack. Hatchet Jack then killed Frenchie. Sean helped me escape from Hatchet Jack."

"I have heard of this white man the trappers call Hatchet Jack," Red Knife replies. "Heard that he is a bad man. That he cheats Indians in trade with whiskey. That he has killed many Indians."

"It was Hatchet Jack that did this to my face before Sean saved me," Chimalis says. "In the storm, we found this cave, not knowing brother bear was sleeping here. Big surprise. Sean killed the bear, and the silver-tip fell on me, breaking my arm."

Red Knife nods, then stands to look out the cave entrance. He ducks back in and announces, "It is not safe here. Lakota Sioux warriors are tracking me. Six nights ago, I snuck into their camp, looking for my missing son. I killed an old warrior out making water. Warriors hunt me, but my spirits are very strong. My spirits make snowfall and Lakota lose tracks in new snow. Now snow has stopped. They will soon find my tracks. No time for more talk." Changing to English, he says to Sean, "Need to leave this place. If Lakota find me, they find you."

Chimalis starts to gather their supplies. "We have meat and pemmican," she tells Red Knife. "Horse is ready. We will go now."

"I will go look for Lakota," Red Knife tells them. "Be careful with the long gun, no shoot Red Knife. You take horses down the mountain into the trees. Then follow the setting sun. I will find you tonight. No light fire." Turning to Sean, he repeats his instructions again in English. "No shoot Red Knife. Red Knife will make the sound of night owl." He gives two hoots of an owl. "You hear night owl, you know it is Red Knife."

CHAPTER  NINETEEN

Sean and Chimalis are wrapped in furs and huddled with their backs against a large pine tree. The two horses are tethered a few paces away. Sean slowly begins to raise his bow after nudging her with his elbow. An arrow waits, nocked onto the bowstring, as he indicates a direction to her by lifting his chin. Sean noticeably relaxes when he hears the soft clear hoot of a nearby night owl.

Red Knife quietly emerges from the moonlit shadows and moves toward them. "Go now," he tells them, "not safe here. Five Lakota warriors camp three arrows away. Much talk over new tracks with two horses. They will attack at sunrise. Go to the next valley. Buffalo there five suns ago. Maybe they are there still."

"Don't need meat," Sean says, puzzled. "Why hunt buffalo?"

"No hunt them," Chimalis replies. "We walk among them. Confuse Lakota with their tracks."

Throughout the long night, they slowly make their way with the help of a three-quarter moon that silvers the trees and grass with its pale light. By sunrise, they are looking down on a small herd of buffalo grazing in the valley below. Chimalis and Sean sit leaning over atop the stallion while Red Knife leans over the neck of his black warhorse. The riders have pulled their buffalo robes completely over their bodies as the two horses slowly pick their way down the steep hillside and into the valley below.

The valley forms a large meadow with a slow-moving stream meandering through it. The buffalo are busy scraping the snow aside in search of grass or simply standing into the wind, chewing their cud.

They don't seem to feel threatened or even take much notice of the two large buffalo walking slowly among them. They simply move aside with occasional snorts, content to just paw the snow with their hooves to reach the sweet grass beneath.

The small stream has been thoroughly disturbed by the herd's hooves. The two horses enter the water and continue down the middle of the stream bed until they reach the far end of the valley.

Once the stream begins to flow into the trees at the edge of the meadow, Red Knife stops his horse. While holding on to his buffalo robe, he turns and removes his snowshoes from the pack behind him. The shoes are long and slender, their edges formed of bent branches polished with beeswax and their lattices constructed of taut leather strips. "Follow the stream as long as you can," the warrior tells them as he hands Sean his reins. "Then head toward the big rock mountain you see toward the setting sun."

"Where are you going?" Sean asks in English.

"Maybe Lakota not continue when they see buffalo," Red Knife replies. "But I'm here to hunt Lakota. If they catch me, maybe they no hunt you." Then he adds, "They have nice horses too. Chimalis needs a horse."

With that, Red Knife dismounts onto a boulder and continues to jump from boulder to boulder into the trees.

Late the next day, Red Knife rides into camp on a brown mustang leading a string of three other horses. He looks surprised to see two horses but only one rider, and when Sean steps out with a bow in hand and an arrow nocked, the warrior nods in recognition. Sean lowers his bow and returns the arrow to its quiver.

Red Knife grunts in Sean's direction and smiles in approval.

Sean strides over to admire the captured horses, but he pauses when he spots the two fresh scalps hanging from Red Knife's saddle. "I guess you added some bones for your necklace," he says in English.

"Yes, but two of them ran off." Red Knife winces before adding, "I don't think they will follow us. One of them is wounded, and now they have only one horse."

"Are you wounded too?" Chimalis asks.

"Lakota hatchet caught me behind my shoulder," he replies. "I think it is nothing."

"You do not have the eyes of an owl to examine your back," she answers. "I will look at this wound and tell you if it is nothing."

Red Knife reluctantly removes his bloody buckskin shirt with her assistance. Sean moves in behind just in time to see a deep, ragged-edged gash behind the warrior's left shoulder. The wound is open and still weeping blood.

"This is bad," she says. "It is cut all the way to the bone. We must stop and treat this wound now or it will never heal. Sean, gather some dry wood for a fire."

"The Lakota may see the smoke," Red Knife replies.

"That is a chance we must take."

Sean gathers wood, then returns just as Chimalis has finished cleaning the wound with hot water. He goes with her, his bow at the ready to protect her as she searches the surrounding forest for a white pine. When they find the tree, she cuts off a few thin strips of inner bark and mashes them into a soft poultice between two stones. Next, she leads Sean back to the camp, where she begins digging through her possibles bag. Finally she produces two small sacks, one containing dried rosehip and the other dried goldenrod. She grinds a little of each into a fine powder and thoroughly mixes it into the pine poultice with a little hot water.

Sean steps aside as Chimalis applies the warm poultice to Red Knife's open wound, then covers and binds it with strips of elk hide. She carefully wraps the remainder of the poultice in a piece of the leather to use again that night.

"This will have to do," she says. "It should stop the bleeding and help you heal."

Five days later, Sean catches sight of a hazy fog of smoke over the next ridge. Just as he moves to point it out, two warriors step out from the trees on either side of them.

"We welcome Red Knife and his guests to our village," the taller warrior says. "We will get our horses and join you."

The two warriors fall in beside them as they continue over the ridge, and Sean feels his nerves begin to fray. Red Knife and Chimalis have been insisting for the past few days that he would be welcomed by the Apsáalooke gathered in this wide little valley, but their assurance has done little to beat down his apprehension.

They ride with their escort past some boys and young warriors out guarding a large herd of horses. Red Knife raises his good hand in greeting.

"Ride into the village and tell Standing Lance that Red Knife comes and would greet him," one of the escorts directs one of the young warriors.

The young warrior gives a whoop and raises his fist in salute as he leaps on his horse and races off to inform the village chief of the trio's arrival. Sean watches the young warrior's horse gallop into the village, smiling nervously at how the numerous dogs start barking and howling as he races past.

Sean sees the village's tepees scattered along the banks of a gently flowing river. Chimalis told him the night before that the little river runs into the bigger one that the white man calls the Yellowstone. Although the air is cold and patches of snow can still be seen in the shady areas, Sean sees children splashing and playing along the river's edge. The sight of the children chasing and laughing after each other causes Sean's heart to skip.

Without thinking, he finds himself scanning through their numbers in search of a young girl with red hair. He scolds himself the moment he realizes what he is doing. He has already asked Red Knife if he has heard of a red-haired girl taken captive by Indians, and as Red Knife said, there is little chance they will find her this far away from home. Still, Sean knows that he will never stop looking for Becky, even if every mile he travels makes it less likely that he will ever see her again.

Men and women alike turn away from their daily chores to watch as the visitors slowly thread their way toward the village center. Some of the warriors grab weapons and follow. Soon the trio is surrounded by warriors and boys, both on foot and on horseback. Sean's discomfort only grows when it occurs to him that most of the gathering crowd's curiosity seems to be directed at him. He involuntarily clutches the rifle in his hand a little tighter, his knuckles white as he nudges the stallion closer to Red Knife.

When the trio arrive at the chief's tepee in the center of the village, they remain patiently sitting on their horses. Sean watches as the village men talk quietly among themselves, nodding to the fresh scalps hanging from Red Knife's saddle and the Lakota horses he leads.

Sean senses the boys crowding in closer around him—sees them point and laugh about his hair. He hears the words for "fire" and "hot," followed by more laughter.

One of the boys pushes through the others to move up beside Sean's horse. He reaches out and pats the stallion's neck. The big bay stamps his front foot and swings his head back to flash an annoyed look at the Indian boy before whinnying and stepping back a couple of paces.

"Nice horse," the boy says as he looks up at Sean.

Sean glances around at the camp, then at the boys gathered around him. He holds up his hand and greets the boy who spoke to him. In broken Apsáalooke, he says, "I am happy to sleep here."

The boys around him look at each other, then break into laughter.

"Welcome to our village," the boy says.

The chief's tepee flap swings open, and out steps a young girl. Sean can't help but stare at her. She must be a few years younger than him, and he is drawn to her pretty eyes and long, silky black hair, but mostly he is curious because it has been over a year since he has seen a girl up close. She holds the flap open for an old man to step through, followed by an old woman.

When the girl drops the flap, she glances over at Red Knife and Chimalis before studying Sean from head to toe. They lock eyes for a moment before she timidly smiles and turns away. Sean tries to imagine what she is thinking. He tells himself that, just like the boys gathered around him, she is probably amused if not repulsed by his hideous red hair. Her legs are long and her neck slender, but the way her fur and hide shift clings to her, it is clear that she is strong. Then she takes one furtive glance back, and he thinks she must be the prettiest girl he has ever seen.

"Welcome to our village, Red Knife," the chief says, startling Sean out of his admiring gaze. "Have you eaten?" Not waiting for an answer, he says, "Come, be my guests. Chimalis and the boy are welcome as well. I should like to hear your story."

Red Knife, Chimalis, and Sean dismount, and their horses are led away by two of the boys. Sean sees the stallion start to act out as the horses disappear behind a tepee.

"It has been many seasons since my eyes have looked upon my friend Standing Lance," Red Knife says. "His name speaks true. I am pleased that he still lives, and I am honored that he knows me by name." He nods. "We have come far, and we welcome his invitation."

While the girl holds the flap open, Standing Lance leads the way into the tepee. Sean is the last to duck inside, and he smiles at the girl as he passes. Everyone takes their seats on worn buffalo robes spread around the central fire pit. An iron pot rests on some rocks next to the fire.

Red Knife sits to the right of Standing Lance, with Chimalis sitting behind Red Knife. When Sean enters, Red Knife indicates for him to sit beside him. The girl steps forward and serves the men wooden bowls of steaming venison stew from the iron pot. Next, she serves the two women seated behind the men before returning to sit empty-handed next to the old woman.

Sean glances the girl's way a few times as he hungrily eats the hot, delicious stew. When the meal is finished, a few other elders step through the tepee flap to join them around the fire. Sean feels a shiver of fear as a muscular old warrior takes a seat beside him.

Standing Lance turns and whispers something to the girl seated behind him. She reaches behind her to retrieve a leather-wrapped bundle. She carefully unwraps the soft leather to reveal a long-stemmed pipe that she hands to Standing Lance. The chief meticulously fills the pipe's bowl with tobacco and lights it with an ember from the fire. While holding the pipe up, Standing Lance offers a prayer to the four directions before sending another down to Mother Earth and another up to Father Sky. He then takes a long, slow pull and hands the pipe to his guest Red Knife.

After taking a pull on the pipe, Red Knife hands it to Sean and indicates with a quick lifting of his chin for Sean to take a puff and pass the pipe on. Sean does so. The tobacco is strong, and he can't help but cough as he hands the pipe to the muscular old warrior beside him. The man grunts at Sean, then nods and accepts the pipe on its journey around the circle.

When the pipe arrives back in Standing Lance's hands, he takes one last puff. Then he holds the pipe straight up and reverently mutters, "Akbaatatdía."

The young girl takes the offered pipe from her chief, cleans and rewraps the pipe.

"My tepee is too small," Standing Lance says. "Many wish to hear your story. Let us move under the heavens for all to hear."

Outside, Sean finds that many have gathered. They have brought their furs to sit on, and a large fire has been lit. Standing Lance indicates places for his guests to sit among the buffalo robes gathered on the damp earth. Sean takes his place between Chimalis and Red Knife in the inner circle. He stares wide-eyed at the Indian faces surrounding him as they take their places around the fire. He nervously notices that most of the men carry knives and hatchets tucked into their belts. The women and children stand behind the men around the circle.

The words now being spoken fade away as Sean's mind flashes back to the bloody handprints on the splintered door, to his mother's lifeless body, and then to the bloody knife from when Two Knives killed his father that rainy night on the trail.

His mind refocuses back to the present. To his relief, the faces studying him are more curious than threatening. He realizes that no one has made a threatening move, or even a sneer in his direction, since they rode in. He turns his attention back to listening and trying to understand what everyone is saying.

Red Knife has just finished telling of his encounter with the Lakota Sioux. The other warriors are grunting and nodding their heads in approval. Sean turns to see the toothless old man sitting next to him smile at him as he nods. Sean returns the gesture.

Chimalis is next to tell her story. "My brother, Elk Horn, and his small band were hunting buffalo," she begins. "We followed some tracks for five days toward the rising sun."

Some of the warriors begin to murmur, stopping only when Standing Lance holds up his hand for quiet.

"Our warriors all knew we were approaching dangerous lands," Chimalis continues. "We agreed to turn back the next day. Then the scouts rode in and said they had located a small herd. The warriors rode off at sunrise to join in the hunt, leaving a few women behind to dismantle the camp. The Dakota surprised us as we broke camp to follow the hunters.

"The Dakota were young and had traveled many days through Lakota lands into Apsáalooke territory to raid for horses. They had not been successful in their quest and were returning home when they came upon us. Little Hawk, the Dakota chief's grandson, was with them. We put up as much of a fight as we could. I saw three women killed. I do not know what happened to the rest of our band. I was taken prisoner, though I pleaded with them to kill me too.

"We traveled many days toward the rising sun—so many that I lost count. We came upon a trapper's camp. The Dakota thought there was only one trapper, and a fight broke out over firewater. The trapper murdered Little Hawk with a knife in the back." Chimalis pauses for a moment to let the gravity of the act be understood. "Another young Dakota was also killed by the trapper before they managed to knock him unconscious. The Dakota were just beginning to torture the trapper when his partner stepped out of the dark and killed all but one with his rifle, pistols, and hatchet.

"That second white man's name is Hatchet Jack, a very evil man. The following year was filled with shame. I did not expect to ever see my home again. The first trapper, Frenchie, did not treat me badly, only using me for his pleasure. I tried to end my shame by cutting my arms, but he stopped me and tied me up. I gave up any hope of freedom."

Sean can feel the sorrow carry through the crowd as most of the listeners, men and women alike, bow their heads.

"My real ordeal came from the other," Chimalis continues. "Hatchet Jack killed Frenchie in a fight, and then treated me much worse. Like the wolverine, he enjoyed giving pain and killing. He would beat me for his pleasure. Sean, the white boy here, was the only light in my darkness. With him, I could escape my torment. He does not see Indian or white man. He sees only good or evil, pain or light."

Sean watches as those gathered around him turn to look his way. To avoid their gazes, he stares down at his moccasins.

"I think there has been great pain and suffering in his young life," Chimalis says as she turns to look at him. "Sean saved my life from Hatchet Jack, helping me escape during a snowstorm. He chose one of the Apsáalooke over his own white blood." Chimalis rises to stand and face Sean. "Three times now, you have saved my life. The last from a great silver-tip bear that broke my arm."

The gathering gasps at her words. Sean feels the eyes of the group watching him. He looks up at Chimalis as she resumes her story.

"I would like to raise Sean as my son and teach him the ways of the Apsáalooke," she says. "I believe the Great Spirit has sent him to us for a reason. I do not understand that reason yet, but I look forward to finding out. I believe Sean will become a warrior of great distinction and renown." She pauses and takes a deep breath. "Sean does not know this, but Hatchet Jack killed his father and blamed it on another. I saw this with my own eyes. That is all I have to say." Chimalis nods her head slowly as she looks Sean's way and returns to her seat.

The Indians around the fire all turn to look at the boy to see his reaction to this startling news.

Sean's eyes grow wide as he jumps up to face her. "Why did you not tell me of this before? Why did you not let me kill him?"

Everyone turns to hear her response. Sean knows that Chimalis has been taught to consider her words carefully, but the several moments it takes her to gather her thoughts are excruciating.

"My people believe that when you are born," she says to Sean loudly enough so that all might hear, "you are born with both good and evil spirits. They wage war throughout your lifetime. Sean, I have watched your spirits fighting this battle since the first day I saw you. The battle has been fought long and hard within you. I have seen this with my own eyes. Now, over the past few moons, your good spirits have grown stronger. Just as my arm is healing, so is your spirit body. I don't know why. Only the Great Spirit Akbaatatdía knows. Your good spirits have finally been able to rise up and defeat the evil ones. I did not want Hatchet Jack's evil spirits to join with your own evil spirits. Your good spirits are not yet strong enough to defeat such an enemy."

Sean clenches his teeth, not wanting to show the sorrow and fear rising up inside him.

"Hatchet's evil spirits were so powerful that they destroyed all of the good spirits he was born with," Chimalis explains. "When we left him, he was pure evil. He killed for pleasure. I did not want that evil to rule your mind. You are different. Your good spirits glow for all to see. I think you could walk a path between enemies." With that, Chimalis turns to nod at Standing Lance as if to indicate that she is finished.

Standing Lance looks her in the eye. "I can hear and feel with my heart that you have suffered greatly. It is with sadness that I now must give you more pain. Your brother, Elk Horn, went out to search for you after the attack. He did not return. I think he has crossed over to the other side." After a few moments of silence, Standing Lance faces Red Knife. "I will look for a tepee among my band for you to call home. I cannot say what will happen to this boy with the fire hair—whether he goes or stays. We do not want the white man to think he has been stolen. The council must give it thought and reach a decision about what to do."

Red Knife tosses a small stick into the fire, then stands to speak. Sean can feel how everyone strains to listen, wanting to know the great warrior's thoughts.

After looking first at Chimalis and then at Sean, Red Knife says, "I have traveled these past many days with this woman and this boy. I have seen their strength and their bravery. I have lost my woman and my boy to the Lakota. My heart has been heavy for many seasons. I have

167

nothing left to return home to." He looks around, nodding at a few of the warriors before continuing. "Many of you knew my father, Diego Arana. He was a proud member of a Mountain band of Apsáalooke. He was a brave man. But he was also a Spanish man. He taught me that the color of a man's skin does not determine the man. It is his heart and soul that defines who he will become." Red Knife pauses to let his words sink in. "I am a strong warrior." He holds up the necklace of finger bones for emphasis. "I am an Apsáalooke warrior. Many Lakota and Blackfeet have found their way to the next life by my blade. My fellow warriors gave me my name because of this—Red Knife. If the band would have me as a brother, and Chimalis would have me as a man, I would gladly welcome her into my tepee.

"I have grown fond of this boy. He reminds me of my own youth. I, too, would like to help teach him the ways of our people. So I will go with him or stay with him, as the council decides. Maybe by doing so, I can find purpose and peace for my wandering soul."

Standing Lance nods in understanding. Then he rises and leads Red Knife, Chimalis, and Sean out of the gathering. A woman steps up and leads them to a tepee. Sean notices that all their gear has been neatly stacked inside, and a welcoming fire burns in the pit. Their horses have been tethered outside.

Sean feels a lump form in his throat as it occurs to him all at once that this might be his new home.

"I have heard and am touched by your words," Chimalis says to Red Knife. "I do not yet know if those words were spoken from the heart or just pity for a lost woman and boy. But I, too, will go or stay with Sean. I owe him a debt of three lives, and I will not abandon him."

Sean's heart skips when her gaze turns to him.

"There is much pain and hurt in all of our hearts," she says. "Perhaps together we can make sense of the world again and make a better future." She looks to Red Knife. "With Sean, I will share your tepee and prepare your meals, but I will not be your woman. Like Sean, your spirits wage a battle within you. I must await the outcome of this spirit battle, for I have been around evil far too long, and I wish to see the good side."

Red Knife's chest swells with a deep breath, and for a moment, Sean fears he may lash out. But then, after a long exhale, the warrior nods and accepts Chimalis's wisdom.

The next morning, Sean wakes to find that Standing Lance has come to their tepee to welcome each of them in turn into his Apsáalooke River band.

The chief tells them that the council has voted overwhelmingly to accept them. He invites them to a celebration to be held tonight in their honor. "Red Knife and Chimalis," Standing Lance says with an air of formality, "the council charges you both with teaching this boy the ways of the Apsáalooke. Sean has just learned the truth of his father's death, and now comes to us with an open mind. The times are rapidly changing, and the old ways are fading into the past. Perhaps, as Chimalis stated, this boy has been sent to us by the Great Spirit to help us through this troubling time."

Sean listens closely, understanding most of what the chief says. Still, he is confused about what they expect of him.

Just before Standing Lance leaves, he faces Sean and places both hands on his shoulders. Sean grows uncomfortable as the old man stares deeply into his eyes. Without saying a word, Standing Lance begins to slowly nod. Moments later, the old chief abruptly turns and ducks out the tepee flap, leaving Sean to wonder just what it was that the old man saw in his eyes.

CHAPTER TWENTY

Over the next two weeks, the wound in Red Knife's back begins to fester, and it is clear to Sean that Chimalis grows more concerned. At first, the warrior tries to make light of her worry by telling her that he has been wounded much worse in the past, but Chimalis will not be put off. When Red Knife begins to fever and the pain increases, they call the medicine man to help with the wound's treatment.

Sean marvels at the medicine man's wise, steady council.

"You must apply hot compresses day and night," the old man instructs Chimalis. "As hot as he can stand. This will help draw the evil out." He leaves some pieces of soft doeskin for Chimalis to use for this purpose. Before he leaves, he looks to Sean and repeats, "As hot as he can stand."

After a day of hot compresses, the medicine man returns to lance and drain the wound of its foul-smelling contents. He thoroughly cleans the wound again with warm water before applying another herb poultice. Sean has his doubts, but to his surprise, Red Knife's fever breaks two days later. It is clear that the rot in the wound is fading, too, as the redness and pain markedly lesson.

"Next time, seek me out sooner," the medicine man says with a wink to Sean before he ducks out through the tepee flap.

Sean is relieved to see Red Knife's recovery, in part because he has come to like the warrior and in part because he will be grateful to have help with the hunting. Of course Sean likes to hunt, but at the same time, he has caught glimpses of other boys in the village engaged in various tests of strength and challenges of skill. He is intrigued by the competitions and would like to join the challenge.

Red Knife is leaning against the backrest outside the tepee as Sean rides up from his latest hunt. "You no hunt tomorrow," he says as Sean dismounts and drops two fat rabbits by the fire near Chimalis. "You should challenge the young warriors. Show them your skill." He nods in the boys' direction. "I'm sure they would welcome the competition."

Sean looks over at the boys wrestling in the open field near the river. Why wait for tomorrow? he thinks. He nods his thanks to Red Knife, then strides toward the boys.

When Sean gets to the spot where the boys are gathered, he notices a circle crudely scraped out on the ground. Two boys are aggressively struggling to throw the other out of the circle. Sean stands and watches as one boy finally succeeds and the others shout a roar of approval.

The boy standing next to Sean is the same one who greeted him on their arrival to the village, the same one who had complimented Sean's horse. The boy turns and taps Sean on the chest, nods to the circle, and says, "Now you try."

Without hesitating, Sean steps into the circle, quickly followed by the boy.

"I am Little Hawk," the boy says.

Sean nods. "I am Sean."

While the surrounding boys yell out Little Hawk's name in encouragement, he shows Sean how to lock wrists. They tentatively test each other's strength with a little pushing and pulling. Sean feels confident that he will win, as he is half a head taller than his adversary. When he begins to push harder, his smaller opponent starts to slide back. The young warrior suddenly falls to his back, pulls hard with his arms, and uses one foot to propel Sean out of the circle with the help of his own momentum. Sean finds himself flying over Little Hawk's prone body to land on his back outside the circle.

The boys around the circle laugh at and tease the big awkward white boy with the red hair. They step up to whoop and holler praises around Little Hawk. Sean's mind flashes back to his fight with Will back in Ohio. He jumps to his feet and pushes his way through the group and back into the circle. He points angrily at Little Hawk, challenging him to a second match. Little Hawk steps in, and they grab each other's wrists.

Sean is determined not to be fooled with the same trick. He circles Little Hawk, careful to stay on balance. Their foreheads touch as they bend at the waist and circle each other. Suddenly, Little Hawk drops a knee on the ground just outside of Sean's foot, ducks under Sean's arm, and rises behind him. Little Hawk locks his hands tight around Sean's waist, repositions his hip outside of Sean's, twists, and flings him out of the circle.

Again the Indian boys laugh and crowd around the victor. Humiliated, Sean's anger overwhelms him. He steps over and punches Little Hawk in the face. The other boys yell and come to Little Hawk's assistance, pushing Sean away and then just ignoring him.

Little Hawk turns to Sean and loudly states, "You will never be Apsáalooke. You should go away." With that, he turns and walks off with the others, leaving Sean standing there alone.

Word quickly spreads through the village that the white boy struck Little Hawk in the face with his fist. It travels so quickly, in fact, that it is clear that Red Knife has already heard the news of the dishonor by the time Sean returns to the tepee and ducks through the flap.

"I sent you to challenge your skills against the other boys," Red Knife says, the anger etched on his face, "not to shame yourself. For an Indian to strike another Indian in the face with his fist is dishonorable. It is not done. You have brought dishonor on yourself, as well as on me."

Sean hangs his head, his shame chasing away his anger.

"Did you not consider that you might lose when you stepped into the circle?" Red Knife asks. "You must always keep your focus and never allow your anger or emotions to control your actions. If you do so when fighting your enemies, you will end up dead."

"I am sorry to have brought dishonor to our tepee," Sean says. "I did not think. I was blinded by anger. What can I do to change things with Little Hawk?"

A short time later, after much thought, Red Knife approaches Sean, "You must give him a horse," the warrior states. "I know Bent Nose, Little Hawk's father. I think a horse will appease his honor."

"I will not give up the stallion," Sean replies hotly. "I can't!"

"I know you are attached to the horse, and I will not ask you to give him up. I will give you the brown mustang I stole from the Lakota, and you will give it to Little Hawk. But for this kindness, I will expect two horses from you in return."

Sean cuts the little brown mustang out of the herd. Then he and Red Knife lead the horse over to stand before Little Hawk's tepee. Little Hawk and his father emerge from the tepee to face them.

After a deep breath, Sean steps up to offer the horse's reins to Little Hawk. "I am sorry to have struck you," Sean says. "My anger has dishonored me. I am still learning The Peoples ways. You were better than me in the circle and deserved to win. If you can forgive my anger, I would like you to help me in learning the warrior's way."

Little Hawk hesitates, but then accepts Sean's peace offering with a smile. He extends his right arm out toward Sean, who tries to shake his hand.

"No, Sean," Little Hawk states. "That is the white man's way. If you wish to be one with the Apsáalooke, you must clasp forearms." As he speaks, Little Hawk takes hold of Sean's forearm.

"Would you like to go hunting with me?" Sean asks Little Hawk. "I will leave just before dawn."

It is late afternoon when the two hunters proudly walk side by side back into the village. Little Hawk leads his horse while the big bay stallion follows on his own a few lengths behind. Both horses are laden with elk meat. Sean and Little Hawk shot the bull elk with bow and arrow, then tracked the wounded animal for hours. They finally found the dead elk in a thicket of aspens.

From that day on, the two young men are inseparable. Over the next few moons, they compete with the other young men in all sorts of tests of strength and skill. Sean excels in any tests dealing with bow and arrow or pure strength. All the boys marvel at his ability to shoot an arrow in the air and then shoot four more arrows accurately into a target before the first arrow returns to ground. Little Hawk can fire off three arrows, but seldom do they all find the target.

One day, it dawns on Sean that he is no longer the shortest in the group. When he looks around, there are only a couple of boys taller, and they are both older. Just as his mother once told him he would, he has been growing, and growing rapidly. His true test of strength comes when he is able to lift the big rock by the river up to his chest and then over his head before heaving it farther than any of the other boys in the group.

Sean's only difficulty is in mastering riding skills. The stallion is simply too tall for him to ride out on the grass at a gallop, reach down, and pick up a short stick stuck in the ground. The first two times he tried it, he fell hard from the stallion's back as he reached down. Of course, the other boys laughed at his clumsiness right along with Little Hawk.

The boys were impressed, though, when the big stallion stopped and trotted back to stand over Sean where he fell, and impressed even more when the stallion wouldn't allow any unfamiliar boys in the group to even come near. The stallion only allowed Little Hawk to approach Sean to see if he was okay.

Despite his failures to date, Sean is determined to show the other boys that he is worthy of their respect. On his third try, he is able to reach down and grab the stick at a gallop. He is so excited with this accomplishment that he abruptly pulls up, turns the bay too aggressively, and falls off yet again. This time, when he stands up, he is laughing just as hard as the others.

"Maybe we should tie you to the horse," Little Hawk suggests as he and the other boys break into uproarious laughter.

This brings even more laughter as the group gathers around the fallen rider.

"It will be okay," Sean says with a laugh in return. "The horse is still learning how to stay under me."

"You have never told me your horse's name," Little Hawk says. "You always just say, 'horse.' For sure, a horse this magnificent must have a name."

"I have never given him a name," Sean answers. "But you are right. I should give him a name. How do you say, Thunder?"

It takes Sean a while to make Little Hawk understand what he wants, but Little Hawk finally catches on and tells him the Apsáalooke's word for thunder. "I think Thunder is a fine name for your horse," Little Hawk responds after considering it. "I think I will call the mustang Lightning. Lightning and Thunder always come together. Yes, I think that is good."

CHAPTER  TWENTY ONE

Sean is surprised at how Red Knife's wounded shoulder has taken all summer to mend. He has witnessed every day how Chimalis has used various medicinal herb treatments from the medicine man, as well as some of her own remedies to fight off the nasty infection that has continuously threatened the weeping, gaping wound. But one day, Chimalis tells Sean that her efforts have finally prevailed. Sean sees for himself that the wound has closed and healed, leaving behind an ugly red scar. Red Knife demonstrates how he has regained complete motion of his shoulder, but he says that the scar aches with the cold wind signaling the coming of fall.

To Sean, the other significant event surrounding the healing is the way Red Knife has been behaving around Chimalis. It has been clear that, throughout his long ordeal, Red Knife has grown to crave the tenderness and attention that Chimalis has shown him.

One night the warrior makes it clear when he removes his gruesome necklace and throws the bones into the fire.

"No longer will I hunt Lakota," he calmly announces to Sean and Chimalis. "My heart is at peace."

No one questions his actions or his motives as he walks around the village. When his friend Standing Lance mentions the missing necklace, Sean hears Red Knife simply state, "The bones tried to choke me as I slept."

Standing Lance merely nods and grunts in understanding.

Chimalis seems pleased. "I think the evil demons may have moved on," she tells Red Knife casually after the three have finished the evening meal. "If you still want me as your woman, I will be honored to share your robe."

Sean grins as the ever-serious Red Knife breaks into a wide smile. He quickly regains his serious nature, grunts once, and slowly nods. "I will ask Standing Lance if he will honor us by presiding over the ceremony."

"Standing Lance is good choice," Chimalis states. "Two full moons from now, I will be ready."

The next morning, Chimalis moves out of their shared tepee and in with a friend, explaining to Sean that she has much to prepare if she wants to look her best for the joining ceremony.

On the day of the ceremony, the men gather near Standing Lance's tepee and wait patiently for the women to escort Chimalis. Sean stands proudly behind Red Knife, admiring his adoptive father's elaborate attire. He particularly appreciates Red Knife's beautifully stuffed falcon, which he has mounted on an elaborate headdress of colorful feathers. Sean looks around and notices that most of the men gathered are also wearing a variety of stuffed headdresses. No wonder the Apsáalooke sometimes refer to themselves as the Bird People. He thinks that he should consider what bird he may want someday.

What little hair Red Knife has been able to grow back from his period of grieving has been tied into a tight bun and painted white in honor of the occasion. Chimalis earlier presented him with the outfit he now wears. His shirt is of intricately beaded soft leather bleached white by the sun in the traditional Apsáalooke fashion. It is clear to Sean that Chimalis spent many weeks making Red Knife's fringed leather shirt so beautiful. It is also finely decorated with porcupine quills to highlight the intricate beadwork.

Finally, the group of women approach, weaving through the village toward the gathering of waiting men. Sean is stunned by the sight of Standing Lance's granddaughter leading the procession. Of course he has seen and watched Burning Moon many times before, but never has she appeared as beautiful as she does at this moment. Her plain white doeskin dress accentuates her body's curves, and he is totally spellbound. He has never thought of her as a woman until this moment, only a girl.

He can't take his eyes off her. When she looks over at him and their eyes lock, she smiles. Then Sean watches in confusion as she opens her mouth, places her finger under her chin, and pushes her chin back up to close her mouth, smiling again. Sean at first is puzzled by what she is doing, but then realizes that his mouth is hanging open. Embarrassed, he closes it and turns his gaze toward Chimalis.

She wears a white doeskin dress as well, but hers is beautifully painted in intricate blue-and-red designs. Blue beads accentuate the edges of her dress, and she, too, wears colorful feathers woven into her long, shining hair.

Standing Lance leads the ceremony. He loops a soft piece of white rawhide over the couple's wrists to unite them. Sean stands proudly, nodding in approval from behind his adoptive parents.

As he looks back to find Burning Moon, Sean suddenly realizes that he is looking over the heads of almost everyone gathered. He thinks back to what his mother told him years before—that he should be patient, because he would probably be a head taller than the other boys one day. It turns out that she was right. He is now much taller than the other young men his age, and the equal in height to all but a few of the warriors gathered. He is no longer the runt with red hair.

Chimalis has often compared his hair to the color of the setting sun. It is a darker red than when he was younger, and he has grown to like it. Days of brushing and applying bear fat to make it shine has straightened out much of his hair's natural curl. Today, Red Knife has shown him how to curl it up into a ceremonial bun instead of letting it hang down his back in the Apsáalooke tradition.

Best of all, Sean's hated freckles have been absorbed by his dark tan. Regardless of his physical stature, Sean has not yet reached warrior status. He has yet to count coup on any of the Apsáalooke's many enemies, nor has he stolen any enemy horses.

CHAPTER  TWENTY TWO

It is three years later when Sean and Little Hawk earn the names that will remain with them throughout their adult years.

They have ridden north for two days, back to a little box canyon at the base of a tall, rocky mountain. A huge rockslide has scarred the mountainside and blocked off one end of the canyon running along the mountain's base. They explored this little canyon while hunting two weeks earlier, and have both been eager to return, having seen so many wild horse tracks on the canyon's sandy floor. They are determined to try and capture some, and now ride up the canyon to the spring seeping out at the base of the slide.

As it is late in the fall, Sean is certain that there will be another hard frost tonight. To the East and overhead, the stars are faintly visible through an eerie mist, but to the West, the skies are growing ominously dark.

"I hope this storm holds off for a few days," Sean says as they begin to unload the sleeping robes and the few supplies they have brought with them. "I can smell rain in the air."

"Getting pretty damn cold too," Little Hawk replies. "Might not be rain, but snow." He nods in the direction of lightning as it slashes the sky over the distant mountains to the Northwest. A faint roll of thunder follows seconds later.

Sean turns to look as the flash silhouettes the distant peaks. "Hear that, Thunder?" he says as he removes his horse's saddle, rubs its neck, and whispers fondly in its ears. "The sky spirits are restless. They call out your name."

After unloading their supplies and staking the horses in the grass growing around the spring, the two young men sit on their robes, uncoiling and checking the braided rawhide ropes they have brought with them.

"Tell me your plan again," Sean says as they inspect the coils of rope.

"This canyon has only one way in and out that I can see," Little Hawk states. "If we wall off the entrance, then when the wild mustangs come to visit the spring, they will be ours. We can rope and break the ones we want right here in the canyon and lead them back to camp."

"Perhaps then I can pay back the two horses I owe Red Knife for Lightning," Sean says. "Your plan just might work. We should leave Lightning and Thunder back here by the spring, to entice the other horses to come join them. There certainly are lots of fresh tracks and dung around here."

The two boys work hard all the next day, cutting brush and long poles to make a brush barricade across most of the entrance to the little canyon. It seems to be getting colder as the day wears on, and although rain threatens, the storm holds off. Finally, the brush fence stretches across the canyon's narrow entrance. They step back to admire their efforts. Long poles lie on the ground to either side of a small, open gap in the brush fence. The boys have left the opening to allow the wild mustangs access to the spring at the far end of the canyon. Once the mustangs are inside, Sean and Little Hawk plan to rush out and use the long poles to close the opening and block the only escape route.

As Sean suggested, they have left Lightning and Thunder staked out by the spring to munch on the lush grass. They now conceal themselves a little way up the canyon walls on either end of the brush fence. It is now just a matter of waiting. They wait through the remainder of the day and into the evening, wrapping their robes tightly around themselves to fight off the cold. They doze off and on where they hide throughout the long, cold night.

Finally, just after sunrise, a black stallion trots up the canyon, leading a small herd of nine or ten mustangs, along with some foals. The savvy stallion doesn't seem to like what it sees. The brush fence is something new, and the stallion immediately senses danger. It stands there, staring and listening for a very long time while its small herd fidgets and nervously mills about behind. Finally, the need for water and the stallion's desire for the sweet grass surrounding the spring overcomes his uneasiness about the brush fence, and he leads the mares and foals through the opening.

Only when the small herd is out of sight around the next bend in the box canyon do Sean and Little Hawk spring forward to close the gap with the long poles. Once they have accomplished this, they clasp each other's wrists and slap each other's backs in celebration.

But what neither one of them considered was the black stallion's reaction to Thunder. Here is a threat to his dominance over his mares, and the black stallion will not let it go unchallenged. The two stallions immediately grow agitated, and within moments, they begin to fight.

Sean's first reaction is to rush forward to help Thunder somehow, but Little Hawk senses his anxiety and catches his shoulder with his hand.

"They will trample you if you go in there now," the young man says.

As much as he wants to pull away from his friend's grip, he knows that Little Hawk is right. Feeling helpless, Sean slumps and rocks back onto his haunches, watching.

Thunder's first violent rearing breaks the rawhide cord free from the stake with a loud snap. The two stallions fight with teeth and hooves until both are bleeding from numerous wounds. The other horses do their best to stay out of their way as the two stallions battle.

The fight is so fierce and so evenly matched that Sean doesn't realize how tightly he has been clenching his teeth until the pain starts in his head. *C'mon, Thunder!* He thinks, just as the other stallion lashes out with its front hoof and cracks Sean's beloved horse in the jaw.

Just when all seems lost, Thunder's hooves right themselves, and the big stallion goes on the counterattack. The next blow lands squarely on the black stallion's neck, pummeling it to the ground, as his front knees buckle.

Finally conceding defeat to the stronger and bigger bay, the black stallion climbs back onto its legs and tries to drive what mares it can back toward the brush fence for a quick escape.

When Little Hawk and Sean see the mustangs coming at them, Little Hawk grabs the buffalo robe he has been keeping over his shoulders and steps through the fence rails. Sean sees what his bold friend is attempting to do, and he steps through the poles to join him. They frantically wave their robes back and forth and holler in an effort to turn the stampeding mustangs. The mares in front are startled and swerve to the side when they encounter the unexpected screaming obstacles blocking their escape.

But the black stallion does not waver. There is no safety if it turns back, only its nemesis, the bigger bay stallion. It has no choice but to charge straight at Little Hawk, the closer of the two antagonists blocking the escape. The stallion screams out a challenge as it rears up, lashing out with its front hooves. Little Hawk and Sean dive for the safety of the fence rails, but Little Hawk's reaction is too slow. One front hoof catches him hard on the side of his head, and the other comes down heavy to stomp on his lower leg.

Seeing his path to freedom now open, the black stallion circles back and successfully jumps the rail fence, knocking the top rail down with its front hooves in the process. The mares turn to follow the lead and bolt to freedom, knocking most of the other rails down as they jump through the gap.

Sean rushes over to his fallen friend's motionless body and drags him clear as the mustangs gallop by. As he kneels to check on Little Hawk's wounds, Sean watches the remaining mustangs and foals panic and stampede through. Lightning has pulled her stake, as well, and has joined the other mustangs in their stampede. Thunder trails after the last of the mustangs. Within minutes, all of the horses the two boys worked so hard to capture, including their own mounts, have vanished into the brush and rolling hills beyond, leaving only a plume of dust to mark their passing.

Gently Sean leans his cheek and ear down close to his friend's mouth. Little Hawk is still breathing, but weakly. Sean picks up his unconscious friend and carries him over his shoulder back to the spring. He gently lays Little Hawk down on the grass, then jogs back to the brush fence and gathers up their weapons and sleeping robes. Once Sean returns to his unconscious friend, he lifts Little Hawk again, placing him gently down on his own sleeping robe and covering him over with his.

After gathering dry wood, Sean soon has a fire burning. He gathers more wood and piles it near the fire, putting Little Hawk's leather rain cape over the dry woodpile to protect it from the threatening weather. He leaves the wood within easy reach, should Little Hawk regain consciousness.

Sean knows that for his friend to have the best chance at survival, he must get help quickly. He sets two more logs on the fire, refills both of their water skins, and leaves Little Hawk's skin by his side, along with a small supply of dried meat.

That is all he can do for his friend at the moment, so he turns and starts his long run back to the village to bring help. He wishes he would have had time to attempt to set Little Hawk's broken leg, but he feels that time is his enemy. Sean simply must reach the village as soon as possible. His rain cape flaps about his shoulders as he jogs, but his bow and quiver ride securely on his back.

As Sean runs, he tries to estimate how long it will take him to reach the village. It had taken them two long days to reach the canyon by horseback, but they were not riding hard. He's hoping to reach the village sometime tomorrow morning, but to do so, he will have to jog through the night, and everything must go right. As he settles into a fast pace, he hopes for his friend's sake that it won't be too late.

When he reaches the pass at the far end of the valley, he comes upon a bubbling stream. There, he stops just long enough to get his bearings and take a quick drink of water before resuming his run to the South. He chews on a piece of dried elk as he runs, his mind consumed with worry about his unconscious friend being visited by marauding animals in the night.

The sun has begun to cast the purple hues of early autumn sunsets against the craggy cliff to the North as he restarts his run. Sean tries to increase his pace while he still has light. Tiny, knife-like stabs of pain shoot through his aching muscles with every stride. He knows these will eventually pass with time if he just keeps running.

He can only hope that the fire he made by Little Hawk will be enough to deter any animals, but he realizes that it will only burn for so long unless Little Hawk wakes. Sean's other concern is the approaching cold front. If the fire goes out, his friend may well suffer from the cold.

With the daylight fading, Sean stops one more time to check his position against the silhouette of the high mountain peaks off to his right. The storm seems to be following him from the North as he runs. He listens again as the thunder cracks and tumbles across the northern sky behind him. He wonders if he can use the thunder to help guide him in the dark. Looking up, he sees dark, broken clouds with a half-moon shining through periodically. He knows that it will be impossible to find his way by the stars if they become hidden by the clouds. The thunder spirits may be his only hope.

The safest thing to do would be to stop, build a fire, and wait out the dark, but that may put Little Hawk's life even further at risk. Sean is determined to continue his jog into the night, keeping the thunder and lightning flashes behind him to help guide him to the South.

His mind turns once again to thoughts of the girl Burning Moon. It seems to Sean that he has bumped into her around the village much more frequently lately. It could just be that he simply did not notice her before. But he sure notices her now, and she always seems to have a smile for him when they pass. He wonders about her long black hair—what it might feel and smell like. But most of all, his thoughts come back to the curves of her body in that white doeskin dress she wore at the joining ceremony. If only he had the nerve to stop and speak with her. He thinks she is easily the prettiest girl in the village.

As the night deepens, the temperature drops, and the air becomes bitter cold. With his thoughts of Burning Moon, Sean has an idea. He reaches into his shirt and pulls out Becky's bonnet. He ties the bonnet carefully over his face, just his eyes peering out above the edge. This will offer some protection for his lips and nose and help with the freezing air.

Sean's jog has slowed to a quick-step walk as darkness closes in around him. With the cloud cover now complete, he is totally reliant on the thunder at his back to guide him in the right direction. The sparsely wooded foothills that he is moving through become dark shadows—so dark now that his eyes begin to play tricks on him in the gloom. He is exhausted, and his judgment is beginning to get foggy.

Did that shadow just move?

Sean studies the shadow as he jogs by. He concludes that it is nothing but a stand of buckbrush, but he now begins to have the eerie feeling that something is following him. He glances over his shoulder to check—nothing. But he still can't seem to shake the feeling.

If he stops now, with only his leather cape for warmth, he will get the cold sickness that Red Knife has often warned him about. He must fight off this urge to stop and rest, for if he does so, he will die.

Sean's mind is just a haze as he stumbles on, his leather cape now frozen stiff and heavy frost covering his shoulders. Will the night never end? His breath comes in ragged gasps and his lungs burn with each one. He wonders why his nose, ears, and hands feel as if they are being held in a fire. He has put his hands under his armpits to suffocate the flames, but it does little good.

His legs seem to have a mind all their own as they continue to rhythmically move forward. He suddenly realizes that he has been watching his feet as he stumbles along. That seems odd to him, and he tries to understand the mystery of it. Sean looks up to see a few faint stars and the moon shining down through a clear sky. His mind lifts out of its dreamlike state as he takes a good look around. The heavy frost on the land glows in a pale silver light, only the trees still in shadow. To his left, the horizon is beginning to faintly glow with the coming of dawn. After trying to focus his thoughts, he realizes that he has not heard the thunder spirits in a long time.

Sean stumbles into the village a short time after dawn. He collapses from exhaustion and cold into the flap of Red Knife's tepee. Chimalis, up preparing the morning meal, yells for Red Knife's help, and they drag him into the tepee. They remove his stiff, frozen face mask and clothes and bundle him in furs next to the fire. Chimalis begins to force him to drink some hot broth while Red Knife gently massages Sean's frozen hands in warm water.

Sean is conscious enough to know that they are working on him, but he can't seem to make himself speak. Finally, he forces words out of his exhausted body. "Little . . . Hawk . . . hurt. Hurt . . . bad."

"Where?" Red Knife asks patiently. "Where is Little Hawk?"

"Little . . . spring . . . in . . . canyon," Sean answers. "Two . . . days' . . . ride . . . north."

Red Knife asks Chimalis what she can remember about the terrain two days' ride to the North. Finally, he asks Sean, "Is there a big mountain with the scar of a rockslide?"

Sean nods, "Yes."

Red Knife tells Chimalis that he knows the location of the spring where Little Hawk lies injured. Sean watches as Red Knife ducks out of the tepee. Then exhaustion overcomes him, and he falls into a fitful sleep.

Five days later, the search party gallops back into the village, and the men are not alone. With Red Knife leading the way, fourteen wild mustangs gallop close behind. Thunder is busy at the rear of the herd, moving from side to side and nipping at the flanks of any horse that falls behind.

When Thunder sees Sean standing outside Red Knife's tepee, the big stallion breaks off from the wild horses and trots over to stand in front of him. Thunder nudges Sean repeatedly in his chest, its big head and nose moving up and down in its excitement.

Sean steps to the side of Thunder to rub the stallion's neck and speak fondly into its ear. "Its good to see you too," Sean says softly to the big bay. "I thought maybe I'd lost you to love." He continues to rub Thunder's neck as the other riders ride through the village on the way to the herd. Sean is becoming concerned that he hasn't seen his friend anywhere.

"Where is Little Hawk?" Sean yells as the last rider passes by.

The man's only reply is to turn and point behind him.

Sean jumps up on Thunder's bare back and rides out in the direction from where the others had ridden. He locates the last of the search party a short distance out from the village. Lightning is pulling a travois upon which Little Hawk lies. Little Hawk's father, Bent Nose, and two other warriors ride beside him.

Sean comes up along his friend's side to ride with him the last short distance into camp. Little Hawk and his father are all smiles when they see Sean approach.

Little Hawk raises his fist and cries out a loud yell of excitement. "We did it," Little Hawk yells up at Sean. "Have you ever seen such fine mustangs?"

"How did you do it?" Sean asks. "The mustangs had all run away when I left you."

"That's just it," Little Hawk replies. "I didn't do anything. I was still sleeping. I think Thunder and Lightning brought them back. When I woke up at midday, they were all just standing there. Thunder wouldn't let any of them leave. Red Knife and my father came two days later. They straightened my leg and said it should be fine by spring."

That night, the village gathers to rejoice and give thanks to the Great Spirit, Akbaatatdía, for sparing the two young warriors' lives.

After the feasting, Red Knife steps forward and raises his arms for quiet. When the shouting subsides, he addresses the gathering. "We, Red Knife and Chimalis, have given this feast, along with Bent Nose and Morning Star, to honor our sons' achievement. They have captured fourteen wild horses to start their herds. My son, Sean, with little regard for his own well-being, has brought much honor with his long run to save his friend's life. Chimalis and I stand proudly by his side. Few warriors could have done more. For this reason, he will no longer be called by his white name, but by his new name, Night Wind. His run through the freezing night to save his friend's life is reminiscent of the night wind, strong and unwavering."

The gathering of guests shouts out and cheers in their approval.

Bent Nose steps forward and holds up his arms to speak. "I think it is only fitting that my son, Little Hawk, also be given a warrior's name. From this day forward, he shall be called Kicking Horse. Night Wind has told me of his bravery in standing up to try and block the black stallion's escape. I think Kicking Horse is a strong name for such a brave warrior."

CHAPTER TWENTY THREE

To get to the fort, Night Wind and Red Knife ride for two days, each leading a packhorse to trade on behalf of the village. Upon their arrival, they decide to pay a visit to the new Indian agent all the tribes have been talking about. Standing Lance requested that Red Knife offer his greetings on behalf of the Apsáalooke.

A soldier at the gate directs them to a small office built along the inside of the palisade wall. They walk their horses over and tie them to a tree outside the wooden structure. Dismounting, they push the door open and step inside.

"How may I help you?" asks a nervous young soldier standing behind a small desk.

"We would speak with the agent," Night Wind replies.

The soldier turns, knocks on the door behind him, and steps through into the next room, closing the door. They wait a few minutes before Night Wind shrugs in Red Knife's direction and they turn to leave the office. A moment later, the closed door opens, and a small man with red hair steps into the room. Red Knife and Night Wind turn back to face him.

"I'm Benjamin O'Fallon, the new Indian agent," the small man says, extending his hand. "Whom do I have the pleasure of meeting?"

Night Wind steps up to shake the agent's hand. "I am Night Wind of the River band of Apsáalooke, the Indians you call Crow, and my father here is Red Knife."

Red Knife merely grunts in greeting, as he often does when meeting a man who has yet to earn his friendship.

Night Wind notes the man's red hair. "You must be Irish."

"Why, yes I am," O'Fallon responds. "And I must say that you don't look Indian yourself. How is it that you come to live with the Crow?"

"The Apsáalooke saved my life from a white man, an' I settled in with 'em," Night Wind replies. "Our chief, Standing Lance, asked us to send his greetings and hope for peace. He does not travel much anymore, but he wanted us to tell you that he plans to attend the treaty signin' at the Mandan Village next summer."

"Your story is one I would like to hear," O'Fallon says. "May I ask what your white name was?"

"Sean, Sean O'Malley, I'm Irish, same as you."

"It is good to meet the both of you. I hope you will attend the treaty ceremony with your chief. It will be good to have someone there to interpret our good words." O'Fallon adds, "That's quite the bow and quiver you have. Don't believe I've seen red-feathered arrows before."

"I have one of those," Night Wind says, ignoring the agent's words, pointing to the Jefferson Peace Medallion holding down some papers on Agent O'Fallon's desk.

O'Fallon looks surprised as Night Wind pulls his Peace Medallion from the beaded pouch hanging on the leather cord around his neck.

"It was my uncle, William Clark, who passed them out on the Expedition of Discovery, nearly twenty years ago," O'Fallon says. "Your too young to have gotten it from the expedition, may I ask where you acquired it?"

"An old Shoshone chief gave it to me many years ago, when I was still a white boy," Night Wind replies. "I forget his name, but he claimed that his sister was part of the expedition."

"The only Indian woman on the expedition that I'm aware of was Sacagawea. Her brother was indeed a chief of the Shoshone. He gave the expedition horses. I came to know Sacagawea in St. Louis when I lived with my uncle many years ago. She was a very interesting woman. Her son was off at the time, visiting France, I believe."

Night Wind nods.

"What a small world," Benjamin O'Fallon says as he extends his hand to shake again with Night Wind. "Very glad to have made your acquaintance. I think you may be of great help to your Crow brothers, and I look forward to seeing you both again at the ceremonies next summer. Be sure you tell all the Crow you meet that they are all invited. We will have many gifts."

Then, just as Night Wind trades a glance with Red Knife that says they should leave, the agent says something that stops him in his tracks.

"Say, did you say your last name was O'Malley?"

When Night Wind nods, the agent looks up at the ceiling as if trying to recall something just on the edge of his memory.

"Seems to me I heard that name somewhere before." The agent pauses as if doubting his own thoughts. " Seems I recollect there was a girl that called herself Malley," he says distantly. "I just assumed that was her first name." But then, when he looks back at Night Wind and sees the conviction in the young warrior's eyes, he seems to steel up with certainty. "Yes, I remember now, a girl with red hair, living with the Dakota Sioux. She claimed she was kidnapped from her Shawnee Ohio tribe, but we all thought that ridiculous, a girl being all the way out here." He sighs as if burdened by the memory.

"Where is she now?" Night Wind asks, his heart pounding in his chest at the thought that he may have finally found his dear sister.

The agent lowers his head. "I'm afraid she passed away of a fever some years back. At least that's what I heard."

Night Wind's eyes widen. "I will have to go to this village to see for myself. Where can I find it?"

O'Fallon shakes his head adamantly. "Oh, I wouldn't advise that, son. The Dakota Sioux are awfully hostile at the moment. They won't take kindly to a visit."

A sudden and overwhelming urge to run to his sister's rescue seizes Night Wind, and it is all he can do to keep himself from bolting from the office. "The girl you speak of," he says tersely, "I believe she is my sister. I must know if what you say is true."

The agent nods knowingly. Then, all at once, he brightens up and raises a finger. "The Dakota chief gave me something of hers that he wanted out of his village. Said it was possessed by an evil spirit. Let me see if I can find it."

With that, he disappears into his office and returns a short time later with a little bundle of cloth clutched in both hands. Night Wind watches in confused apprehension as the agent unwraps what he is holding. His heart skips when he sees it—a crudely made, indigo cloth bag. Night Wind immediately recognizes the cloth from the indigo dress his sister was wearing on the day she disappeared. He quickly pulls out the indigo bonnet from inside his shirt to confirm his fears.

The tears surge to Night Wind's eyes so quickly that he has no hope of stopping them. O'Fallon looks on with concern written plainly on his face as Night Wind sinks to one knee and Red Knife rushes over to comfort him. For the first time, after all these years of silently searching, Night Wind knows that his sister is dead. With her goes the last threads of the family he once knew, that final hope that he would ever be able to piece back the identity of his childhood.

"May I keep this?" Night Wind asks.

The agent solemnly nods his head as he hands the bag to Night Wind.

Night Wind feels the lump inside the bag and reaches inside. He brings out a finely carved wooden head. The wood is smooth and polished shiny from years of handling, but he recognizes the small head instantly: the head from Becky's doll!

A sense of mourning hangs over Night Wind's head as they finish trading their winter's catch at the fort's trading post. When he notices a couple of old trappers leaning up against the outside wall, he steps over to ask the same question he has asked all the trappers he has met over the past few years.

"Have either of you come across a trapper called Hatchet Jack?"

One of the men stands up straight, his anger showing in his response. "If I did, he'd be dead. That yellow-bellied skunk murdered me partners an' stole me furs."

"Sounds like Jack, all right," Night Wind replies. "How long ago did this happen?"

"Been goin' on seven or eight winters back, maybe more," the old trapper relates. "Bastard come staggerin' in ta camp outta a blizzard. Face a real mess too. Bad enough ta scare the quills off a porcupine— one half all burned up an' such. Asking if we might spare some vittles. Said that he ain't ate in a week. When we tossed him a joint of buffalo ta gnaw on, he said he was lookin' for a white boy with red hair travelin' with a squaw that stole his gear. Wanted ta know if we'd seen 'em. Got all friendly an' such, then pulled out a hatchet an' kilt me partners an' shot me in the head. Next mornin', when I come to, me partners lay scalped, an' everythin' else was gone." The old trapper pulls off his hat to show Night Wind the scar running along the side of his bald head. "Lucky for me, I ain't got me no hair." He squints in the direction of Night Wind's red hair. "Say, you must be that white boy he was lookin' for, ain't-cha? Reckon ya went an' gone full Injun."

Night Wind ignores the trapper's last statement. "Did he say anything about where he was headin'?"

"I recall he did mumble somethin' 'bout havin' to cross a desert to get to Oregon," the trapper answers. "But best be careful if ya do run into him, 'cause that bastard's crazy—just plumb loco. Be sure to tell him for me that ole Henry's still lookin' to kill him."

"You won't have the pleasure if I see him first," Night Wind replies.

Flashes of lightning and the rumble of thunder echo through the nearby foothills. Red Knife and Night Wind were hoping to shoot a buffalo on their return from the fort, but so far, they haven't spotted a thing on the open buffalo grass of the rolling prairie. Night Wind thinks that if they don't see anything tomorrow, they may be riding into their village empty-handed tomorrow night.

But now they need to get off the prairie and find shelter from the coming storm. They know that it is not a good idea to be the highest point in the tall grass when a lightning storm moves through. They again hear the thunder growl a warning in the distance.

Suddenly, five Lakota Sioux warriors appear at the top of the nearby ridge. Seeing their enemy so close, Night Wind glances around for an escape route. Red Knife points to a line of trees, and they begin to gallop their horses and packhorses toward the nearby river.

The Lakota shout out their war cries as they spot their ancestral enemies and urge their ponies forward in pursuit. Night Wind looks up to see that they have angled their pursuit in an all-out effort to cut them off.

"Cut the packhorse free if you have to," Red Knife yells to Night Wind as they make for the river.

Night Wind can see that it is going to be close. With Thunder under him, he is confident that he and his pack horse can outrun the Lakota horses to the river, but he looks back to see Red Knife's horse struggling to keep up. The pack horse seems to be holding them back. Lakota arrows fly by Red Knife's head as the Lakota make a futile effort to bring one of them down with a lucky shot.

Thunder and the pack horse splash across the shallow river as Night Wind guides them over to a jam of washed-out trees lying along the opposite bank. Red Knife pulls up beside him moments later, grabs his rifle, and leaps from his horse's back. Red Knife's pack horse is pulling deep for air. Night Wind has already pulled out the big Hawken rifle from its scabbard by the time Red Knife joins him behind the trees. Red Knife takes aim and fires just as the first Lakota rider hits the river with a great splash of flying water. The impact of the lead ball hits the warrior in his shoulder, driving him in a backward somersault from his saddle.

The other Lakota pull up their horses when they hear the formidable boom of the heavy rifle and see their leader go down. The fallen warrior is quickly up on his feet, and with the helping hand of another, is pulled up behind his rescuer. Hanging on with his good arm, blood streaming from his wound, the warrior is taken to safety behind some trees.

Red Knife turns to Night Wind. "Why did you not shoot?"

"We are on Lakota land," Night Wind replies.

"The Lakota will not tell the Apsáalooke where they may or may not go," Red Knife answers heatedly, looking confused by his adopted son's answer.

One of the Lakota warriors calls out from across the river in broken Apsáalooke. "Do the Crow run like the coyote, just to hide and shoot the white man's long gun? We know it is Red Knife who hides like the badger in its hole. My uncle would have his revenge for his friends killed at Big Stoney Mountain. Will the mighty Red Knife not come forth from his hiding place and fight him man-to-man as a true warrior? Or are all the stories I hear true, that he just kills men while they sleep in the dark of the night?"

Night Wind watches as a regal looking Lakota warrior rides forth from behind the trees to stand in the open along the river's bank. He is carrying a lance and shield. He wears a red-stained war shirt. Holding his lance and shield up high, he lets out a war cry, "*Hoka-hey!*"

Red Knife turns from watching the Lakota to face Night Wind. He hands his adoptive son his rifle. "He questions my courage. I must fight. If I fall, leave the packhorses and take these rifles back to our people. Thunder can outrun their ponies. You must not allow the Lakota to capture them."

After swinging up onto his horse, Red Knife rides out from behind the log pile to stand across the shallow river from his adversary. Night Wind sees that the Lakota's shield will put Red Knife at a distinct disadvantage, but he has little choice. It is a matter of honor.

Red Knife yells out his challenge. "Is this the coward that ran off in the night while his friends fought and died as true warriors? The shame you carry must be great!"

Night Wind doesn't know if the Lakota warrior understands Red Knife's words, but the tone of Red Knife's voice makes the insult clear. After drawing out his hatchet, Red Knife kicks his horse into a gallop across the shallow water. At almost the same time, the Lakota kicks his horse into action.

The two warriors charge by each other. The stone lance tip of the Lakota barely misses as Red Knife ducks away, while his own hatchet blow is easily deflected by the Lakota's thick leather war shield.

As the horses whirl, Red Knife's horse reacts quicker, and he charges into the enemy horse's shoulder before it has fully turned. Both horses and men fall into the shallow, muddy river. The Lakota's horse goes down screaming as it snaps its fetlock on the rocky river bottom upon impact. The injured horse immediately rises and tries to run off, only to fall again in shrill agony. It continues to try to stand up, all the while screaming in pain.

The Hawken rifle booms out lead, smoke, and flame, and the injured horse collapses in a heap, dead. Night Wind quickly works to reload his rifle while the two warriors regain their feet to continue the fight.

Red Knife's horse moves off to stand nearby in the shallow water. The two warriors crouch and face each other with drawn knives. The Lakota still holds part of his lance, broken in the fall, but he now tosses it aside to float down the river. They both charge simultaneously, and the two lock in a struggle of wills and strength.

Red Knife stumbles and falls into the water, still gripping the Lakota's knife wrist as he pulls his enemy down with him. The evenly matched opponents roll over and over in the deadly struggle. Finally, the thrashing ends as both warriors remain partially submerged. They break apart from each other, each falling backward with a splash. The Lakota warrior rises up first in a sitting position and looks over at his Lakota companions before toppling over on his side, dead.

Red Knife rises and stumbles over behind his fallen enemy. While holding his dead foe up by the hair, he deftly scalps him. The Lakota's body rolls slowly down the river as Red Knife holds the scalp aloft and screams out a savage victory cry. "Aiee!"

A young Lakota warrior comes riding around the trees directly at Red Knife. Pulling his horse up at the river's edge, he yells out in broken Apsáalooke, "Hear my name, Red Knife. I am called Broken Horn, and now you will join my uncle in the afterlife!"

Night Wind's Hawken booms out again from behind the log jam. Broken Horn's stone lance head explodes from the tip of his lance, shattered by the ball's impact. Startled, Broken Horn wheels his horse and retreats back to cover.

Red Knife grabs the reins of his nearby horse and walks back over behind the fallen trees. They both watch as the Lakota mount their horses and ride off, taking the wounded warrior with them.

Upon seeing the questioning look on Red Knife's face, Night Wind simply states, "The boy did not need killing. He spoke in the words of the Apsáalooke."

CHAPTER  TWENTY FOUR

Night Wind squats to look at the remains of a recent fire. Kicking Horse crouches beside him and turns to his friend. "I think there were three warriors. The fire's totally cold, but it appears to be recent. Possibly last night."

After rising to his full height, Night Wind carefully scans the surrounding forest. Both of them hold their horses' reins. Night Wind reaches up and pulls the bow from his back and tightens the string. "No, there were four, Lakota most likely. They were brash to make their camp so close to Apsáalooke lands."

Kicking Horse nods as Night Wind points out the different prints. "You may have mastered our language and are a good tracker," Kicking Horse says, "both at home and in the forest. But you still do not understand the Lakota. We are not in our land, but in Lakota land. My uncle says a warrior will die five times over if captured by the Lakota. I think maybe we should turn back."

"Do you know that the white man says that about all Indians?" Night Wind says. "Anyway, how can just four Lakota frighten two Apsáalooke warriors? There are only four of them. Red Knife alone killed three of them at one time." He pauses to scan his surroundings one more time before swinging up on Thunder's back. "Besides, we still have not found the wild horses we seek. Are we to shame ourselves by returning to the village empty-handed?"

Kicking Horse stands and mounts Lightning. "My brother forgets that fear is a friend. It helps keep a warrior alert and alive. This is now the second time we have seen Lakota sign. We have come too far north, five days from our village. I think we should turn back. It is better to return empty-handed than to have our scalps decorate our enemy's lodgepole."

"Red Knife taught me never to fear my enemies—only to respect them. A warrior is born to fight the enemies of his people. Only the sun and wind live forever." Night Wind turns and starts to walk his horse north. "Let us look for horses one more day. If we do not find any, then we will turn back."

Kicking Horse nods with what looks like reluctant approval.

From behind a stand of trees, Night Wind sees a doe step forth from the brush and into the small clearing. He and Kicking Horse nock arrows and slowly rise from their prone positions to kneeling ones. They each draw back on their bows, and with a quiet word from Night Wind, both arrows fly through the air as one. The deer takes one leap into the air and falls to the ground. Kicking Horse is about to run out into the clearing when Night Wind touches his arm to stop him. While nocking a second arrow, Night Wind quietly peers around at the surrounding forest. Finally satisfied that all is indeed quiet, the two young warriors move out into the clearing.

When they reach the dead doe, they kneel to determine which of the two arrows protruding from the deer's side was the killing shot. A smiling Kicking Horse triumphantly points out that his arrow made the kill.

With one hand on the deer's side, Kicking Horse says a prayer to the deer's spirit. "Forgive us for taking your life. Your flesh will nourish us and make us strong for our fight with our enemies. We thank you for the gift of life, and we wish your spirit a safe journey."

Later that evening, Night Wind is sitting with Kicking Horse under a small rock overhang while their horses are hobbled a few yards away, grazing on the little grass available. Off in the distance, lightning gouges the sky, and thunder rolls across the valley below.

Kicking Horse studies the rocky surface below his buffalo robe. "I do not like this campsite. We should have stayed where we roasted the deer. The ground there was soft with pine needles."

Night Wind shakes his head. "One thing I learned from the evil one, Hatchet Jack, was that if you sleep where you eat, you make yourself an easy target for your enemies. Red Knife agrees. My father also told me the day you assume to know where your enemies are is the day you die with an arrow in your back. That you should always be thinking, where might my enemy be lurking? Face all directions."

Kicking Horse grunts and nods before pulling his buffalo robe tighter around his shoulders.

"I wish my father would teach me as much about girls as he has about the wilderness." Night Wind glances down and then turns to his friend. "How do I show a girl I like her without making a fool of myself?"

"It is better to let the girl make the first move," Kicking Horse is quick to offer. "That way, a warrior need not face defeat." A hint of a smile creeps onto his face. "Who is this girl that has so caught my friend's eye that his mind wanders from the joy of the hunt?"

"Her name does not matter." Night Wind feels his face grow warm. "I just thought you might have some advice to help me ease my ache."

Kicking Horse's expression falls in disappointment.

Night Wind sighs. "If you must know, it is the granddaughter of Standing Lance. The girl called Burning Moon."

"I thought this was so," Kicking Horse says with a laugh. "Do not worry, my friend, for Burning Moon has been falling all over herself trying to catch your eye. The whole village knows this. Are you really that blind that you have not seen how she looks at you?"

For the second time, Night Wind feels his face flush. "But she has always just stared at me—ever since the very first day Red Knife and Chimalis brought me to the village. I thought maybe she was just curious about my white skin and red hair."

"My friend, you are now almost as dark as I am. She's more than just curious." Kicking Horse gives him a nudge. "You have become one with the Apsáalooke. Your ugly green eyes are clouded over by your eagerness to become a warrior. Go and speak with Burning Moon. You will know I speak true."

Night Wind nods and gets to his feet. "Maybe you are right." He gathers his robe and gestures with his head toward the forest. "I will take the first watch. I can't sleep now, anyway. You have given me much to think about."

Night Wind follows the line that Kicking Horse points out. Down the valley, there is a wisp of smoke rising above the trees.

"It must be the same four Lakota whose trail we crossed earlier," Kicking Horse says. "We should head back to the Musselshell River before they cross our trail."

Night Wind smiles as an idea forms in his head. "My friend, this is a gift from the Great Spirit Akbaatatdía himself. We came to find horses, didn't we? Well, these Lakota have fine horses. We will take theirs."

"We came to find wild horses, not Lakota horses. We don't even know how close their main camp is."

"But the Lakota have done us a favor. We do not have to travel to their main camp. They have brought their horses to us. We don't even have to break them."

Kicking Horse nods reluctantly. "It is settled then. We will thank the Lakota for their horses tonight. Our people will sing a song about us."

As the sun sets on the enemy camp, the two young warriors are watching from a distance. Night Wind points with hand signs, indicating the route they each will take to get down to where the Lakota have tethered their horses. Their own horses are tied up a short distance away. Kicking Horse has left his bow and quiver tied to Lightning's saddle. For some reason known only to the Great Spirit, Night Wind has chosen to bring his bow and quiver of arrows with him, but has left the Hawken rifle with Thunder. The two warriors have been taking turns watching the enemy camp and resting.

The Lakota fire is just a warm glow of embers as the two begin to inch their way toward the tethered Lakota horses. They have watched the moon move halfway across the heavens since the enemy warriors wrapped themselves in their sleeping robes. The Lakota clearly feel secure in their own hunting grounds and have not posted a guard. Their camp is quiet.

Night Wind and Kicking Horse move quietly among the tethered horses. The horses nervously begin to move around and nicker at the unfamiliar scent of the two strangers. Night Wind selects one and rubs the nose of the horse in an attempt to reassure it and settle the nervous animal down. This seems to calm the horse a little. As he continues to rub the shoulder and chest of the horse, he reaches down with his knife and slices the leather thong that hobbles the animal's two front legs.

While quietly leading the horse away, Night Wind looks in the direction of his young companion. To his surprise, Kicking Horse is no longer among the horses, but stalking into the enemy camp itself. He looks intent on stealing the war lance stuck in the ground near the head of one of the sleeping Lakota. This certainly was not part of the plan the two had worked out, but there is little that Night Wind can do now except pray that his impulsive friend will not cause them serious trouble in his reckless foolishness.

His worst fears come to pass when a strong arm shoots out from under the robe and sweeps Kicking Horse off his feet. The Lakota camp instantly springs to life with a shout of alarm. All four Lakota are on their feet with their knives drawn. Surprisingly, Kicking Horse does not make any attempt to get up.

As two Lakota race to the horses, Night Wind has no recourse but to leave his chosen horse and quietly fade back into the protection of the darkened forest around him. Within moments, he has vanished among the shadows of the trees. Two of the warriors move cautiously into the darkness as the other two secure the loose horses and tie up Kicking Horse.

Unwilling to abandon his friend, Night Wind makes his way through the darkness around to the other side of the camp. He has no other choice but to observe the camp from a distance. Night Wind is uncertain what has happened to Kicking Horse, other than that he fell hard and is now tied up. His friend appears to be unconscious. He watches in shame as the two Lakota warriors emerge from the forest, leading Thunder and Lightning. The stallion's head is thrashing about, straining against his reins. One of the warriors holds up Night Wind's rifle and yells out in triumph.

Night Wind is tempted to put an arrow into the one holding the rifle, but he is worried that they would then kill Kicking Horse in retaliation. He will have to be patient and pick his spot carefully if he is to retrieve his friend alive.

After much gesturing and arguing, the Lakota gather and begin to break camp. One of them takes Kicking Horse's bow and quiver from his horse and tosses it into the fire to burn. The Lakota swing their prisoner's unconscious body across the back of his own horse and tie him in place. They then mount their horses and cautiously begin to make their way down the valley.

Night Wind waits until they are out of sight. Then he moves down to the abandoned campsite. Quickly he moves to the fire and knocks the burning bow and arrows from the flames. He is too late. They are burned beyond saving.

After letting out a deep sigh, Night Wind ponders his next step. He realizes that he has little choice but to attempt to save Kicking Horse. This is reinforced by Red Knife's words back at the battle by Dead Horse River the year before. "Do not let your long gun fall into your enemy's hands. Many more of our people will die if your long gun remains with the Lakota." He wouldn't be able to face his father if he didn't at least try to rescue his impulsive young friend and retrieve his rifle.

Night Wind climbs up the side of the valley and into the high trees above. Once there, he turns and begins to jog downstream in the direction the Lakota took his friend. He follows the mountain's contours, weaving his way through the trees. As he jogs, he tries to keep an eye through the trees and on the game path that runs along the small stream on the valley's floor.

Three times during the long, hot day, he moves cautiously down to study the path for sign. Satisfied that he is indeed still following the right trail, Night Wind quenches his thirst from the little stream before climbing back up the valley's side to resume his pursuit.

After jogging steadily into the late afternoon, Night Wind is just about to move back down to quench his thirst and examine the path again when his eye catches movement coming up the trail. He squats down beside a tree to wait. Within seconds, he is surprised to see Thunder trotting by, pursued closely by one of the Lakota warriors.

Night Wind smiles to himself. He knows just how much the stallion hates to be led, and knew it was only a matter of time before Thunder broke free. He swells at the thought that his horse just might have given him the opportunity he has been waiting for. After the Lakota passes on the path below, Night Wind turns and starts to jog back in the direction from which he came.

Certain that his enemy has not seen him, he begins a gentle descent down to the valley's path. He fingers his knife handle as he watches the back of the warrior vanish up the path and into the trees below. Now it is simply a matter of waiting.

The sun has left the valley floor, and the light is beginning to dim when Night Wind hears the first sounds of horse's hooves coming his way. He nocks an arrow on the bowstring. For some strange reason, he does not want to kill the Lakota unless it becomes absolutely necessary.

Upon carefully peering around the trunk of the large cedar where he waits, he can't help but chuckle to himself at the sight of his enemy trying to lead the big stallion. It is only when they slowly draw closer that Night Wind notices that his enemy is but a boy. When the boy turns his head back to try to control the unruly stallion, Night Wind steps out from his concealment, knife in hand, and begins to sprint toward the struggle.

The boy's horse and Thunder have come to a standstill in a stubborn test of wills. The end result is inevitable. The larger stallion, with his ears cocked back, rears back against the lead rope, yanking hard with his big head, one way and then the other, in an effort to dislodge the rope that restrains his freedom. The young Lakota boy desperately pulls on the lead rope in a futile attempt to control the enraged horse.

Before Night Wind reaches the battle to intercede, Thunder frantically rears back and comes down hard with one of his hooves on the braided leather rope restraining him. The Lakota youth is violently yanked from his saddle and tumbles back, head over heels, landing hard upon his back.

Night Wind yells, "No, Thunder—easy there, big boy." But he is too late. Before he is able to reach the prone boy and pull him to safety, Thunder has reared again, and his hooves come down hard on the youth's legs.

Night Wind continues to talk soothingly to the agitated stallion, trying his best to calm Thunder down. Thunder bounces and kicks at the fallen youth's body with his hooves. Then the horse suddenly stops, putting his ears forward at the sound of Night Wind's soothing voice. Thunder's nostrils flare less and less as his heavy breathing abates. While continuing to speak softly, Night Wind walks over to rub Thunder's neck and shoulder as he removes the braided rope.

Kneeling down beside the unconscious Lakota, Night Wind sees a young boy, much younger than the warrior he accidentally shot when he was a young boy himself. Past memories come flooding back to him. He almost expects this boy's eyes to suddenly open and reach a hand up to him. He can't help but think of this boy's parents, like many before him, never knowing what happened to their missing sons.

Night Wind knows he is expected to kill and scalp his fallen enemy, but he is unable to do so. He drags the youth over to some grass and examines his wounds. One leg is horribly broken, the bone crushed below the knee. Nothing else is obvious, but there are bruises on the boy's body and a red mark on the side of his temple.

The boy needs assistance, but Night Wind can't stay any longer. He asks Akbaatatdía to help guide the youth's spirit back to this life or help him on his journey to the next. After breaking the Lakota's bow and arrows, he ties the fallen youth's horse to a nearby tree and heads back on the trail of Kicking Horse.

Dusk finds Night Wind riding Thunder along the path in cautious pursuit. He is leery that the Lakota may return in search of their young companion. All of his senses are focused as he quietly rides through the night's gloom. Night Wind stops as soon as he sees the flicker of a fire in the distance. He moves off the trail and tethers Thunder to a small tree before cautiously approaching the Lakota, bow in hand. He circles around to the far side before settling down to await an opportunity a mere thirty paces from the little campfire. With a simple plan in mind, Night Wind hopes and prays that the remaining Lakota are not all boys.

He watches the three by the fire. They are engaged in a heated discussion. Night Wind has located Kicking Horse, bound hand and foot and tied to a small tree nearby. He bides his time as the tallest of the three Lakota looks disgustedly at the other two. First, the tall Lakota gestures with his hands back up the trail and then over at Kicking Horse. It is obvious to Night Wind that the warrior wants them to go and look for the missing boy. He wonders if the boy could be a younger brother.

After a few angry words, the tall warrior pulls a heavy stone war club from his belt and starts to walk over to where Kicking Horse is bound. Night Wind knows he must act, and he raises his bow to release an arrow. But then another warrior jumps to his feet and runs over to grab the taller man's arm. They loudly exchange some more words before the taller warrior grudgingly replaces his war club and moves off in the direction of the horses.

Night Wind seizes the moment. He draws two arrows from his quiver and jams them in the dirt in front of him. Kneeling, he takes aim at the closest of the three warriors, the only Lakota still sitting near the rifle and other weapons left lying near the fire. As the warrior reaches forward to check on the roasting meat, an arrow thumps into his chest, and he silently falls to his side, dead.

Within seconds of releasing the first arrow, Night Wind releases his second. He is not as lucky with the second arrow as he was with the first. His second intended victim, upon seeing his companion die from the first arrow, dives headlong for the rifle. The arrow catches him in the shoulder, embedding its steel tip in the bone. The Lakota screams in pain while making a valiant attempt to raise the rifle with his good arm. He is trying to pull back the hammer when the third arrow thumps into his chest to cut his scream short.

The tall warrior by the horses sprints back to dive behind Kicking Horse, knife in hand. He places his knife at his captive's throat and, not knowing where his enemy is, starts to scream out his challenge into the dark. Night Wind steps out of the shadows and approaches the fire. He strides toward the Lakota warrior, an arrow nocked ready on the bowstring. When it is clear that his enemy will cut Kicking Horse's throat if he comes any closer, Night Wind stops and sets the bow down near the fire. He draws his knife from his belt and challenges with a motion of his free hand for the Lakota to step forward and fight him.

As the Lakota springs forward with his knife in one hand and his war club in the other, Kicking Horse sweeps his tied legs to the side and trips the charging Lakota warrior. The warrior falls heavily and awkwardly on his chest and lets out a stifled moan. He makes a feeble attempt to rise, only to collapse back again to the ground.

Kicking Horse yells for Night Wind to kill him, but Night Wind approaches cautiously. He pushes on the Lakota's shoulder with his foot, getting no reaction. He then puts his foot under the prone man's shoulder and roughly rolls him over. The warrior is like the others—just a boy, a few years younger than Kicking Horse. It looks like when he tripped and fell, he landed on his knife, which is now protruding from his stomach.

"What are you waiting for?" Kicking Horse yells. "Kill him!"

"He is only a boy," Night Wind says as he cuts his friend's binding. "Where is the honor in killing him?"

"That bastard was ready to brain me with his war club," Kicking Horse replies. "Nits eventually grow into lice."

"Go get Thunder," Night Wind says as he finishes cutting his friend's bonds. "He's a little way up the trail. Make sure you talk to him first so he hears your voice. And don't try to lead him. He's had a bad day. Just let him loose, and he'll follow you on his own."

As Kicking Horse leaves, Night Wind kneels by the wounded youth's side. The boy's eyes are wild with pain, fear, and uncertainty. Night Wind reaches down and yanks the bloody knife from his gut. The young warrior does not cry out, but loses consciousness from the pain.

After cutting off the buckskin shirt from one of the dead Lakota, Night Wind uses it to tightly bind the boy's wound. When he pushes the boy's shirt aside, what he sees astonishes him. Hanging from the wounded youth's neck is a beaded leather medicine pouch. Night Wind grabs the leather pouch in one hand and examines it closely.

He retrieves his own beaded pouch from the cord around his neck—the pouch where he keeps the Peace Medallion—and holds it up next to the dying Lakota's pouch so that he can examine it by the firelight. Except for a slight difference in size, and a big difference in weight, the beaded designs on both pouches are identical. After returning the boy's pouch and dropping his own back inside his buckskin shirt, Night Wind hurriedly finishes binding the boy's wound.

"Why do you bother with that boy?" Kicking Horse asks as he returns to camp with Thunder following a short distance behind. "He is our enemy. I say we kill him now and take his hair before the other returns."

"Can you not see that they are all boys out on a hunt?" Night Wind asks. "I do not take pride in taking the lives of boys. I will wait here to see if this one lives through the night, then decide what I must do."

"What about the other one? He could be—"

"You need not concern yourself about the other one," Night Wind interrupts. "Thunder broke his leg. Anyway, he is even younger than these boys. You may go or you may stay—as you wish."

"I think your horse has more sense than you do," Kicking Horse answers. "I cannot forget that these so-called boys were taking me back as Lakota warriors, not as boys. I still say you should kill him now and take his hair. He will not live through the night, anyway. Besides, we don't know where their village is. Their own warriors may be out searching for these boys as we speak."

"Maybe you should run away then," Night Wind responds angrily. "And you will not take their hair. I killed them, not you, and I say they will not be scalped. You seem to forget that if you had not foolishly gone into their camp, and had instead followed our plan, we would be riding into our own village now with two new horses. Instead, I had to rescue my impulsive friend from the four young boys that captured him. Like

I said before, I do not like fighting boys, and you will not scalp them. It is beneath us as warriors. I will stay until morning to see if this one lives or dies."

"You are right, brother," Kicking Horse replies. "I owe you my life. I will wait with you until morning's light. Come, let us see your new horses."

With the coming of dawn, light filters down through the canopy to the forest floor. Night Wind is still at the wounded boy's side when Kicking Horse awakens. Night Wind has moved the wounded boy over next to the fire and wrapped him in a buffalo robe. While keeping the fire burning, he has tended to his enemy's wound throughout the night. First, he heated his Hudson Bay knife in the coals and used it to cauterize the unconscious boy's open wound. The boy's body jerked as he did so, but luckily, the youth did not awaken.

At first, it appeared that the wounded youth's spirit flickered between life and death. But as the night passed, the young warrior's pulse and breathing grew stronger, and now the Lakota youth is sleeping quietly. As Kicking Horse approaches, Night Wind offers his companion some roasted meat from the fire.

"I don't know why my brother bothers with this enemy. Even if he does live, he will still face the agony of torture when we return to our village. The same fate I would have suffered, had they brought me to their village. For his sake, it would be better to kill him now." Kicking Horse turns away to start packing any weapons or robes of value onto one of the Lakota horses.

Night Wind walks over to stand beside Kicking Horse. "That is why we must leave the boy here with one of the horses," he says to his friend. "We will also leave him with some meat and water. He has lived through the night and seems to be regaining some of his strength and may yet live. His life's spirit is strong. It is now up to the Great Spirit, Akbaatatdía, to decide both of their fates between living or dying."

Kicking Horse sighs but does not argue.

"You were right last night when you said we should ride quickly," Night Wind says. "We must avoid other warriors out looking for these boys. Only now I hope they find them before it is too late."

When the two young warriors return to their village four days later, leading two Lakota horses, there is much rejoicing. Many have been speculating that the worst has happened. Few seem to have believed that the two young men would ever return.

That night, Red Knife, Chimalis, and their friends gather together in front of Red Knife's tepee to feast and honor the promising young warriors. Night Wind has decided not to attend, preferring instead to sit alone by the river and think. He doesn't get much time to himself before Red Knife quietly approaches and sits down beside him.

"You should come and join us," Red Knife says. "After all, the celebration is being held in your honor. It is not often that a warrior defeats four Lakota. Chimalis and I are proud of your great victory."

"I do not feel honor in killing young boys who were just out on a hunt in their own lands," Night Wind says. "They were not looking for trouble. I feel something, yes, but it is not honor. More like anger and shame. Kicking Horse's stupidity brought this trouble upon us and cost these boys their lives. Now our people will only have more trouble with our enemy to the North."

"The Apsáalooke and the Lakota have been enemies for generations," Red Knife explains. "You are mistaken if you think your actions have brought any new dangers upon our people that they did not already have. Besides, if we didn't have worthy enemies, how would our young men prove their valor and their bravery? Only the weak love their enemy. Our greatness can only be measured by the greatness of our enemies. I am giving this celebration feast in your honor. Do not embarrass me with your absence."

"I will do as you wish, Father. As always, my wish is to make you proud and walk the warrior's path in your footsteps."

Red Knife stands and turns to walk back up to the festivities. Night Wind smiles and moves forward to stride beside his father. When they reach the celebration, bonfires are burning and people are eating from various dishes. It seems that everyone has pitched in and brought a favorite food. Warriors and young men step forward to greet and congratulate Night Wind on his accomplishments.

Kicking Horse is also surrounded by a number of young warriors. He is obviously relating his version of the past few days. As Night Wind approaches the gathering, Kicking Horse steps over to his friend. After placing a hand on Night Wind's shoulder, he lets out a loud war cry, Aiee!" The crowd begins to gather in closer as Kicking Horse whoops it up around his friend.

Red Knife steps forward and raises his hands for quiet. When the shouting quiets down, he addresses the gathering. "We, Red Knife and Chimalis, have given this celebration in honor of our son, Night Wind. His cunning and bravery have saved the life of a fellow warrior brother and brought much honor on himself.

"Once again, Night Wind, as his name implies, has had a chilling effect with his strength and determination. This time the chill fell upon our Lakota enemies." He turns to Night Wind. "You have proven yourself a warrior. You have demonstrated bravery, determination, and cunning, all without cruelty. As such, you now shall have your own tepee." Red Knife turns back to Chimalis, and she hands him two eagle feathers. With pride on his face, he affixes the two eagle feathers into his son's hair. "Night Wind, I present these feathers as one warrior to another. Wear these symbols of a warrior with pride, my son."

Then Chimalis steps past Red Knife to stand before her adopted son. She pulls from the doeskin pouch at her waist a beautifully beaded bear claw necklace, which she places over Night Wind's head. "My son, for many years now, I have saved these claws from the silver-tip bears you killed while saving my life. I have been waiting for the proper moment when you would again demonstrate such bravery and become a true warrior of the Apsáalooke. You now have done so, and I am proud to call you my son."

The gathered group of friends and warriors shout and whoop in their approval. Night Wind looks from Chimalis back to Red Knife and then raises his hand to speak. "My mother and father do me great honor, as I honor them in turn. Red Knife, my father, brings me honor first with my name and now with these eagle feathers." He turns to Chimalis. "I will always treasure the bear claw necklace from Chimalis, my mother. I am proud to be a member of the Apsáalooke." He pauses and looks at Kicking Horse. "My heart rejoices in being able to help in my friend's escape. However, I do not feel honor in the killing of these Lakota boys. It is beneath a warrior to acknowledge such feats as bravery. Therefore, I give away the captured horses and weapons and will not wear the eagle feathers until such time as I have truly earned the right in battle."

Night Wind reaches up and removes the two eagle feathers from his hair. He will not wear them, but he will not discard them, either. Night Wind then turns and walks away from the celebration. The friends that have gathered are left to discuss the surprising turn of events among themselves.

Standing Lance is among the gathered guests who hear Night Wind's words. As Night Wind walks past the old chief, he turns to glance back at Standing Lance and sees the old warrior watching him with a confused expression. Night Wind hopes that his sense of honor did not ruin any chance he has with Burning Moon.

CHAPTER  TWENTY FIVE

Along the footpath by the little stream, Night Wind carries the heavy buck across his shoulders. The early morning stillness is suddenly broken by the nearby sound of girls' laughter. Night Wind is well aware of the small pool below the little waterfall a short distance ahead. He often bathes there himself, but this is the first time he has heard girls there.

Drawn to the sounds of their giggles, Night Wind stops at the top of the waterfall and gazes down at the girls below. Three young women are kneeling along the edge of the pool, playfully laughing and splashing each other as they clean their faces and hands. Night Wind is pleased to see Burning Moon among them, doing most of the splashing. He has stumbled on the very girl that has been consuming his thoughts and twisting his heart into knots both day and night. She seems to be teasing and daring the other two with her giggling and playful splashing.

Then, to Night Wind's utter surprise, Burning Moon suddenly pulls her doeskin dress up over her head, flings it up on the grassy bank, and plunges into the cold water. All the while, she continues to splash the other two girls, daring them to join her.

Night Wind is mesmerized by what he sees. Of course, he has seen Chimalis naked many times over the past few years, but the sight has never made him feel like this. He knows that he should slip away and allow the girls their privacy, but he can't take his eyes off Burning Moon. He can't imagine how a girl's body could possibly be more beautiful.

The other two girls are moments away from joining Burning Moon in the pool, having removed their moccasins, when one of them sees

Night Wind standing above the falls. They react in startled fear, but quickly relax as they both recognize who the intruder is. With much giggling, they slip their moccasins back on and gather their bundles of firewood. After glancing back at their friend standing naked in the water, they giggle and chatter excitedly as they follow the path to the village.

Burning Moon looks confused by her friends' sudden change in expressions, and she turns to find the source of what startled them. When her gaze meets Night Wind's, she ducks down in the water to conceal her nakedness. But then she, too, seems to relax when she realizes who it is. "Must I get up before the sun in order to bathe without being spied upon?" she calls out.

"It was not my intention to spy on you, Burning Moon," Night Wind replies. "Though, now that I am here, I don't regret the view. I just watched the sunrise, and you are far more beautiful."

"I am surprised you even know my name. I was beginning to think you preferred boys."

"It is hard not to notice someone so lovely."

"That is very sweet, but you don't really expect me to believe you, do you?" Burning Moon blushes. "I bet you say that to all the naked girls you see."

"You are but the first naked girl of the day," he replies. "But the day is still young."

"How is it that you just happened to be walking in the woods at sunrise? That is pretty hard to believe."

"As to why I am here, you may believe what you wish, but the truth is that I was just returning from a night of hunting in the forest. As it is, you were the one I was seeking to speak with. I just didn't expect it to be such a nice opportunity."

"This water is cold. Perhaps you could turn your back so I could come out?"

Night Wind grins impishly. "But then I would miss a most beautiful view. The early morning views across the valley are often beyond words from here. Besides, have you not been trying to catch my eye this past year?"

"You have me at a disadvantage," Burning Moon says. "So I guess I have no choice. Could you at least come down and give me a hand? These rocks can be slippery."

His heart skipping, Night Wind hurries down the slope to the water's edge, where he drops the buck from his shoulders and sets the bow and quiver down next to it. He steps forward and extends his hand to Burning Moon. She clasps his wrist with both hands and jerks backward, pushing off from the rock bank.

Night Wind loses his balance and falls forward into the pool with a splash. Burning Moon climbs out of the pool and quickly pulls her dress over her head. She picks up a couple of small rocks and flings them at Night Wind, striking him on the shoulder with one. Then, leaving her bundle of wood where it lies, she turns and hurries off with her moccasins in hand.

Night Wind pulls himself out from the water. He picks up his weapons and her bundle of wood and, hoping to get in front of her, darts off into the forest. He sneaks past her through the forest and waits along the path behind a large fir tree.

When he spies her coming up the trail, he is about to step out, but Burning Moon suddenly stops and turns to look back. After a few moments, she audibly sighs, pulls on her moccasins, and turns to continue along the path.

As she comes to the fir tree, Night Wind steps out in front of her, dropping the bundle of wood at her feet. He startles her, and she moves to strike him on the chest.

He catches her wrists. "You should be more grateful to someone who carries your wood," he says. "That wasn't a very nice trick you played on me back at the falls."

"I thought you wanted a closer look." Burning Moon looks as if she is stifling a giggle. "Did you enjoy your bath?"

"No, but the view was indeed stunning." Night Wind's face grows hot despite his soaking wet buckskins. "I truly did plan on talking with you, though. That is, if you are not in too much of a hurry."

She looks down at her wrists and answers softly. "It seems I have no choice, since I am being held against my will."

"I am sorry," Night Wind says, releasing her wrists. "You are by no means a captive. I have never been very good when it comes to girls." He studies her face. "I was really hoping I could see more of you."

Laughing, Burning Moon replies sarcastically, "I don't think there's much more to see."

Night Wind, hurt by this remark, starts to turn away.

"But I would like that," she blurts out, setting a hand on his arm. "I would like to see you too. I will speak with my grandfather."

She squeezes his arm, smiles, and picks up her bundle of wood. She then steps past him on the trail back to the village, and he turns to watch her go. She glances back and smiles before continuing on her way. When she turns away again, he punches the air in his excitement. Talking with any girl has always made him uneasy, but Burning Moon has somehow been different. He turns and heads back to retrieve his buck at the waterfall.

He remembers Red Knife's words about how a man can count all of his life-changing events on the fingers of one hand. Night Wind has thought about his life-changing days quite often, and he hopes that today might be one of those days. He also thinks that he may be switching to his second hand very shortly.

After swinging the buck back onto his shoulders, Night Wind wonders what Burning Moon's grandfather might say. He has noticed the strange looks the old chief has thrown his way, and how Standing Lance always seems to be watching him. Now it seems that Burning Moon's grandfather may very well decide his fate.

It is late the next morning when Burning Moon steps from behind a nearby tepee and catches Night Wind's eye. She smiles in his direction and nods vigorously. She vanishes as suddenly as she appeared, but Night Wind could not be more pleased. He takes a deep breath as a smile spreads across his face.

The early afternoon sun sparkles on the slow flowing river. Burning Moon is beating some buckskins on the rocks along the water's edge as Night Wind sits watching her from a log by the bank.

"My grandfather tells me you are different," Burning Moon says over her shoulder. "He warns me that I shouldn't put too much hope in a relationship between us."

"I will have to prove him wrong then," he replies. "Standing Lance is a traditionalist. I think my white skin frightens him."

"He did tell me he worries that if it comes down to having to choose between the whites and the Apsáalooke, you will have difficulty."

"Yes, I have thought of that. Thought about that a lot, actually. But I now consider myself a member of the River band of the Apsáalooke. I think the question would more likely come down to a choice between right or wrong."

"Grandfather also wonders why you spend so many nights out alone in the forest."

After taking time to organize his thoughts, Night Wind finally replies. "I want to speak true with Burning Moon. I only ask that my words stay with her." He throws a couple of rocks into the river. "My heart is deeply troubled, for I carry many heavy burdens. I often feel the need to be alone, to find myself. I prefer to think my torments through in solitude. It sometimes feels as if I am caught in a snare, knowing my fate and yet helpless to avoid it. The sight of simple things, even tepees or arrows, sometimes seem to overwhelm me. I don't expect you to understand because I don't truly understand myself."

"Grandfather stills cautions me you are not truly Apsáalooke," Burning Moon says as she pounds the buckskins against the rocks. "You do not take scalps, nor follow the customs of our people."

"Red Knife and Chimalis have always been good to me. I honor and respect them. But even though I want to please them with all my heart, I still see a white man when I look at my reflection. I see a white man with green eyes and red hair."

Burning Moon steps away from the washing rock and moves to stand beside Night Wind. "A man cannot choose how he is to be born. The Apsáalooke judge a man not by his skin, but by his deeds. You have shown through your actions that you have a true and brave heart."

"I have never told this to anyone," he says through an intense stare. "Not even Chimalis." He sighs and looks out over the river. "My white mother, brother, and grandparents were all killed by Indians. My little sister was taken, and she died from a fever in a Dakota village, far to the East. Indians may even have killed my father, though Chimalis would have me believe that my uncle did. But I truly believe they all died as a result of my actions, and I have carried that burden with me for many years."

"I do not understand. Explain this burden that lies so heavy on your shoulders. If Indians did this deed, how could the blame be yours?"

"Not even my true father knew, but I accidentally killed a young Indian warrior when I was out hunting with my grandfather." Night Wind shakes his head mournfully. "It seems like such a long time ago now. I must have been only ten or eleven summers. Grandfather took the young warrior's bow. It is the same bow I use today. My grandfather and uncle both called it a Spirit Bow. I did not believe in the bow's spirits at first, but I do now. I believe the bow's spirits have guided my actions throughout my long anguish. It has guided my spirits to help the Indians—not just the Apsáalooke, but all Indians. Do I dishonor my family's memory now by wanting to live as an Indian? To be an Apsáalooke warrior?" Night Wind's eyes begin to tear up.

"If your parents' hearts were as good as yours," Burning Moon replies, "then I think they would simply wish for your happiness. You must move away from the past. Let it go. The future is just beyond the next sunrise. You need to look forward to a better, brighter future, not live in the darkness of the past. I say let your bow's spirits guide you, for it is a blessing."

"But my burden is even greater," Night Wind responds, "for now I believe I have found Red Knife's long-lost son. I think he was the wounded Lakota I spared. I do not know whether he has lived or died, but he wore Red Knife's beaded design on his medicine pouch."

"How can you be certain? The Lakota boy may have simply taken it or been given it by Red Knife's true son." Burning Moon places a hand on Night Wind's shoulder. "Have you spoken of this with your father?"

"No, I have not told Red Knife," Night Wind answers. "At this time, I must not, for he would once again take up the lance and knife. For the vision the spirits have shown me, I cannot allow this to happen. But the bow's spirits have told me that it is his true son. I have left the Lakota boy a message, something to open his mind in the direction of the truth. If he has survived his wound, he may reach the same conclusion. For now, I must let the future play itself out to the will of the Great Spirit."

"For your sake, I hope this happens sooner rather than later," Burning Moon says.

"For now, though," he says, taking her by the hands, "you have given me a new reason to look forward to the future. I will prove to Standing Lance that I am a good match for his granddaughter. Then we will have a great feast at the summer gatherings to celebrate our joining."

Burning Moon steps closer and squeezes his hands. "Even as a young girl, when you rode into my life, I knew that you would be the only man for me. You do not have to prove anything to my grandfather, only to me. What's meant to be will always find a way, for it has been that way for all eternity."

Overwhelmed by her words and his feelings for her, Night Wind draws her closer and wraps her tightly in his arms. He lowers his head, and their foreheads touch. After a moment, she turns her head up. Their lips touch, and they tenderly kiss for the first time.

The kiss quickly becomes one of passion and desire as she returns his embrace in kind. Finally, they break their kiss and embrace a moment longer, looking into each other's eyes. As they step apart, Burning Moon turns to gather her wash. They slowly walk side by side back up to the village.

That night, Night Wind sits before the fire outside Standing Lance's tepee while Burning Moon absently stirs the coals with a long stick. Night Wind is deep in thought as he stares into the flames.

"Do you remember your white family's faces?" she asks him. Before he can respond, she adds, "It is sad, but I can't remember my mother's face. My grandmother, Moon Shadow, says she was very pretty. She died in childbirth, along with my baby brother. That was a long time ago. Moon Shadow says I was just four summers old when they died. All I remember of my mother is that she had a kind, soft way of speaking."

"I remember my family," Night Wind answers. "My mother was always cleaning me up after a fight. I was always fighting because I was teased a lot by the other boys. They made fun of me because of my red hair and freckles, and because I am Irish. They especially teased me about being so small for my age." He slowly nods his head as he thinks back. "I miss my older brother, Jake, the most. He was always there defending me when I needed it."

"It's hard to believe you were ever small," she says. Then she scrunches up her nose. "What is Irish?"

Night Wind smiles. "Irish people come from Ireland. Ireland is an island that lies across a wide water, far, far toward the rising sun. My family was Irish, and some people just don't like new people coming to their land."

"We don't like the Lakota or Blackfeet coming onto our lands," Burning Moon says matter-of-factly. "You must have been lucky the other white tribes didn't kill you. Maybe since the white tribes allow the red-haired Irish tribe to live with them in peace, they will allow the black-haired tribe of the Apsáalooke to do so as well."

Night Wind smiles at her reasoning.

"Why does Chimalis say your white father was killed by your uncle?" Burning Moon asks. "A brother does not kill a brother."

He stares at the fire for a while before answering. "My uncle is a bad man—a man filled with hate—a fur trapper called Hatchet Jack. He was actually my father's step-brother." He looks from the fire to Burning

220

Moon. "Chimalis told me she saw my uncle kneeling by my father's body, holding my father's scalp in his hands. She also claims that she later saw the same scalp with my uncle's belongings." He takes a deep breath and sighs before continuing. "Chimalis is a good woman, but she had good reason to hate my uncle. The night was dark and stormy. Maybe what she saw has another explanation. That is one of the mysteries that troubles me."

"Do you know if this Hatchet Jack still lives?"

"I am sure he does. An old trapper claims he may have gone to Oregon, and that he is still looking for Chimalis and me. My spirits also tell me he lives, for his face has tormented my dreams too many times."

"Do your dreams show you any answers to what troubles you?"

"My dreams are very confusing. They only tell me that Hatchet Jack and I will meet again. They have never shown me how or where this meeting will take place." He feels uncomfortable thinking about his dreams of his uncle and changes the subject. "Tell me. Do you remember your father?"

"No, not really," Burning Moon says softly. "I only remember that he was very serious. I feel sad not being able to remember my father and mother. I have been told that my father never got over my mother's death. He started taking unnecessary chances in his encounters with the Lakota. When I was seven summers, he rode out of camp and never returned. Grandfather is certain that he died a brave warrior." She sighs deeply. "My grandparents raised me after my mother and father died. I do remember my father's feather headdress. Grandfather once showed it to me. I think he still has it somewhere." After pausing a moment, she says, "My father counted many coups and earned many eagle feathers."

"I sometimes dream about my white father," Night Wind says. "He was a big man, a kind man. Above all, I remember that he was an honorable man. In my dreams, I can see his red hair, but his face is always blurry. I try to picture his face when I wake up, but I can no longer remember it."

They sit quietly by the fire for a long time.

"You said you had reckles," Burning Moon says finally, looking like she is having trouble pronouncing the white man's word. "What are reckles? Is it some kind of white man's disease I should be afraid of?"

"I said I had freckles," Night Wind corrects with a laugh. "White men with red hair sometimes have little dots on their body called freckles. It is not a disease. My little sister had them too. They go away as you get older. I still have a few on my back."

"I have seen these freckles once, before you came to our village," Burning Moon states. "A woman from another band had a baby with spots. I do not remember the baby having any hair, though. The elders said the baby must have been left outside under the stars too long, and the stars burned his skin. Were you burned by the stars? Is that why you always keep your shirt on?"

Before he can answer, Moon Shadow calls for her granddaughter from the tepee flap.

"I must go now. Grandmother is old and needs my help in preparing the evening meal. Will I see you in the morning?"

"I hope you see me in your dreams. I certainly will search for you in mine."

Burning Moon gives him a smile and rises to go. He watches her as she turns and ducks through the tepee flap.

CHAPTER TWENTY SIX

Wrapped in his grizzly bear robe, Night Wind sits under a large pine tree. He has once again retreated to the sanctuary of the mountain forest to clear his head and think. As he has so many times before, he holds Becky's indigo bonnet and carved doll head in his hands. Below him, the valley is shrouded in mist. He glances over at the moon, which hangs lazily just above the horizon. Its faint light dims as an evening mist begins to rise, bathing the surrounding trees in silvery shadow.

Nearby, an inquisitive owl questions the night. Another night bird calls out in reply from deep within the forest. Night Wind immediately takes notice and sits up, questioning the night's stillness and concentrating hard on the surrounding darkness. In his mind, something is wrong. He stuffs the bonnet back inside his shirt and the small head in his leather bag. The forest sounds that he has become so finely attuned to are different. That last call he heard was entirely wrong. Burrowing owls live out on the prairie, not in the forest. His senses tell him that an enemy may be close. Either that or somebody is playing a joke on him.

He hears the soft crack of a small branch nearby and focuses all of his attention in that direction. *That sounded close.*

After quietly gathering his bow and quiver, Night Wind moves deeper into the forest's shadows. His movements are like the mist itself as he glides silently through the trees, just a shadow lost in the gloom.

Night Wind stops beside a large tree, sensing that he is nearing the source of the mysterious sound. He stands quietly for a long time, all of his senses focused on the forest around him. He can smell horses nearby but can't clearly pinpoint their location. Suddenly, he hears a soft whinny a little off to his left. He moves two trees closer. Around the trunk and down into a small gully, he sees three shadows in the night. Two of the phantom warriors continue up the gully, leaving the third behind with the horses.

The warrior being left behind begins to whisper a protest directed at his two companions. One of the two turns and jerks his hand up for silence. The protesting man is left behind, rubbing the nose of one of the horses that is shifting restlessly. The young warrior does not seem aware of any immediate danger, as he is leaning against the head of the agitated animal in an effort to calm it.

The only sound Night Wind makes is the soft thud of the broken tree branch striking the side of the young warrior's head, knocking him unconscious. The warrior crumples to the ground as Night Wind steps past him to grab the reins of the horses he was holding.

"You should have listened to your horse," Night Wind whispers to the prone Lakota warrior. It takes him a few moments to calm the startled horses.

After binding the unconscious warrior's hands with a piece of rawhide cut from the reins, Night Wind picks the warrior up and throws him across the back of one of the horses. Next, he leads all three horses a short way back up the ravine before turning them up the slope to tether them in a new location. Once the horses are securely tethered, he moves off in a different direction in an attempt to intercept the other two Lakota warriors.

Night Wind knows that part of the village's vast herd of horses is grazing in a nearby mountain meadow, so he loses no time in making his way in that direction. He knows that Kicking Horse has sentry duty at some point tonight, and Night Wind hopes to arrive before the Lakota. He knows where the sentries are posted, so he quietly moves to the side of the herd from where the enemy warriors will most likely approach.

Night Wind spots the sentry's shadow-like outline leaning on his lance as he watches the horses. Some horses softly whinny, drawing the sentry's momentary attention. Night Wind watches as the sentry moves a couple of steps closer as if to ascertain the reason for the horses' uneasiness. After listening and watching for a few moments, the sentry turns and moves back under a tree. He picks up a skin robe and throws it across his shoulders before sitting down with his back against the tree trunk.

Night Wind continues to study the dark shadows of trees and brush around the sentry for any signs of movement. Suddenly, the shadow he originally thought was a bush in the gloom, moves a few paces closer to the sentry. Night Wind knows he must warn this sentry of the danger.

The soft hoot of a night owl breaks the stillness of the night, and the sentry takes note, sitting up straight. His robe drops from his shoulders. Again, Night Wind makes the hoot of the night owl. Drawing his knife, the sentry quietly rises to his feet. Night Wind watches as the sentry suddenly spots the Lakota warrior about to spring from the shadows.

With a loud war cry, the sentry turns to meet his challenge. Knife in hand, the Lakota warrior rushes forward out of the gloom. The sentry drops to his back at the last second, and with his foot, propels his charging adversary over his head to land hard on his back. Both men instantly spring to their feet. When the village comes to life with nearby shouts and dogs barking, the intruder turns and vanishes into the night.

The sentry regains his feet, looking undecided about whether to follow or stay as the first warriors run up from the village. The sentry points and shouts out, "Lakota," and the warriors turn to begin their pursuit. They hesitate about running into the darkness when a loud thump breaks the night's stillness.

By the time the other warriors reach him, Night Wind is standing like a shadow over the prone figure of a young Lakota warrior. He has just struck the boy in the head with a large branch. The warriors that have rushed from the village stand uneasy before him, as if they do not know whether he is friend or foe.

In the dim light, Night Wind identifies himself: "Night Wind, Apsáalooke."

The tension in the air releases, and the warriors gather closer.

"I was hoping to capture all three of the raiders," Night Wind explains, "but one is still out there." He points down the ravine. "He will head that way. That is where they left me their horses."

All but one of the Apsáalooke warriors takes off running in the direction Night Wind indicated. The remaining warrior turns to face Night Wind.

"That is the third life I owe my friend," Kicking Horse says. "This Lakota would have killed me if you had not given the hoot owl warning. What will I do when you are not there to save me?"

"You are an Apsáalooke warrior," Night Wind states. "Why do you think your enemy is so superior? You are still young and learning, but your enemy is just a man." He lifts his chin in the direction of the unconscious Lakota on the ground. "You see? He sleeps like any other man."

Kicking Horse nods in agreement.

"Come and help me bind him," Night Wind says. "Then we will gather their horses. I have hidden them in the forest with another sleeping Lakota."

The villagers have gathered at the end of the village nearest the horse herd. Everyone is loudly discussing the morning's excitement. Night Wind watches them turn as one, as he and Kicking Horse step into camp leading the three Lakota horses. Tied and draped over the backs of two of the horses are Night Wind's captives.

Upon arriving at the center of the village, Night Wind pulls the captives from the horses and drops them unceremoniously to the ground. Although one of the captives lands on his back, he quickly regains his feet to stand glaring at his enemies. The other lies as he has fallen, still unconscious.

For the first time, Night Wind gets a look at the young captive defiantly standing before him in the morning light. He steps closer to get a better look. The captive stands taller and holds his head high as Night Wind studies his features. Night Wind pushes aside the warrior's buckskin shirt to reveal a recently healed scar visible on the front side of the Lakota's stomach.

The captive's eyes get a little wider when Night Wind looks at the scar. Night Wind abruptly turns and walks away. The last thing he sees before he departs is two warriors stepping forward to force the prisoner back to the ground beside his unconscious companion. Even as he strides off, Night Wind hears war cries and shouts as another group of jubilant warriors return to the village. High on a lance point, hangs the scalp of the third Lakota raider. The villagers crowd around the returning warriors and join in their triumphant yells.

Drums beat, and the roar of the village celebration carries into Night Wind's tepee. He stares into a small fire, deep in thought. He hears a scratch and low clearing of the throat outside the tepee flap, and he beckons the visitor to enter. Red Knife ducks through the flap and sits across the fire from his son. Night Wind nods solemnly at his father.

"The village speaks of your whereabouts," Red Knife tells his son. "You should come and join in the celebration. The prisoners have been made ready to be tested."

"They must not!" Night Wind shouts as he jumps to his feet and exits the tepee. He pushes his way through the shouting throng of warriors and onlookers to the Lakota prisoners. They have been stripped down to their breechcloths and tied to upright stakes. Night Wind sees that they are bleeding from a few small cuts where some of the women have already started to torment them.

The conscious captive breathes deeply, but still stands defiantly when Night Wind approaches. His companion is still only semiconscious as he sags against his bindings.

Night Wind steps to the front of the two Lakota and turns to speak loudly. "These men are my prisoners. They will not be tortured without my say-so. There has been too much bloodletting between the Apsáalooke and the Lakota."

The stunned crowd falls quiet at his words, only to erupt moments later in shouts of protest and disapproval. They have gathered to see the hated Lakota suffer and die—and hopefully begging in the end. Now it seems it will not be, as Night Wind steps forward with his knife and slashes the rawhide bindings holding the prisoners' arms above their heads. He leaves their wrists bound securely.

After indicating for the prisoners to follow him, Night Wind turns, picks up their discarded buckskin clothing, and leads them back to his tepee. The surprised captives follow him, one helping the other stumble through the shocked villagers. On the way, Night Wind stops in front of Standing Lance and speaks a moment with him.

When Night Wind ducks back into his tepee, he is followed by Standing Lance, the two Lakota captives, Kicking Horse, and Red Knife. When they are all seated, Night Wind offers the captives some water from a wooden cup. The semiconscious one readily drinks when the cup is put to his lips. The defiant one turns his head away.

"I do not understand what my son does," Red Knife says. "Does he wish the other warriors to follow his lead or turn their backs on him?"

"I am glad that my father, Red Knife, is here," Night Wind says. "I thank Standing Lance and Kicking Horse for their presence as well. Standing Lance's wisdom is well known. You three can assist me in my talks here with the Lakota." After a pause, Night Wind continues. "In response to my father's question, I do not seek to lead the Apsáalooke's warriors. I do not choose the path of war, for I must answer to my own spirits first." Night Wind pauses and looks to Red Knife. "In this, you may think you have failed in your teachings, Father. You have killed many of our enemy, so I ask you now, do you think they all needed killing? When will the killing stop?" After turning to look at Standing Lance and then back at his father, Night Wind asks, "You both have made war all your lives. What do you have to show for it?"

Red Knife looks surprised by his son's questions, and he seems to consider his answer carefully. "At one time, when the Lakota took my son, I thought it necessary to kill all of our enemies. Then I grew tired of the killing. I did not recognize the man I had become. But we alone cannot change the customs of our people. The Lakota and the

Apsáalooke have been sworn enemies from before the time of my grandfather's grandfather. I think my son asks too much. What would you have us do?"

"My spirits have been guiding me for many moons," Night Wind says. "Only now do I understand their direction. Last night, I had the vision again, as I have had many times before. This time, it was very clear to me as I contemplated this vision for a long time. I finally realized that it all comes down to one question. Are we more like our Indian enemies or more like the white man?" He looked at all those seated. "If we do not stop the needless killing of our Indian brothers, then our way of life will not survive the coming of the white man. While we fight and kill each other, the white man will overrun us. They will take our hunting grounds, kill our buffalo, and then kill our people. When we finally realize what is happening, it will be too late. That is the vision my spirits have been showing me."

Standing Lance turns to Night Wind. "Visions can be sacred. But they can also be misleading if one does not interpret them correctly. Why is Night Wind so sure of this vision?"

Pointing to the young warrior sitting across from him, Night Wind answers, "Because I see the face of this Lakota warrior in all of my visions. He may be the key to peace between our people. I am sure that if the Indians continue to fight among themselves, we will be sealing our own fate. I come from the white man's land, and I cannot begin to tell you of their numbers. None of you would believe me."

"I have heard the whites are as numerous as the stars in the sky," Red Knife says.

"That is where my father is wrong," Night Wind says. "The whites are easily as many as the stars. The whites are more like the blades of grass on the prairie." He pauses to let his words sink in before continuing. "If you can find truth in my words, perhaps my father and Standing Lance can better understand what worries me. Our future is playing out before us, and we still fight among ourselves. I need your help in trying to make the Lakota understand my concerns."

Standing Lance does not seem convinced. "Night Wind's view of the white man must be wrong. They would not be able to hunt enough meat to fill their bellies."

"I wish my chief was correct. But my view of the white man is not wrong. They do not hunt their meat, but grow it. This story is for another time. Will you help me speak with the Lakota captives? My vision shows me that it is only a short breath of time before the Indian tribes will be pushed from their land. It has been that way everywhere the white man has gone."

Red Knife and Standing Lance both nod their agreement. Night Wind has seen how Standing Lance knows a little of the Lakota language and will be able to assist him in talking to the captives.

After turning to the Lakota, Red Knife signs quick introductions of those present.

The Lakota warrior indicates that his name is Broken Horn and his companion is Eagle Eye. Speaking half in Lakota and half signing, Broken Horn explains, "I have seen Red Knife fight before. He is well known to my people as a shadow that kills in the night. Why does Night Wind save my life? How does he know of my wound?"

Night Wind nods solemnly. "I have saved Broken Horn's life before, when he and his companions captured my friend here, Kicking Horse. It was not my desire to kill Broken Horn's companions, but I had to save my friend. I did not kill Broken Horn because I find no honor in killing." He pauses, then adds, "I know you speak our tongue. Why do you not do so now?"

Red Knife, Standing Lance, and Kicking Horse all look at Night Wind and then at one another with this revelation.

With anger burning in his eyes, Broken Horn says in Apsáalooke, "Your friend here was caught trying to steal our horses. You killed my older brother that night. Why do you not let your women kill us?"

"As Broken Horn well knows," Night Wind replies, "I also spared him and one of his young companions that night. I do not feel the need to kill, especially one so young. I spare your lives today because I need your help. I wish you to carry a message to the Lakota people. You have just heard me speak of my vision. It is a vision in which you play a large part. I truly believe that the Great Spirit has sent you to me as his messenger."

"I thank you for sparing my younger brother's life," Broken Horn says. "He walks with a limp, but at least he still walks. Our warriors could not understand the meaning of this thing. They think it must have been some sort of Crow trick." Broken Horn then says loudly, "Maybe it was a trick! Maybe the Crow fear the Lakota? Maybe they wish to change their enemies into friends with their sweet words and then kill them. But the Lakota do not fear the Crow, nor do they fear the white men. We have killed many whites that have come into our lands uninvited."

As Broken Horn rants, Night Wind remains still. When the captive finally grows quiet, Night Wind calmly states, "I am white. The whites have people beyond number. I have seen them, and I have seen their cities. While we fight among ourselves, the whites are beginning to move across the buffalo grass to the place they call Oregon Country. When the land runs out there, and all the Indians there are dead, the whites will return to the lands of the Apsáalooke and Lakota. Unless we stand together, we will be no match. One bee cannot drive away the badger raiding the hive, but a swarm of angry bees can make the badger look elsewhere."

"We have seen the white wagons to the South," Broken Horn replies. "They are not a threat. They fear us when we draw near. The Lakota do not need the help of the thieving Crow. We can fight our own battles, as we have done since the beginning. Why should I trust the words of my enemy? Your vision, too, is probably just a trick."

Red Knife turns to his son. "He does not believe you. Perhaps I should kill him now."

Calmly, Night Wind addresses his father. "It is hard to gain the trust of one's enemy. I understand that this will take time." He turns back to Broken Horn. "I have already spared your life two times now. This will make the third life I return to you. Because of this alone, you should give my message some serious thought and carry it back to the Lakota elders. My words are not a trick. A brother does not lie to a brother."

Red Knife looks over at his son, clearly confused. "How can you call our enemy your brother?"

From inside his shirt, Night Wind produces the beaded medicine pouch with the sign of Red Knife. He hands it to his father.

Red Knife looks at his son with a questioning frown. "I gave this to you years ago, when you became my son."

Night Wind nods in Broken Horn's direction. Broken Horn is staring at the pouch with astonishment. From the edge of the tepee, Night Wind picks up Broken Horn's buckskin shirt and belongings. After looking through them, he locates the beaded medicine pouch he saw earlier. He tosses it to his father. "As you can see, they are the same. We are both sons of Red Knife. Broken Horn is your lost son. Do you not recognize him?"

Red Knife looks shocked as he stares over at Broken Horn. He slowly rises to step over to the Lakota captive. After examining Broken Horn's face a moment longer, he lifts the young warrior's hair from behind his left ear. Night Wind can see the scar by the young warrior's ear, and he can see Red Knife's eyes begin to moisten as well.

"Black Bear, my son," Red Knife says in a voice just above a whisper.

In Lakota, Broken Horn says unconvincingly, "I am Broken Horn." Then, weakly he adds, "My . . . father . . . is . . . Shining Light of the . . ."

Eagle Eye, who has looked confused during the past few minutes of the conversation, suddenly rises to his feet. He angrily asks a question of Broken Horn in Lakota.

Broken Horn shouts something back and Eagle Eye slumps back down. Broken Horn then stares at Red Knife and then questioningly looks to Night Wind. Red Knife sits down, looking overwhelmed. He lifts the medicine pouch from around his own neck and tosses it to Broken Horn so that the young warrior might study the design.

"Only a father would know of your scar," Night Wind says softly. "I did not know of it myself."

"But, the stories . . ." Broken Horn says weakly.

"Stories are but stories. Remember the fight at the river we now call Dead Horse Creek? Red Knife proved to you then that he is a great warrior, a warrior with honor. Your eyes do not lie. If I can shoot the stone point off of your lance, do you not think I could have easily killed you? And ask yourself, how do you speak the Apsáalooke language?"

"Broken Horn was the second warrior that challenged me?" Red Knife asks.

"Yes, the one I would not shoot," Night Wind says. "He was also the warrior who captured Kicking Horse. That is where he received the scar on his side. I sat with him through the night and tended his wound. That is when I found the medicine pouch. The Great Spirit did not call him home that night, even though he was gravely wounded. Akbaatatdía clearly had other plans for him." Night Wind pauses, slowly shaking his head. "The spirits have been putting us together for a reason. That is what I have been trying to explain. That is my vision."

"Why did you not return my son to me then?" Red Knife asks.

"Father, you have taught me that when a decision is made, it must be kept. Even if it is against a brother. The truth takes time. Broken Horn was not ready yet. The medicine pouch planted the seed, but the seed needed time to sprout."

Rising, Red Knife steps over to Broken Horn and cuts the bindings on his wrists. He indicates for Broken Horn to follow, and he ducks out through the tepee flap. The others look at each other, then rise to follow. Only Eagle Eye is left behind. Many of the villagers have gathered around the tepee, talking quietly among themselves. Everyone looks curious about the progress of the talks.

Perhaps now they will learn, Night Wind thinks.

The gathered crowd grows quiet when Red Knife raises his hands to speak. "It is a day for great rejoicing. My long-lost son, Black Bear, has returned. Night Wind has found Black Bear!"

In stunned silence, the villagers stare at the Lakota captive standing beside Red Knife. Finally, one warrior lets out a shout, which is quickly picked up and followed by other shouts of excitement. A few of the elders step forward to welcome Black Bear. Then Red Knife motions for his two sons to step back inside the tepee. Standing Lance and Kicking Horse duck back in, as well, and they all sit again.

Eagle Eye is still bound, and Broken Horn asks his father if he may have his friend's bonds cut. Red Knife assents with a nod of his head and hands Broken Horn a knife.

After Eagle Eye's bonds are severed, he sits there in clear confusion and rubs his wrists and sore head. He looks questioningly at Broken Horn.

"It seems I am destined to be both Lakota and Apsáalooke," Broken Horn replies in both languages. "Destined to live two lives with both tribes."

"My brother," Night Wind says to Broken Horn, "I am glad that the Great Spirit has led us to each other. I know that our father has searched long and hard for you for many years, and that he has greatly mourned your loss. Akbaatatdía led Red Knife to find Chimalis and me when we were lost and had little hope. He then crisscrossed Broken Horn and my paths until we found the truth. But now our greatest challenge still lies before us.

"Broken Horn, will you join me in seeking peace between our peoples? Only then can the tribes stand united and strong enough to resist the white men when they come. Together our tribes would be a force of strength in our dealings with the whites. If the Lakota elders would like to talk about peace between our people or about my vision, I would be honored to come and stand before them in their council lodge."

Broken Horn takes some time to explain to Eagle Eye what has happened and what is being asked of him.

Eagle Eye doesn't look convinced that this isn't some kind of trick. He asks Broken Horn another question.

Night Wind hears the doubt in Eagle Eye's question, but he doesn't wait for a translation before replying. "My brothers are the Apsáalooke. But they are also the Lakota, Cheyenne, and Shoshone. I am white in skin only. My heart and mind lie with the Indian."

Broken Horn translates Night Wind's words to his companion, who looks surprised and confused.

"We will speak to our council and share your vision," Broken Horn says. "Since you have given us the gift of life, they will consider your vision and words carefully. Your words are strange to our ears, there meaning distant, but I believe they come from the heart. Only time will tell if the seed will sprout." Broken Horn rises to his feet and turns to his father. "I will speak from my heart with my Lakota father." He clutches the medicine pouch tightly. "The spirits have cleared the mist from my mind, and I have seen the truth. I must become two men with two tribes and two families. If permitted, I will move between my people, both the Lakota and the Apsáalooke, for I cannot walk away from my Lakota family so easily. But I will return as Black Bear to learn from Red Knife, my Apsáalooke father, the ways and customs of the Apsáalooke. From this day forward, I will fight the Apsáalooke no more."

Night Wind feels his heart pound with pride as Red Knife rises and clasps his long-lost son's forearm.

"And I will fight the Lakota no more," Red Knife says. "Now I must take you to meet Chimalis, my woman. She will be overjoyed to learn that my son has returned."

Never in his life has Night Wind felt so thrilled about the prospect of what the future holds, nor as frightened.

CHAPTER TWENTY SEVEN

Night Wind takes in the sight of the River Crows' summer camp, which lies spread out along the banks of the Musselshell River. Three bands have gathered together for the annual buffalo drive at nearby Long Ridge.

Because of his exploits during the year, Night Wind has been selected to serve as this year's buffalo runner. This is an undeniable honor for such a young warrior, and he still can't quite believe it has fallen to him. But as the crowd watches from the ridge, he takes a deep breath and slings the buffalo robe over his shoulders. He sprints toward the herd, adjusting his course with each step so that he might judge the distance between the cliff and the herd perfectly.

His heart pounds in his chest as he nears the edge of the cliff. He knows if he arrives too early, the herd will not follow him over, and if they veer away from their fatal leap, he will be blamed for the hunt's failure. Of course, this kind of failure would be preferable to what will happen if he arrives too late and the herd plows him over the cliff to die with them.

The roar of the hooves gets louder as Night Wind closes the gap. Such is the deafening noise that he can hardly hear the cries of his fellow drivers charging from all sides with their fire sticks and waving robes meant to frighten the heard into panic. His lungs burn and his legs ache as he nears the edge, but like always, he presses on. He can feel the ground shake as the herd closes in behind him, their numbers in the dozens. They are following Night Wind's lead, who, in his buffalo skin robe, they have taken for one of their own.

His feet move swiftly across the prairie, never breaking stride even as they meet with the rocky ground just before the outcropping that signals the cliff's edge. At the last instant, Night Wind slides to his knees and paws at the stony surface even as he tumbles over the edge. There, just five feet below, is the rocky outcropping that will serve as his cover from the herds lumbering run overhead.

Night Wind slumps down for safety, pressing his body tightly against the cliff's face. In the dusty air he struggles to catch his breath. Moments later he watches as the herd, being pushed by those behind, leap out above him into emptiness and their death on the rocks far below. As the ground shakes, the deafening roar of hooves is only an arm's length above his head. By the time the last of the shaggy beasts passes overhead and all is silent, it is clear that the drive has been an overwhelming success.

Hours later, Night Wind strides proudly through the camp to take in the sights. The women are busy with their scrapers and knives as they flesh out the buffalo hides and cut the meat up for the drying racks. Night Wind smiles at how they laugh and chat with their friends as they work. Dogs run everywhere, fighting over the scraps of flesh and fat being tossed aside. The drying racks sag with heavy strips of buffalo meat, and Night Wind knows that the dancing and feasting will last far into the night.

Everywhere he goes, people offer their praise and their thanks for his crucial part in the drive's success. By the time the sun reaches its peak, Night Wind has been stuffed with choice pieces of meat and special dishes from all corners of the combined camps. Even when he holds up his hands and pats his stomach in polite refusal to their offerings, the villagers insist. The 180 tepees run along both sides of the river, and Night Wind still has the other side to visit. He fears that it is going to be a long afternoon.

Later that same day, with the shadows growing long, Night Wind turns to see a lone scout riding hard into the camp, shouting. His horse is lathered from exertion as Night Wind and a few other villagers gather to hear the scout's news. Among much loud talking, the scout gestures back toward the ridge from which he came. The villagers move around his horse and take a few steps in the direction the warrior points. Night Wind mounts Thunder and prepares to face whatever danger might come.

A short time later, down from the ridge strides a mountain man leading two packhorses. A pack of dogs runs out from the village to challenge the approaching stranger, barking and snarling. Resting at the ready across his arm, the trapper carries a Kentucky long rifle. Two pistols are tucked under his belt, along with a knife and a hatchet. He wears a patch over one eye. As he rides in, he is shouting out self-praises, as well as praises about the mighty Crow warriors.

He kicks a moccasin out at one of the snarling village dogs that is getting too close, striking it hard in the head. The dog gives a sharp yelp and cowers away. The rest of the dogs continue barking, but now keep a respectful distance from the stranger's foot.

When the mountain man reaches the center of the combined villages, the villagers crowd in closer, looking curious and excited to see what he has brought for trade. Other traders have come into their villages this year, but not for many moons.

Night Wind watches as the fur-covered man dismounts from his horse, his rifle still clutched in his arms. Night Wind wasn't entirely sure when he first saw the trader riding down the hill, but now he is certain. This is his uncle, Hatchet Jack.

The mountain man raises his left hand in greeting, then begins speaking in very broken Apsáalooke. "Greet, friends, River Crow of mighty Crow Nation. Look for great chief Standing Lance. My name Jack. Trade much with Crow friends."

Night Wind clenches his teeth, unsure of what to do.

Standing Lance steps forward from the group that now surrounds the trader. "I am Standing Lance, and I have heard of you. You are the mountain man some whites call Hatchet Jack."

"Many names," Jack replies, sounding hesitant. "Come far. Trade with Crow friends. Gift of firewater to big chief Standing Lance, and

Crow friends. Make strong." Jack turns to his packhorse and produces a pair of whiskey jugs.

"No, you keep crazy water," Standing Lance says. "You no cheat village with crazy water. I have seen warriors with many furs drink white man's crazy water. In morning, they wake up with no furs, no powder and shot, and no beads for their women. The only thing they have left are sick bellies and hurting heads. It would not be pleasant for Hatchet Jack if my warriors were to think bad thoughts of him in the morning."

"Suit yourself," Jack replies in English before he begins to unpack his trade goods from the packhorses and spread them out on the ground.

The villagers move in excitedly.

Night Wind whirls Thunder around and gallops back to his tepee to collect his animal pelts for trade. A short time later, he charges up at a gallop, taking a line directly at the trader. Hatchet Jack's hand moves down to one of the pistols at his belt. Night Wind abruptly pulls Thunder up at the last moment and throws a bundle of beaver, martin, and otter pelts at the feet of his uncle.

Ignoring the man he has been bartering with and not looking up, the mountain man kneels to examine the new pelts. Apparently satisfied by the fine quality of the furs, Hatchet Jack reaches over to the jug of whiskey. He offers it up to Night Wind, who marvels that his uncle seems to have mistaken him for just another Apsáalooke warrior.

"Good pelts here," Jack says. "Drink good whiskey. Then we talk trade."

Night Wind dismounts from Thunder and steps toward the trapper. Hatchet Jack sits and beckons with a hand for Night Wind to join him. Night Wind waves his hand to indicate that he will stand. He ignores the offered whiskey jug, and the trader shrugs and pulls it back.

Jack takes another drink before setting the jug down beside him. "I see strong warrior. Many fine furs. You need new scalping knife? Beads for woman?" Jack hands up a knife in Night Wind's direction. "Good knife—strong steel."

"I do not need knife," Night Wind answers. "I have a good knife." He pulls the Hudson Bay blade from his belt and holds it up for Jack to admire. "This was passed down to me from my father. A few trade beads do not interest me." After looking around at Jack's display laid out on the ground, Night Wind asks, "What else do you have in your packs to trade?"

"Have many scalps from fierce warriors." Jack reaches deep into a pack on one of his horses and pulls out a leather bag of scalps. Most of the scalps have long black hair, but two are light brown, one is blond, and another is reddish. "For furs, you choose five scalps. Good trophies for lance. Jack give your woman beads as gift."

"Only one of those scalps interests me, Uncle Jack!" Night Wind answers in English.

Hatchet Jack keeps his head down for a moment as if gathering his thoughts. As he slowly looks up to study Night Wind, he quickly stuffs the scalps back into the leather bag as if hoping the red one hasn't been noticed. He switches to English as he says, "This child'l be a boar grizz, if'n it ain't little Sean. Thought you'd gone under. And I'll be damned if'n ya haven't went an' gone all Injun like. This calls for a drink."

Jack takes a pull on the jug and offers it up to Night Wind, who knocks the jug from his uncle's hands. It crashes to the ground, spilling its contents. Night Wind continues to stand as he tests with his thumb the sharpness of the blade in his hands.

"Now that ain't very sociable like," Jack says with a bit of a snarl.

"Chimalis told me a story 'bout me uncle Jack that I found hard to swallow," Night Wind says, marveling at the sound of his own voice speaking English exactly as he had as a child. "The story was 'bout me pa an' his step-brother on a dark, stormy night out on the prairie."

"Chimalis? Chimalis! Was that the squaw's name? Sure was a panther under robes. 'Bout the only thing she could do better was lyin'. No telling what stories she's thought up to tell ya. Didn't exactly favor me none. Damn squaw never did know how good she had it. Whatever happened to that bitch?"

"Oh, Chimalis is still 'round 'bout. Maybe you should meet her man, Red Knife. He used to collect fingers from his enemies. Had a couple necklaces' worth before he grew weary, it bein' so easy an' all. I'm sure he'd like to speak with ya 'bout Chimalis. Should I call him, Uncle?"

Jack looks as if he is growing more nervous by the moment. "Now, boy, listen 'ere. Ya wouldn't believe some squaw's lies over your own uncle Jack now, would ya? That squaw was nothin' but trouble from the get go. Should've left her for the Lakota long ago."

While fingering his knife, Night Wind answers in English. "I didn't want to believe her, but then again, she never gave me no reason not to. But that red hair in your bag here kinda clears everything up now, don't it? Did ya really have to kill him? Your own step-brother an' all?"

"Your pa was just gonna hold us back. He was hurt bad, an' ya ain't gonna keep your hair for long in Lakota country draggin' a gut-cut man 'round. Just lookin' out after your hide as well as me own!"

"Tell ya what I'm gonna do," Night Wind says. "Since you're a trading type, I'll make ya a trade. Ya leave everything here, 'cept your knife. Walk on out, an' I won't kill ya. Everything ya got here for your life, and that would be a deal."

A number of warriors have moved around the two men, clearly anticipating from the tone of the conversation that something is about to happen. Night Wind notes how Hatchet Jack fingers the butt of the pistol tucked into his belt, then looks nervously at the gathered warriors.

"Ya got sand in ya, boy," Jack says, glancing around at the surrounding warriors. "After I kill ya, what's to keep these heathens from killin' me?"

Night Wind turns to the other warriors and says to them, "This man killed my father. I aim to kill him and feed him to the village dogs. If he should kill me, it is finished. I trust my brothers here will allow him to safely leave the village."

The surrounding group of warriors grunt and nod their heads in understanding.

Kicking Horse, who has joined the onlookers, mutters quietly to Night Wind, "I cannot speak for Red Knife, though."

"They will not interfere," Night Wind tells Hatchet Jack. "This is between us."

"I went all the way to Oregon lookin' for ya," Jack says, "an' all this time, your hidin' in me own backyard. Okay, boy. I've kilt a lotta men. Some needed killin', an' others maybe not so much. Just found it a might pleasurable at times. Ya might say I kinda have a talent for it. I'm gonna have fun killing you! Ya ready ta meet your thievin' old man in hell?"

Standing at ease, knife in hand, Night Wind waits for his uncle to get up. Hatchet Jack slowly stands and removes his pistols from his belt. He pulls his knife with his left hand and his hatchet with his right. The surrounding warriors expand their circle to give the combatants more room. The two crouch low and begin to slowly circle one another, looking for a weakness.

As they circle, Night Wind says, "Life is like the breath of the buffalo on a winter's day. It is not meant to last forever."

Suddenly, Hatchet Jack steps and swings his hatchet in a downward arch. Night Wind blocks the weapon's flight with his knife blade and immediately ducks past the sweep of Jack's knife as it slashes through empty space just above his head. Momentarily off-balance from his wild slash, Jack is knocked off his feet by the sweeping kick of Night Wind's foot. He falls hard onto his back. Night Wind lunges with this advantage, only to find Jack's moccasin thrust upward into his gut. Night Wind slashes wildly at Jack's leg as he is knocked backward into the packhorses.

Jack regains his feet. "I see Jack's little nephew filled out with a bit of spunk in him," Jack says, glaring at Night Wind through hostile eyes. "Not like your pa. Your pa was always a coward when it came to standin' up like a man."

Hatchet Jack feints a rush, and Night Wind leaps away. Circling to the right, both men make short feints with their knives. Finally, Night Wind fakes a rush, and Hatchet Jack swings his hatchet harmlessly through the air. Night Wind follows up his feint with a slash of his knife blade, and his uncle's hatchet falls to the ground. Jack screams in pain as Night Wind's knife rakes his right forearm, laying it open to the bone.

His eyes wide at the severity of his wound, Jack dives for his things. He drops his knife, grabs a pistol with his left hand, and fires at the onrushing warrior. The lead ball crashes into Night Wind's right shoulder and spins him backward to the ground.

Night Wind hits the earth knees first, the pain in his shoulder urging him to stay down. He looks back just in time to see Hatchet Jack, his arm gushing blood, grab his knife again and charge. Night Wind surprises his uncle with his strength. The moment they clash, despite the pain in his shoulder, Night Wind lurches to his feet, holding Jack's knife at bay with his wounded arm while Jack does the same to Night Wind's knife. They struggle for a moment before breaking free again.

As Jack wildly lunges, Night Wind steps to the outside and slams his foot down hard against the outside of Jack's left knee. He feels Jack's kneecap dislocate, along with tearing ligaments and flesh. The old trader's eyes widen in pain as his leg crumples beneath him. Night Wind doesn't waste any time leaping onto his uncle as he falls back over some trade goods, but Jack catches his knife blade just inches from his chest.

Night Wind sees his uncle's eyes grow wide with pure, naked fear as he stares up at his nephew.

Jack starts pleading, out of breath, his strength clearly wavering. "Ya wouldn't kill your own uncle, would ya? Your pa was just as good as dead anyway!"

"This is for Pa an' Chimalis," Night Wind says. He straddles his adversary and gives one last hard shove with all his weight. The knife plunges home into Hatchet Jack's chest. Quickly Night Wind reaches over to grasp his uncle's fallen hatchet in his good hand. Then he raises it high and slams it down into the forehead of the dying man. "An' this is for me!" he yells.

The deed done, Night Wind collapses onto his back in pain and exhaustion. The first face he sees when he looks up belongs to Burning Moon, who has rushed past the warriors to kneel by his side. Pushing himself up, Night Wind crawls over to his uncle's body, pulls out the knife, and deftly scalps his fallen enemy. Burning Moon assists her man as he attempts to stand.

As he holds the scalp over his head, Night Wind gives a bloodcurdling war cry. The surrounding warriors let out a series of whoops and war cries of their own, as Night Wind crumples back to the ground.

Night Wind wakes to the comfort of Burning Moon gently wiping his forehead with a soft piece of doeskin soaked in a wooden bowl of cool water. She doesn't seem to notice how his eyes flicker open, for she turns to tend to some other things. When Night Wind reaches out to touch her elbow, she gasps and turns back.

He smiles at her as he stares through half-opened eyes. "It seems I will always need someone to take care of me," he says weakly.

"I'll always be here to take care of you," she replies, tears running down her cheeks. "This time, you scared me."

"How long have I been unconscious?"

"You've been with fever now for two days. Luckily, the ball passed right through your shoulder. I don't know how it is possible, but I don't think it hit any bone." She offers him a wooden bowl. "Here, drink this warm broth. You have lost a lot of blood."

"My Spirit Bow watches over me," Night Wind says as he takes a long drink from the bowl. He lays his head back down on the grizzly bear robe. Burning Moon pulls the woolen trade blanket up over his chest.

After a few minutes, Night Wind asks, "Do you have the red-haired scalp from my uncle Jack's bags?"

"Yes," she says. "Chimalis retrieved it. She knew you would want it. It is here, along with a flintlock rifle she says also belongs to you. But those things can wait. You must rest now."

But Night Wind will not rest—at least not until his questions are answered. "What has become of my uncle's body?"

"I saw Chimalis drag the body out into the forest. No one has seen it since. She was carrying his hatchet and a big knife when she left, and she stayed away all day." Burning Moon furrows her brow. "There was much blood on her clothes when she returned. She did not greet anyone, but went straight to the river and sat down in the water for a long time."

"You must help me," Night wind says. "There is one more thing I must do." He tosses the trade blanket aside and starts to rise up on his sleeping robe. Struggling to sit up, he turns to Burning Moon for help.

She rushes to his side and tries to prevent him from climbing to his feet. "Whatever it is, I am sure that it can wait until you are stronger."

"It has waited far too long already. I can rest later. This thing I must do will take a big burden off of my heart. Hand me my eagle feathers and bring me my father's scalp. And, bring me the dark blue cloth bag."

Burning Moon returns with the feathers. Night Wind carefully places them in a small leather headband so that they stand upright. While this is happening, Burning Moon pulls the red scalp from among some furs and hands it to him. He takes the offered scalp and tucks it carefully inside his shirt. She looks hard to find the indigo cloth bag, finally locating it.

Night Wind, followed by Burning Moon, ducks out the tepee's entrance. He uses her shoulder to lean on as they start off in the direction he indicates. They soon leave the village and walk off into the nearby forest. Night Wind notices how a small group of villagers watch them curiously as they leave. Standing Lance and Red Knife stand side by side among the group.

After walking quite a way into the forest, Night Wind finally stops under a large pine tree. "This is where I have spent many sleepless nights, deep in thought over my sister's and father's fates." He looks up at the tall pine. "Here, under this pine tree, my bow's spirits have spoken to me. I need your help putting their spirits to rest. I would do this myself, but I fear I cannot climb."

Burning Moon nods.

Night Wind takes his father's scalp from inside his shirt and offers it to her. He then hands her the small wooden head. "You must climb the pine and tie my father's hair high in the branches. This way, the wind can carry its spirit back to reunite with the rest of my father's wandering spirit. Put the wooden head into the blue bag and tie the bag next to his hair. The doll's spirit eyes will help locate my sister. Only then will my father's spirit be whole, find peace, and be free to join his wife, and family."

"I have not climbed a tree in many years," Burning Moon says, "and even then, not very well. But I will try." She places the scalp and doll's head in the indigo cloth bag and secures it over her shoulder. With a great deal of effort, she carefully climbs halfway up the tall pine.

Night Wind watches from the ground as she removes the scalp from the bag and ties the red hair to one of the limbs. Then she ties the bag to hang next to the scalp. Night Wind kneels and raises his one good arm in silent prayer. Becky's bonnet seems to grow warmer inside his shirt next to his heart.

They return to the village a short time later. Night Wind is in considerable pain as Burning Moon assists him back to his tepee. Standing Lance and Red Knife are sitting outside the old chief's tepee. Night Wind can feel their gaze follow them as they pass.

"You have a fine son, Red Knife," Standing Lance says loudly enough for Night Wind to hear. "He is a true warrior of the Apsáalooke. Such a strong, brave man will make a fine match for my granddaughter."

Through the pain and exhaustion, Night Wind's heart soars.

CHAPTER  TWENTY EIGHT

The sky is darkening with threats of an afternoon thunderstorm as Night Wind leans against the willow branch backrest outside his tepee and plays a quiet game with his young son. Burning Moon is sitting next to him, sewing some soft leather garments. Her belly is swollen large as she nears the birth of their second child. Occasional thunder rumbles along the horizon.

"It makes me happy to see you enjoying our son," Burning Moon says. "He will grow to be a fine warrior someday. I just wish you had more time to be with Jake. He needs his father."

"It makes my heart heavy that my duty calls me away," Night Wind replies. "The days are too short to do everything I would like."

"I do not blame you. Your son and I just miss you. The council seeks your advice more than ever." Burning Moon pats him on the thigh. "And I think it is good that you and Black Bear travel between the Apsáalooke and Lakota to seek peace."

"I did not tell you, but something strange happened yesterday at the big council meeting." Night Wind raises his chin. "Did you see the dark warrior who rode in yesterday? The one in the red shirt?"

She nods. "The one that paints his face black?"

"He is the great war chief Jim Beckwourth of the Mountain band of the Apsáalooke. Only he doesn't paint his face black. His skin is black." He waits for her reaction before continuing. "He led the Mountain band to one of their greatest victories over the Blackfeet."

"How can a man have black skin?" Burning Moon asks. "Was he burned?"

"He is an African," Night Wind says. "I was friends with a African family back in Ohio. Then I saw lots of them when I was coming out here with my white father and the evil one. I don't know what tribe African is or where their African homeland is, but Jim Beckwourth looked at me yesterday and immediately said he knew me."

"Did you remember him?"

"I do not recall having met him before, but he insisted that I did," Night Wind replies. "He said that the Great Spirit works in mysterious ways, and that our lives have been woven together in the great web of life."

She nods as she continues with her threading.

"I asked him to visit our tepee for our midday meal," Night Wind adds, pausing to judge her reaction. "This way, we can both hear his story."

"You said he was a chief," she protests. "I have nothing prepared to feed such a distinguished guest."

"The venison stew I smell cooking right now will be fine," he replies. "Beckwourth does not seem to be the kind of man who needs or expects fancy things."

Burning Moon frowns and turns to duck into the tepee to prepare for their guest.

A short time later, Night Wind sees Jim Beckwourth approaching. He sets his son down on the grass and stands to greet the black chief. Night Wind indicates for his guest to sit, then pushes the tepee flap aside to tell Burning Moon that their guest has arrived. He then takes a seat across from Beckwourth and picks Jake up again.

"You have a fine-looking son there," Beckwourth says as he nods toward little Jake.

"Thank you. His name is Jake, but his grandfathers both call him Curly."

"No greater gift can a man receive. I have been fortunate to have many wives, and I am blessed with many sons."

"Then I have some catching up to do," Night Wind replies as Burning Moon ducks through the tepee flap carrying the iron stewpot.

"We are expecting our second child sometime in the next moon. A boy or a girl, as the spirits decide—it does not matter."

Beckwourth gives an approving smile.

"Jim Beckwourth, this is my woman, Burning Moon," Night Wind says, gesturing toward his wife.

Burning Moon smiles at their guest before ducking back into the tepee for wooden bowls and spoons.

After their meal, Jim Beckwourth compliments Burning Moon on the delicious stew. She begins to get up, but he indicates with his hands for her to stay seated. "Night Wind does not remember our past meeting," Beckwourth begins, "but it was one of the five turning points in my life." He looks to Night Wind. "You were but a boy—a boy who did not speak. You were on the boat I slaved on, coming down the Missouri River."

When Night Wind's eyes widen in surprise, Beckwourth nods and looks in the direction of the stallion tied to a nearby tree.

"I see you still have the same great horse," the chief says. "I had never seen such a spirited animal up close, and I envied you. You and your father did something that I will never forget. I was hoping to have the chance today to thank him myself. Is he with you in the village?"

"My father died many years ago," Night Wind replies. "Killed on the trail coming out to this beautiful country. But I still do not know what my father or I could have done for you."

"Your father stopped the whipping man from giving me another lash. That act gave me faith that there were still good men living in this wicked land. Then you, Night Wind, gave me renewed hope. You stepped up with compassion and kindness and gave me and my friend, Matu, something so sweet that I can still remember the taste of it in my mind."

"You're the slave from the boat!" Night Wind says excitedly. "The one who jumped to shore and tied the boat to the tree!"

Beckwourth beams.

"I remember you now," Night Wind continues. "Matu must have been the big man with all the scars on his chest. My father told me that your friend was a proud and brave man, much braver than he was. The captain said he was some sort of big chief back in Africa."

"I do not know about that, but what your father did for me was very brave as well. Most men would have just turned away."

"How did you end up here with the Mountain band?"

"You and your father gave us new hope—new strength in our desire for freedom." The black chief sighs. "A short time after you left us, the captain and the whipping man got drunk on the firewater that whites call rum. The captain drank himself into a sleep. Matu yelled something at the whipping man to trick him into using his whip. I do not know what Matu said, since he yelled it out in his old language, but he managed to grab the end of the whip and yank the whipping man off-balance. Matu then had his revenge. He made the whipping man swallow his whip by ramming it down his throat before tossing him overboard. Luckily, I was able to get the whipping man's keys before he became fish food."

"Such an evil man deserves such a death," Night Wind states with a nod.

"Yes, he earned his fate with the scars on our backs," Beckwourth agrees. "We unlocked our chains and rowed the boat to the western bank. Matu pushed the captain's head down deep into the mud, and we all ran. I have not seen Matu since."

Night Wind looks to his wife, who listens in rapt attention.

"I wanted to see my father one last time," Beckwourth continues, "so I made my way up to St. Louis. I traveled by night, stealing what food I could from farms along the way."

"You probably followed the same path we did," Night Wind says.

"Perhaps, I would not know," Jim Beckwourth answers. "When I reached my father in St. Louis and told him my story, he said he met the man with the red-haired boy. He told me you had left five days earlier, heading west. My father heard that William Ashley was gathering men to go trapping, and I took a chance. He didn't ask if I was a free man, although he could easily tell by the scars on my back. Some other trappers took an interest and staked me with a horse and gear, and I headed west with Ashley. A season later, because I am black, I was sent by Ashley to buy horses from the Indians. I became lost, and was saved from starvation when some Blackfeet found me wandering on the prairie. I ended up living with the Blackfeet for a year."

"What was that like?" Night Wind asks.

"They are a defiant people, more warlike than the Apsáalooke," Beckwourth replies gravely. "They want to kill anybody that comes into their country. They wanted me to help kill my white trapper friends. That was something I could not do, so I left them and returned to Ashley. I later became good friends with some of the Mountain band I traded with. The white trappers who had staked me when I left St. Louis demanded that I pay back my debt. Since I did not have the money to do so, I went to live with my Mountain band friends. Here I sit today."

"Your life has taken many turns," Night Wind says. "I wonder what the Great Spirit has in store for you next."

"I have given that some thought, myself. Indeed my life has been a strange journey. I started out in a faraway land, living in a mud hut and helping my father grow yams and rice. Then I was captured by tribal enemies and sold into slavery. I crossed a vast water only to be sold again as a slave, and yet now I sit here a contented man with many wives and horses and live free with the Apsáalooke."

When Jim Beckwourth rises to his feet, Night Wind follows, helping Burning Moon rise as well. Beckwourth thanks Burning Moon for his meal and turns to extend his hand to Night Wind. They grasp forearms.

"I thank you for your support at the council last night," Beckwourth says. "I believe you have a clear understanding of what the Apsáalooke face in the future. I will say a prayer for your father's spirit." He nods, turns, and walks off.

"That was an amazing story," Night Wind says to his woman. "I had no idea our lives were so intertwined."

"What did you say in the council last night?" Burning Moon asks.

"In the council, Beckwourth said that the whites are coming in greater numbers than even I anticipated. Even the Lakota are finally beginning to be concerned. The Mountain band is having difficulty keeping their young warriors away from the wagons. Beckwourth fears it is only a matter of time before a young warrior's desire to show off and their natural feelings of invincibility will put us all at risk. I simply agreed with him." Wanting to change the subject, Night Wind turns to Burning Moon and holds up Jake to face her. "Don't you think Jake looks more and more like Standing Lance every day? Look at his eyes, how dark and scary they are."

"Jake does not have scary eyes, and neither does my grandfather," she answers with a grin. "If anything, he looks more like you. No one else around here has reddish hair."

"Your grandfather does too have scary eyes! You never had to ask him for his granddaughter's hand. I thought his eyes were going to burn right through me."

"He just does that to test people's character." She laughs. "He wants to see if they will meet his glare or turn away. He once told me that you can tell a lot from looking into a person's eyes—glimpse into their soul."

"Well, you might have warned me that my soul was going to be examined. I almost turned away and walked out." Night Wind chuckles. "You don't know how lucky you are."

"You should be relieved he would even talk to you about me," she replies in good humor. "You were not his first choice. Nor his second, for that matter. Now, though, I think he is quite fond of you. It just took him a while to become accustomed to your unusual ways."

Before he can respond, Night Wind feels liquid warmth bloom over his chest. With a laugh, he holds his son away at arm's length. "Well, there is nothing unusual about our son. He just peed all over my shirt! I didn't know he had such a powerful stream." He watches proudly as the boy finally finishes peeing. "He truly will be a mighty warrior. He may be able to drown his enemies."

"If you spent a little more time with him, he could show you other surprises." Burning Moon rises to take baby Jake while Night Wind goes into the tepee to change shirts.

Night Wind senses the change in the winds just before they arrive at the village. As the rain begins to fall, he watches the four warriors trot their tired horses into the village. The last of the four leads a fifth horse carrying a body. Angry shouts go up from the riders as they weave through the village. Like Burning Moon, who comes out to join her husband, people are emerging from their tepees to stand in the rain and see what all the shouting is about. A young woman screams and rushes forward, clutching at the body of the fallen warrior.

Burning Moon gasps, and Night Wind can see why. The woman in anguish is her good friend Shooting Star. Burning Moon rushes off to join the other women in consoling Shooting Star as she sobs and cries in her grief. Night Wind stands back at his tepee for a moment, pondering how he will face the horror that awaits him on that horse. There is only one reason Shooting Star would react in this way: her husband, Kicking Horse, must be the dead warrior.

The other warriors dismount and approach a group of men that have gathered in front of the chief's tepee. His grief rising in his heart, Night Wind strides out to join them as Standing Lance steps forward to speak with one of the young riders.

"Whites have murdered Kicking Horse!" Buffalo Leg yells out for all to hear. "They shot him from his horse for no reason. We were not threatening them! We demand our revenge. The ones responsible for this cowardly act cannot be allowed to go unpunished!"

"The council shall meet to consider this thing," Standing Lance says. "You are all welcome to speak your thoughts. This matter affects the entire tribe. The council will decide what is best to be done."

With a heavy heart, Night Wind steps forward to cut his best friend's body down from his horse, Lightning. He lays the body gently on the grass, then kneels beside his longtime friend.

Lightning steps over to lower her head and sniff at Kicking Horse.

"I am sorry, my friend," Night Wind says to his departed friend. The bullet wound in Kicking Horse's chest is large and jagged, the blood watery over the torn flesh. "I should have gone with you as you asked.

I will look after Shooting Star and your beautiful baby girl. They will never be in need."

Rain begins to beat down harder on the mourning villagers as the women carry the body away so that the council might assemble. Night Wind watches in sorrow as his dear friend passes over the hill and out of sight.

CHAPTER TWENTY NINE

The village is immediately thrown into turmoil at the terrible news of Kicking Horse's shocking murder. His life was at a high point with the recent birth of his daughter just three moons past. Night Wind has heard Shooting Star's wailing cries of anguish from the direction of their tepee. Burning Moon has remained with her, and other women have gathered to help her face her grief and prepare Kicking Horse's body.

Night Wind heads in another direction with the rest of the village men, plodding through the sheets of rain. They are angrily talking among themselves as they make their way to Standing Lance's tepee, where the council is gathering to determine what the village response should be. Many of the warriors are holding up weapons and shouting war cries, clearly having already reached their own conclusion as to what must be done. Within a very short time, even in the driving rain, a large contingent of agitated warriors has surrounded Standing Lance's tepee. Night Wind stands near the back of the gathering, but when they spot him, they usher him to the front so that he may join the others inside the tepee.

Here, Buffalo Leg is heatedly relating the incident to the council. "It is as I have stated. We were riding through the buffalo grass down by the big bend in the muddy river. Kicking Horse had spotted three wagons camped on the far side of the river last night. He asked me if I wanted to go with him this morning to ask the wagons for coffee. We have always been friendly to the whites. Many of you here have done this very thing in the past. Just so we would not seem a threat to them, we four stayed back as Kicking Horse went forward by himself. Before he even had a chance to ask, a shot rang out from the last wagon. The wagons then began to run.'"

A long-dormant fear roils in Night Wind's mind.

"Did Kicking Horse charge toward the wagons?" Red Knife asks. "Some whites do not appreciate good riding."

Buffalo Leg's gaze searches the group before settling on Night Wind. "No, Kicking Horse was trotting on Lightning. Night Wind told us of the white man's fearfulness. That is why we chose to stay back."

"I would like to hear Night Wind's thoughts on this matter," Standing Lance says.

Night Wind draws a deep, sorrowful breath. "You all know that Kicking Horse was my friend," he begins, shaking his head slowly from side to side. "I do not doubt Buffalo Leg's account, but I do know that different eyes see the same thing in different ways. Kicking Horse was full of a young warrior's pride that made him take chances. You have all seen this, as I have. I just cannot envision Kicking Horse begging for coffee. My eyes do not see his pride allowing this thing. Even if this was what he said to his companions, it casts a shadow on my thoughts." While looking at Buffalo Leg and the other young warriors sitting behind him, Night Wind says, "Perhaps my young friends missed something, some movement or gesture on Kicking Horse's part that the whites in the wagons misunderstood as a threat. You were at a good distance from the wagons. Perhaps you might have missed something Kicking Horse did."

"We talked about what we saw as we rode back to the village," Buffalo Leg answers. "It is as I have stated. We saw Kicking Horse do nothing to bring on his death." The young warrior scowls, and when he speaks again, it is with threat in his tone. "Night Wind speaks as if his friend deserved to be murdered! I think he has become too much of a peace man—or perhaps his white skin is shining through!"

At this affront to his honor, Night Wind leaps to his feet and glares at Buffalo Leg. When he feels the disapproval of the elders closing in on him, he quietly sits back down.

Everyone looks back at the fire as if nothing has happened.

Night Wind looks around at the other members of the council before turning to glare again at Buffalo Leg. "Kicking Horse was my best friend. He was first to befriend me when I came to live among you. I, too, grieve his death, perhaps more so than any gathered here. I was not there. I simply want to be certain about what you saw. I do know that he was brash at times, as he was when he tried to take the lance from the four sleeping Lakota warriors."

Silence hangs over the tepee as the men tumble into deep thought.

Night Wind listens to the crackling fire for a time as he ponders how to say what he must say. "Just consider my words carefully," he begins finally. "If we fight the whites, we cannot win. Our children will cry out with hungry bellies if our warriors pursue the path of war. Sure, we may avenge Kicking Horse, but there will be consequences to our actions. The blue soldiers will be sure to follow. Word that the Indians are attacking the trappers and supply wagons will spread quickly among the whites. Then the whites will not hesitate to shoot. They fear the unknown, and so they fear the Indian." To Buffalo Leg, he asks, "Would you have all our brothers shot on sight over what may be a misunderstanding, or worse, just one scared white man?"

Some of the surrounding elders murmur and grunt in agreement.

Buffalo Leg jumps to his feet and starts gesturing wildly with his hands as he protests. "If we do nothing, then that word will spread too! The whites will think they can kill Indians at their pleasure without fear of reprisal. I would rather die a warrior, with my pride intact, than die a coward in fear of the future." To Standing Lance, he says, "We do not ask the council's permission to seek our revenge on these wagons. We only seek your wisdom and understanding."

As Buffalo Leg returns to his seat, one of his comrades shows his support by putting a hand on his shoulder.

After waiting through a few moments of silence, Standing Lance asks, "Does anyone else wish to address this matter?"

From the outer circle, Jim Beckwourth rises to speak. Until this moment, Night Wind had not noticed the chief. He suspects that Beckwourth and his contingent from the Mountain bands must have been preparing to leave just as Buffalo Leg and his companions rode in.

"I am Beckwourth," he says, "war chief of the Mountain bands of the Apsáalooke. This matter concerns all of the Apsáalooke, not just this River band. I have lived among the whites. I have been their slave for most of my life, so I have more reason than most to hate them. My desire would be to rid the world of them. Stamp them all out like biting ants where you lay your robes. But I know this is not possible. The words Night Wind has spoken ring true. There are far too many whites, like the ants. Kill a few and more will boil out of the nest to bite you until you move your sleeping robes elsewhere. We will stand with you when the time comes to fight, but is this the right moment?"

With that, he sits back down.

Night Wind nods, glad to have had his unlikely friend to support him.

When it becomes clear that no one else will speak, Standing Lance rises. "I have listened to Buffalo Leg and have heard the words of others. Though my heart rests with Buffalo Leg's words, wisdom makes my mind look elsewhere. We all have known that this day would come. We spoke of it just one day past." He pauses, looking around at the others gathered. "The times are changing, and we must change with them. It is not as simple as the past, when we would follow our hearts, kill the guilty party, and it would be finished.

"I have made my mark on the Friendship Treaty, as some of you gathered. I will not break my oath, even to the white man. We will send word to the Indian agent, Benjamin O'Fallon, at the white man's fort. We will ask him to punish the ones responsible. We also must find the wagon."

When a murmur of disapproval rings out from the young warriors, Night Wind draws a breath to argue on his chief's behalf, but before he can get the words out, Standing Lance raises his hand for silence, and the warriors obey.

"Night Wind was with me at the Friendship Treaty signing," Standing Lance says. "He knows Agent O'Fallon. It would be best that he speak with the agent, since they are of the same Irish tribe. They both have the Peace Medallion given out by the white father, Jefferson. Maybe Night Wind will be able to explain to O'Fallon that we do not seek trouble, only justice for the murder of Kicking Horse, as promised by the treaty."

Others in the council grunt in understanding. With a nod, Night Wind accepts the order from his chief.

"We must not send a large group to find the wagons," Standing Lance cautions. "We do not want another confrontation. They are headed to the new trading post the whites call Fort Hall. Red Knife and Buffalo Leg will go in an attempt to find the white wagons responsible."

Five days later, the council meets again. When all the members are seated and the pipe has been passed, Night Wind stands to address the gathering.

"I spoke with Agent O'Fallon at the white man's fort. He said there was little he could do without knowledge of who fired the shot. He said that he would ask General Atkinson to send soldiers to speak with traders in any wagons that recently arrived at Fort Hall, but O'Fallon didn't think anything would be found. I told him that if an Indian had murdered a white man, the blue soldiers would be sent to punish the Indians. I added that the soldiers would not be overly concerned if they punished the guilty Indians or not." Night Wind pauses before adding, "O'Fallon did not have words to say in response to this, other than to say that he was sorry."

The others at the gathering rumble their disapproval.

"I pointed out the Peace Medallion on his table," Night Wind continues, feeling his anger flashing across his face. "I told him that I, too, still wear the Peace Medallion. I, too, seek peace among the tribes and with the white man, but that peace must come from both directions."

Now the group murmurs their agreement.

"O'Fallon again said that he would do his best," Night Wind continues. "But I do not think anything will come of it. He did ask for the council's forgiveness, and said again how sorry he was for this tragedy."

As the others contemplate his words, Night Wind sits down.

It seems that many of those present were not aware that Night Wind carries a Peace Medallion, for several ask to see it. He pulls it from the beaded medicine pouch hanging around his neck. The men pass around the heavy medallion as the council continues.

"Buffalo Leg and I tried to follow the tracks of the three wagons," Red Knife explains. "But with the heavy rains, we could not track them. We searched for two days, but the wagon tracks have vanished. We rode well beyond Apsáalooke lands in our search of the wagons before turning back."

As Red Knife sits back down, Buffalo Leg rises. "Since we cannot find the wagons responsible for my friend's death, I say we attack the next whites or wagon we see. Night Wind spoke with O'Fallon, so the whites will know why this has happened. The word will spread and the issue will be settled. Kicking Horse's death will be avenged, and his spirit will be able to roam free in the next life."

Red Knife rises again and turns to Buffalo Leg. "You listen, but you do not hear. Night Wind and Jim Beckwourth, a great war chief, both have said we cannot win a conflict with the white man. They both have lived among the whites. The whites will take an attack on any wagon as the excuse they need to drive us from our lands. Where would you have us go?" Red Knife looks around at those assembled. "The Apsáalooke are in good standing with the whites at the fort. We trade our furs at the trading post for the white man's goods that make our lives better. If we cannot trade, where will we get our powder and lead to defend ourselves against our enemies?"

Without standing, Buffalo Leg says, "We have all heard the stories of the greatness of Red Knife. I have long admired him as a great warrior. Now, it seems, he is getting old and does not clearly see the warrior's path. His spirit hesitates where once it would cry out. Is his spirit taking the easier path of the coward?"

Red Knife looks down at the young warrior. "It is true that my spirit does not rush forward without thinking, blinded by blood, as it did when I was less experienced. I look more to the good of my people rather than my own glory." He shakes his head at Buffalo Leg. "Consider your actions carefully before you act. Are your actions for the good of the Apsáalooke? Night Wind and I will not attack whites that know nothing of Kicking Horse's murder. You have been foolish enough today, first to insult my son, and now to insult me. If you think I am a coward, I will fight you with knives until first blood, and I will do so right now."

Buffalo Leg stands but ignores Red Knife's challenge. "Enough talk! It is time for action. We all knew O'Fallon would do nothing. Night Wind has just said so. A shiny medallion will not avenge Kicking Horse's spirit, and I say his spirit must be avenged. I did not put my scratch marks on the white man's paper treaty."

Night Wind grows uneasy at the sense of stirring among the gathering. They are listening to Buffalo Leg, and some of them are agreeing.

"I have been told that there are some whites living along Singing Creek," Buffalo Leg continues passionately. "On land promised to us by General Atkinson in the same Friendship Treaty that Chief Long Hair and Standing Lance both signed with Atkinson and O'Fallon. Singing Creek is only a short day's ride. That is where I will ride in the morning, and if we do not see any other white men on the way, I will kill those living at Singing Creek. If O'Fallon and the whites will do nothing, then I will enforce the treaty. Any who wish to follow, I will welcome them as warrior brothers."

Without waiting for approval, Buffalo Leg turns and walks out of the council. Night Wind knows an urge to chase after him—to try to stop him and talk sense into him—but he has seen this same look in a man's eyes often enough to recognize that it is no use.

Late that night, Night Wind goes to speak with his father before leaving the village. Red Knife is sitting with Chimalis by a dying fire when he walks up. Thunder follows on his own, trotting a little way behind.

"There is something I should tell you that I have only told Burning Moon," Night Wind says to Red Knife. "Something that has shamed me for my entire life." He takes a deep breath before going on. "When I was a boy, I was out deer hunting with my grandfather. I saw a movement in the woods. Thinking that it was a big buck, I fired a shot. The antlers went down, and my grandfather and I moved forward to see the buck I had shot. When we reached the spot, my grandfather was looking at a bow and quiver that he had taken from the Indian boy lying at his feet. The boy was just a few years older than I was. The bow my grandfather was looking at is the same bow I use today." Night Wind can't tell how Red Knife is taking the news, but he feels like he has no choice but to continue. He takes another deep breath. "I had shot the boy in the chest, and he was still alive. As he lay dying, he stared up at me and reached out a hand for help. My grandfather just told me, 'Nice shot,' before turning and walking away. I followed. We took the boy's bow and quiver and the buck he had been carrying, and we left him to die alone in the snow. The ghost of the boy reaching up and my grandfather's words, 'Nice shot,' have haunted me since that day so long ago.

"On the way back to our cabin, my grandfather and I were both almost killed by the storm that followed us home. Lightning struck a tree right next to me, and I would have been killed for certain if I had not tripped at the same time. I am sure now that the bow's spirits tried to kill us both on the way back to our cabin—tried to get their revenge. Neither of us ever mentioned the storm or the dead Indian boy again."

Red Knife and Chimalis trade a glance but say nothing.

"That means I am the one responsible for my white mother, brother, and grandparents being killed by Indians," Night Wind says, tears forming in his eyes. "And, ultimately, I am responsible for my white father's death, as well, and the death of my sister, Becky." Night Wind looks at his father and mother.

Both are staring into the fire's dying embers, allowing their son to continue without judgment.

"For a long time, when I closed my eyes at night, I would see the flashes of lightning and hear the angry growl of thunder. I would see the ghost of the Indian boy reaching up to me. See those eyes and hear my grandfather's words, 'Nice shot.'"

Finally, Red Knife speaks. "Why do you tell us this now? Why after all these years?"

Tears trickle over Night Wind's cheeks as he draws a breath to reply. "Because I want you to understand that my grandfather thought the way most white men think about Indians. They do not see us as people. We are but animals in their eyes. A nuisance, like the wolf, to be shot dead." He takes another deep breath, muttering quietly, "Nice shot."

When Chimalis reaches out a hand as if to comfort him, Night Wind rises, feeling unworthy of her affection at this moment.

"This is all happening too fast," he says as he turns and moves toward Thunder. "I need more time to try and unite the tribes. I must warn those people on Singing Creek. Otherwise, the whites will wipe out the Indians. Do you understand? I am not trying to save a few whites. I am trying to save the Apsáalooke!"

Night Wind mounts Thunder as Red Knife steps up to the stallion's side.

"I am beginning to better understand your vision of the future," Red Knife says. "You must do what your spirits tell you. That has always been your path to follow. We cannot avoid the future, but perhaps you can bend it a little."

With a tearful nod in thanks, Night Wind takes his bow and quiver from where they hang on the saddle and arranges them on his back. He looks down at his father one last time before nudging Thunder into a trot out of the village and into the night.

CHAPTER THIRTY

An afternoon thunderstorm is brewing over the mountains off in the distance to the West. The clouds are churning angrily as they tumble and roll across the heavens, darkening as they draw nearer.

Night Wind has ridden through the long night, hoping to arrive well ahead of the war party. He follows Singing Creek upstream for most of the morning and has just made up his mind to turn around and head downstream when he climbs this last gentle rise and gazes down on the little homestead below. With the delay, he fears that his warning might be too late. He is certain that the war party has to be close behind him.

From his position on Thunder, he looks down from the ridge at a house standing under the partial shade of a large grove of cottonwoods. It appears to have been dug into the ground a couple of feet, then crudely constructed of sod, mud, and poles. Grass grows from its sod roof. Night Wind knows that the house will probably flood when the stream becomes a raging river in the spring runoff.

A makeshift corral stands alongside the house, where two oxen and a skinny milk cow are confined. Near the front door of the cabin, a broken-down wagon leans awkwardly to one side. Night Wind sees that the front axle is supported by a large rock. He can guess that this is why the travelers stopped here in the first place. More than likely, they plan to push on next spring, if they can get the wagon wheel fixed.

Two young boys are busy emptying buckets full of soil and mud handed up to them from what appears to be a new grave. A man is stooped over in the hole, scraping the dirt out with a long piece of wood. Next to the grave are two other fresh graves with little wooden crosses.

Night Wind wonders what has been killing the family. Upon seeing the two brothers, his mind flashes back to the graves of his own family he left back in Ohio. Only they were killed by Indians, and here the Indians have not yet arrived.

Are these people sick?

Night Wind thinks that if they have some sort of disease, he may be trying to warn the wrong people. Night Wind has heard about what the white man's diseases can do to the Indians, so he knows that he will have to approach the homestead carefully.

The storm has finally reached them, and the rain begins to fall just as he nudges Thunder down off the ridge in the direction of the homestead. The younger of the two boys is first to see his approach. The boy drops his bucket and immediately grabs the sleeve of his older brother before moving to stand behind him.

Night Wind raises both of his hands in friendship. "Hello, the house!" he calls out from his horse as he continues to walk Thunder through the rain in the direction of the homestead.

He pulls Thunder up to a halt when a woman comes to stand in the cabin's open door. Night Wind sees her weakly leaning against the doorframe. Her face is covered with red splotches.

The older of the two boys looks down at his father scraping out the grave before grabbing the rifle lying on the ground nearby. He aims and fires.

Night Wind is just starting to turn his horse when the ball strikes his chest. The force of the impact knocks him from the saddle, and he falls hard to the ground on his side. He rolls over to his back and glances down at the blood forming on his chest.

"Why did you shoot?" he whispers to himself. "I was coming to warn you."

A short way off, as the two boys run up the hill toward him, Night Wind faintly hears the younger boy yell out congratulations to his older brother.

"Ya got him, Joe. Ya done shot an Injun!"

The father yells up at his sons as he weakly jogs to catch up. "Nice shot, son. Nice shot. You done got us a horse. Now maybe I can fetch

Ma an' little Mary a doctor an' get us the hell out of this godforsaken, pox-infested place."

Night Wind stares up at the angry sky, the rain splattering his face as he struggles to breathe. The pain in his chest is excruciating. His mind drifts back to the ghost of the young Indian warrior he accidentally killed so many years ago. He sees the mortally wounded boy reaching up to him as before, but this time the ghostly vision holds a slight smile for Night Wind.

The man and his two sons have slowed to a cautious walk as Night Wind sees them faintly approach through the rain. Night Wind wants to ask them why, and he wants to tell them to stay away, but he can't seem to summon the strength to speak.

"Wow, Pa!" one of the boys says. "Look at that bow! What a shame it's been busted."

Night Wind watches as the man grabs the reins of Thunder and begins to lead his horse away. He wants to warn him about the horse, but only a whisper passes his lips. The youngest boy rushes up to grab an arrow from his quiver.

The last words Night Wind's mind hears as he fades in and out of consciousness are those of his grandfather. *"Nice shot!"*

CHAPTER THIRTY ONE

From his state of half-consciousness, Night Wind faintly hears the cries of warriors and the occasional boom of a rifle, but they all sound somewhere way off in the distance. He stares at a bright light in the far reaches of his mind, watching as the light fades to a dim glow.

Nearby, he hears a death chant, and he wonders who has died. His body feels numb and exhausted. Each shallow breath he takes is a painful struggle, like something heavy is pressing down on his chest, trying to crush the life from his body. His mind is all in a fog.

"Nice shot," plays over and over in his thoughts. The chanting is coming closer. Has his spirit passed over into the next life?

He feels his mother holding him, rocking him in the old rocking chair, but how can this be? He desperately wants to see his mother's face, if only to tell her how sorry he is for what he has done. His body struggles with his mind to open his eyes. He takes a deep breath as his eyes slowly flutter open, but all he sees is a blur. As the blurry image slowly clears, Night Wind sees that it is not his mother holding and rocking him, but his father.

Red Knife is rocking him and chanting his death song.

"My son! My son!" Red Knife's image whispers as he holds and stares down at Night Wind with disbelief in his eyes. "How can this be that Akbaatatdía has interrupted your journey and returned you to me in the present world?"

Night Wind feels his father gently lower him onto the damp grass. He strains to watch while Red Knife lifts his bloody shirt to examine his wound. The hole is in the center of the bloody leather shirt, and at the sight, Night Wind assumes the worst.

Now Red Knife uses some wet grass to gently wipe his son's bloody chest. As if trying to keep himself calm, the old warrior describes what he sees as he looks for the small entry point of a lead ball. But through all the blood on Night Wind's shirt, Red Knife explains that the wound is instead a series of deep lacerations in a circular pattern. Night Wind has never heard of such a thing, but he can sense that it will not help him in his chances to recover.

Red Knife disappears for a moment before returning with Night Wind's medicine pouch. When he holds it up, Night Wind can see that the beadwork Chimalis did so beautifully on the pouch is ruined in the center. Showing through the torn hole in the leather is a shiny object. Red Knife reaches inside the medicine pouch and pulls out the deformed bronze Peace Medallion.

Through his barely open eyes, Night Wind looks on in disbelief at how the medallion he received from the old Shoshone Indian chief so many years before has been dented in the middle by the impact of the lead ball. The Peace Medallion, it seems, has saved his life.

In his confusion, Night Wind thinks about his broken bow lying in pieces on the grass nearby. He wonders about the bow's powers, wonders whether the spirits it carries will disappear into the wind. If his life has been spared, and if he indeed has a future, what might it hold now that his bow is gone?

Red Knife stands and strains to help his semiconscious son up into his saddle. "It is a good thing Thunder is so well trained," he says to his son. "I watched as the white man tried to lead him away. He didn't get very far."

Red Knife then turns and begins to slowly lead the two horses up and over the ridge.

Night Wind is slumped over the saddle, struggling to hold on. Thunder, the old stallion, makes one halfhearted tug back on the reins before walking on. He really doesn't like being led.

Night Wind faintly hears behind him the sound of the other warriors whooping and yelling down by the sod house. The gunfire has stopped, replaced by screams. It is too late to warn them about the pox.

The rain eases into a light drizzle as the storm passes over the region just as rapidly as it began.

CHAPTER  THIRTY TWO

Spring - 1836

It has been three weeks since the massacre at Singing Creek. Night Wind and Red Knife are sitting quietly staring into the flames of a small fire between their two tepees. They listen to the soft babble of the nearby creek. Night Wind takes in a deep breath and grimaces at his discomfort.

"Your chest still hurts?" Red Knife asks his son.

"Sometimes it is worse than others." Night Wind replies as he gently rubs his chest. "I'm sure the ball must have broken some ribs. Each day it seems a little better then it was. It will just take some time."

The two men sit quietly for a spell before Night Wind looks over and states, "You and Chimalis should not have left your people. Maybe the village will take you back."

"They were yours and Burning Moon's people, too," Red Knife responds. "Besides, Chimalis would never leave Burning Moon to have the baby herself."

Red Knife slowly shakes his head as he stirs the coals with a stick. "The council was wrong when they banned you from the village. They do not understand your vision. You did not choose the white man over the Indian."

"I know Standing Lance did everything he could." Night Wind sighs as he continues, "He thought the same way about me at one time. It's just, Burning Moon is very upset that Moon Shadow and Standing Lance will not see their new great grand-baby."

"Some of the young warriors blame you for Buffalo Leg's death, but it will work itself out eventually. It may be better this way. It is not pleasant to stay where one is not wanted," Red Knife states. "The baby is coming now and it is good that Chimalis is here to help. The second one is always easier, you'll see."

Red Knife carefully places another small piece of wood on the fire. "The whole matter was not your fault. Buffalo Leg was a fool. He caused his own death with his blind hatred of the white man," Red Knife states again in disgust.

"Kicking Horse was my best friend. Everybody knows that." Night Wind throws a stick in the fire in anger. "Now who will look after Shooting Star's little girl?"

Thunder, picketed with the other horses nearby, stomps one of his front hooves and gives a faint whinny. Night Wind grabs the Hawken rifle leaning against the nearby log and peers into the failing light of dusk. Red Knife instantly grabs his rifle as well.

Out of the fading light, a voice yells out in English, "You men best drop your rifles. We don't want no trouble."

Night Wind calls back in English, "Who are you? Show yourselves."

"United States Army, and we have you surrounded," the voice calls out from the dark. "We'll show ourselves when you set your rifles aside. Now put 'em down or we'll be forced to shoot! I ain't gonna tell ya again."

Night Wind starts to translate for Red Knife, but Red Knife is already lowering his rifle to lean it back against the log. Seeing this, Night Wind reluctantly does the same. "Come on in, and we can talk."

Once the two warriors have set aside their weapons, seven soldiers step out from the surrounding darkness and into the flickering light of the campfire. Each has a rifle leveled at Night Wind and Red Knife. As they step inside the circle of light, Chimalis ducks out of the nearest tepee. Two of the soldiers turn their rifles in her direction, and one quickly steps over.

"You two injuns don't look all that tough," the lieutenant states sarcastically. "O'Fallon inferred you two might be some kind of big problem."

"Just what is it you want?" Night Wind asks, already sensing the answer.

The lieutenant nods his head and chuckles before answering, "It ain't what we want, it's what O'Fallon wants. I reckon O'Fallon has a hankerin' to hang ya, that's what."

A yell from inside the tepee breaks the tension of the moment. Chimalis turns to duck back into the tepee, but her way is barred by a soldier's rifle. The lieutenant nods his head in the tepee's direction. "Miller, see what all the fuss is about."

The soldier steps out a moment later and says, "Looks to me like some squaw is havin' a baby," adding with a grin, "real pretty little thing, too. There's another little nit in there as well."

Another muffled cry comes from inside the tepee, and Chimalis yells out in her native tongue, "She needs my help!," as she attempts to push past the soldier. The soldier pushes her back hard with the rifle across her chest. Night Wind bolts to intervene and is quickly struck on the side of his head with the heavy brass butt of a rifle stock. Blinding white lights explode in his head as he sinks into black oblivion.

Night Wind slowly regains consciousness and moans with the effort to lift his head. He attempts to push himself up to his knees. With the effort of every movement, his head throbs with shooting pain, as if his skull is going to split in two. He opens his eyes and tries to look around, trying to understand where he is. He listens hard to hear the babble of the nearby stream and glances up to see the stars above. But, he hears and sees nothing. Dark stillness surrounds him.

Night Wind has a vague recollection of soldiers, but can't understand why. The ground is hard underneath, and with the feel of his hands, he soon realizes he is kneeling on a wooden floor. He senses he is in a room—a room engulfed in darkness. He slowly turns his head and sees a faint beam of light emanating from a tiny hole in what must be the wall. Focusing on the pin of light, he feels along the plank floor until his hand touches a log wall, just a few feet away. His head pounds with excruciating pain. Slowly making his way over to the wall, he realizes his ankles are shackled together with a chain. He sits, leaning against the uneven wall, and runs his hands over the chain and iron shackles. Only then does he remember—they want to hang him. O'Fallon wants to hang him.

Night Wind tries to remember what happened through the searing pain in his skull. His thoughts are jumbled and fuzzy with the foggy mist of returning consciousness, but slowly he begins to sort through the night's drama.

Burning Moon! His baby! What has become of them? He tries to yell out, but the pain is too intense. He pushes himself to his feet and makes his way over to the source of the dim light, shuffling his feet as the heavy chain drags on the floor. The air is cold and stale around him. The room turns out to be a lot smaller than he thought. He pounds his fist on the wall next to the light, but the logs are solid and he hears no response. Placing his ear to the wall, he again hears nothing. He moves his eye to the small speck of light, but can only make out vague shadows on the other side. Night Wind cannot even be certain if he is looking outside or into another room. He quickly realizes he has overexerted himself as a sudden dizziness washes over him in a nauseating wave. He slumps back down to all fours and vomits before collapsing back into unconsciousness.

"Rise an' shine, Injun," a soldier says as he opens the stockade door and kicks Night Wind in the side. He sets a plate of beans and piece of hard bread on the floor next to Night Wind. "Don't reckon why O'Fallon wants to feed ya. Just gonna string your sorry ass up anyway."

The pain explodes in Night Wind's chest, to match that of his head. With much effort he whispers, "Water. Can I have some water?" All the while shielding his eyes from the sudden light.

The soldier points to the opposite corner, where a flask of water and a wooden bucket already sit. "Ya already got water."

"How is my wife, Burning Moon?" Night Wind asks. "How is my baby?"

"Couldn't say," the soldier answers as he turns and walks out. Night Wind listens as the key is turned in the heavy door behind him. Night

Wind can now see little streaks of light, dimly cast about the windowless room, filtered through cracks between the logs. He must have first awoken during the dark of night. He also saw that the heavy door did indeed open onto some other room. He is now certain he is being held at the fort.

Ignoring the food, Night Wind shuffles over to the door and calls out, "I want to see O'Fallon!" He receives no response other than a swelling pain in his head. He kicks on the door with his foot and yells again, "Take me to O'Fallon!" He hears someone walk over to the door.

"Shut up, Injun! Yell out one more time an' you'll end up accidentally choking ta death on your supper." As he walks away, the soldier adds, "Be dead, just like your damn horse!"

Four days later, Night Wind is finally taken to see the Indian agent, Benjamin O'Fallon. His guards have shackled his wrists as well, before he is shuffled into another log building and pushed down onto a bench in front of the agent's desk.

"I must say, I'm a bit disappointed in you, Sean." O'Fallon states without looking up from the papers on his desk. When the agent finally does look up, he adds, "I thought we were of the same mind—peace. But, as I recollect, you were plenty angry the last time we spoke."

"My name is Night Wind. Where are my wife an' children?" Night Wind asks. "Are they here at the fort? And, what has happened to Chimalis an' Red Knife?"

"Your boy is safe with Chimalis. Red Knife is locked up here, like you. He has already admitted to going on the raid and being present at the settler's killings and will be hung." The agent takes a deep breath before he continues, "Your squaw and baby, I'm afraid, are dead. She died in childbirth, along with the baby. I'm sorry to.... The agent continues to talk, but Night Wind does not hear. He cannot believe what he has just been told. Burning Moon, gone? How could this be? Everyone had told him, the second baby was always much easier than the first. He drops his head into his hands in grief, his eyes filling with tears.

"But, you Sean, have much bigger worries," O'Fallon adds as he regains Night Wind's attention, "The settlers want justice—revenge. Their piece of flesh, so to speak."

Night Wind slowly rises to his feet, his temper momentarily overcoming his grief. "You mean, like when the Apsáalooke wanted justice for a white man murdering Kicking Horse?" Night Wind shouts. "I came to you then for justice, an' you did nothin'! And, don't call me Sean. That ain't my name." Night Wind feels the dizziness and nausea beginning to return, and he takes a deep breath.

A guard starts to step over to force Night Wind to sit back down, but the agent waves him away with his hand.

"General Atkinson may be more lenient if you became a white man again, rather than an Indian." Agent O'Fallon calmly continues, "Sean, I know you were at the massacre. You left behind your bow and one of your arrows."

"I never said I weren't there," Night Wind states, regaining his composure as he sits back down. "I was there. I was tryin' to warn the settlers when one of 'em shot me."

Agent O'Fallon opens the drawer and slides a dented peace medallion across the desk for Night Wind to see. "Is this your peace medallion?"

Night Wind's hand jumps to his neck. "Yeah, how did you get it? An' where's my medicine pouch?"

"I searched you when Lieutenant Mullens brought you in. I found no medicine pouch." O'Fallon continues, "If you were truly trying to warn them, why would they shoot you?"

"I don't know." Night Wind adds, "As I said, it was one of 'em settler's boys. Probably got scared, an' all. I never even pulled my bow from my shoulder."

The agent pulls out an arrow from his desk drawer and slides it across the desk toward Night Wind. "Then how do you explain one of your red-feathered arrows ending up down by the cabin?" Agent O'Fallon smiles. "You see, I remembered your pretty arrows."

Night Wind stares at the arrow, trying to understand how this could be. He slowly shakes his head at the puzzle. "I don't know. All

I know is Buffalo Leg, the warrior that led the attack, is dead. He was killed in the attack. I did not fire a shot with either my rifle or my bow. I did not see Red Knife until he took me away. The attack came after I was shot—after Red Knife took me away. Hell, Red Knife, Jim Beckwourth, Standing Lance, an' I all stood up in council to argue against the raid."

"Beckwourth and Red Knife both said the same thing. Against my better judgment, I believe you. But, of course, General Atkinson will have to make the final decision. He's not expected here for at least another two weeks. He's out at Fort Hall dealing with the Blackfeet."

Agent O'Fallon next pulls Becky's blue bonnet from the drawer and offers the bonnet and the dented peace medallion back to Night Wind.

Night Wind pushes the medallion away. "I don't want it. It is based on white man's lies." He holds the bonnet a moment, rubbing the material between his fingers before dropping it back on the desk next to the medallion. "It seems now, I no longer have a need for this."

The agent frowns and shakes his head before returning the two objects to his drawer. "I'll send Chimalis over to see you. She can tell you more about your wife than I can."

"One of the guards said my horse was killed?" Night Wind asks.

"Yeah, Lieutenant Mullens got a little carried away with the whole detail. I've reprimanded him." O'Fallon continues, "Seems that when you were hit on the head, one of your horses broke free and went a little crazy. He reared up and stomped the soldier that struck you. Stomped him good. Mullens had to shoot the stallion in order to stop it. The injured private is still in the hospital ward. Doc doesn't think he'll make it. The general may hold that against you as well, but I'll make sure he knows you were already unconscious."

Chimalis comes to the stockade later that same day. His shackles have already been removed at O'Fallon's direction, and they greet each other by holding forearms and touching foreheads before sitting against the wall. Chimalis reaches inside her leather dress and pulls out some pemmican and hands it to Night Wind.

His eyes are red from crying prior to her visit, and he is grateful for the room's dim light. He feels as if his heart has been torn from his chest over the loss of Burning Moon. His eyes quickly begin to tear up again as she relates Burning Moon's ordeal.

"When the lieutenant finally allowed me back into the tepee," Chimalis says, "Burning Moon was frantic with pain. The baby was coming in the wrong position. The bottom was coming first instead of the head. I tried to turn the baby, but I was too late, the contractions were coming too close."

Tears run down her cheeks as she continues. "Burning Moon was a small woman and she was being torn up inside. When the baby finally arrived, the cord was tightly wrapped around the baby's neck and she was still-born. I tried the best I could to revive the baby and stop Burning Moon's bleeding but I could not. Perhaps, if I had reached her a little sooner, I might have been able to do something." Chimalis takes Night Wind's hand and adds, "She asked me to tell you she was sorry and that she and the baby will be waiting for you in the spirit world. I used some poles from the tepee, wedged between two trees, to make a burial scaffold. I wrapped Burning Moon and the baby in her sleeping robes so they would arrive together in the spirit world."

"I swear, I will kill Mullens." Night Wind says between sobs. "If I get out of here, I will kill him, and he won't die easy."

Chimalis holds him in her arms. "It may not have been entirely Mullens' fault. Remember, Burning Moon's own mother died in childbirth."

Night Wind takes a long, deep breath as his sobbing subsides. "How is little Jake?"

"He is well for now, but he needs his father."

"Have you heard they plan to hang me and Red Knife?"

"Yes, but you must live for your son. I trust in Akbaatatdía to do the right thing." Chimalis takes a deep breath before saying, "There is one more thing I must tell you."

Night Wind looks at her and realizes the seriousness of what is coming.

"The Apsáalooke are sick with the pox. Some from our village arrived at the fort last night. They say many have died, including Standing Lance and Moon Shadow."

Early the next morning, Night Wind again is ushered into the agent's office. This time, they are not alone. Standing to one side of the room is Red Knife, Jim Beckwourth, and a tall mountain man he has never seen before. Benjamin O'Fallon indicates with his hand for Night Wind to sit on the bench in front of him. Night Wind remains standing.

"It seems, you and Red Knife's being held here at the fort has somehow stirred up the Lakota," the agent begins. "I don't rightly understand what's going on, but they are demanding we release the two of you or they threaten to make trouble. They refer to you in particular, as the 'peace warrior.'"

The agent nods toward the mountain man leaning against the log wall. "Jim Bridger arrived late last night with the news that a few hundred Lakota warriors, led by a warrior named Broken Horn, have stopped a group of sixty trappers and six Indian missionaries, along with their ten wagons. Bridger here is guiding the trappers who are led by Melton Sublette. Bridger claims the group could easily shoot their way out, but Sublette fears that would be bad for trade. They're headed to the Green River rendezvous, and the last thing he wants is any Indian trouble.

"The missionaries are traveling with them to the Green River, and then they'll head on up to Fort Hall and then on to the Oregon Country. Some do-gooder by the name of Dr. Marcus Whitman leads that bunch. They adamantly refuse to even consider shooting at the Indians. Hell, they've even brought their wives with them." Nodding toward Night Wind, O'Fallon asks, "Can you shed any light on any of this?"

"Broken Horn is Red Knife's son an' considers me his spiritual brother," Night Wind states. "I spared his life three times an' I reckon he feels he owes me."

The Indian agent's eyes open wide in astonishment. "I see. That is an interesting twist indeed." O'Fallon smoothes his mustache as he thinks, studying the men around him. A few moments later he turns back to Night Wind. "Will you ride out there with Bridger here and look into the matter? Maybe try to soothe things over some? If you could, the general might be more inclined to overlook your transgressions."

"Why should I help you?" Night Wind states with a heavy heart.

"Well, I really don't want to hang you, and I assume you don't want to be dead."

"Red Knife rides with me," Night Wind replies.

"No, Red Knife stays here at the fort," The agent responds. "If all goes well and nobody gets killed, he'll be free to go upon your return. You have my word."

"I'll have two hundred angry Lakota, that's what I'll have. Broken Horn won't take less than Red Knife's freedom." Night Wind adds, "There's one other matter that I need to speak with you about, but I think I need the fort's doctor as well."

When the army surgeon arrives, Night Wind holds up his left arm and points to a small, faint scar just above his wrist. "When I was a small boy, an old army doctor cut my brother and me to stop us from gettin' smallpox. My father told me the story years later. Pa was fighting for the Ohio militia against Tecumseh, an' all the soldiers were cut for pox by the doctor. The doctor was a friend of Pa's so he agreed to do me an' Jake, too."

"The old doctor told Pa that he was a young soldier at Valley Forge with George Washington himself when Washington's doctors made the same cut on the soldiers there." Night Wind continues, "Pa said Washington later claimed stoppin' the smallpox was the main reason America won the revolution. But, I don't rightly know how this small cut could stop smallpox."

The surgeon slowly nods his head, eyes squinted in thought, before speaking. "I seem to remember reading something about this in one of the medical journals. I believe the name for it is 'inoculation'. You make a small cut on the arm and then rub pus from smallpox into the cut. The patient may end up getting a very mild case but then he cannot get the disease again." He thinks for a second and then says, "It just might work. We certainly do have a developing problem here."

"I'll ride with Bridger here only if the surgeon agrees to cut my son, Red Knife an' Chimalis," Night Wind states. Benjamin O'Fallon nods his head in agreement, reaches behind him and hands Night Wind his Hawken rifle, knife, and gear.

CHAPTER THIRTY THREE

Ten days later, a guard on the wall spots a dust cloud off in the distance. Within an hour, wagons, trappers, and missionaries begin to trickle through the fort's gate. The trade wagons are heavy, pulled by six mules each, and the going is slow. This group is followed at a distance by a large contingent of Lakota. They turn away from the fort to set up camp upriver, away from their traditional enemy camped near the fort.

Night Wind, Broken Horn, and Jim Beckwourth ride through the gate and up to the agent's office. Night Wind's long auburn hair has been cut off short in mourning. Broken Horn leads a second horse but does not dismount when his companions do. "I will wait here for my father and see if O'Fallon honors his spoken words."

Night Wind and Jim Beckwourth push open the agent's door and stride in.

"Welcome, welcome indeed," the agent greets. "Looks like a job well done. I trust you had no trouble?"

"Broken Horn waits outside for his father, Red Knife," Night Wind stoically states. "I think it best not to make him wait long."

O'Fallon nods over to the guard, and the soldier exits out the door. Turning back to Night Wind, "Your suggestion for fighting the smallpox epidemic seems to be working. I thank you. Of course, we've had a number of soldiers desert rather than face the fear of inoculation, but we now have the outbreak under control. I thought Lieutenant Mullens had run too before his body was found behind the outhouse. It was probably one of his men that slit his throat. You might say, he wasn't real popular with his men. Just thought you'd like to know."

"His mind was twisted with hate," Night Wind responds. "What about the pox with the Apsáalooke?"

"I'm afraid, the doc says they haven't responded as well. Most of them had already contracted the disease before the doctor could help them." O'Fallon adds, "I'm sorry to have to tell you, Chimalis has the pox. The doc has done all he can, but he doesn't think she'll make it. My wife has been taking her food and is caring for your boy. He's been inoculated and seems to be fine."

The side door opens and Red Knife walks in with the guard. O'Fallon turns to face them. "You're both free to go. All charges are dropped, and Night Wind's arrow will be lost."

As the two warriors turn to go, O'Fallon says, "Hold on a second. There's one more thing."

They turn back as O'Fallon opens his desk drawer and pulls out his own peace medallion. Pushing it across the desk toward Night Wind, he says, "I really think you should have this. You've earned it, and I truly believe you are a man of peace. Someday, Night Wind, if you have the time, I'd very much like to hear the story of how you came about the name of 'peace warrior.'"

Night Wind hesitates before finally picking the medallion up from the desktop and slipping its rawhide loop over his head. Tucking the peace medallion inside his leather shirt, he is somewhat comforted that it is back in its proper place.

Benjamin O'Fallon follows the three men out the door. The agent steps up to Broken Horn, still sitting on his horse. "It is an honor to meet such a mighty Lakota warrior."

The agent states, as he waves his hand in the direction of the Lakota encampment, "To have so many warriors follow your lead is a great tribute to you." He steps forward and offers up his hand to shake.

Broken Horn stoically ignores the agent's offered hand and turns to Night Wind for translation. After Night Wind translates, the

Lakota turns back to face O'Fallon. "Tell the agent to keep the wagons from going any farther north. Honor the spoken words of the treaty."

Night Wind translates what his brother has stated before asking the agent, "Just where is Chimalis?"

Night Wind notices his father stiffen as O'Fallon answers, "She's down by the river. Near the corral."

"Have our other horses brought to the corral." Night wind tells the agent.

Night Wind, Jim Beckwourth, Broken Horn, and Red Knife are all quietly sitting by a small campfire, each deep in his own thoughts. They found Chimalis earlier, dead from the pox, under a small brush shelter. She was lying on a makeshift bed of dried grass, clutching Night Wind's medicine bag to her chest. Red Knife was devastated. Jim Beckwourth had located a buffalo robe, and Night Wind and Red Knife worked together to wrap her body. Because of the pox, they would not allow Broken Horn to come near.

"I'm going to take Chimalis back to the place we left the tepees when the soldiers came," Red Knife quietly states. "She always liked to camp at that little stream, and then she will be with Burning Moon and the baby. I will use my tepee to build a burial scaffold for all three."

"I will go with you and help," Night Wind states. "I would like to spend the day to honor and pray for all three. But, we should use my tepee for the burial scaffold. I will no longer need it."

"Where will you go from there?" Red Knife asks, before quickly adding, "I plan to find my brother's band, and I think you would be welcome."

"The Mountain band of the Apsáalooke would take you in, too," Beckwourth offers.

"Wherever I go with the Apsáalooke or even the Lakota, there will always be the same doubt," Night Wind replies. "Too many think I have betrayed the Indian." He remains quiet in thought before speaking again. "I have given the agent my word to guide the mission-aries as far as Fort Hall, and I have spoken at length with Marcus and Narcissa Whitman. They lead the missionaries I will be guiding."

"They plan to open a school to teach Indian children in Oregon Country the white man's way." Night Wind turns to his father and sighs. "Father, it is with a heavy heart I tell you now, I plan to continue west with the Whitmans. With Burning Moon and the baby gone, and me being an outcast, there is no life left for me here. Living alone is no way to raise Jake. Narcissa Whitman has promised to look after Jake at the school until I get settled. I will take Jake to them in the morning, and catch up with the wagons in a few days, after I have mourned Burning Moon, Chimalis, and the baby."

Night Wind can see tears in his father's eyes as Red Knife nods his head in understanding.

"Perhaps one day you will return?" his father asks.

"We will try," Night Wind replies.

Pointing over to the young bay stallion, standing with the other horses, Night Wind states, "I'm going to raise horses. I am good at it, and these horses carry Thunder's bloodline. The young stallion I believe will become a great horse."

Night Wind then holds up the beaded medicine bag from around his neck. Burning Moon had repaired the damage caused by the lead ball the best she could. The bag now bulged with the heavy gold coins held inside. "I don't know how Chimalis retrieved my medicine bag from Mullens, being weak with the pox, but with all the gold my uncle Jack left behind, I should be able to get a good start when I reach Oregon."

A short while later, Red Knife rises and walks over to his son. He carefully removes his own medicine pouch from around his neck. He runs his fingers over the beautifully beaded design on the leather pouch before solemnly handing it to Night Wind. "I would like you to give this to my grandson when he gets a little older. Tell Curly the stories of his grandparents, Chimalis, and Red Knife, so he will know of his Apsáalooke heritage."

Broken Horn quickly adds, "And, tell him of your Lakota brother and how you became known as the 'Peace Warrior.'"

The End

AUTHOR'S NOTES

Although my story is purely fictional, I did attempt to weave the narrative around some actual people and places, while taking some liberties with dates.

Tecumseh: A Shawnee chief who became the leader of a large, multi-tribal confederacy in the early 1800s. He worked with his brother, Tenskwatawa, also known as 'The Prophet,' to unite American Indian tribes in the Northwest Territory in defense against the white intrusion. They sided with the British in the War of 1812.

Cincinnati: First settled in 1788 under the name of Losantville. General Arthur St. Clair, the governor of the Northwest Territory, renamed the small village "Cincinnati" in 1790. This was in honor of both the Roman citizen-warrior Lucius Quinctius Cincinnatus and for the Society of the Cincinnati. The society was an organization of American revolutionary army officers. After the revolution, Cincinnati became the departure city of choice for settlers heading into the western wilderness. The introduction of the river paddle-wheeler on the Ohio River after the war of 1812 turned Cincinnati into a center of river commerce and trade. At the time of my story, the population was approaching ten thousand, with a large population of African Americans, both free and slave.

St. Louis: Founded as a French fur trading post in 1763 under Auguste Chouteau, St. Louis became the capital of the new Louisiana Territory from 1805 until statehood. Increasing population led to incorporation as a town in 1809. A volunteer fire department and a police department were founded, with a jail established in the new fortifications being built around the city. After the War of 1812, St. Louis became the new "Gateway to the West." The increasing population stirred interest in statehood, and with the Missouri Compromise of 1820, statehood was achieved on August 10, 1821.

Missouri Compromise: The Missouri Compromise of 1820 permitted Missouri to enter into the Union as a slave state and Maine to enter into the Union as a free state. The compromise outlawed slavery in the remainder of the Louisiana Territory north of the 36°30′ parallel.

Jefferson City/Lohman's Landing: Jefferson City, the new capital of Missouri, was created specifically to serve as the state capital. In 1821, Daniel Morgan Boone (the son of the frontiersman Daniel Boone) was commissioned to lay out a new capital city halfway between St. Louis and Kansas City. The site chosen was the old trading post of Lohman's Landing. The new town was incorporated in 1825 and named in honor of Thomas Jefferson.

Jacob and Samuel Hawken/Rocky Mountain Rifle: The Hawken .50-caliber rifle was a muzzle-loading rifle built by gunsmiths Jacob and Samuel Hawken. The heavy-caliber rifles were popular with mountain men and hunters during the fur-trading era and became widely known as the "Rocky Mountain Rifle." Each rifle was handmade in the Hawkens' St. Louis workshop, which they ran from 1815 to 1858. The earliest known .50-caliber rifle was made for William Henry Ashley.

William Henry Ashley: When Missouri was admitted to the Union, William Henry Ashley was elected its first lieutenant governor. In St. Louis in 1822, Ashley and his partner, Andrew Henry, formed the Rocky Mountain Fur Company. They advertised that they "sought one hundred enterprising young men" to commit to a trapping adventure lasting two to three years. They planned to follow the Missouri River to its source to trap fur. Between 1822 and 1825, the Rocky Mountain Fur Company completed several large-scale fur trapping expeditions. Ashley devised the rendezvous system in which trappers, Indians, and traders would meet annually at a predetermined location. Many of these annual rendezvous were located along the Green River in Wyoming. Ashley's men, led by Jedediah Smith, William Sublette, and David Jackson, claimed to have discovered the South Pass over the Rockies in 1824.

John Jacob Astor: A German immigrant, Astor was once considered to be America's richest man. Once Lewis and Clark's expedition showed it was indeed possible to trek overland to the Pacific Ocean, Astor devised and financed a business plan to settle the Oregon Country. He felt that if he could ship furs to China in exchange for tea and other Far-Eastern goods, he could sell these goods in New York City for a huge profit. Although Astor financed and devised the plans, he never left New York City.

First, he founded the American Fur Company. Then he sent out two groups of men with plans to meet in Oregon Country. One group would travel overland, while a second group would sail around South America and found a trading post in Oregon on the Pacific Coast. Fort Astoria (present day Astoria, Oregon) was founded in 1811 by the crew of Astor's ship, the *Tonquin*. The following year, while fur trading farther north, *Tonquin's* crew was massacred by hostile Indians, and the ship was destroyed.

The overland group of four dozen men reached Fort Astoria early in 1812, shortly after the loss of the *Tonquin*. Due to the distant location and the outbreak of the War of 1812, his grand scheme ended up a business failure. Fort Astoria was sold to the British to avoid complete losses. His men felt it best to let Astor know of this failure, and a party immediately headed back overland. These men, led by Robert Stuart, discovered the South Pass over the Rocky Mountains in 1813, prior to Ashley's men. The mountain men tried their best to keep the pass a secret, but that was not to be.

Chief Cameahwait: Considered by most to be the brother of Sacagawea, although the Shoshone word for "brother" and "cousin" are identical. On August 13, 1805, the Lewis and Clark expedition met a group of Shoshone Indians. Sacagawea recognized her brother, Cameahwait, who had become a chief of the Shoshone. He gave the expedition horses as a thank-you for reuniting him with his sister. Sacagawea had been kidnapped by the Hidatsa Indians when she was twelve. Cameahwait went along with the expedition as a guide over the mountains. He received a Peace Medallion from the Lewis and Clark expedition. Later, he died at the hands of the Blackfeet Indians in a battle at Bloody Creek, Montana, but the year is uncertain. In my story, he gifts his medallion to young Sean O'Malley, either as a trade or a thank-you for helping the Shoshone in their time of need.

Jim Beckwourth: My story takes liberties with the character and life of Jim Beckwourth. In true life, he was the son of a prominent Virginia slave owner, Sir Jennings Beckwith, and one of his slaves, known as "Miss Kill." Beckwith moved to Missouri in 1806 and took Jim and his mother with him as house slaves. Jim was freed by his father on his nineteenth birthday, and immediately changed his name to Beckwourth. He joined William Henry Ashley's trading expedition to the West in 1822.

While sent out to purchase horses from some local Indian tribes, he became lost and was saved from starvation by the Blackfeet Indians. He remained with this tribe for only a short time. He later went to live with friends in an Apsáalooke band in order to avoid paying a debt. He found a permanent home among the Apsáalooke and claimed to have married eight Apsáalooke women. He helped lead the Apsáalooke to victory in a great battle against the Blackfeet and was subsequently made a war chief of the Apsáalooke. He continued to trap while living with the Apsáalooke, selling his furs to the American Fur Company. There are many stories told about him, but he was also well known for his extreme exaggerations.

Benjamin O'Fallon: Orphaned as a child, Benjamin O'Fallon went as a teen to live in St. Louis with his uncle, Governor William Clark of the Lewis and Clark Expedition. In 1817, he was appointed US Indian Agent to the Sioux. He later became the Indian agent for the upper Missouri in 1819. He built his headquarters at Council Bluffs, Iowa.

The Friendship Treaty: This treaty between the United States and the Crow (Apsáalooke) Nation was signed at the Mandan Village on August 4, 1825. Major representatives of the United States included General Henry Atkinson, United States Army, and Major Benjamin O'Fallon, Indian Agent. Chief Long Hair of the Apsáalooke and numerous sub-chiefs, including Standing Lance, made their mark for the Apsáalooke Nation.

Article 2 of the treaty shows the overall attitude of the United States for the Native Americans. It reads as follows:

> *The United States agree to receive the Crow tribe of Indians into their friendship, and under their protection, and to extend to them, from time to time, such benefits and acts of kindness as may be convenient, and seem just and proper to the President of the United States.*

Directly relating to my story is Article 5, which reads as follows:

> *That the friendship which is now established between the United States and the Crow tribe should not be interrupted by the misconduct of individuals, it is hereby agreed that for injuries done by individuals, no private revenge or retaliation shall take place, but instead thereof, complaints shall be made, by the party injured, to the superintendent or agent of Indian affairs, or other person appointed by the President; and it shall be the duty of said Chiefs, upon complaint being made as aforesaid, to deliver up the person or persons against whom the complaint is made, to the end that he or they may be punished, agreeably to the laws of the United States. And, in like manner, if any robbery, violence, or murder, shall be committed on any Indian or Indians belonging to the said tribe, the person or persons so offending shall be tried, and, if found guilty, shall be punished in like manner as if the injury had been done to a white man.*

Smallpox outbreak: I took liberties with the time frame of the smallpox epidemic. It would be another three or four years after Night Wind's encounter with the settlers before the smallpox epidemic would strike the Apsáalooke Nation. The outbreak of smallpox was devastating to the Apsáalooke. Prior to the outbreak of the disease in 1840, the population of the Apsáalooke Nation was estimated to number ten thousand. Ten years after the outbreak, the population had declined to two thousand.

The Spirit Bow: The idea of the Spirit Bow is entirely of my creation. Many tribes gave a trial of manhood to young men hoping to be initiated into various warrior societies. These trials often included physical tests of endurance in the wilderness, survival, and attempts to see a vision by depriving oneself of food, water, or sleep for days at a time. In this manner, the warrior might create the necessary mental state to bring on a vision. The young warrior accidentally shot by Night Wind back in Ohio was engaged in just such an initiation test.

Dr. Marcus Whitman: In 1836 a small group of missionaries drove the first three wagons across the continent to Oregon Country. Prior immigrants had abandoned their wagons at Fort Hall and preceded on by pack horse. Narcissa Whitman and fellow missionary, Eliza Gray, became the first two white women to travel overland across the continent. The missionaries did indeed travel as far as the Green River with a group of seven wagons and sixty fur trappers, led by Milton Sublette with the help of Jim Bridger.

The Whitman's established a settlement and Indian school near present day Walla Walla, Washington. Marcus Whitman returned east for the third time in 1842 and led the first large group of one thousand immigrants and wagons overland to the Oregon Country.

AUTHOR'S BIO

Jim Lettis grew up in Mountain View, California. He graduated from San Jose State University in 1969 and went on to teach thirty-three years of middle school in Sunnyvale, California. Jim was very proud and honored to be named Sunnyvale Elementary School District's Teacher of the Year in 2001.

Writing under the pseudonym Grandpa Peeps, Jim is the author of two wonderful children's books in verse, *The Squire and the White Dragon* and *How to Catch a Whopper*. The novel, *Spirit Bow: The Saga of Sean O'Malley* is his first. He hopes this work of fiction will help bring history alive for his readers.

When he isn't writing, Jim enjoys photography, traveling, gardening, reading, and playing poker. He currently resides in Cave Junction Oregon, with his wife, Celia.

YOU CAN HELP!

First, thank you very much for purchasing my novel, **Spirit Bow: The Saga of Sean O'Malley.**

Since I am a little-known author, I would greatly appreciate your help in getting the word out. I'm sure some of you realize, it is very difficult breaking into the industry. If you know of an agent or publisher looking for a new client, please, feel free to mention my name.

There are two very easy ways you can help.

If you have enjoyed reading my book, please post a short review on Amazon, Bookbaby, Barnes and Noble, or Good Reads. Favorable reviews are critical in helping to create interest and drive sells.

Second, it would be greatly appreciated if you could put a book recommendation out over your social media accounts to your friends.

Thanks again for your purchase, and hopefully, your help. Sincerely, James Lettis.